# PSYCHE

A novel

# PSYCHE

by Phyllis Brett Young

Introduction by Nathalie Cooke and Suzanne Morton
Foreword by Valerie Young Argue

McGill-Queen's University Press
Montreal & Kingston · London · Ithaca

McGill-Queen's University Press 2008
ISBN 978-0-7735-3490-2

Legal deposit fourth quarter 2008
Bibliothèque nationale du Québec

Printed in Canada on acid-free paper that is 100% ancient forest free
(100% post-consumer recycled), processed chlorine free

McGill-Queen's University Press acknowledges the support of the Canada
Council for the Arts for our publishing program. We also acknowledge the
financial support of the Government of Canada through the Book Publishing
Industry Development Program (BPIDP) for our publishing activities.


**Library and Archives Canada Cataloguing in Publication**

Young, Phyllis Brett
    Psyche: a novel / by Phyllis Brett Young ; introduction by Nathalie
Cooke and Suzanne Morton; foreword by Valerie Young Argue.

Originally Published: Toronto: Longmans, Green, 1959.
ISBN 978-0-7735-3490-2

    I. Title.

PS8547.O58P7 2008          C813'.54          C2008-903929-7

# CONTENTS

Studio portrait of Phyllis Brett Young, circa 1959, used for publicity and book jackets. Courtesy Valerie Argue

# FOREWORD

## PHYLLIS BRETT YOUNG

Phyllis Brett Young was born in Toronto in 1914 to English immigrant parents. Her father, George Sidney Brett, was head of the Department of Philosophy, University of Toronto; her mother, Marion Brett, was an avid reader and a talented woodcarver. Educated in both public and private schools, Phyllis attended the Ontario College of Art before marrying her long-time sweetheart, Douglas Young. The early, depression-era years of their marriage were difficult financially, but after World War II Douglas began a successful career in personnel that led to a five-year stint with a branch of the United Nations in Geneva, Switzerland. Their only child, Valerie, attended the International School there, while Phyllis had the freedom and perspective to write her first novel, *Psyche*, and plan her second, *The Torontonians*.

By the fall of 1960, when, after a two-year relocation in Ottawa, the Youngs returned to Toronto, Phyllis Brett Young's writing career had taken flight. Between 1959 and 1969 she published four novels (*Psyche*, *The Torontonians*, *Undine*, and *A Question of Judgment*), a fictionalized childhood memoir (*Anything Could Happen!*), and a thriller (*The Ravine*, published under the pseudonym Kendal Young). Her novels, positively received by readers and reviewers alike, appeared in numerous editions and languages in Canada, the United States, and England and other European countries. *The Ravine* was made into a movie under the title *Assault*.

Over the years, the Youngs lived in variety of apartments and houses (both urban and suburban), eventually retiring to their dream home in the country near the town of Orillia, Ontario. Phyllis Brett Young died in 1996, Douglas Young just eighteen months later.

## *PSYCHE*: SOME REFLECTIONS FROM THE AUTHOR'S DAUGHTER

An emotionally gripping story, an intellectually challenging idea, and a contemporary Canadian setting are the three basic elements of my mother's novels. In *Psyche,* her first novel, each plays an essential role. The book was greeted with huge critical acclaim and quickly became a national and international best-seller, published in more than a dozen hardcover, paperback, bookclub, and magazine editions, in many different languages. People seemed to fall in love with Psyche and her compelling story. As the following sample demonstrates, reviewers repeatedly commented on how absorbing and affecting they found the novel: "a powerful, exciting, and thoroughly moving book" (*Globe and Mail*, 31 Oct. 1959), "completely absorbing" (*Ottawa Journal*, 28 Nov. 1959), "a fast-moving intriguing story" (*Penticton Herald*, 5 Dec. 1959), "irresistible" (*Halifax Herald*, 13 May 1960), "read on without interruption until it was finished long after midnight" (*Toronto Daily Star*, 13 Feb.1960), "a book that ruthlessly holds the attention of the reader from first to last" (Mazo de la Roche, on the jacket flap of the 1959 Longmans Canadian, 1960 Putnam American, and 1961 White Lion British hardcover editions), and "Start to read *Psyche* only if you have the time to lose yourself completely!" (*Chicago Tribune*, on the back cover of the 1964 Lancer American paperback).

More than just a good read, *Psyche* revolves around a thought-provoking and still topical question: which factor has the greatest influence on character development, heredity or environment? In the early 50s, when it was still the norm for families to dine together and in my home it was felt that conversation should focus on topics of "general interest," the nature/nurture debate came up frequently. No doubt my mother had already followed such dinner-table discussions when she was young. Clearly my grandfather, who as head of the Department of Philosophy, University of Toronto, introduced a new course in 1931-32 that included in its description "the influence of heredity and environment," had given the matter a great deal of thought. A firm believer in science as philosophy's companion in the quest for knowledge and author of the three-volume *History of Psychology*, George Sidney Brett would have kept abreast of every new finding and point of view.

For Phyllis Brett Young, the subject ultimately led to a novelist's "What if ...?" What if a young child – perhaps two or three years old – was stolen from her parents and grew up not knowing anything about her roots? Would her genes or the events of her childhood and adolescence shape her character and her future? The major clue to the answer lies in Young's choice of title. Like her beautiful namesake from Greek mythology, who wandered the world looking for her lost love, the novel's heroine, Psyche, whose name has come to personify the soul, journeys in search of her physical and psychological identity. Assisting her in this search is the genetic legacy she carries. "In modern parlance," the author tells us (p. 8), "the 'psyche' is the most complex and most important component of any given human being. It is the sum of the infinitely varied intangibles which make every living man and woman unique in his or her own right."

Most readers have seen heredity as the hands-down favourite in the novel. My mother, intelligent and strong-willed, would certainly have found it difficult to imagine herself (or her daughter) as anything but a survivor. Nonetheless, having read and considered everything she could find about the subject, like Psyche's mother she does not discount environment as at least a partial determinant. "I can know – perhaps," Sharon says of her daughter, "that her chances are better than even. No more than that" (p. 99). Psyche finds kindness and help along the way: from her unofficial foster-parents, Mag and Butch, from the young school inspector with his precious gift, from Bel, the madam with the heart of gold, and last but not least, from the newspaperman, Steve Ryerson; even the egotistical artist, Nick, plays a positive role, opening a door to the outside world and her long-lost beginnings. She also has the early-childhood influence of her biological parents, with "chords of memory, touched from time to time by vaguely familiar harmonies of sound and colour"(p. 43).

Psyche's odyssey is played out against a contemporary Canadian setting, deliberately chosen by the author because of two strongly held beliefs: one, that the development of a distinctly Canadian literature was necessary for Canada to become known in other countries, and two, that the novel was paramount to the preservation of our social history. As she says in two of numerous interviews, "We must become interested in ourselves and then we'll interest other people" (*Montreal Gazette*, 13 Jan. 1960) and "What our writers should be doing is reflecting ourselves as we are now" (*Star Weekly Magazine*, 24 Feb. 1962).

Unlike my mother's second novel, *The Torontonians*, first published in 1960 by Longmans Green and reissued in 2007 by McGill-Queen's University Press, *Psyche* contains no dates or place names. Although the central themes in *The Torontonians* (the perils and pitfalls of a materialistic, suburban life, especially for middle-class women in the pre-Betty Friedan 1950s) were, and still are, relevant to any large North American city, the novel is firmly grounded in time and place, with real names used for every location except one neighbourhood and a couple of streets. In *Psyche*, not specifically identifying any of the locations allows the author to take creative liberties with her closely described settings – though readers from outside the country will at the very least recognize them as being in Canada, while most Canadians will recognize Toronto as the inspiration for the noisy, never-sleeping metropolis and Sudbury for the northern mining town. Some may also be able to identify such

Valerie Argue (Phyllis Brett Young's daughter), early
1960s. Courtesy Valerie Argue

areas as Muskoka (site of the kidnapper's rented cottage) and
Caledon (the artist's studio). Having lived most of her life in
Toronto and vacationed either at her family's cottage on Lake
Muskoka or, with her husband and daughter, in Algonquin
Park, all of these locations were well known to my mother.

By not providing explicit dates, the author is free to play with
the timeframe of the novel. A few clues – in particular, the fact
that as a World War II veteran the kidnapper would have been
eligible for generous government grants (page 12) that were not
available after World War I – suggest that Psyche is probably
stolen around 1945 and that her story moves forward, through

a compression of time, into the 1950s, with her flight from the city at age nineteen occurring sometime before March 1954, when Toronto's streetcar service to its northern limits (p. 281) was shut down in favour of the new subway. Along the way there are flashbacks to 1930s Depression-era phenomena, such as hoboes riding the rods (chapter 3), and premonitions of dramatic changes in a city whose population has already exceeded one million (p. 133). By not providing dates and not giving the places in her novel any names, even fictitious ones, the author contrives to draw the reader in and to create a more enclosed fictional world for Psyche's timeless story. That the technique is deliberate can be seen in the novel's opening description where, in the front hall of Sharon and Dwight's home, a shaft of sunlight hitting the chandelier scatters a shower of prismatic colours over a maid's black-and-white uniform, "transforming it momentarily into motley out of place in time and locale."

If Psyche captured the hearts of millions of readers, it was probably in no small part due to the fact that she also captured the heart of the author. Before starting to write a novel, my mother would live with her characters for up to a year, until they took on a life of their own – propelling the plot. In the case of Psyche, I think she must have fallen in love with the beautiful child she created and rejoiced in her remarkable courage and resiliency.

Valerie (Brett Young) Argue
March 2008

# INTRODUCTION

*PSYCHE* is a terrific read. A captivating view of popular psychology in the 1950s, it sweeps readers into a fictional world of crime, suspense, and romance. But the novel is more than a popular romance or mystery since it both uses and queries the conventions of those popular forms, just as it scrutinizes some of the most hotly debated topics of twentieth-century psychology. *Psyche* is a thoroughly modern novel, with a fiercely proud and independent heroine who experiences life on her own terms. Published in 1959, the same year as Hugh MacLennan's *The Watch that Ends the Night* and Mordecai Richler's *The Apprenticeship of Duddy Kravitz*, Phyllis Brett Young's *Psyche* has largely disappeared from public consciousness. This new edition of the novel allows us to reintroduce a work set in mid-century Canada and to suggest ways in which it sheds light on its place and time. *Psyche* speaks to the age-old tension between nature/nurture and to questions about the influence of heredity and environment. It also challenges generalizations about postwar democratic and egalitarian values as well as those surrounding Canadian literature and popular genre literature at the end of the 1950s.

*Psyche* is out of step with the stereotypes of democratization and egalitarianism associated with postwar Canada. The post World War Two years are generally characterized as a time of rapid social change in which social attitudes about class, ethnicity, and gender were transformed, with Canadians beginning to internalize the ideals of international human rights protocols that led in the 1960s to the end of previous restrictions on immigration and elitist educational and legislative impediments to equality of opportunity. *Psyche,* however, speaks to the tenacity of older values surrounding class, elitism, and heredity.

The innate intelligence of the novel's heroine, Psyche, is a central theme throughout the novel. While postwar psychology was preoccupied with personality development or the effect of obsessive mothering, Psyche is remarkable for how little she changes – she was confident and self-assured as a little girl and is just the same as a young woman. Rather than being over-mothered, her surrogate mother, Mag, although kind, leaves her pretty much alone. Mag teaches by lived example and "perfect" Psyche provides few instances for reprimand, so explicit moral training on fundamental matters such as honesty and feminine virtue amount to a brief warning about how theft would lead to a "stomache-ache [sic] created expressly by the Lord" or vague admonishments "to be a good girl."[2]

Young's decision to go against the tenets of the time in creating her heroine reminds us that there was less consensus of opinion in the 1950s than we often think and suggests that she was well aware of the various aspects of complex questions about psychological development and values. Although it would be inappropriate to focus exclusively on her father in thinking about why she structured the novel as she did, given his role as a prominent public intellectual, he cannot be ignored. George Sidney Brett was one of the most influential English-language philosophers in Canada during the first half of the twentieth century. A 1902 Oxford graduate in Classics and Humanities, he arrived in Canada after four years teaching philosophy in Lahore, India (now Pakistan).[3] While in India, Brett learned to speak Hindustani and read Sanskrit and Arabic and, according to historian Michael Gauvreau, continued to write about India in the 1920s and 1930s, disagreed vehemently with Gandhi and the Congress nationalists, and "was an advocate of the princely states."[4] While this may have been the result of his Britishness and allegiance to the Empire, this elitism was out of step with his liberal contemporaries. Brett came to Trinity College, University of Toronto, in 1908, first as librarian and lecturer in Classics. Almost immediately, he was promoted to professor of ethics and ancient philosophy and soon moved "temporarily" to the university Philosophy Department to "shore up its psychology subfield."[5] At the time, psychology was a branch within philosophy and in 1912 Brett had published the first volume of his most important scholarly work, *The History of Psychology*. The appointment in philosophy and psychology became permanent and full-time in 1921 with the publication of the second and third volumes of *The History of Psychology*. At the same time, Brett was named the university's director of psychology. Brett understood psychology as the "science of the soul." He believed the discipline required a humanist tradition as "History alone, can adequately unfold the content of the idea denoted by the word 'Psyche' or explain the various meanings that have from age to age been assigned to the phrase 'science of the soul.'"[6] This was not the direction the discipline was taking, however, and from the time of his appointment he advocated that psychology be made a separate department, a step the university took in 1927.[7] Brett's support of the partition of psychology from philosophy reflected his opposition to the evolution of the discipline. He was opposed to all forms of behaviourism in psychology, an approach that was becoming dominant in the United States in the 1920s. Behavioural psychologists rejected the study of consciousness, focusing instead on what could be observed, predicted, and controlled.[8] In Canada, behaviourial psychology was dominated by the mental hygiene movement, which emphasized heredity and adopted a eugenicist framework toward both "bettering the race" and preventing its degeneration. One of the tenets of this set of beliefs, which came to dominate English Canadian social reform in the 1910s and 1920s, was a belief in innate intelligence and the "overriding influence of heredity upon capacity."[9] Through the Canadian National Council for Mental Health (1918) and later the Toronto-based

Eugenics Society of Canada (1930), prominent citizens, academics, and social reformers influenced immigration policy and public understanding of the issue.[10] Mass intelligence testing and the educational experiment surrounding the Dionne quintuplets captured the public's imagination. The Dionnes, born in 1934 and legally stolen from their parents when they were made wards of the Province of Ontario, became part of the twenty-four hour a day psychological developmental program of Dr William Blatz of the St George's School for Child Study and the expanding Psychology Department, University of Toronto. The young girls were not only Ontario's most important tourist attraction but were also seen as an extraordinary research opportunity for exploring the impact of nature/nurture: as the girls were believed to be genetically identical, differences between them had to be explained by environment.[11]

Even after Brett moved away from psychology, he maintained links with the discipline. In 1926 he was appointed to the Board of Directors of the St George's School for Child Study, operated by Dr William Blatz and funded by the Canadian National Committee for Mental Health.[12] In 1927 he was one of the founders, with Carl Murchison and Edward Titchener, of *The Journal of General Psychology*. Brett also maintained an interest in nature/nurture debates. Philosophy 1A, his course on "Introduction to Ethics" instituted in 1931-32, was described as a study of "The basis of morals in human nature; the influence of heredity and environment; standards, motives, and sanctions of conduct; application to the problems of personal conduct and social relations."[13] Ultimately, however, Brett believed in education and culture. Michael Gauvreau has described him as concerned that "modern civilization was the fruit of a fine balance of humanistic and scientific knowledge; here was the high road between freedom and determinism. At stake was the question of how to preserve that freedom in the face of the knowledge that much of human behaviour was determined by biological and environmental forces." For Brett, who rejected psychological behaviourism, "philosophy and history assured the possibility of rational action."[14]

This view may have been seen as slightly old-fashioned at the time, but Brett was not the only social scientist in the 1930s to oppose the behavioural trends in psychology and the wide public support for eugenics that was eventually destroyed by Nazi German's extreme application of its logic.[15] Brett's rigid adherence to a scholarly agenda focused on intellectual unity is a striking contrast to the independent and "natural" character of Psyche, who is "unbiased by ready-made social strictures."[16] His very public presence among Canadian intellectuals is a complete contrast to the emotional absence of Psyche's father, whose loss is registered only through his wife's pain. Psyche's emotionally removed father differs from the emotionally present father expected in the postwar period.[17]

It might seem that a link with Brett could be found in Psyche's gradual understanding of her name. She is aware of her given name because it was printed on the nightshirt she was wearing on the day of her kidnapping. But the word, with its opening two consonants, is unrecognizable to her foster parents and hard for the young child to pronounce. However Psyche's intuitive sense that the word holds a profound significance for her never wavers. She accepts the other names she is given only as a matter of necessity or as a function of familiarity, as when she answers to "Maggie" at school, to "Rosalie" at Oliver's restaurant, or to Bel's affectionate diminutive, "kid." For years, she is condemned to spell rather than pronounce her own name, a limitation symbolic of the lack of information she, as victim of a kidnapping, has about herself and her personal history. Psyche's gradual understanding of the name's pronunciation and implications seems, at first glance, to emphasize the way in which the self develops over time and is shaped by experience, rather than springing into existence fully formed. Such a privileging of process is consistent with Brett's own emphasis on the importance of taking into account "growth and development" in order to understand the "real activity of the mind."[18] However the novel itself emphasizes that Psyche both believes in and illustrates the way an individual's personality can remain intact despite the vagaries of circumstance.

*Psyche* also fails to conform to stereotypes of the late 1950s in its direct focus on sexuality. The 1953 publication of *Sexual Behavior in the Human Female* by Alfred Kinsey et al focused public attention on the female libido, claiming that women were not different from men in seeking sexual satisfaction. Psyche's natural and magnetic appeal to both men and women reinforces and underscores the link to Kinsey's findings. Are there suggestions of lesbian sexuality in the sympathetic portrayal of Kathie, with her elite private school background and experiences of "an incessant warfare between mind and body"[19] and "strife that had torn her apart since adolescence,"[20] who seems to have an unrequited love for Bel and perhaps for Psyche as well?

While the question of what shapes a person is a key theme, the novel's plot revolves around a kidnapping. Modern kidnapping in North America is often considered to begin with the 1874 abduction of four-year-old Charley Ross. The mystery of Ross's disappearance was never solved and for the next fifty years men came forward claiming to be the "lost boy." Lost boys were not uncommon in the late nineteenth century, in both real life and in fiction. The most famous fictional Lost Boys were probably those in J. M. Barrie's *Peter Pan*. Historian Paula Fass describes "lost and found" newspaper ads for children and reports that tens of thousands of American children disappeared in late-nineteenth-century cities, taken into institutions, abandoned, murdered, or abducted.[21] The grieving parents of lost children worried not only about a child's survival or safety and the abuse of innocence but also about how his or her identity would be altered by the experience. This concern for the effect on a child's character can be seen in texts ranging from colonial "captivity narratives" to those describing the 1974 kidnapping of Patty Hearst. It is very different from Psyche's mother's hope, indeed the belief she clings to despite reading opinions to the contrary, "that her child could have shaped her environment to her own inherent needs, rather than allowing her environment to be the principal factor in determining the kind of person she would be."[22]

The idea of the "lost boy" was gradually replaced by the fear that children were vulnerable to harm not only from strangers and misfits but also from elite, successful, educated young men. Fass argues that by the 1920s kidnapping was the "ideal criminal form," with the best example of this the 1924 high-profile kidnapping/murder of Bobby Franks by college students Nathan Leopold and Richard Loeb.[23] The senselessness and brutality of the abduction and murder both shocked and fascinated North Americans. Contemporary ideas of psychology were sufficiently influential that these "abnormal" self-confessed killers received life sentences instead of death. Public opinion was that children were not safe outside the house and predators could take any form.

The next kidnapping to become a public obsession proved that children were not safe even within their homes. The most famous kidnapping of the twentieth century is the 1932 abduction of Charles A. Lindbergh Jr. who, like Psyche, was taken from his home when parents and servants were nearby. The Lindbergh child was only twenty months old and, like Psyche, blonde and blue-eyed. His parents were wealthy and famous: Charles Lindbergh had made the first solo flight across the Atlantic. Unlike earlier American kidnapping cases, Charles A. Lindbergh Jr.'s mother, Anne Morrow Lindbergh, played a prominent role in the public view of the tragedy, where she was portrayed as the dignified, grieving mother.[24] The fear of death and mutilation present in all child kidnapping cases was indelibly imprinted on the public mind when the toddler's decomposed body was found over two months after his kidnapping.

After the 1930s, kidnapping of children for ransom became less common. Fears now focused on sexual exploitation. The non-familial abduction of children, while tragic, was relatively uncommon in the United States, but its possibility loomed large in the imagination of anxious parents. Fass has written that the possibility of "kidnapping threatened the physical and emotional integrity of the family and the sanctity of child life, which was the modern family's central responsibility."[25]

In the 1950s, Fass argues, kidnapping was transformed from a crime to an American "fixation" as "some of the psychological currents stirred up in the 1920s were attached to general uneasiness about sexuality and gender and a recharged familialism."[26] Babies and adolescent girls were regarded as particularly vulnerable. Psyche, both as an infant and an adolescent girl, reflects this anxiety. The significant deviation in Psyche's story, however, is that her mother expresses no fear that her identity might be permanently altered.

Although not intended to be interpreted too literally, the context of the novel evokes a particular time and place. Young acknowledges the novelist's responsibility to "catch our way of life now" before it is lost to memory.[27] The maid wears a proper black and white uniform and refers to her employer as "the master." Coffee is not "to go" but drunk at a counter out of a proper cup. Radio and television have not flattened out local accents, and the author writes the northern Ontario working class rural accent in dialect. Unemployed, itinerant men are described as "Hoboes" moving from "jungle" to "jungle" where transients congregated and camped. A wrapper was a house dress, loosely cut and designed for hard domestic work, even if little of this actually happens in Mag's shack. *Fanny Farmer's Boston Cook Book,* first published in 1896, was the most popular American cookbook, so it is not surprising that it and the Bible share the distinction of being the only books in Mag and Butch's home. Although never stated explicitly, it is difficult not to associate the slag surrounding the mines with Sudbury, Ontario, the city with Toronto, and the location of Oliver's Restaurant with Muskoka towns such as Gravenhurst or Huntsville.

That Phyllis Brett Young attended the Ontario College of Art (OCA) during the 1930s not only accounts for some details in descriptions of the city in the novel but also provides clues about the artistic context in which readers might situate the novel's heroine. Still today, on Grange Park in Toronto, you find the University Settlement and the Art Gallery of Ontario (AGO), the latter bearing a resemblance to the gallery in

*Psyche* and known for buying and displaying the work of Ontario artists during the time period of the novel. The novel's artist figure, Nick, is certainly reminiscent of those who taught Young at the OCA, spending their winters working from sketches done during the summer months in the wilderness north of the city. Charles Comfort, for example, who taught at the OCA in the late 1930s and produced both landscapes (including of the country surrounding the mines) and portraits, might have been the model for Young's artist.[28] While the artistic context is certainly Canadian, the title of Nick's portrait of Psyche – "The *American* Venus" – signals the artist's desire to move outside national paradigms. That title, in addition to conjuring echoes of the great masters and their renderings of mythic figures (Venus being closely associated with love and classical beauty[29]) might have evoked other connotations in the minds of Young's readers. The 1926 silent film *The American Venus*, about a Miss America beauty pageant and starring Louise Brooks, was very popular at the time of the book's release. (Ironically, given the significance of the mother-daughter relationship in *Psyche*, contemporary audiences may be more familiar with the 2007 film *The American Venus*, which focuses on a dysfunctional mother-daughter dynamic that contrasts sharply with the idealized relationship depicted in Young's novel. Like *Psyche,* the film also involves the daughter's absence from her mother – but where the novel focuses on the kidnapping of the young child, the film involves her escape from her demanding mother.[30])

For the most part, the novel privileges the deep structures of plot – the complication and resolution of the trajectories of archetypal quest and popular romance – over the socio-economic specifics of mid-twentieth century Ontario. *Psyche*, as its title suggests, is the archetypal story of an individual's search for herself. Vladimir Propp's influential *Morphology of the Folktale* appeared in English only in 1968, but Young's novel, published almost a decade earlier, amply illustrates its primary finding: stories draw their momentum and force from the specific configuration of a limited set of fundamental plot elements. While the number of particular narrative elements varies depending upon different accounts – Propp identifies twenty-one in the Russian folk tale, for example, Janice Radway identifies thirteen in the popular romance[31] – such approaches share a sense that readers experience a certain catharsis when encountering familiar narrative paradigms and following them through the various stages of complication and resolution. How then can we account for Young's placing specific details within a novel that seems, at one level, to discount the significance of detail? Why does Young insist on capturing the cost of fuel, a pair of shoes, or a second-hand car, when working in a genre that seems to dismiss such detail as trivial? Analyzing the popular romance of the twentieth century, Lynne Pearce provides a useful distinction between the general category of "romantic fiction" and that of "popular romance," arguing that the former seems to have an interest in "creating rather 'loosely observed' locations (spaces and places that are recognizable and yet *not*)." By contrast, "it is clear that *popular* romance also has an interest in making its 'scene-setting' more precise: an interest that might, indeed, be seen to distinguish the 'popular' from the 'classic' and 'middle-brow' and which is probably best understood as the genre's more explicit commodification of romantic love. In other words, while the more classic romance may be seen to use its 'romantic locations' to prompt or fulfill the desires and 'expectant emotions' of the lovers, popular romance tends to make them into a 'lifestyle statement' which is (in part) the undisguised *object* of the romance."[32]

Young's novel would thus be a "popular romance," rather than "romantic fiction," with the potential to act as a powerful rhetorical vehicle for a particular view of life. But to what end? Certainly, few would disagree that the novel makes a case for nature over nurture, the trumping of environment by heredity. The heterosexual romance plot seems to centre first on the obstacles imposed by economic circumstances, next on the peril posed by a wealthy mine owner's immoral son who sees himself above the conventions of civilized behaviour, then on the injustice of seduction and adultery, and, finally, on the possibility of a happily-ever-after ending with an honest man. That most of these characters remain flat reinforces the reader's sense that their significance is as character types, not as complex individuals; *Psyche*, in other words, is not a work of psychological realism. It is a novel centred on plot rather than character, more the descendent of the novelistic tradition of Henry Fielding than of Samuel Richardson, an observation implied by the text on the cover of the 1964 Lancer Books edition, where Psyche is described as a female Tom Jones, referring to the titular hero of Fielding's picaresque novel.

The novel raises readers' expectations of a plot common in popular romances – the story of a beautiful heroine whose quest for love and happiness is thwarted by villains and socioeconomic hardships. At one level, those expectations are rewarded. But the novel also "unwrites" the popular romance plot, systematically raising and challenging readers' expectations. Most important, Psyche seems far more motivated to find the truth about herself than to establish a strong and lasting connection with a love interest. She is driven to better herself and sees the men she encounters largely as a means to that end. From the school inspector, for example, she receives a dictionary. From Nick, she learns how her own powers of observation fit within the context of the history of visual art, as well as how to speak eloquently, in a subplot that shares much with the popular musical *My Fair Lady*, a smash hit on Broadway when it appeared in 1956.[33] From the journalist, Steve, she receives the greatest assistance of all.

The significant bond between mother and daughter also challenges the conventions of popular romance. Psyche's quest for self-knowledge is ultimately a quest to find her way home to her mother.[34] In turn, Psyche's quest is paralleled by her mother's search to find her daughter. As the narrative shifts from the perspective of the mother to that of the daughter and back again, it is apparent that their thought patterns mirror one another. Their unrelenting search also allows Young to show that love – and maternal love in particular – is a powerful force in human interaction. Sharon and her fortitude, the practical and endearing Mag, and the generous Bel are ultimately what sustain Psyche and allow her to weather the storms of her various encounters with men.

The presence of so many men is another way in which this novel undermines popular romance's focus on the development of a relationship between a heroine and her love interest. Psyche, whose beauty attracts a number of potential suitors, finds herself subject to violence and seduction. Some of the dangers she encounters are clearly a function of the reduced circumstances in which she finds herself as the foster child of a couple living in poverty on the outskirts of a poor mining town. This is very different from the exotic locales that provide popular romance readers with leisurely escape. Instead, Young's readers are made aware of the lack of beauty in the slag-heaped environment in which Psyche is raised. Glimpses of Sharon's blue delphiniums or the field of wild flowers surrounding Nick's studio come as a welcome change of scenery and serve as contributing elements to readers' sense of catharsis at the novel's conclusion.

Psyche's natural appreciation of beauty and Sharon's more cultivated understanding of aesthetic principles signal at least one other aspect of the novel. Young, a trained visual artist herself, creates characters who situate themselves in a world in which the aesthetics of modernism exert a considerable influence. Psyche is able to see that the scenery around the shack she shares with Mag and Butch is replete with a whole prism of colours. This vision, so startlingly at odds with common assumptions about the wasteland aesthetics of the slag-heaped landscape, emphasizes Psyche's sophisticated artistic eye despite her lack of education. Small wonder then that, under Nick's tutelage, she is able to absorb the rudiments of art history during the course of one summer, inhaling knowledge as though in a single deep breath. What she comes to understand is akin to the argument expressed by T. S. Eliot in his watershed essay "Tradition and the Individual Talent" – that works of art engage in a dialogue with one another, benefiting and building upon the insights of earlier works of the "Tradition" as well as reflecting the outside world. Such an insight is distinctly modern and suggests that the novel should be read as speaking to and about aesthetic traditions.

One of the remarkable insights of this novel is its valorization of the appreciation of beauty, whether natural or cultivated. Even those characters the novel judges harshly, such as the mine owner's son, have an aesthetic sense. Psyche comes by her appreciation of beauty naturally, never having had the opportunity to visit an art gallery or admire the works of the great masters during her childhood. Sharon is keenly attuned to her daughter's natural preference for the colour blue, not coincidentally the colour of Sharon's eyes. There is one notable exception, however – the kidnapper's environment is clearly ugly and he lacks any interest in rectifying the situation. Against this bleak portrayal of a individual devoid of human sympathy and aesthetic sensibility, Young's other characters, moral and immoral, appear colourful and engaging.

RECEPTION OF THE NOVEL

Phyllis Brett Young's early success with *Psyche* gave her financial independence and the title, according to Donald Goudy of the *Star Weekly Magazine*, of "Canada's bestselling novelist."[35] While a bestselling novel in Canadian terms was in the order of 5,000 copies, *Psyche* reached a much larger audience and, as described by a *Toronto Star* columnist, promised the "pulsating longevity achieved only heretofore among Canadian works by Mazo de la Roche's *Jalna*."[36] Serialized in the German magazine *Stern*, which typically reached 2,000,000 readers, Young's work had incredible exposure abroad.[37] It was also serialized in the magazine *Woman and Beauty*, with vivid illustrations by Walter Wyles, the first installment of a condensed version appearing in the April 1961 issue.[38] The novel was published in 1959 in Canada and then released in the United States in the fall of 1960 and in Britain in the spring of 1961. By 1962, the novel appeared in a German edition as *Die Tochter des Zufalls* and had been translated into a number of other languages for audiences on the Continent. *Psyche* is thus one of Canada's most successful bestsellers, described variously as "a contemporary tale that brought both urban and rural Ontario into view,"[39] one that provided evidence of the "increasing exportability of our literature,"[40] and "an excellent suspense story set in Toronto."[41] Film rights were quickly sold, with Victor Saville as producer and British actress Susannah York in the role of both mother and daughter (a casting decision that appropriately underscored the similarity in appearance and character of these two characters). Ironically, given Young's patriotism and her conviction that the novel is distinctly Canadian,[42] she is quoted by Toronto reporter Lotta Dempsey as agreeing that Saville's plan to shoot the film in Great Britain will enable him to capture "the complete essence of the milieu." "I've seen the mining areas in England and Wales, and they're perfect for background," she explains, "And when I found Victor Saville wanted it, the man who did 'Goodbye Mr. Chips' and 'Mystery Ship' was good enough for me."[43] Unfortunately, Saville was ultimately unable to make the movie.

Despite the novel's success, its ability to evoke a tingle of recognition in Canadian readers who recognized "a realistic background so palpably our own,"[44] and its exploration of a theme that emerged as a key concern of Canadian writers and critics alike during the latter-half of the twentieth century (the search for identity), *Psyche* has been out of print for a number of years, little mentioned in histories of Canadian literature, and notably absent from *The Oxford Companion to Canadian Literature* as well as surveys of bestselling genre fiction in Canada. Particularly striking in this regard is *Psyche's* absence from the *Chronological Index of Crime Fiction by Canadians* compiled by Skene-Melvin. Its absence is all the more curious when one realizes that all Young's other books – with the exception of *The Torontonians* and *Anything Could Happen!* – are listed: *The Ravine* (1961) by Kendal Young (an alias used for that one novel) is listed as crime fiction written by a Canadian but set elsewhere *Undine* (1964) and *A*

*Question of Judgment* (1969) are also included. One wonders whether, had *Psyche* been listed, it would have appeared as fiction written by a Canadian and set in Canada, or whether the absence of particular place names and privileging of plot over locale would also have placed it within the category of Canadian fiction set "elsewhere." That *Psyche* was not categorized as crime fiction per se is not entirely surprising. Whereas *The Ravine* (which appears in a film version as *Assault*) focused on the criminal act, *Psyche*, by contrast, used the initial criminal act only to set in action the chain of events that drive the novel – a chain of events that subsequently involve other crimes (a shooting, prostitution, and the various deceptions of everyday social interaction). Skene-Melvin's very useful and broad definition asserts that crime fiction "encompasses adventure, crime, detective, espionage, mystery, suspense, and thriller fiction and includes tales of intrigue and violence as well as those of crime and investigation, with or without a solution."[45] He identifies four particular branches of crime fiction: crime, detective and mystery, espionage, and the thriller. *Psyche*, on Skene-Melvin's scheme, belongs to crime literature, which draws its inspiration from the picaresque – a narrative tradition in which the protagonist gathers experience and self-knowledge as s/he moves from one place to another. Skene-Melvin points out that Canada has a long history of crime fiction with a strong and vibrant writerly community. While it "hasn't lacked artists ... it has lacked the audience,"[46] and many Canadian crime writers found themselves publishing abroad and appealing to British or American audiences. During the twenties and thirties, for example, Canadian writers often masqueraded as British or American, a subterfuge adopted even by members of the Montreal Arts and Letters Club. William Lacey Amy, for example, who wrote as "Luke Allen," set his Blue Pete series in Canada but all his detective stories outside Canada, with the exception of *The Black Opal* (1935). But a number of Canadians, even early in the twentieth century, wrote under their own names and set their fiction on Canadian soil, including Morley Callaghan, who set *Strange*

*Fugitive* (1929) in Toronto, and Leslie McFarlane, who set *Streets of Shadow* (1930) in Montreal. By the 1940s, Skene-Melvin argues, crime fiction in Canada was typically set in urban locales – Margaret Bonner's 1946 *The Shapes That Creep* in Vancouver, Janet Layhew's *Rx for Murder* in Montreal – with detectives linked to particular cities – Toronto for E. Louise Cushing's Inspector MacKay and Montreal for David Montrose's detective Russell Teed, for example. Long before the watershed appearance of Howard Engel's Benny Cooperman in 1980, Canadian writers were exploring the potential of crime fiction and experimenting with the appeal of Canadian characters and settings to audiences at home and abroad.

We use the term "writers" here, rather than "crime writers," because some of Canada's most enduring crime fiction was written by authors who moved between genres and aimed their work at a wide variety of audiences from general readers to scholarly audiences. Sheila Watson's *The Double Hook* (1959), long recognized as both a pivotal example of Canadian modernism and a challenging read on any standard, is one of the novels included in Skene-Melvin's chronological index as a work of Canadian crime fiction. Other well-known and respected texts set in Canada include Malcolm Lowry's *Under the Volcano* (1947), Timothy Findley's *The Last of the Crazy People* (1967) and *The Butterfly Plague* (1969), Marie-Claire Blais' *L'Exécution* (1970), Robertson Davies' *Fifth Business* (1970), Anne Hébert's *Kamouraska* (1970), and Rudy Wiebe's *The Temptations of Big Bear* (1973) and *Where Is the Voice Coming From?* (1974). With the exception of *The Butterfly Plague*, all are set in Canada.

CANADIAN CONTEXTS

Phyllis Brett Young used the opportunity of the earliest media interviews for her successful first novel to underscore Canada's potential as both the setting for literature and a context for the emergence of talented writers. But, since she insisted that Canadian writers should advocate for their own country and on Canada's remarkable potential for a fictional setting, why is she reluctant to identify specific locales in *Psyche*, her first novel? Like many other writers of her day, in the decades prior to the institutionalization of Canadian literature and a sense of confidence in Canada as a viable setting for literature, not to mention as a country able to nurture and support Canadian writers, Young establishes a balance between the particular and the general. At one level, then, Young's intentions and her content are in opposition: although the Ontario setting is clear to anyone familiar with the slag heaps of Sudbury, for example, the specific locale is never mentioned. Her second novel, *The Torontonians*, is explicit not only about its urban Canadian locale but also about the socio-historical context of its pre-Betty Friedan era setting. Young's advocacy for Canadian content is consistent with the Massey Commission that, in 1951, signaled the need for a national literature, and argued that "to be truly national, [a literature] must be recognized as characteristic of the nation by other nations, and that it must in consequence have the human appeal and the aesthetic value to awaken the interest and sympathy, and to arouse the admiration of other peoples."[47]

The Massey Commission cites a number of factors behind the lack of a national literature in mid-century Canada, including the isolation of Canadian writers. The response to its report was not only the establishment of funds and mechanisms to support Canadian author travel abroad but also the shipment of Canadian books abroad and, in the longer term, a recasting of Canadian studies as a vehicle for cultural diplomacy. As Robert Fulford points out, this was the second part of Vincent Massey's vision. "The Massey Report politicized the subsidy of the arts. Its central argument was that the nation should support the arts so that the arts could support the nation."[48] The report triggered a number of events, including the creation of the Canada Council and the National Library. It also fostered the creation, recognition, and publication of works focusing on Canada and the creation of a national identity. It was in the post-Massey Report era that the critical work of Northrop

Frye, Margaret Atwood, and D.G. Jones found an immediately receptive audience.[49] Arguably, until 1990 the institutionalization of Canadian literature and the direction of publishing were shaped by the initiatives launched by the Massey Report. As Robert Lecker notes, the emerging Canadian canon, with relatively few exceptions, privileged works that represented the realities of Canada – its landscape, people, and search for its own identity. Books that failed to follow this formula tended to slip off the course lists, particularly off McClelland and Stewart's influential and inexpensive list of Canadian books in the New Canadian Library (NCL) series.

Young's comments on the need for Canadians to recognize and nurture their own literature anticipated those of Margaret Atwood in her watershed book of criticism, *Survival*. In that 1970 publication, Atwood introduced Canadian audiences to their own literature and literary tradition and, as the book's title implied, focused her attention on the emerging theme of the individual's survival in the face of obstacles. From Atwood's *Survival*, as well as Northrop Frye's *The Bush Garden* and D. G. Jones' *Butterfly on Rock*, Canadians began to get a sense of their literature as not only deeply rooted in the great scripts of western civilization, particularly of the Old Testament, but also as bearing witness to the socio-cultural shifts of the day.

As Canadian literature gained recognition, the works being taught in university classrooms tended to be those mentioned in the critical trilogy (Frye, Atwood, and Jones) and had a doubled perspective – one eye on history and the deep structures of myth, the other on the contemporary moment. Sinclair Ross's novel *As For Me and My House*, for example, was intended to capture the dustbowl depression era as well as explore the individual's relationship to God captured by the closing phrase of the title's originating context, "as for me and my household, we will serve the Lord."[50]

Other works appearing on course syllabi in the early decades of the institutionalization of Canadian literature included novels by Morley Callaghan, whose archetypal characters walked the streets of twentieth-century Canada; Robertson Davies, whose Deptford trilogy evoked Jungian archetypes and also depicted Ontario in the twentieth century; Margaret Atwood, whose novel *Surfacing* opened with a road trip that served both to introduce its readers to an archetypal quest story and also to remind them of the particular landmarks of a highway leading to northern Quebec; and Hugh MacLennan, whose works captured socio-political events of the twentieth century in generalized patterns of binary opposition and dialectic while also portraying Canadians, with their admirable tendency towards moderation, as a valuable paradigm for diplomacy. This Canadian literary canon or shortlist of works of significant cultural currency emerged for practical as well as for intellectual reasons. Drawing on a questionnaire distributed to Canadian writers and academics, three shortlists of works to be included in the NCL list were announced, to heated controversy it must be said, at the now infamous 1978 Calgary conference: "the most 'important' 100 works of fiction" (List A); the ten most important novels (List B); and the ten most important works of various genres (List C).[51] Of the ten novels appearing at the top of the "most important 100," Montreal figures as the setting in four (Roy, *The Tin Flute*, 1945; MacLennan, *Two Solitudes*, 1945; Richler, *The Importance of Duddy Kravitz*, 1959; MacLennan, *The Watch that Ends the Night*, 1959), Toronto in one (Davies, *Fifth Business*, 1970), and rural Canada in the other five (Ross, *As For Me and My House*, New York 1941, Toronto 1957; Leacock, *Sunshine Sketches of a Little Town*, 1912; Buckler, *The Mountain and the Valley*, 1952; Mitchell, *Who Has Seen the Wind*, 1947; and Laurence, *The Diviners*, 1974). List B, the ten most important novels ("novels," that is, as opposed to "books") replaces *Two Solitudes* with Sheila Watson's 1959 *Double Hook*, and Leacock's *Sunshine Sketches of a Little Town* with the first novel of Laurence's Manawaka Series, *The Stone Angel*, 1964.[52]

The impact of the NCL series cannot be underestimated. For practical reasons, these inexpensive paperbacks quickly entered circulation in classrooms across the country, and the works themselves became cultural currency for audiences quickly learning to appreciate their own literature. However, as a result of the NCL choices, a number of very well received and valuable works of Canadian literature, and of Canadian modernism specifically, fell out of favour and out of the public eye. There is currently a concerted effort to revisit the canon and to reclaim and reissue important works that are unavailable. For example, Gwethalyn Graham's *Earth and High Heaven*, first published in 1945, was reprinted by Cormorant Press in 2003. Phyllis Brett Young's second novel, *The Torontonians*, first published in 1960, was reissued by McGill-Queen's University Press in 2007. A large initiative called the "Early Modernisms in Canada" project was launched in 2008, with support from the Social Sciences and Research Council of Canada, to encourage and support the reissue of modernist texts that are currently unavailable.

Taken together, Canadian novels of the 1970s and 1980s articulated the persistent query, best expressed by Northrop Frye, "Where is here?"[53] If the novels charted an individual's search for his or her own place in the world (such as Atwood's *Surfacing*, Laurence's Manawaka Series, specifically the novels framing it, *The Stone Angel* and *The Diviners,* Munro's *Lives of Girls and Women* or her aptly entitled *Who Do You Think You Are?*), then the novelistic canon posited the search for an identity (personal, communal, regional, or national) as a pressing and persistent concern for Canadians. Young's *Psyche* fits well within this literary landscape.

Young's career was launched at the moment Canadian literature was on the verge of becoming institutionalized, when Canadian books were soon to be available in homes and classrooms, when Canadian writers were beginning to see that writing was a viable career and that it might just be possible to stay in Canada and make a living as a writer rather than being forced to flee to another country and direct their books towards the larger audiences in Britain or the United States. If the early 1960s found Atwood, Laurence, and Richler abroad, the 1970s found them back in Canada. Young followed a similar trajectory, but a decade earlier. As with other writers who claim to have come to a new appreciation and understanding of their Canadian home while abroad, Young discovered much about Canada from the vantage point of Geneva. "Living in an international colony taught the Youngs a lot about Canadians," writes Mary Jukes after an interview in which Young explained that "the only two names everyone seems familiar with are Mike Pearson and Mazo de la Roche." As Jukes explained, "In searching for a reason she came to the conclusion that it was because we have so little Canadian literature – not enough novels, plays, for, by, and about Canadians."⁵⁴ While she wrote *Psyche* in Geneva, taking advantage of the time afforded by the staff available to her as wife of a United Nations employee, she and her husband also recognized that they were not willing to spend their lives abroad, that "something vital was missing."⁵⁵

The theme of lost or missing things has reverberated throughout this introduction. The novel is about a missing child, and has itself been missing from the contemporary literary landscape. By reissuing *Psyche* we invite readers to rediscover and recover one of Canada's bestselling novels.


EDITIONS OF *PSYCHE*

- *Psyche.* Toronto, Longmans, Green & Co., 1959. (Hardcover, English language edition)
- *Psyche.* New York: G.P. Putnam's Sons, 1960. (Hardcover, English language edition)
- *De Tijd Zal Hat Leren,* Utrecht, Uitgeverij de Fonetin, [1960?] (Hardcover, Dutch language edition)
- *Psyche.* London: W.H. Allen & Co., 1961. (Hardcover, English language edition)
- *Psyche.* Hamburg: Wolfgang Krüger Verlag, 1962. (Hardcover, German language edition)
- *Tochter des Zufalls.* Vienna: Buchgemeinschaft Donauland, 1962. (Hardcover, German language edition)

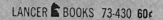

# Phyllis Brett Young

# PSYCHE

Like a female Tom Jones she
was tossed into the world
alone. And, every man who
saw her—wanted her.

"Excellent novel. outstandingly well written." *Hartford Courant*

# Phyllis Brett-Young

# Die Tochter des Zufalls

- *Die Tochter des Zufalls*. Stuttgart, Deutscher Bucherbund, 1962. (Hardcover, German language edition)
- *Sokea Leikki*. Helsinki: Kustannusosakeyhtiö Tammi, 1963. (Hardcover, Finnish language edition)
- *Psyche*. London: Pan Books Ltd., 1964. (Paperback, English language edition)
- *Psyche*. New York: Lancer Books Inc., 1964. (Paperback, English language edition)
- *Psyche*. Munich, Wilhem Heyne Verlag, 1965. (German paperback edition)
- *Psyche*. Toronto: Paperjacks, 1976. (Paperback, English language edition)
- *Psyche*. London: White Lion Publishers Ltd., 1976. (Hardcover English language edition)
- *Psyche*. Munich: Wilhelm Heyne Verlag, 1976. (Paperback, German language edition)

Approximate translations:
*Tochter des Zufalls*, "The Daughter of Chance"
*Sokea Leikki*, "The Blind Game"
*De Tijd Zal Hat Leren*, "The Time Will Teach"[56]

NOTES

1 We wish to thank Michael Gauvreau for his assistance on G. S. Brett, Gwendolyn Owens for her assistance on Charles Comfort, Michele Rackham and Christine Mervart for their research assistance, as well as Valerie Argue for her foreword and personal photos. Phyllis Brett Young's papers are available at the Howard Gotlieb Archival Research Center at Boston University and we are grateful to Adam Dixon, archival assistant, for facilitating our access to the collection and its treasures. Thanks also to Kathleen Holden and Joan McGilvray for their close readings.

2 Young, *Psyche*, 51.

3 Slater, *Minerva's Aviary: Philosophy at Toronto, 1843-2003*, 237.

4 Gauvreau, Personal communication, 9 April 2008. See also Irving, "The Achievement of George Sidney Brett (1879-1944)."

5  Fass, *Kidnapped: Child Abduction in America*; Slater, *Minerva's*.
6  G S Brett. *A History of Psychology Volume 1: Ancient and Partristic* (London, 1912), 4-5. Quoted in Gauvreau, "Philosophy, Psychology, and History: George Sidney Brett and the Quest for a Social Science at the University of Toronto, 1910-1949," 228.
7  Before the 1940s, Toronto and McGill were the only universities in Canada that made this disciplinary split. Gleason, *Normalizing the Ideal: Psychology, Schooling and the Family in Postwar Canada*, 22.
8  Gauvreau, "Philosophy."
9  Raymond, *The Nursery World of Dr Blatz*, 28.
10  Dowbiggin, *Keeping America Sane: Psychiatry and Eugenics in the United States and Canada, 1880-1940*, 183; McLaren, *Our Own Master Race: Eugenics in Canada, 1885-1945*.
11  Raymond, *Nursery*, 105.
12  Gauvreau, "Philosophy," 230.
13  Slater, *Minerva's*, 244.
14  Gauvreau, "Philosophy," 236.
15  Slater, *Minerva's*, 264-5.
16  Young, *Psyche*, 57.
17  Dummitt, *The Manly Modern: Masculinity in Postwar Canada*; Seeley, *Crestwood Heights: A Study of the Culture of Suburban Life*.
18  Brett, "Introduction."
19  Young, *Psyche*, 196.
20  Young, *Psyche*, 225.
21  Paula Fass, *Kidnapped: Child Abduction in America* (Oxford: Oxford University Press, 1997), 43.
22  Young, *Psyche*, 98.
23  Fass, *Kidnapped*, 63.
24  Fass, *Kidnapped*.
25  Fass, *Kidnapped*, 134.
26  Fass, *Kidnapped*, 18.
27  Bishop, "Phyllis Brett Young: With the Canadian Slur."
28  The authors are grateful to Gwendolyn Owens for this suggestion.
29  Grant and Hazel suggest that Venus was "identified from very early times with the Greek Aphrodite, and endowed with her mythology," Grant, *Who's Who in Classical Mythology*, 341. Grant and

Hazel identify Aphrodite as "The Greek goddess of love," Grant, *Who's*, 36.

30 Buchanan, "American Venus: Synopsis," http://tv.msn.com/movies/movie.aspx?m=2077071&mp=syn.

31 Radway, *Reading the Romance* (London and Chapel Hill: University of North Carolina Press, 1984), 150.

32 Pearce, "Popular." 533.

33 That Psyche is a heroine destined for greatness is evident in her remarkably self-possessed demeanour, even as a child. That her speech does not reflect the sophistication of her lineage and thought is realistic. However, it is relatively unusual in literary convention. Consider Pip of Dickens' *Great Expectations*, who speaks in Standard English despite his working-class background.

34 One wonders, as Michele Rackham points out, whether "the plot structure, the novel's post-war context, and references to Venus (Aphrodite) might suggest that *Psyche* positions itself as a rewriting of *The Odyssey* and, within the context of the twentieth century, engages in a dialogue with the quintessential Modernist novel, Joyce's *Ulysses?*" Certainly *Psyche*, like *Ulysses*, makes effective use of shifting narrative perspectives, the latter moving between the perspectives of Stephen Dedalus and Leopold Bloom. *On the Subject of Psyche*, email correspondence with the author (2008).

35 Goudy, "The Case of the Reluctant Writer."

36 Dempsey, "Private Line."

37 "Boston University Begins Collection of Phyllis Young Manuscripts, Letters."

38 Brown, "George Sidney Brett." April 1961, 64-7, 127, 129, 131.

39 Goudy, "The Case of the Reluctant Writer."

40 Bishop, "Without the Canadian Slur," 13.

41 Bishop, "Without the Canadian Slur," 12.

42 "In that the people are absolutely Canadian," Mitchell, "Writer Denies Need for Inspiration, Lazy Streak Her Only Problem." Her novels more generally have a "wholly Canadian background and outlook," Goudy, "The Case of the Reluctant Writer."

43 Qtd. in Dempsey, "Private Line."

44 Bishop, "Novel of the Week."

45 Skene-Melvin, *Canadian Crime Fiction, an Annotated Comprehensive Bibliography of Canadian Crime Fiction from 1817 to*

1996 and *Biographical Dictionary of Canadian Crime Writers, with an Introductory Essay on the History and Development of Canadian Crime Writing*, x.

46 Skene-Melvin, *Canadian Crime Fiction, an Annotated Comprehensive Bibliography of Canadian Crime Fiction from 1817 to 1996 and Biographical Dictionary of Canadian Crime Writers, with an Introductory Essay on the History and Development of Canadian Crime Writing*, xv.

47 "Chapter Xv: Literature," 223.

48 Fulford, "The Massey Report: Did It Send Us the Wrong Way?," 1, robertfulford.com/MasseyReport.html.

49 Key texts include Frye's *The Bush Garden*, Margaret Atwood's *Survival*, and D.G. Jones' *Butterfly on Rock*.

50 "Joshua," 24.15: 351.

51 Steele, ed., *Taking Stock: The Calgary Conference on the Canadian Novel*, 151.

52 Steele, ed., *Taking*, 153-4.

53 Frye, "Conclusion," 826.

54 Jukes, "Once over Lightly."

55 Qtd. in Jukes, "Once over Lightly."

56 Thanks to Valerie Argue for providing bibliographical details from her home library as well as approximate translations of titles.

WORKS CITED

Archer, Eugene. "Susannah York Gets Dual Role." *New York Times*, 226 August 1961, 1.

Bishop, Dorothy. "Novel of the Week." *The Ottawa Journal*, 28 November 1959, 1.

Bishop, Dorothy L. "Phyllis Brett Young: With the Canadian Slur." *Ottawa Journal*, 4 June 1960.

"Boston University Begins Collection of Phyllis Young Manuscripts, Letters." *The Globe and Mail* 1964.

Brett, G. S. "Introduction." In *Introduction to Psychology*. Toronto: MacMillan, 1929.

Brown, Harcourt. "George Sidney Brett." *Isis* 36, no. 2 (1946): 110-14.

Buchanan, Jason. "American Venus: Synopsis." http://tv.msn. com/movies/movie.aspx?m=2077071&mp=syn.

"Chapter XV: Literature." *Royal Commission on National Development in the Arts, Letters & Sciences*, 222-43. Ottawa: King's Printer, 1951.

Dempsey, Lotta. "Private Line." *Toronto Daily Star*, Tuesday, 3 October 1961, 1.

Dowbiggin, Ian. *Keeping America Sane: Psychiatry and Eugenics in the United States and Canada, 1880-1940*. Ithaca: Cornell University Press, 1997.

Dummitt, Christopher. *The Manly Modern: Masculinity in Postwar Canada*. Vancouver: University of British Columbia Press, 2007.

Fass, Paula. *Kidnapped: Child Abduction in America*. Oxford: Oxford University Press, 1997.

Frye, Northrop. "Conclusion." In *Literary History of Canada, Canadian Literature in English*, edited by Carl F. Klinck, 821-49. Toronto: University of Toronto Press, 1973.

Fulford, Robert. "The Massey Report: Did It Send Us the Wrong Way?" robertfulford.com/MasseyReport.html.

Gauvreau, Michael. Personal communication, 9 April 2008.

– "Philosophy, Psychology, and History: George Sidney Brett and the Quest for a Social Science at the University of Toronto, 1910-1949." *Canadian Historical Association: Historical Papers* (1988): 209-36.

Gleason, Mona. *Normalizing the Ideal: Psychology, Schooling and the Family in Postwar Canada*. Toronto: University of Toronto Press, 1999.

Goudy, Donald. "The Case of the Reluctant Writer." 24 February 1962 1962.

Grant, Michael and John Hazel. *Who's Who in Classical Mythology*. Oxford: Oxford University Press, 1993.

Irving, J A. "The Achievement of George Sidney Brett (1879-1944)." *University of Toronto Quarterly* 14, no. 4 (1945): 329-65.

"Joshua." In *The New Oxford Annotated Bible*, edited by Michael D. Coonan, 314-52. Oxford: Oxford University Press, 2001.

Jukes, Mary. "Once Over Lightly." *The Globe and Mail*, Monday 21 December 1959, 1.

Lecker, Robert. *Making it Real*. Concord, ON: Anansi, 1995.

McLaren, Angus. *Our Own Master Race: Eugenics in Canada, 1885-1945*. Toronto: McClelland and Stewart, 1990.

M████ Beverley. "Writer Denies Need for Inspiration, Lazy ▃▃▃blem." *Montreal Gazette*, 13 January 1960.

▃▃▃ ubject of Psyche." 2008.

▃▃▃ ance and its Readers." In *A Com- Classical to Contemporary*, edited ▃rd: Blackwell Publishing, 2004.

*Subject of Psyche*, email correspon- o April 2008.

*ursery World of Dr Blatz*. Toronto: ress, 1991.

Reid, ▃▃▃ Good Excuse." *The Moncton Daily Times*, 31 May ▃▃

Seeley, John R., R Alexander Sim & E.W. Loosley. *Crestwood Heights: A Study of the Culture of Suburban Life*. Toronto: University of Toronto Press, 1956.

Skene-Melvin, L. David St C. *Canadian Crime Fiction, An Annotated Comprehensive Bibliography of Canadian Crime Fiction from 1817 to 1996 and Biographical Dictionary of Canadian Crime Writers, with an Introductory Essay on the History and Development of Canadian Crime Writing*. Shelburne, Ontario: The Battered Silicon Dispatch Box, 1996.

Slater, John G. *Minerva's Aviary: Philosophy at Toronto, 1843-2003*. Toronto: University of Toronto Press, 2005.

Steele, Charles R., ed. *Taking Stock: The Calgary Conference on the Canadian Novel*. Toronto: ECW Press, 1982.

Toye, Eugene Benson and William. "The Oxford Companion to Canadian Literature, Second Edition." edited by Eugene Benson and William Toye, 1199. Toronto: Oxford University Press, 1997.

Young, Phyllis Brett. *Die Tochter des Zufalls*. Stuttgart: Deutscher Bucherbund, 1962.

– *Psyche*. Toronto: Longmans, 1959.

# PROLOGUE 1

THE child's cry floated softly down the well of the circular staircase; plaintive only because it seemed wordless; coaxing because it so obviously sought an answer from the thick, warm silence of the house.

A maid stepped through an archway under the stairs, to wait for a repetition of a call she was not quite certain she had heard. And, as she stood there, a shaft of late afternoon sunlight, falling athwart the chandelier above her head, scattered a shower of prismatic colours over her black-and-white uniform, transforming it momentarily into motley out of place in time and locale.

Again the child called, still gentle, not yet insistent.

Moving quietly away from beneath the soundless fall of colour, the maid crossed the hall diagonally and traversed a long livingroom to French windows and a garden which dropped in terraced levels to a bank of delphiniums as blue as the blue sky above.

Sharon, in a deck-chair close against the delphiniums, saw the girl immediately, and rising, walked swiftly to meet her.

"Is she awake?" she asked, as soon as she was within earshot, and her husky voice betrayed an overtone of anxiety.

"Yes, ma'am. She's not crying, ma'am. Just calling for you."

With a smile more brilliant than her wheat-gold hair, Sharon thanked the girl and dismissed her. Then, schooling her feet to a decorous walk, she made her way toward the house, while inwardly she derided her impulse toward haste.

Dwight is right, she thought wryly. I behave like a featherbrained young duck with one very young duckling, suspecting danger behind every clump of reeds, scenting trouble on every breeze that blows. That my little one is, and forever must be, my one, my only duckling, is no excuse, makes her in no way more vulnerable. It is I who am vulnerable—and I am a fool. Nothing will happen to her. So carefully watched, so much loved—what *could* happen to her?

# THE KIDNAPPER | 2

I

HE sat on an unmade bed in an attic of a second-rate boarding-house, and stared at the cracked plaster wall opposite him. It was not a prepossessing view, a fact of which he was well aware. He hated the room, and everything in it, not for what it was but for the dingy condition of living it represented. A more fastidious man would have disliked the unclean sheets because they were unclean; he resented them solely on the grounds that they were poor quality cotton rather than good quality linen.

A figure at once repulsive and pathetic, he was not unlike a gaunt grey wolf which should have been reaching its prime, but which instead, because of inherent weaknesses, already fought a losing battle against the invisible adversaries of starvation and cold. A wolf without the courage to bring its glaring animosity out of its cave to face anything but the smallest and most helpless game, without enough perception to distinguish friend from foe.

And as he sat there, scattering cigarette ashes across already soiled bed-linen, tension revealed itself in a muscle, at the corner of a thin, bloodless mouth, which twitched with the regularity of a metronome; in pallid skin drawn too taut over high cheek-bones; in the pin-point pupils of black eyes that reflected the light as reluctantly as a mountain tarn on a sunless day.

Brooding, as he had taken to doing more and more often, over the unfairness of his lot, he became convinced that he had not been treated as a veteran should have been.

Although he had spent less than two of his thirty-three years in the army, he thought of himself exclusively as a veteran, as a hero who had given his all for an ungrateful society. That he had joined up under the influence of too much whiskey, and regretted it immediately he was sober again; that he had, during his brief sojourn in uniform, been better clothed and fed than ever before in his life; that he had seen no fighting; and that he had been provided with a liberal rehabilitation allowance, were not factors to be considered at all in his simple theorem of resentment. He was a veteran. He had no money. Therefore he was discriminated against. It was as elementary as that.

He could not have said when it first occurred to him to collect, by force, this imaginary debt owed him by society, for it was an idea that ripened slowly. Petty law-breaking was by no means unknown to him, but crime on a large scale, with proportionate risks, was a new departure, and he approached it with caution. His present employment, electrical installations in private houses, made robbery at first seem the obvious answer to his problem, but he shrank from ordinary domestic thieving because it would, if it were to yield a worth-while amount, involve jewellery, and jewellery could be too easily traced. What he wanted was to make one grand coup and retire. He envisaged, when thinking of this retirement, a fast car, a service apartment, and a decorative young woman who would do exactly what she was told to do at all times.

That he should finally decide on kidnapping was almost inevitable. In spite of all existing evidence to the contrary, it seemed a comparatively simple method of acquiring considerable riches in a very short space of time. To abduct a child, even the child of wealthy parents, is rarely impossible. The crux of the matter, in his opinion, lay in selecting a child old enough that its care and feeding need present no particular difficulties, yet not so far matured that it would be able to talk coherently upon its return to its home. He decided, however, after due consideration, that the choosing of the actual victim ought to be left until all other preparations had been completed.

He laid his plans with deliberation, employing a careful cunning almost as effective as native intelligence, an asset with which his ancestry had not too liberally endowed him.

From a pawnshop he acquired a rectangular black suitcase which would pass as a tool-box to the uninitiated. Under the handle of this object he cut two ventilators shielded by neatly inserted wire screening. From a lady of doubtful virtue, who might have been expected to know better, he borrowed two hundred dollars which he invested in an old Ford, bought for cash from a used-car lot. This vehicle he stored in a downtown car park under a fictitious name, at no time bringing it anywhere near his lodgings or the building that housed the firm for which he worked. The problem of where to keep the child while he negotiated with the parents he settled to his entire satisfaction by renting a cottage, through the mails, under still another alias. He looked this acquisition over during the early hours of a Sunday morning. In spite of precise written instructions from the absent owner, he had some difficulty in locating it. He was sorely tempted to ask a solitary farm labourer for a true compass bearing, but, after only the briefest hesitation, he drove on without stopping. It was impossible, he decided, to be too careful.

When he finally found the place, a dilapidated frame house trapped between the end of a weed-grown track and a swamp that had been advertised as a lake, he knew with cynical amusement that he had been cheated. Any indignation he might have felt was based purely on principle, for the house was in every way ideal for his purpose.

On this occasion he stayed only long enough to repair a faulty lock on the back door. The job took him no more than twenty minutes, and was a perfectly legal undertaking in all respects. Nevertheless, by the time he returned to his ancient car, his narrow forehead was damp with sweat, and his bony fingers were trembling to such an extent he could scarcely fit the car key into the ignition.

He came back a week later under cover of darkness in order to install sufficient supplies for a stay of, if necessary, three weeks' duration. A bundle of cheap, new blankets, a case of whiskey, a meagre assortment of clothing, and several cartons of canned goods which included Carnation Milk and Clapp's Baby Foods, comprised the sum of preparations which he considered not only adequate but inspired.

The mechanics of his plan for collecting the money—he intended to demand two hundred thousand dollars—were simple enough, and involved nothing more complicated than a paper parcel, neither registered nor insured, addressed to Mr. V. E. Teran, Box 3005, General Post Office, City. He thought, and quite wisely, that the crowded anonymity of a public place offered more cover than any country hedgerow at midnight. A pawn, who would actually open the box, could easily be found, and hired on some slight pretext, within the precincts of the Post Office itself.

The ransom note, which he also wished to have prepared in advance, proved an unexpected stumbling block. Sitting, as he invariably did when he was in his room, on the edge of his untidy bed, he struggled evening after evening with the composition of this piece of literature. And, as the waste-basket filled with abortive attempts—later to be flushed down a communal toilet—his unhealthy skin grew red with frustration, and the unruly muscle in his cheek increased the tempo of its rhythm.

It was, curiously enough, the threat that must accompany the practical directions that bothered him so much. If he failed to make the child's death the alternative of a safe return for payment received, the whole scheme would deteriorate into a comparatively mild game of hare and hounds, with time no longer a decisive element, and the odds therefore in favour of the hounds. The parents must be frightened into acting at once and without calling in the police. Yet, psychopathically sensitive to the opinion of others, he shrank from branding himself in black and white as a possible murderer. The very word terrified him. He was no baby-killer—merely a man who had been unfairly treated, a man who had Never Been Given a Chance.

With a vision of feminine legs rampant on a heraldic motif of new cars on the one hand, and a very realistic hangman's noose in bas relief against a sea of accusing faces on the other, he was still struggling in a quagmire of indecision when the opportunity for which he had been waiting presented itself, made to order down to the last detail.

## 2

*The chimes of the grandfather clock at the foot of the circular stairway, announcing to the household that it was seven o'clock, coincided with the single deep tone of the dinner gong.*

*Sharon put her cocktail glass down on the inlaid table in front of the fireplace, but she was slower in relinquishing the object she had been holding in her left hand.*

*With a small, half-apologetic grimace at her husband, she said, "I'll take it up to her after dinner. She would be unhappy if she woke and it wasn't there."*

*With mock ceremony, she placed the small teddy-bear in the exact centre of the lounge on which she had been sitting. And the firelight caught not only his wise glass eyes, but also the shimmering mass of Sharon's hair as she stooped and then straightened again.*

*"You spoil her," the man said softly, "as much as you spoil me."*

*Sharon was tall, but she had to look up to meet her husband's grey eyes. "And why shouldn't I spoil you both just a little?" she asked, smiling. "You can't guess how much pleasure it gives me. Dwight—oh, darling—I think I must be the happiest woman in the world."*

In the shadows of the high box hedge bordering the back driveway to the house, a small flashlight winked once, no more noticeable in the gathering darkness than a firefly. A moment later the gaunt man was striding purposefully up the drive to the back door, while in his mind's eye he reviewed the layout of the house as he had seen it on two previous occasions. Yet, having reached the door, he hesitated at this, the eleventh hour, his hand suspended above the iron door-knocker, while his opposing desires and fears engaged in a last desperate encounter over a battleground of nerves still raw from previous skirmishes.

He could never afterwards recall making the actual decision. His hand, moving apparently without his conscious volition, lifted the knocker and dropped it back into place with a heavy reverberation which rippled across his cold skin like the first deep growl of an approaching storm. From that instant on it was as if he moved in a trance, doing and saying, with a cool precision quite foreign to him, everything he had so painstakingly planned.

It was the stout cook who answered the door, and he could see that she recognized him at once, even in the diffuse light of the small electric lantern above his head.

Taking the initiative with bold assurance, he said, "Sorry, Missis. It's that there special fixture for upstairs."

"Couldn't you 'ave come——" the cook began, but she got no further with her protest, for—a conscientious workman not to be deterred from finishing his job—he was already manoeuvring an over-large tool-box through the open doorway. Almost perforce she moved back to let him pass.

"Won't be but a few minutes," he told her quietly. "No need to disturb the folks if they're at dinner."

On the far side of the large, brightly lit kitchen, a swing door opened as a maid came through with an empty soup plate in either hand, and he had a glimpse of candlelight and flowers, and heard a man's deep voice and a woman's laughter.

With a quick surge of elation he realized that he had timed his actions perfectly. Walking neither slow nor fast, he crossed the kitchen toward the door that he knew concealed the back staircase.

The cook, uncertainty written clearly on her broad face, wavered between the necessity to serve a roast at once, and the knowledge that this was no proper time for an electrician to be at work in a private house. The roast won; in part because she took a pride in her cooking; in part because the man's assured familiarity with the house reminded her that he had been given right of entry twice before.

Turning toward a gleaming white stove, she said, over her shoulder, "Greta, tell the master that electric chap's here when you go in the dining-room."

The young maid, filling silver entrée dishes, nodded her neat dark head. "Hope he don't wake the baby," she said absently, and, a chap of her own to occupy her thoughts, promptly forgot the "electric chap" completely.

In the upstairs hall the man paused, listening intently. The light from a lamp on a small table against one wall accentuated the razor-sharp contours of a face devoid of all expression, and found no compassion in eyes as dark as the purpose that sent him moving, furtive and silent, into the west wing of the house.

The knob of the child's door turned noiselessly under a hand now protected by a thin cotton glove. The door opened, and closed again behind him.

A tiny night-light, which he himself had installed, showed him blue curtains, patterned with white lambs, billowing softly on a gentle night breeze; a flaxen-haired doll at rest on a blue carpet; a small pink dressing-gown hung over the back of a small chair; small pink bedroom slippers side by side under a low white cot.

"Mum—Mum?" a small voice whispered.

The black bag was set down on the blue carpet. The man's hand went to his pocket. An instant later small legs thrashed beneath blue blankets, and small hands plucked ineffectually at a dark, suffocating terror, while the sweet, sickening odour of choloroform drifted through the room.

Repressing an almost overwhelming need to cough, the man waited until he felt the small body go limp. He snapped open the lid of the black bag; snatched a down comforter from the foot of the cot, folded it, placed it in the bottom of the bag; straightened the child's now unresisting arms and legs; rolled her in her blankets, and laid her in the bag. The lid was shut and locked. A grubby envelope was placed on the empty cot. A small pillow was dropped out of the open window—a red herring to confuse a privileged class for whose intelligence he had no respect—and he was ready for the second, and in a sense, most nerve-wracking part of his scheme.

The nursery door opened and closed again. The lamp in the hall at the mouth of the west corridor cast a distorted shadow as he crossed into the east wing. In another bedroom, the black bag between his legs, his fingers working like lightning, he attached a chrome bracket to exposed wires hanging from a hole in a dove-grey wall. Using no tool other than a screw-driver, he completed the task in less than two minutes, but, when he left this room and its justification for his presence in the house, his thin lips were working and his face was a dirty ashen white.

At the top of the back stairs he removed the cotton gloves, pulled his peaked cap low over his forehead, and lit a cheap, strong-smelling cigarette. The first inhalation of acrid smoke steadied him considerably, but its chief purpose was to cover any lingering smell of chloroform. In so far as he was capable of doing so, he had thought of everything.

The cook was alone in the kitchen, and her back was toward him, a circumstance which made it possible for him to cover half the distance to the outside door before she turned and faced him directly.

" 'Night, Missis." His voice did nothing to betray him, and the hand he lifted to his cap concealed his face adequately.

The cook, affronted by the cigarette, found herself to some extent mollified by the respectful salute, and, outflanked for the second time in fifteen minutes, allowed the black bag to be carried out into the night.

The man was sweating freely by the time he reached his car. The child had appeared delicate, even fragile, and her weight had come as an unpleasant surprise to him.

He wedged the black bag on the floor between the back and front seats of the car, and climbed into the driver's seat. The engine caught, as it did not always, as soon as he put his foot on the accelerator, and he knew his first flash of triumph, but his supreme moment arrived when he reached the road, and, switching on the lights, rattled away toward his hide-out. Intoxicated by power, as he never had been by whiskey, he felt as though he had defeated the whole world single-handed. His fevered imagination conjuring up visions of barbaric luxury, he almost forgot that he had not yet exchanged his small, unconscious hostage for the thick packets of currency that he thought of as already his.

*Sharon rose from the dinner table, and, blowing out the candles, slipped her hand into Dwight's as they walked into the hall.*

*In the long living-room the cocktail tray had been replaced by a silver coffee service, and fresh logs had been placed on the fire.*

*With scarcely perceptible hesitation, Sharon sat down and lifted the heavy coffee urn with a slender hand much stronger than it appeared to be. But, before she began to pour, Dwight, who missed very little where she was concerned, said, "The coffee can wait."*

*Her glance went to the teddy-bear beside her, and then to the man watching her with affectionate amusement. "I——" she began.*

*"Never mind," he interrupted gently. "I can wait, too. Fate made a mistake when she gave us more than a single room where you—cross-eyed, my darling—could watch both members of your family at one and the same time all the time. Run along to your papoose, but don't be long."*

*When she had left the room, he sat down, and, content to be idle for a short time after a busy day, waited for her to return.*

*As long as he lived he was never to quite get the sound of her heart-breaking, agonized cry out of his ears. Piercing, terrible in its anguish, scarcely recognizable as his own name, it ripped through the quiet house like the knell of all human happiness.*

Until he reached the outskirts of the city, the man forced circumspection upon himself, observing the speed limit, going out of his way to avoid main intersections and the normal hazards of thick traffic, and watching—although reason told him that this was foolish—for policemen. But when pavement gave way to a gravel surface, and the road was flanked not by lighted houses but by a dark expanse of fields and woods, he increased his speed, and the old Ford swayed and bumped noisily along increasingly narrow and unfrequented roads.

His landmarks had been carefully memorized by now. A right turn after passing a broken-down stone stile; a farm-house in a grove of pines; a wooden bridge over a small stream; and then the straggling outposts of the willow bush which surrounded the old cottage and the swamp which extended its own unwholesome welcome, a rank smell of damp and rotting vegetation, more than a hundred yards up the track, which petered out at its margin.

Exercising what should have been an unnecessary caution, he negotiated the last stretch of this forlorn imitation of a road with his lights out. Thus he did not see the car already parked behind the house until he was so close to it that he had to jam on his brakes in order to avoid running into it.

The snapping of his nerve was an almost audible dissonance echoing and re-echoing deep inside him. Padded bills, back-bedroom trysts with other men's wives, and an unfortunate habit of cheating at cards had not been a sufficient preparation for major crime. To have come upon any car at all would have shaken him badly. To recognize, even by starlight, the uncompromising markings of a police cruiser, was to lose his head completely. That its presence there could not possibly have any adverse connection with himself, that as lessor of the property it was his right to question the presence of the police on the premises, rather than the contrary, did not begin to occur to him.

His teeth chattering with terror, his heart threatening to burst out of its bony rib cage, he threw the car into reverse with a harsh grinding of gears, and zig-zagged backwards along the track with a recklessness born of utter, uncontrolled panic. That he should regain the main road without wrecking the car against tree trunk or boulder was sheer good luck, coupled perhaps with the instinct for self-preservation which, run amok, had precipitated him into a flight as senseless as that of an animal who flees while as yet unpursued.

For nearly an hour, escape his only coherent thought, he drove at breakneck speed through a night which offered no haven and no security.

The knowledge that he was not being followed gradually making an impression on him, his frenzy slackened, and he experienced a return to something approaching reason.

He pulled the car over to the side of the road and turned off the motor. Taking out a grease-stained brown handkerchief, he mopped his face and neck, and then felt in his pockets for cigarettes. His hand encountering the small bottle of chloroform, he pulled it out and threw it from the open car window in one convulsive movement, as if by so doing he could rid himself of everything it represented. Almost crying, he beat his fists against the steering-wheel, while he thought of the fortune which had so nearly been his. I've been robbed, he thought hysterically, robbed —robbed—robbed!

It was frustrated anger rather than courage that led him to consider the possibility that all might not be irretrievably lost. He had derived a sense of security from the slow evolution of his original plan, had felt himself protected by its careful framework, and it took him some time to acclimatize himself to the idea of continuing the undertaking upon an entirely different and much more perilous basis.

Holding a cigarette in one hand, attempting to quiet the muscle in his cheek with the other, he stared blankly ahead into the night, and tried to think of what he might still do to recover the ground he had lost.

He had very little money, and he swore violently under his breath when he thought of what he had spent on the cottage and the provisions now beyond his reach for all time. On the credit side he still had the car and the child. His main objective must be to find a place where he could hide, and it seemed to him that the further he went the more safely might he accomplish this. Somewhere to the south of him lay not only the city but the lake with its almost continuous chain of towns running both east and west. The only hole that would stay open for long in the net which would soon be spread out to catch him was to the north where, no more than four hundred miles away, civilization, as such, met and was defeated by the great, rolling tides of the northern forests. On the fringes of this wilderness he should be able to find a temporary sanctuary where, for a small price, no awkward questions would be asked.

He looked at the luminous dial of his watch. Thinking it must have stopped, he put it to his ear, heard its steady tick, and was forced to believe, although it seemed fantastic, that it was no later than nine o'clock. That he should have a greater margin of time than he had thought did a lot to restore his confidence, and the quite reasonable assumption that the child had not yet been missed made him feel almost safe again.

By God, he thought, taking a deep breath, he'd beat the bastards yet. Let them find out, as they probably would—bloody nosey-parkers that they were—that he had done it. They could trace him to the cottage and think how bloody smart they were, but they weren't going to be smart enough to get him and the kid. They could have the kid when they were ready to kiss good-bye to two hundred thousand bucks, and not before. He'd show them, the whole stinking, bloody lot of them, how smart they were.

He had already started the engine and engaged the clutch, before it occurred to him to think of the child as a living creature who might need attention. Suddenly as concerned for her well-being as he had recently been careless of it, he jumped out of the car, and, turning on his flashlight, opened the back door and hastily unlocked the black bag. His relief when he found that she was still breathing, and therefore still negotiable, was intense.

She had freed her arms from her blankets, but she had not regained normal consciousness. That she had been much too hot in the close confines of the bag was evidenced by her flushed cheeks and the dampness of her fair curls, but apart from this he saw nothing in her appearance to cause him any alarm.

Kids are tougher than they look, he thought callously, and closed and locked the black bag again. Then, climbing back into the car, he settled himself as comfortably as he could for the all-night drive ahead of him.

He was able to take his bearings from the first small town through which he passed, and not long after that was on the main highway to the north.

He encountered very little traffic, and for two hours made good time without admitting to himself that eventually he would be forced to make a stop in order to buy gasoline. It was nearly midnight, and the needle of the gauge was hovering close to the empty mark before he would face the necessity. Then, as irrational in this as in everything else, he became terrified lest the tank run dry before reaching a service station. When he next saw the glimmer of lights ahead of him this fear had become, for the moment, so much greater than any other, that he drove up to the pumps they had signalled without the slightest hesitation.

It was a girl who came out to serve him; a stocky, dark-haired girl wearing a blue smock with 'Pete's Place' emblazoned on one sleeve.

"Fill her up," he said briefly.

"You want the oil checked?"

"No."

Beyond the pumps he could see a brilliantly lit lunch counter with windows open to the warm night, and he realized that he wanted a cup of coffee as much as he had ever wanted anything in his life. Running his tongue over dry lips, he wondered if he dared go in. The place was empty; he could sit at the counter and watch the car at the same time; and the fact that a girl was looking after the pumps seemed proof that she and another smocked figure he could see inside were the only people around.

"That'll be four sixty-five."

He watched her narrowly while she counted out change for the five-dollar bill he handed her. She did not appear to take the slightest interest in him.

He waited until she had gone back inside before making up his mind. Then, getting out of the car, and locking it, he followed her up a shallow flight of steps and through a screen door which he failed to shut properly.

It was not until a cup of coffee had been set down in front of him that he noticed the radio, which he realized had been on ever since, and probably before, he came into the place. The sweat breaking out on his forehead, he heard the opening sentences of a midnight newscast.

Swinging around, he addressed the two waitresses who were idly talking to one another at the further end of the counter. "Turn that thing off, will you. It gets on my nerves."

The dark girl replied. "The boss don't like——"

"Turn the bloody thing off!"

The girl shrugged, did as he asked, and, deliberately turning her back on him, resumed her conversation.

Radios, telephones, police—soon, if not already, they would all be his mortal enemies. He took a scalding mouthful of coffee, and spat it back into the cup. The radio silenced, the girls' voices were perfectly audible to him. He was tempted to tell them to shut up. They made it difficult for him to listen for approaching cars, and he was not going to risk staying if another car drew up outside.

"—don't think he could have really meant it."

"Oh, he meant it right enough. It's just the way he is."

"Well, if you ask me—say, did you hear that?"

"What?"

"Listen! I could've sworn I heard a kid crying."

The man's stool crashed backwards to the floor, and coffee poured across the marble counter from an overturned cup, as he leaped for the door.

Fumbling frantically with his car keys, he could hear that the child was not only crying, but also beating small fists in wild desperation against the walls of her black prison.

His foot pressing the accelerator to the floor boards, he swung the car violently away from the pumps and sent it hurtling into the darkness ahead. Again he had escaped; but there was no escaping from the sobbing of the child whom he took with him.

"Shut up—shut up—shut up!" he muttered savagely. "Do you hear me, you bloody little bastard—shut up!"

*The clock at the foot of the circular stairway struck three in a house normally, at that hour, quiet and dark, tonight blazing with lights.*

*Sharon heard it, and thought: "She has been gone eight hours now." First it was one hour, then two, then three—now the black gulf stretching between her and her baby was eight hours wide. How much wider was it going to get? "Oh, God—God, in Your mercy, bring her back to us! Christ—help me to bear the unbearable!"*

*Dwight, standing behind Sharon's chair, bleak grey eyes fixed on the ashes of a fire that had died unattended nearly eight hours earlier, heard the clock, and thought: "She can't go on much longer like this. God, show me how best I can help her."*

*The police inspector, sitting across the room from them, heard it, knew he should have been in bed long ago, and wondered what it was about these people that had brought him back to this house for the third time that night, when he could have delegated this last visit to a junior officer.*

*He ran his finger down the side of his long, deeply creased face, while he wished he had more and better news to give them.*

*Clearing his throat, the sound loud in a house too quiet since the tread of many feet had ceased soon after midnight, he told them that the kidnapper had been identified one hundred and forty miles north of the city. Speaking quickly and concisely, he gave them an account of the long-distance call received from a dark-haired waitress who had seen more than she had appeared to see, and whose photographic memory had produced a description even more exact than that on the nation-wide broadcast which she had picked up at two o'clock.*

*Dwight's voice was steady. "Someone will see this girl personally?"*

*"A special detective is already on his way."*

"You're setting up road blocks?"

The inspector nodded. "By seven o'clock this morning every car moving on a main road within four hundred miles of that lunch counter will be stopped and searched."

"It can't be done any faster?"

The inspector did not resent the question. He had asked it himself, and with more heat, at headquarters. "It's a big country, sir, and when you look at it where we're looking, a very empty one. We're moving men in as fast as we can."

Sharon saw an army of blue-coated men marching down into a gulf now nearly nine hours wide, and knew that she must go with them, down, down into the darkness——. With a whisper as meaningless as the soft whisper of her silk dress, she crumpled forward on to the floor.

The child's frenzied, piteous crying was a steady assault on the man's nerves for more than an hour and a half. Cursing himself for the crazy impulse which had moved him to throw away chloroform he would willingly have employed any number of times, he raved and shouted at her in a hoarse voice which occasionally rose to a scream. His black eyes, fixed on the narrow band of light always just in front of the car, were scarcely sane, and, at about the time when she finally became silent, he was very close to quieting her for good with a spanner that lay on the floor beside his feet. The ransom was all that had prevented him from doing so earlier. Money was his only remaining reality in a nightmare in which life and death had become equally inconsequential, in which there had never been a day, never anything but darkness and fear and an empty road that curved and twisted and straightened, only to curve and twist and straighten again.

At first he had been relieved when he noticed how infrequent the towns were becoming, and how insignificant, no sooner approached than lost in the chasms of the night behind him. And trees, interspersed less and less often by clearings, had seemed to provide cover for a flight which would evade all pursuit. But now, the quiet black palisades of forest, pressing in on him from both sides, unbroken for miles by any sign of human habitation, became a menace in themselves. Born and bred in the noisy, never-sleeping heart of a great city, this vast silence appeared as inimical to him as the dark, unexplored silence of outer space.

If he had been told then that a full-scale man-hunt had already been launched against him, that the hunters were at that moment setting up their traps ahead of him, and that only by a miracle had he escaped those even now in place behind him, he would not have believed it.

Mesmerized by the steady hum of the car engine, so unvarying a rhythm it scarcely qualified as sound any more, his brain fogged by lack of sleep, he was unaware that his speed was decreasing, and that his driving was becoming more and more erratic, the old car wandering from one side of the road to the other like a drunk unlikely to reach home safely.

As the stars began to fade, and darkness was diluted by a thin promise of dawn, the trees fell back to give way to what at first appeared to be rolling pastureland; pastureland that grew, with sudden, appalling lack of forewarning, into squat, unnaturally smooth mountains rearing up in stark silhouette against the dying night.

The mines, the man thought dully.

The hydro pole into which he crashed two miles further on seemed to come to meet the car, rather than the car going toward it. He was aware of a sickening jar and a sharp agony in his left side, while his ears rang with the harsh discord of splintering wood, tortured metal, and shattered glass.

The rippling echoes of a disturbance too slight to affect the grim slag hills that had borne witness to it, had long since dissipated before he was able, or even dared, to move.

Dragging himself out of this trap of his own devising, a wounded animal concerned now with nothing beyond its own immediate safety, he took stock of a situation which, bad though it was, could have been considerably worse. Once on his feet, he found that he had sustained, apart from cracked ribs, nothing more than minor bruises. His hand pressed to his side to ease the

pain there, his pallid mouth funneling a steady stream of obsceni-
ties, he examined the car.

In a grey light, belonging neither to night nor to day, he saw
that it had fared, if anything, better than he had himself. One
headlight was smashed, the grill was buckled, and the front
bumper, embedded in the shredded side of the wooden pole, had
been torn loose, but there was no really serious damage visible. If
the wheel alignment was still true, it could be driven with safety.

Hope flaring up in him again, he struggled into his seat, started
the motor, and, in reverse gear, roared the engine. The chassis
vibrated noisily, and the wheels spun, but the car did not move.
Flinging open the door, he got out to discover what was the
matter.

On first sight of the front wheel overhanging the edge of the
ditch, he thought it would be comparatively easy to push the car
free of both ditch and pole. Five minutes later, blind with sweat,
his side a torment he wished he could tear out with his bare hands,
he knew he was beaten: even uninjured he could not have done
it. Wildly he looked up at the lightening sky, desperately searched
with bloodshot eyes a landscape devoid of life or movement of
any kind, a world in which nothing grew and no birds sang.
Shivering with cold and fear, his breath coming in short laboured
gasps, he knew he must run, and made an enormous effort to pull
himself together sufficiently to think of what must be done before
he started running.

The license plates—he must get them off. With the spanner he
did this as fast as he could, and then, bending and hammering
them, reduced them to a size he could stuff into his pockets.

Taking out a comb, he ran it through lifeless dark hair, combed
too often and washed too little, while he wondered confusedly if
there was anything else he could do to remove any possible connection between himself and this wreck he should leave behind
him as quickly as possible. The black bag—he dared neither leave
it nor open it. Eventually, his connection with the car would be
established: to abandon the black bag would be madness. Yet—
the fear which he had been forcing into the farthest recesses of his
mind leapt gibbering into the light—if the child were dead he did

not want to know it, and what but death could have kept her silent so long? Why had she not cried out when the car struck? Why was she not crying now? He took two steps away from the car, and then stood still. He could not, must not leave that glaring clue. And what if the brat was dead? He hadn't killed her—they couldn't say he had killed her. He could open the bag without looking at her, could dump her on to the floor without even touching her. If they ever caught him he could say she was alive when he left her—they would have to believe him, because it would be true—it would be true—it would be true——

Mumbling incoherently, he opened the rear door of the car, pulled the black bag up on to the seat, unfastened the catches, hesitated an instant, and then, his eyes screwed shut, turned it upside down above the gap between front and back seats. There was a slithering sound, a soft thud, and silence. A horrid, wordless noise escaped from his slack mouth, and he sprang backwards as though from a pestilence, slamming the door with such force that the windows rattled and fresh fragments of glass from the broken headlight fell to the ground with a cold, musical tinkle.

Briefly, he stood frozen where he was, his teeth chattering audibly in a silence now unbroken by any other sound. Then, the empty black bag bumping against his legs, he turned and ran down the road pursued by devils which would never again be far behind him.

# 3 | THE HOBOES

THEY came along the deserted road that wound through the slag, just as the first yellow streaks of dawn were staining the eastern sky. There were two of them, and they employed a shambling walk that covered the ground with a minimum of effort while producing a very fair rate of progress. They were on their way south to a "jungle" in a city ravine, and an autumn conference of their kind in which it pleased them to play a yearly part. Like migrating birds, they had habits. Following the sun, propelled not only by their own whims but by a constabulary that wasted neither sympathy nor affection on them, they steered a seasonal course that varied amazingly little from year to year. This time it had taken them longer than usual to beat their way across the continent, and they were in a hurry lest they be late for their conference and the always interesting debacle that ensued when the police, spurred by an irate citizenry, moved in to break it up. Normally they rode the rods, but a small incident involving a brakeman now suffering from a sore head had made it advisable to desert the railroad in favour of the highway.

Approximately the same height, dressed in much the same *mélange* of cast-off clothing, they were scarcely distinguishable one from the other. They were neither of them young, but their faces, weathered and not unamiable, had an ageless quality common to men who carry no responsibilities heavier than the light packs on their backs.

They both saw the car at the same moment, and without need

for verbal communication became host to the same speculations. Anything was grist to their mill, and a deserted and partially wrecked car promised, to the enterprising, a number of small items that could later be negotiated for beer, cigarettes, or even cash.

Glancing casually over their shoulders, they quickened their pace, and approached the car. Sharp eyes alert, they noted its age and make, the dust that lay thick over it, the extent of its damage, and, most particularly, the absence of license plates.

"The heap's hot."

"I reckon."

There was evident satisfaction in both their voices. A stolen car was anybody's prize, to be looted as thoroughly as was humanly possible.

Before touching anything, they prowled around it like stray dogs around an intriguing garbage can, while a possibility, so glorious they were at first afraid to entertain it, began to dawn on them. When they saw the keys, an open invitation, in the ignition, they wasted no time on making an inventory of the car's contents.

"Think we can shove her out?"

"Nothin' to it."

"Enough juice to get her there?"

Distrusting the gauge, a rusty nail was attached to a piece of string, lowered into the gas tank, drawn out and examined.

"More'n enough."

They had said all that was necessary. Less than sixty miles further south was a wrecker who had the good taste not to ask questions, and whose establishment could be reached via rural roads unprofaned by police patrols. Laying down their packs, they put their shoulders to the fenders, and a minute later the car rolled backwards on to the highway.

Smiling broadly, they recovered their packs, and climbed in.

"Damned if I ain't forgot to renew my drivin' license," remarked the man who had elected to drive. Stepping on the starter and rewarded by an engine that turned over at once, he settled back with an air that royalty in a Rolls Royce might have attempted in vain. He was on the verge of throwing in the clutch when his eye was caught by the dislodged bumper lying at the foot of the mutilated hydro pole. He looked up at the sky. It was nearly morning, and he knew that it was tempting an already too beneficent fate not to get the hell out in a hurry, but it was not in his nature to leave anything behind that could be turned into profit. He pointed to the bumper, and his shabby companion, in agreement with him on this, as on most other matters, immediately got out and retrieved it.

"Shall I throw it in back?"

"Good enough."

"There's some right nice blankets in—Christ Almighty, there's a kid in here!"

In an instant the driver had eased his bulk out from behind the wheel and opened the rear door on the far side of the car, to find himself looking down at a small, tear-stained white face, and fair curls not thick enough to cover the ugly swelling on one side of a small head. A slow, hot wrath suffusing his blunt features with red, he said heavily, "Afore God, I'd like to kill the bugger that done it."

"She's out cold, but she's breathin' all right."

"Let's git her up off the floor."

With horny hands, clumsy but amazingly gentle, they lifted the unconscious child on to the back seat.

"You reckon she was left for dead?"

"I reckon."

"You remember what I done to Alf when he kilt that little dog?"

It was a memory the other man had no wish to resurrect. "Forget it," he said abruptly. "It's the kid we got to think about. She ain't hurt real bad. What are we goin' to do with her, though?"

Their two faces a study in disturbed perplexity, they stared at the child whom they both assumed had been wantonly abandoned by its own kin. Theirs was a world that acknowledged no ties of any kind, but it bordered at times on a more domesticated existence where such a thing was a not uncommon occurrence. They were angry and upset, but they were not surprised. Man's inhumanity to man was not the least of the causes that had driven them away from society. They were unquestionably shiftless, immeasurably lazy, and could not, by the wildest stretch of imagination, have been called honest men, yet they never for an instant thought of leaving this little creature in the ditch for someone else to find—or not, as the case might be.

The man who had discovered the child pushed a battered felt hat back from his face, and rubbed his hand slowly across a square, unshaven jaw. Then his eyes sought something fifty feet further along the highway which he had earlier noticed and dismissed as of no interest. Now he pointed to it, automatically using a thumb on which he had traveled thousands of miles, and said slowly, "See that old mail-box over there a ways? Probably a shack back a piece from the road."

# 4 | THE MINER AND HIS WIFE

I

THE first rays of the rising sun struck across a lost world of slag that could have been a surrealist's conception of prehistoric times; a barren, repellent landscape of unheroic peaks and valleys filled with purple shadows; a tarnished earth's surface as unyielding as volcanic lava, too raw, too sterile to produce growth of any kind, stranger and bleaker than the fabled mountains of the moon, shaped in haphazard ridges melting one into another without drama or individuality; a treeless, grassless, man-made desolation, naked in a crude, inhuman beauty uniquely its own.

In a gully still unwarmed by the flaming orange of a sunrise slashed with thin black streamers of cloud, the shack crouched against the inhospitable slag like the last relic of a forgotten, and unsuccessful, civilization. A low wind, overlooked by the night in its passing, whined around its box-like contours and tore with idle malice at its tattered tarpaper sides. A twist of newsprint, blown against a ramshackle outhouse, pawed at a half-open door, and fell back, again inanimate. In a crevice in the slag devoted to refuse, a can clattered as a rat lifted its head from its scavanging to gaze with cruel ferocity at the bundle lying on the single, shallow doorstep of the shack.

As daylight strengthened, the formless shadows in the gully became absorbed by the dark grey slag. The air, heavy with minute dust particles, took on a copper-coloured hue, and the sun, its brilliance muted as though by the smoke of many forest fires, revealed itself as a burnished copper disc.

Inside the shack, the miner's wife turned over in bed, opened eyes still bleary with sleep, and looked at a battered alarm-clock on a bureau of necessity so close to the bed she could have reached out and touched it. It was a purely automatic gesture, for the clock was never right, was, in fact, rarely wound. With a prodigious yawn, she swung her feet out on to the worn board floor and heaved her great bulk upright, her hair a soiled red banner cascading to her waist. From a row of nails, on which hung an assortment of clothing, she took a faded pink wrapper, and, still yawning, struggled into it.

"Butch!" Her voice was hoarse but not unpleasant.

No reply was forthcoming from the mountainous hump on the farther side of the brass bedstead.

"Butch! You hear me, you big ape? It's time you got movin'."

Like an amiable hippopotamus rising from a wallow it had no desire to leave, Butch sat up and blinked at a new day from under shaggy black eyebrows. "You say somethin', Mag?"

"You hear'd me."

"You got breakfast ready a'ready?"

By the light of a single, long-unwashed window, Mag scrutinized herself in the clouded mirror of the bureau while she took ineffectual swipes at her vivid hair with a brush whose bristles were worn down almost to the wood. Her voice as tranquil as her fat, good-humoured face, she said, "Don't you go a'wastin' time askin' no stoopid questions. Get up."

"Who's askin' stoopid questions?"

Bunching her hair in a careless knot at the back of her head, and skewering it with a few large hairpins, Mag did not bother to reply. She dabbed pink powder on the end of her nose, more from habit than from any remnant of once warranted vanity. Then, prepared to face a renewal of the few daily tasks her life demanded of her, she pushed aside a limp green curtain in the partition that divided the bedroom from the main room of the shack.

Ashes still warm from the previous evening made the lighting of a fire in the coal stove a relatively simple business. Moving heavily, but with a certain slow efficiency, she filled a kettle from one of the two pails of tepid water standing on the back of the huge stove. A few dirty dishes were collected from amongst an accumulation of odds and ends on a long trestle table and put into a primitive sink. Clean dishes were taken from open shelves above the sink and set on the table in a space which she cleared with a sweep of a large freckled arm. Knives and forks were sought for, and found, in a cardboard box in the top drawer of a golden-oak dresser that was her chief pride and joy. Aluminum salt and pepper shakers were set down between a greasy pack of playing cards and an unfinished piece of brown knitting whose purpose defied conjecture, and she was ready to prepare bacon and eggs. These were kept in a refrigerator that was much too frigid during the winter months, and totally useless in the summer, consisting, as it did, of nothing more than a hole in the floor reached by a trap-door.

She was already on her knees, for her a difficult process in itself, when she paused, the trap held partly open, and listened for a repetition of a sound so alien in those surroundings she thought her hearing must have been playing tricks with her. Protesting floor boards and an unhappy grunt told her that her lawful wedded husband was dutifully wrestling with the uncomplicated garments in which he was soon due to set out for the mine. The crackling of the fire, and the hiss of a kettle about to come to the boil, assured her that his breakfast would be ready as soon as he was ready for it. These were the familiar sounds she heard every morning of her life, and, unless the weather were bad, almost the only sounds, for the unproductive slag gave birth to no stir or rustle, no change or movement, simply an immense silence as profound as that which must have preceded the creation. Occasionally, high against the sky, the cry of a bird could be heard, a lonely repudiation of the brutally arid land over which it passed. But that was all.

"It musta been a bird," Mag told herself. "It couldn't have been nothin' else."

And then she heard it again, and knew that it was no bird.

Puffing with the effort involved, she got to her feet, and, walking with unaccustomed speed, crossed to the door and jerked it open. For a moment, bereft of the power of speech, she simply stared at the child who, having struggled free from her blankets, sat upright on the doorstep looking up at her with miserable, blue-eyed bewilderment.

Taking in the smudged evidence of many tears, and the ugly lump on the small head, Mag felt her heart turn over.

"For the luvva Mike," she breathed softly, "it were a stork." And without further hesitation, she stooped, picked the child up in warm, competent arms, and carried her into the shack.

"Butch! Come out here quick. Somebody's been and dumped their kid on us in the night."

There was a wordless rumble of shocked disbelief from behind the green curtain, followed immediately by Butch himself, his head thrusting forward from his great shoulders, his small eyes blinking rapidly as his limited intelligence attempted to accept the unacceptable.

The child was heavy, but Mag continued to hold her, rocking her gently, murmuring quiet reassurances in a wordless language no child could fail to understand.

"Well, I'll be——" Butch began, and, unable to finish the sentence, was forced to find it complete as it was. Shaking his bullet head from side to side, he gaped at his large spouse as if she had at that moment outdone all past performances in the way of miraculous conceptions.

Feeling the child's tense body begin to relax, seeing fear replaced in wide eyes by an instinctive, touching trust, Mag put her down, settling her against lumpy pink cushions on a sagging red couch. "There now, you feel better, don't you, kid?" Over her ample shoulder, she addressed Butch. "Get her a cuppa milk."

"Are you sure——"

"That she'll drink milk? Don't be so damn dumb. All kids like milk. Here, baby, what's your name? Tell Mag, What's your name?"

"Are you sure it's a girl?" Butch roared in a deep, bull-like voice that was curiously unterrifying for all its volume. "Them blue eyes and yellow curls don't mean nothin'. Why, when I was a kid, I had——"

The big woman regarded him with a withering contempt that reduced him to silence. "Do I look like I was born yestidday, you big baboon? Now, get a hustle on with that milk."

Butch was, and always had been, more than satisfied with Mag. She suited him. But there were times when he felt dimly that she did not accord him quite the deferential respect he deserved as man of the house. This was one of those times, but he nevertheless did what he had been asked because he could not think of anything else to do.

Mag, leaning close to the child, narrowed long-sighted eyes to look at the embroidery on the front of the simple white nightgown. "I believe you got your name right on you, haven't you, kid? Now, hold still, and let Mag take a look." Frowning, she concentrated on a pattern of letters which she actually had no trouble in deciphering, but which made no sense to her, could not be formed into syllables she could pronounce. "P—S—Y— No, t'ain't possible. Mebbe it's the kid's initials or somethin'."

Butch, by this time standing beside her with a slopping cup of milk in his large, hairy hand, said, "Mebbe it's some furrin' name."

"Could be," Mag replied doubtfully. "For the luvva Mike, what would the kid be wantin' with a saucer!" Leaving him to decide for himself what he would do with the saucer, she took the cup from him and carefully held it to the child's mouth.

Psyche took a tentative sip, said "Milk!" in a pleased tone of voice, and, putting her own small hands on either side of the cracked white cup, proceeded to dispatch its contents as fast as she could.

Standing back, her hands on her hips, Mag said, with a pride she was quite unaware of, "Why, the kid can talk some. She's real bright, ain't she?"

"How old you reckon she is?" Butch asked.

"More'n two, and less'n two and a half."

"You sure?"

"Sure I'm sure. Ain't I helped my old woman to raise eleven kids?"

"What you aimin' to do with her?"

Psyche, having finished the milk, climbed down off the couch, and, walking with a not quite certain balance, carried the cup over to the table which was level with the top of her head. With enormous care, she reached up and set the cup down. This done, she turned to look up at Mag with a radiant smile. "All done. Go home now?"

*The pages from the calendar on Sharon's rosewood desk fluttered into the wastebasket, days falling into eternity as irresistibly as the bronze leaves drifting down from the oak trees in the garden. Fourteen—fifteen—sixteen—the gulf which could no longer be measured in hours was now sixteen days wide.*

*On the morning of the sixteenth day Sharon sat in the office of a police inspector whose long, tired face reflected a defeat he would not admit in so many words.*

*Looking over his head at a large wall calendar as cruel as her own, she avoided his eyes and the message in them which she could not—would not—accept. As long as she lived, it was a message she would refuse to accept from anyone, ever.*

*The policeman, seeing the unconscious firming of her delicate mouth, and the desperate determination in blue eyes beneath level dark eyebrows, read her thoughts as clearly as if she had said them aloud. He knew her quite well now; knew that her apparent fragility masked strength; knew that there was warmth behind the cool reserve with which she usually faced the world; knew that she possessed not only imagination and a quick perception, but a mind as clear and keen as any he had ever encountered. And, knowing all these things, he was afraid she might—because of rather than in spite of her unusual gifts—perhaps destroy herself in the unending pursuit of a hope which he already saw as hopeless.*

*In the sixteen days following the kidnapping, the kidnapper* had been twice identified with reasonable certainty, the second time more than half-way across the continent; but there the trail had ended. That he had parted company somewhere along the way both with the child and the car he had been driving, was accepted by the police as fact rather than conjecture. But in what order, or where, or under what circumstances he had done this, it had been impossible to discover. All they knew was that, somewhere across a staggeringly wide course, the child, with a fawn's protective colouring and lack of scent, had disappeared without leaving a trace behind her; had, despite the scope and efficiency of the machinery set in motion to find her, vanished into thin air. She might be still alive—or she might be dead.

For the first time, the policeman found himself thinking of her as an individual, and estimating her chances of survival, not simply in terms of days and years, but as a person whose heredity and environment might well be diametrically opposed in their twin influences on her.

He became aware that the young woman opposite him had risen to her feet, and that the long silence that had fallen between them marked the termination of an interview as painfully fruitless as the many that had preceded it.

Getting up quickly, he shook hands with a formality he found both foolish and oppressive. If she had thanked him for anything at all, he felt he could not have borne it.

"We will continue to do everything in our power," he told her quietly.

"You have done everything—already, haven't you?"

She is telling me that we have given up, he thought bitterly, and really she is right. "We will continue to do everything in our power," he repeated.

Her shoulders very straight in a black coat whose sombreness she had deliberately defied with a frivolous red hat, Sharon walked to the door.

"Good-bye," she said, and then added, with soft violence, "I will never give up—never!"

During her first ten days at the shack Psyche often bumped a hurt on her head which took that long to heal, but to Butch and Mag's awe and amazement she never once cried on these occasions. She rarely wept at all. When she did, her tears were like a summer storm, coming in a brief, fierce deluge, without warning or apparent cause. The second time this happened, Mag, casting around for something with which she could be diverted, gave her a multi-coloured feather duster that she had ordered from a mail-order catalogue and never used. The feather duster failed in its immediate purpose, but Psyche was rarely to be found without it after that. She caressed its soft brilliance, talked to it by the hour, dragged it behind her both inside and outside the shack, and never went to bed without it. At night, when Mag tucked her up on the ancient couch in a corner of the tiny, cluttered store-room that paralleled the bedroom, its motley harlequin head would be on the pillow beside her fair one. And when the oil lamps were lit, and the miner and his wife were settled in the main room, if they listened they could hear the gentle murmur of an unintelligible, one-sided conversation that never seemed to reach a conclusion, that would cease only when Psyche fell asleep, and would be resumed in the morning as soon as she woke.

"It's kind of like a doll for her, ain't it?" Butch said.

"More like a person, almost," Mag answered slowly. "It's like as if it were someone she's known before."

"She's a good kid."

"Yeah, she's a good kid."

"It don't seem right that a kid like that should be in one of them orphan places."

Mag sighed. "There ain't no other place for a kid whose folks don't want it."

During the daytime Psyche kept very busy exploring the shack, a pastime that seemed of consuming interest to her. It was almost as if she were looking for something. Returning again and again to the places through which she had just methodically searched, she seemed unable to convince herself that the next time it would not, miraculously, be there. When the game became simply a game, and nothing more, it would be difficult to say, but as time went on her repeated examinations of the limited premises became more leisurely than they had been, and she would pause to rattle things that would rattle, and to attempt to rattle things that would not. Having found her way under the sagging couch, she would stay in hiding there and make small noises until Mag goodnaturedly chased her out with a broom not often used for any other purpose. Given a spoon to lick, or a dry crust on which to sharpen her few small white teeth, she would linger on the doorstep in the sunlight talking to Feather Duster.

"She ain't much trouble," Butch said.

"She ain't no trouble at all," Mag told him firmly. "Kids an' dogs an' cats, they're all much the same when you come right down to it. You gotta feed 'em an' give 'em a place to lay down, that's all."

They had had a dog once, and a number of cats which had gone on to their reward in a variety of ways, all of them abrupt. But they liked small creatures, and, though they were not consciously aware of any lack in their lives, were lonely when they were without one. Unfettered by the doubts and fears that would have been theirs if they had been more gently reared, they tackled the crisis that fate had seen fit to send them with direct simplicity. Equally simply, they drifted into a decision that was never declared in so many words.

During a hot Indian summer, Psyche grew brown beneath a brassy, cloudless sky, and, allowed to trip and fall and pick herself up again unaided, learned how to walk steadily on bare feet whose soft soles gradually assumed the consistency of shoe leather. In a face the colour of an over-ripe peach, her eyes were startlingly blue, and her short curls were bleached by the sun to palest gold. She grew thinner, the baby fat melting away from straight, strong bones, but otherwise she appeared to thrive on a diet consisting chiefly of pies, fried meats, and canned goods. Small hands, never entirely clean, became useful instruments adept at buttoning the weird costume that Mag had fabricated for her out of a vast pair of pink cotton bloomers.

That this outfit would have to be improved upon if she were to stay at the shack was obvious, and the evening when Mag sat down with a department-store catalogue and laboriously wrote out a clothes order, she inscribed, in so doing, adoption papers as formal as any that would ever be taken out.

## 2

THE first snows of that year, falling early in December, found Psyche an integral part of a way of life that was to be hers for nearly fifteen years. Chords of memory, touched from time to time by vaguely familiar harmonies of sound and colour, would occasionally upset and bewilder her, but, too young to retain specific mental images of any other existence than the one she now knew, she was on the whole perfectly happy.

Trusting, friendly, but even as a small child physically undemonstrative, she met the rough kindliness and unspoken affection of the miner and his wife with a response that was, by chance, exactly right. Independent, easily amused, increasingly loquacious, she fulfilled their need without demanding anything of them that they could not give. Her natural, and almost immediate, adoption of their own vernacular served to identify her with them as nothing else could have done. That she should, in addition to this, take a childish pride in the shack and its well-worn contents, pleased them enormously and added a lustre to it which it in no way deserved.

The shack, practically indistinguishable from dozens of other tarpaper habitations scattered across the broad swath of slag surrounding the mines, differed from these others only in that it was more remote than most. Sufficient unto themselves, Butch and Mag had chosen to separate themselves from the herd, and had, in this way, achieved the dignity of independence; the single dignity possible under circumstances against which they rebelled only in theory. They shared, in common with their kind, a fatalistic recognition of the harsh fact that they lived in a world that could exist only as long as the mines continued to produce; a conjectural span that might just possibly last a man's working lifetime, but that might, equally possibly, terminate as abruptly as a turned-off fountain. Big business, manipulating stocks and shares, could ill afford long-term advance notices of the death of a mine; and the men who first laid hands on the rich ore destined for so great a variety of transmutations, were cogs in the machine too small for any real consideration.

It was not an atmosphere conducive to permanence of any kind, yet the shack, cut off from corroborative visual proof that it was part of a community as flimsy as its own four walls, seemed to have acquired a timelessness as immutable as the slag hills which sheltered it; offered a security that, though false, was nevertheless a sufficient protection for the three who called it home.

The mechanics of life at the shack were of the simplest nature, for both Butch and Mag, essentially lazy, did things the easy way whenever there was one to be found. Though their housekeeping was sketchy to the point of non-existence, they housed no fleas or other vermin, chiefly because the surrounding trerrain effectively discouraged such forms of life. The garbage, accumulating during the week in a convenient crevice in the slag, was burned on Sunday mornings, a pagan ritual observed summer and winter alike. This task, delegated to Butch, was one that he rather enjoyed. Paying cursory attention from time to time to an acrid column of yellow smoke, he would perambulate heavily around the circumference of the small valley he looked upon as his own. That it was his only by squatter's rights he had long ago forgotten, and he favoured its few barren acres with the benign approval a member of the landed gentry might have bestowed upon rich farm and wood lands.

"Come on, kid," he would say, "it's time to walk around the propitty."

The "propitty" boasted, in all, three landmarks, the shack itself just managing to dominate outhouse and well.

The outhouse, which embodied the sanitary conveniences of the establishment, stood some forty feet behind the shack. In fine weather it served its purpose well enough. From inside one could see a pleasant rift of blue sky through the air space above the door, and an inconveniently placed leak in the roof could be temporarily forgotten. In the winter, however, it provided a deadly pilgrimage postponed as long as was physically possible, the knowledge that at least the leak was frozen over proving of small comfort.

The well, from which they drew their water supply, was not far from the front door, and had cost more to drill than the price of the shack and everything it contained; the water table, lowered by the impermeable quality of the ground above, having been finally reached at a depth of sixty-five feet. The labour involved in cranking buckets up and down was one of the reasons why washing was considered a luxury to be indulged in only after careful and lengthy consideration.

The official "front door" of the shack, to which all deliveries other than coal and kindling were made, was the mail-box on the highway a quarter of a mile away. A forsaken scarecrow, maintaining its lopsided balance by some unexplained miracle, its name long since erased by time, it was by its very loneliness an unmistakable sign-post to the truckers who laid their expected tributes at its single wooden foot. Deliveries of food were made four times a week, and new orders—often reduced to a terse 'the same'—withdrawn by the truckers from the box itself. Once a week the Liquor Control Board parted with an offering consisting invariably of two cases of beer and two bottles of the best Scotch whiskey, for Butch and Mag concurred in the belief that 'good stuff was easy on the guts'. These things came from the small mining town four miles away. Consumer goods such as clothes, household implements, and, in fact, every other item that ever found its way to the shack, came from further afield through the medium of a city department store lavish in its gifts of seasonal catalogues and monthly circulars. These advertisements were the only mail as such ever to reach the mail-box. At one time there had been an occasional ill-written missive addressed to Mag, but now her sole link with the past was her own tenacious memory, and the department store stood alone as representative of what they vaguely spoke and thought of as the "outside".

Mag, her own great weight a sufficient burden in itself, made the necessary excursions to this "front door" with voluble protests that began when she set out, and terminated only when she could again collapse, wheezing, on the couch where she spent most of her time. Psyche, on the other hand, looked forward to the visits to the highway with an eagerness that increased as she grew older. Nearly always they saw a car, sometimes more than one, sweeping briefly across their periphery, glamorous meteors on their way to or from the outside, following a road that Psyche saw as a never-ending ribbon stretched to infinity across space and time.

One day, after deep thought, she asked, "Mag, which way's the outside?"

Without hesitation, Mag pointed south. "Thataway."

"Then where's t'other way go?"

"Nowheres in partic'lar, that I knows of."

Psyche's level and surprisingly dark eyebrows drew together in a small frown of concentration. "Nowheres must be sorta like here."

Mag cast a disparaging glance at the slag which pressed against the highway on either side, grim and forbidding even at high noon. "Couldn't be no worse, anyway. Come on, kid, you're gettin' big enough to help tote some of these here things.'

Mag never made any pretense of liking anything about what was, pro tem., her home. On rainy days, after the housework was done—a chore consisting of a few idle flicks with a duster—she would settle down on the couch, and, a faraway look in her light-blue eyes, relive for Psyche's benefit her experiences before she came to the mines, dwelling with real nostalgia on such simple, and to Psyche unknown, pleasures as picking wild flowers and walking leaf-shadowed country lanes.

By the time she was seven Psyche knew every detail of these

reminiscences, if anything better than Mag did herself. A critical audience who brooked no deviation from the original text, she would interject corrections when she deemed it necessary, and demand that the answers to her innumerable questions be incorporated as part of chapter and verse.

"I ain't never known nobody with a memory like the kid's," Mag told Butch. "She never forgets nothin' she ever hears or sees."

Psyche was fascinated by all Mag's stories, but the ones she liked best were those that concerned her days in service when, first as general housemaid, and then as cook, she had worked for a family whose manner of living was beyond belief. Because Mag's vocabulary was nearly as limited as Psyche's experience, they hit upon a scheme, which afforded them both an equal pleasure, of illustrating these memoirs with the help of mail-order catalogues.

Seated on the floor beside the couch, her long thin legs tucked under her, a curtain of uncut hair falling forward over her face, Psyche would search well-thumbed pages for the article which was apropos at the moment. Nothing she could find was ever quite good enough, but this was to be expected, for Mag's past was clothed in all the splendour of King Solomon's court in its heyday.

Referring to the house in which she had worked, and in modest contradiction of the picture she had just painted of it, Mag would say, "It wasn't no palace, mind you, kid, but they did do things real nice. An honest-to-God Irish lace cloth when company came, flowers arranged real pretty for a centre-piece like, and them little glass bowls for washin' the hands in when they was finished eatin'."

One winter's day when the slag lay deep buried beneath a covering of snow whose crystalline surface cracked audibly in a temperature of more than twenty below zero, Psyche laboured at producing a facsimile of this grandeur.

When Butch and Mag sat down to a table, not only cleared of its usual attendant clutter, but embellished with candles and carefully fashioned paper flowers, Psyche's eager expectancy was more than rewarded by praise which made up in heartiness for what it lacked in variety. However, when she produced, at the end of the meal, brown paper doilies on which reposed jelly glasses filled with water, Butch failed her.

Seeing Mag's portentous wink, he knew that something extraordinary was expected of him, and, his low forehead a field fresh furrowed with perplexity, did the best he could.

Picking up the jelly glass in front of him, he drained it in one great gulp, and said, "Dee-licious, damned if it ain't."

It was the first time he had wilfully drunk water for many years. He had exhibited gallantry beyond the call of duty, and it was not his fault that it was a mistaken sacrifice.

Butch had been a rookie on the police force when he met and courted the red-headed cook who lived within the circumference of his beat, but, try as she would, Psyche could not see him in uniform. A Butch with neatly combed hair, polished brass buttons, and shining shoes, was a vision which even her lively imagination refused to conjure up. Nevertheless, the knowledge that he had been a policeman, even if long ago, gave her a certain respect for him that she might not otherwise have had. The law in itself, however, together with all its official representatives, became fixed in her mind as well-meaning, kindly, and not particularly intelligent.

"Did he like being a policeman?" she asked Mag, curiously.

"Sure."

"Then why did he quit bein' one?"

"He got flat feet," Mag told her matter-of-factly.

Her own dramatic arrival at the shack was an anecdote to which Psyche was willing to listen as often as Mag could be persuaded to retell it. She was nine years old, and it was a hot autumn day very like the one on which she had come to the slag, when, to Mag's intense astonishment, she interrupted the story with a violence quite out of keeping with her normal behaviour.

"I don't wanna hear that one no more!"

"Why, kid—you always——"

"I don't wanna hear it, see!"

Mag was not entirely without perception. "You're thinkin' of the other side of it, ain't you, kid?" she asked gently. "You're thinkin' of the folks what left you here."

Her mobile face unchildish and set, Psyche said, "I ain't thinkin' of nothin'."

"You mustn't be that way about it, kid. You got folks right here who think a heap of you, and if there was others what didn't —well, it don't make no difference now."

"It do so make a difference!" Psyche cried, and suddenly sobbing convulsively, turned and ran for the door.

## 3

LOOKING back, years later, Psyche was to realize that she had, in many ways, been extremely lucky in her odd foster-parents.

She was always to remember them together as an inseparable unit, but Butch was the shadow where Mag was the active force and substance.

Mag was a woman who would have been strikingly handsome if she had not been so grossly overweight. Her forehead, beneath the never-dying flame of her untidy red hair, was broad and peaceful, her fleshy nose straight, and her generous mouth well-shaped. Her expression usually revealed both her easy-going kindliness and her complete satisfaction with a life primitive in its simplicity.

She was illiterate, and capable of a hearty vulgarity which a scrubbed intelligentsia would undoubtedly have found distasteful. Basically, however, she was vulgar in the classical sense only. She was one of the common people, and, unashamed of this, possessed an integrity which revealed itself in very real moral standards. Her conversation was often generously peopled with bitches and bastards, but, believing in God, she never allowed His name to be taken in vain under her roof. When her normally dormant temper was aroused, she could, and did, throw moveable pieces of household furnishings at her slow-moving helpmeet; but marriage was to her, most truly, an Holy Estate, into which no third person might be allowed to wander with impunity. In her opinion adultery was the pastime of those already damned beyond any last-minute Judgement Day redemption. Slovenliness, drunkenness, gambling and fighting, all these were frailties to be accepted with benevolence; but tampering with the truth, the careless acquisition of another's property, and cruelty or oppression visited by the strong upon the weak, were sins undeserving of any lenience.

Her father had been a God-fearing Baptist, who, while failing to transmit any lasting religious fervour to any of his twelve children, had by example as much as anything else bred in all of them an abiding respect for practising truth and honesty which they never quite outgrew.

Mag, lazy though she was, had a conscience that would not allow her to deny Psyche what were, according to her lights, the advantages of a proper upbringing. Her one great stumbling-block in the instrumentation of this worthy aim was that Psyche did not appear to need correction in any way. In a situation where temptations simply did not exist, she committed no crimes. Full of energy, always anxious to please, she not only did what she was asked to do but did it at once. With what appeared to be an inherent belief in individual rights, she never touched the few things in the shack which she was forbidden to touch, such as Mag's prized damask tablecloth which was used only on Christmas day. And when Mag roused herself from her lethargy sufficiently to walk the four miles into town to see a movie or 'visit a while', Psyche, far from being a nuisance, was, in these foreign surroundings, unnaturally quiet. She might well have been told to wash her neck, comb her hair, and refrain from slamming doors and swearing, but it would never have occurred to Mag to criticize these particular sins of omission and commission.

Finally, despairing of finding a concrete example for what she considered her most important lesson, Mag fell back on theory.

"Look, kid, if you was to take a nickel that was some person else's, would you be better off than you was before?"

"Sure. I'd have a nickel, wouldn't I?" Psyche answered reasonably.

"And what would you spend it on?"

"A choclit bar," Psyche replied at once.

"It would give you a stummick-ache."

"Why? T'other ones never did."

"This one would, because you would be a thief and God would send you a stummick-ache for sure," Mag told her triumphantly.

Psyche knew that a stomach-ache created expressly by the Lord to chastise one would be something to be avoided at all costs.

Mag, watching her expressive face, felt satisfied that 'honesty is the best policy' had been planted in fertile soil. Her eyes misting with easy, sentimental tears, she felt that her old man would have been proud of her. What she did not realize then, or ever, was that she had already, as her father had done, taught her lessons by example, and that she was wasting her breath by continually cautioning Psyche, "Always tell the truth, kid," and "Don't ever forget to be a good girl." The difference between good girls and bad girls, and the facts of life which had to be understood before this difference could be fully comprehended, were hurdles she crossed while Psyche was still a small child. Again, she had no idea that the steady, protective affection she and Butch had for one another was to have a far more lasting effect on Psyche's future reactions and behaviour than any of the lurid tales she told her about Girls Who Went Wrong. Syphilis, and starvation in gutters, meant nothing to Psyche. To be 'loved, honoured and kept' on the other hand meant a great deal to her, for she was increasingly aware of the fact that she did not really belong anywhere. Butch and Mag's obvious dependence on each other, though it became part of an unrecognized ideal, yet served to emphasize her own lack of any true identification with them. Unconsciously compensating for this lack, she began to identify herself with her unknown beginnings rather than with the shack, and to think more and more often of the 'outside' as a source to which she must inevitably return.

At night, when she lay in bed, her eyes fixed on the store-room's one tiny window, watching the single star it framed too briefly, she would try to picture the family to which she might once have belonged. A fair-haired mother and a dark-haired father became constant, but she eventually gave up attempting to fill in brothers and sisters who never seemed to stay the same age and sex from one night to another, and who—drawn, though she did not know it, from a variety of catalogues—insisted on turning up in clothing which made it quite impossible for them to be living in either the same place or the same season of the year.

Thinking of her parents, she would tell herself fiercely that they must be nice. But if so—then how had she come here? It was an unequal equation with which she would struggle until the tears came, and it was necessary to bury her head under rough blankets so that Butch and Mag, on the other side of the thin partition, might not hear her choked breathing. Steadfastly refusing to discard her original hypothesis that her parents, solely because they were her parents, must be good in all ways, she fabricated solution after solution to account for their apparent desertion of her, no one of which she could find wholly convincing. If she could have thought of them as dead, it would have been easier to exonerate them of all blame. She could not bear to do this.

Naturally enough, it did not occur to her then to search in herself for clues to the heritage which had come to mean so much to her. She was eleven years old before she ever objectified herself at all.

It was late in November of that year that heavy rains during the night, combined with a sudden, sharp frost in the early hours of the morning, together produced the illusion of another ice age. When the sun rose, its rays struck a blue-white ice crust from which they glanced off in rainbow colours. To Psyche it was a glimpse into fairyland, a fairyland into which she sallied forth immediately breakfast was over. Skating without skates, floating between vividly blue sky and a world caught fast beneath a prison of glass, she turned her back on the shack and felt as if she were suspended, bodiless, between heaven and earth.

Would this, she wondered, be the way she would feel if she were dead? If she were nothing more than a soul on its way up to heaven? Would she still be herself? And what, after all, was herself? Was it bright hair, straight nose, and thin arms and legs, or was it something more than that? Suddenly she had to find out. Whirling around, keeping a slippery balance with difficulty, she made her way back to the shack as fast as she could. Once inside, she went straight to the clouded mirror above Mag's untidy bureau. Disregarding dusty red hair combings, spilled face powder, and a pin-tray full of cigarette stubs, she stood on tip-toe and leaned as close to the mirror as possible.

Carefully she took stock of her features, one by one, in search of something elusive which they might betray if she stared at herself long enough and hard enough. But, as she stared, her face became gradually that of a stranger, frighteningly unfamiliar. The eyes—which could not be her eyes—seemed to be getting larger, the pupils wide and black within a thin banding of blue iris; opaque, unfocussed, those eyes not only gave her back nothing of herself, but seemed to threaten her very identity as a person.

With a real effort of will, she wrenched herself free. As she moved back, the edge of the bed caught her behind the knees, and she sat down with unexpected suddenness. She felt, though more keenly, as she had on the night when she had tried to see how long she could hold her breath. She had experienced on that occasion the same floating vagueness, the same feeling of being a long way off from anything known, and had had the same awful fear that she might not be able to come back into herself again.

Now, glad to be sitting down, she tried to think out what she had discovered about herself. At first, it seemed to her that the answer to this was nothing. And then the very fact that she had learned nothing became an answer of sorts in itself. Her face, it seemed, was a mask which not only hid her real self from herself but also, probably, from other people. From this she moved on to the realization that no matter what she thought, no one need know her thoughts if she did not want them known. There could, it would seem, be no trespassing on a 'self' without the owner's consent. Why she should be so pleased, and even comforted by this quite remarkable but, as far as she could see, not very useful discovery, she could not make out. It was, of course, nice to know that you belonged to yourself in rather a special way, but it would be much more helpful to know exactly what it was you belonged to. Probably this was something you could learn only if you watched yourself for a long time; watched what you did when you did it, and thought about what you thought. And if you shouldn't like what you finally saw as your real self, would it be possible to change it in any way, or did you just have to stay the same always whether you were satisfied with that or not? Then again, if you could change, would you still be able to feel that you were you?

Finding this all very confusing, she decided to see if Mag could be of any help to her.

Mag, her sleeves rolled up, was baking a pie. On the corner of the table nearest the stove. *Fanny Farmer's Boston Cook Book* lay open at the correct page. Mag neither looked at it nor needed it. It was simply a badge of office, a reminder that when she had first walked out with a heavy-set young policeman she had been not only a cook but a good one. Her pies, usually apple, were now her single exercise in this proficiency.

Psyche hitched herself up on to the table, and, picking up a small piece of dough, absently kneaded it into a grimy ball between her fingers. "Mag, if you was changed—I mean, if you wasn't yourself exactly, what would you be?"

"Tight," said Mag.

"No—no. I mean if you was changed on purpose, sort of?"

"I dunno, kid. I ain't never wanted to be nothin' that I ain't."

Getting down from the table, Psyche went slowly over to the window. The ice on the crests of the slag hills was already melting: as impossible now to recapture its sharp, clear, many-coloured beauty, as to feel again the inner excitement it had engendered.

"I am me," Psyche said experimentally under her breath. It did not seem to mean much any more.

"You want to cut up them apples, kid?"

Small rivulets of water were tracing dark veins down the sides of the slopes and gathering in shallow pools which reflected a sky blurred by the return of a haze rarely absent for long.

With an oddly fatalistic shrug, unconscious period to a broken spell, Psyche said, "Sure, if you like, but I can't never find the damn knife."

"Try dumpin' the box out on the table," Mag advised.

Falling in with this suggestion, Psyche happily fetched the cardboard cutlery box and allowed its heterogeneous contents to rain out upon the table with all the clatter possible. Neither she nor Mag ever objected to a noise.

In what was essentially a silent corner of the universe, sounds of any kind had a real significance. When a thick cloud ceiling pressed close against the slag, the passing of cars on the highway could be heard, and Psyche, scarcely knowing she did it, would count the number that went by in a morning or an afternoon. In the spring and fall, when wild ducks called as they steered a course high above the shack, their migrations would be remarked upon and referred to again and again in the days that followed. The strident reveille of the old alarm clock, ringing at odd hours during the night and day, was greeted as a pleasantly familiar, rather than an irritating, punctuation to sleep or conversation. And when storms broke in a tumult of wind and rain, thunder and lightning, around the tiny house, its inmates enjoyed the disturbance of a peace at times oppressive in its tranquillity.

Neither Butch nor Mag, however, began to comprehend the extent of Psyche's loss when the old gramophone broke down, perhaps because music was of no importance to them, and perhaps because, as Psyche had been forced to play it, it had been inaudible to them.

Resurrected from amongst a stack of equally useless articles in the storeroom, it had been set up on an orange crate beside her bed, and had become overnight a possession that ranked second only to Feather Duster. The lid of the imitation-leather case was gone; the few records that remained were worn and scratched; and since there were neither needles nor tone arm, it could only be operated with a pin held in a hand, both mobile and steady, that learned how to follow a revolving, threadlike course without independent wavering. But this was enough. Leaning close against the machine, listening with absorbed concentration, Psyche was able to capture ghostly music that had the remote perfection of a scene looked at through the wrong end of a telescope; music, stripped of all mechanical impurities, which was the thin skeleton of a past which became for her an enthralling present. "After the Ball", "Moonlight and Roses", "Alexander's Ragtime Band"—she smiled, and grew sad, felt a queer restlessness, and smiled again.

The night when Butch came home to find Mag alone in the main room of the shack, and only two places laid for the evening meal, his broad face became creased with immediate, dumb anxiety.

"Where's the kid? She sick?"

Mag shook her head. "No, she ain't sick. She just don't want nothin' to eat."

"Wassa matter with her?"

"The phono's gone on the bum," Mag told him laconically.

Butch scratched his head as he always did when thought of any kind was demanded of him. "She set great store by that old thing, didn't she?"

"Yeah, but we ain't got the money to go gettin' another, so don't go athinkin' of anythin' stoopid like that," said Mag, revealing that she had already thought of it herself.

"Mebbe there might be somethin' else?" Butch asked hopefully. He had a great respect for Mag's ability to cope with any crisis needing more than brute strength, the single contribution he himself was ever in a position to make. That this would, on a future occasion, be all that was required of him in one of the most awful crises of the kid's life, he could not foresee, and so he was humble in his reliance on a judgement he knew to be superior to his own.

Mag, in both their opinions, was equal to the occasion. "We'll give her one of them mouth organs. I already wrote the letter."

Psyche treasured the mouth organ, when it came, because it was shiny, new, and hers, but as a gateway to music it was a complete failure. Although moved by, and responsive to music of any kind, she had no inherent creative talent for it, and the discordant noises which were all she was able to extract from her new toy were actually offensive to her. They tended, if anything, to thrust farther away, rather than to bring back, her lost puppet world where tiny figures laughed and wept and danced to rhythmic harmonies now dissolved like smoke in a rising wind.

With no one to call her a baby, Psyche still took Feather Duster with her wherever she went. His once bright face was grey with age, and his plumed head was balding in spots, but his value as a companion was as great as it had ever been. She was growing like an exotic young weed, and her shapeless pullovers and denim trousers were always too small for her; but even with this and Feather Duster thrown in, she was already essentially too beautiful to be found laughable by any but others of her own age, and as yet she had had none of these to deal with. When they went into the town, a place more depressing than the slag surrounding it, and as devoid of growth, it was to find a world of adults, for they always went in the evenings when the children were in bed. And the social life of the shack itself was limited to Saturday nights, when three miners, who worked the same shift as Butch, came in to play poker with him.

It was Butch, in closer contact with civilization than Mag, who one day uneasily broached the subject of "schoolin' for the kid".

Mag disposed of this radical idea. "I ain't never had no proper schoolin', an' I done all right, ain't I?"

"I went to school," Butch reminded her with no little pride.

"An' you can't read nor write no better than me," Mag told him tartly. "I've teached the kid how to make her letters and how to read some. Anyway, girls is different."

After some consideration, Butch conceded that, in certain respects at least, girls were different. There, for the time being, the matter was dropped, and Psyche was left to her own devices for another year.

Free to wander pretty much as she pleased, to come to careful conclusions unbiased by ready-made social strictures, she developed an independence of mind and spirit rarely achieved by a child as young as she was. But, denied the tests that not only give proof of special ability but also provide stimulus, her physical growth was far in advance of any possible intellectual maturity. Having absorbed all that Butch and Mag could teach her, their limited fund of knowledge dredged to its shallow depths, her naturally active intelligence was stirred only occasionally, and only by something seen, felt, or observed outside the shack itself.

Butch and Mag might waste no love on the slag, but Psyche was fascinated by the elemental emptiness of a land that owed its changing moods to the slow rotation of the earth itself. It was exciting to her to discover that, even here, no day was quite the same as any other, that the pewter-coloured hills reflected nuances of colour as perceptible as the differing hues of the great, unobstructed span of sky above it.

Exploring the four points of the compass, she found that the wastelands seemed to continue to the north indefinitely; certainly beyond her courage or desire to go. To the west were the mines, the core and source of the blight that devastated the countryside. From a vantage point higher than most, she would stare at tall derricks rising out of haze that thickened here to the density of a dark cloud, its heart pierced by the unholy glow of huge smelters. Feather Duster clutched tightly to her, she would listen to the rattle of winch and chain, the harsh gears of heavy trucks, and the hoarse scream of whistles implementing spoken commands beyond her hearing. She came often to the miniature mountain top from which she had first surveyed this scene, but she never lingered long, and never approached any closer to a sound and fury that repelled her as much as it interested her. Although she knew that Butch went there every day, she rarely thought of him in connection with this patternless turmoil. She preferred to pretend that it was the home of dragons, a witches' cauldron stirred deep in the earth, a threat from which—when she was ready—she must flee as fast as her long legs would take her.

Eastward she discovered the outer fringes of the slag, and a stunted, leafless tree-line; a foreign country that genuinely frightened her by its dissimilarity from anything she knew or had imagined.

"Is them woods, yonder to the east?" she asked Mag. "They don't look like you said woods did."

Mag glanced up from knitting one of the shapeless woollen bags that Butch must accept as socks, and sniffed audibly. "Them's not proper trees. Why, kid, like I told you, a proper woods has leaves, an' grass, an' little flowers growin' everywheres, just wild like."

"You mean with nobody havin' planted them?"

"Sure."

Psyche's voice was no more than a whisper. "You mean free— for anyone to pick what wanted to?"

"Ain't I told you that a hundred times?"

"Yeah, but I can't never believe it. Is some of them blue, perhaps?"

"Most like. You're sure crazy over blue, ain't you, kid?"

"I always was," Psyche said, and it was almost as if she were telling the big woman something she might not otherwise have known.


*Leaving his car in front of the house, Dwight walked around to the gardens at the back where Sharon was nearly always to be found at the end of a summer's day.*

*She was there, and, rising from her chair, came to meet him, graceful and unhurried.*

*He is back, she told herself. Another day has gone, and he is home again. I must not run. I will not run. He is there. I can see him, and in a moment I will be able to touch him. There is no need to run, and I will not do it.*

*Watching her, seeing the blue of her dress reflected in the blue of the delphiniums behind her, Dwight thought, what would I do if ever she were not here? Then, his quick stride slowing, his eyes swept the wall of blue which extended across the entire back of the garden, and he realized with shocking suddenness the significance of something that he had not even noticed before. How long had it been going on, this steady, purposeful planting?*

*When had the pink and white of phlox and carnations first begun*
*to be submerged in this sea of delphiniums?*

*A hurt that he steadfastly refused to dwell upon, a hurt now*
*eight years old, became mingled with fresh pain caused by the*
*knowledge that whereas he had once shared Sharon's every*
*thought, now there was a corner of her mind she kept locked*
*against him, and which he dared not try to explore. If she had*
*done this, what else might she not have done to fortify memories*
*for a child whom he did not believe they would ever see again; a*
*child whom he did not believe was necessarily alive.*

*His arms, when they closed around her, held her almost too*
*forcefully, but all he said was, "Sharon—my darling."*

*Sharon, her face pressed hard against his shoulder, said nothing*
*beyond his name. "Dwight."*

The direction in which Psyche most often set out when she left
the shack was south. This was not only because she now fetched
most of the deliveries left at the mail-box—sometimes making
three or four trips in a single day for this reason alone—but because the highway was a magnet that she neither tried nor wished
to resist. It was her road to Damascus, her way to Mecca, the
actual, tangible starting point of the long journey to the 'outside' on which she had become more and more certain that she
herself would some day set out.

Lying on the further side of the first of the two uneven ridges
which, with intervening depressions, separated the highway from
the shack, she would wait with infinite patience for the appearance of a car, any car, going south. Those going north she paid no
attention to, scarcely even saw. Old cars, chugging past with
difficulty, worried her, for she doubted if they had the strength
and stamina to reach a goal too nebulous and visionary to be
other than worlds away. The real rewards of her vigils were the
swift, bright chariots, flashing with chrome, which only a heretic
would have believed incapable of reaching their enchanted
destination.

She came to know the truckers well, and they watched for the fair head usually to be seen peeping over a slate-grey rise a hundred feet back from the mail-box. They took to bringing her little presents of candy and gum, and, when the summer sun beat down on the unprotected slag, bottles of pop chilled against fast-melting blocks of ice, chips of which she would still be sucking when they had gone. At another season of the year, when bitter winds blew across wastes of arctic white, she would be invited into the warm cabs of the trucks to drink scalding tea or coffee from thermoses which always seemed to contain enough to allow their contents to be shared with her.

These rough and ready men were, without exception, kind to her. They were her friends. And she saw nothing odd in the fact that they were her only friends; her only continuing association with anyone, other than Butch and Mag, until the day when the truant officer for the district discovered both her presence at the shack and her absence from school.

It was on a warm September morning that Psyche came into the shack to announce that there was a "funny lookin' man outside."

Mag pushed a loose strand of hair from one side of her moist forehead to the other, gave a wriggling hitch to her crumpled calico dress, and advanced impressively to challenge the uninvited intruder. He proved to be a slight, bald man of fifty-odd in a neat, dark suit. He wore gold-rimmed glasses, and carried a leather dispatch-case. Dormant memories of travelling salesmen, whom it had once been her duty to dispense with while in service, satisfied Mag that this was a situation which she was more than competent to handle.

"We don't want nothin' we ain't got, bo," she said with hauteur, and wheeled about in order to re-enter her residence. She was arrested, however, in mid-manoeuvre, by a voice which was, considering its apparently mild source, surprising in its forcefulness.

"You have a child here, madam, of school age. Either you will make immediate arrangements to send her to school, or you and your husband will appear in court on Thursday of next week."

# 4

PSYCHE was twelve when her formal education began. She was nearly fifteen when she herself assumed the responsibility for an abrupt and final departure from an odorous, overcrowded classroom that she hated from the first moment she stepped into it.

Her preparations that first morning were of the simplest nature. Her one skirt was pressed. A faded blue shirt was patched. And Mag provided her with a yellowed block of writing paper and a carefully sharpened pencil.

Butch, who had been deputed to take her on her first morning, asked, "Who do I say the kid is?"

Mag had thought of this. "You better say she's Moran, like us. Make out she's a relative like. We don't want no nasty little kids askin' no questions of her."

Butch began to scratch. "What about t'other name?"

Mag was nonplussed. "I ain't thought of that."

Psyche, who had been silent up to this time, astonished them by saying quite fiercely, "I got a first name. It's writ plain on that there little dress I come in."

"We ain't sure that that's——" Mag began.

"I'm sure!"

"Now, look, kid, there's no call to go gettin' excited."

"I ain't excited. I'm just sayin' I got a name, that's all."

Mag wavered, moved by the desperate insistence she saw in Psyche's thin, brown face. "Well, you may be right, kid, but it ain't no name nobody round here's goin' to recognize like."

"That don't matter. I can spell it. I've learned it good."

"I ain't goin' spellin' no names," Butch said.

Mag looked at him doubtfully. "You could, mebbe."

But Butch was for once not to be moved. "I ain't goin' up to no fancy-pants teacher an' say I can't say the kid's name right. I'll be buggered if I will."

Psyche pleaded and coaxed to no avail.

"I ain't agoin' to make no more of a fool of myself than what God done a'ready," he said stubbornly.

Mag, eventually settling the problem, said, "Margaret's a good name, kid, even if it's my own. It ain't goin' to hurt you none to answer to Maggie."

"But I ain't Maggie!"

"You'll get used to it," Mag told her firmly. "See if you don't."

Psyche had often seen the school, a one-storey, flat-roofed, brick building on the edge of the town, encircled by a bare expanse of sun-baked mud. A long plank walk led from the road to the front door and a blackened stone portico that failed to lend dignity to architecture depressing in its squat, four-square lack of imagination. Following Butch up the walk, concentrating on boards that lifted and fell under her reluctant feet, she tried unsuccessfully to overcome nervousness that made the palms of her hands sticky and the roof of her mouth dry and sore. It was early, and the barren playground was still deserted, but even so she could not raise her eyes from boards that rose and fell until, too soon, she found herself climbing four worn stone steps.

It was dim in the entrance hall, and it smelled.

Butch, if possible even more uneasy than Psyche, stood still and looked uncertainly around him. On his left, through an open door, he could see a large class-room; opposite him were two doors, side by side, labelled respectively, "Boys" and "Girls"; on his right was another class-room. Mag, coaching him carefully, had told him to go to the office. That there should be no office was a blow that left him floundering, incapable either of going on or of going back. He would have continued to stand there indefinitely if the heavy silence had not been broken by a short, dry cough from the class-room on the left.

Clearing his throat loudly, he said, "Come on, kid. That'll be Teacher."

Propelled by the shocking echoes of his own hoarse voice, as much as by his failing courage, he lumbered through the classroom doorway with Psyche close behind him.

The next hour, culminating in a humiliation she would never forget, was one of the worst Psyche ever had to live through. Tongue-tied, she heard herself introduced.

"This here's Maggie Moran."

Dumbly she shook hands with the tall, spare woman who was to be her teacher. Agonized, she watched Butch leave, and then went to the desk assigned to her, at the back of the room. Haltingly she answered the questions that the tall woman asked her, knowing that each time she opened her mouth she was being further condemned by cold grey eyes that found her wanting in every possible way.

But if this had been bad, how much worse it was to sit, biting her nails, while the room filled up with noisy, laughing children who, while seeming to ignore her, yet studied her with sly, curious glances, followed by spoken asides which, although she could not hear them, she knew instinctively were uncomplimentary. Only one of them spoke to her, a big black-haired girl of fourteen or fifteen.

"Hello, who let you in?"

The words were not unfriendly, but Psyche, although she wanted desperately to reply, was quite unable to utter a sound.

"Snooty, huh?" said the girl. And the remark, falling across a momentary lull, was a brand Psyche was destined to carry for as long as she went to the school.

"I gotta get outa here," she thought incoherently. "I gotta get out. I can't not bear it!" She had actually half risen from her seat when the sharp, peremptory period of a hand bell reduced the tumult of the previous moment to a stillness in which any sound or movement would have been so conspicuous she could not contemplate making one. Sinking back, her hands clenched beneath her desk, she sat rigidly staring at her pencil and writing block.

"We will now repeat the Lord's Prayer."

The prayer was repeated, exactly that and nothing more, by over sixty voices intoning the required phrases with an automatic, monotonous precision which robbed them not only of beauty but of meaning.

"We will now sing the National Anthem."

Scrambling to her feet long after all the others had done so, Psyche, her cheeks flaming with embarrassment, for the first time heard vocal homage paid to her country.

"We will now call the roll."

When her own turn came, Psyche knew precisely what was expected of her. As all the others before her had done, she had only to stand up, say 'Here, ma'am', and sit down again. It was perfectly simple.

"Maggie Moran."

Psyche stood up.

"Maggie Moran!"

What combined folly and courage drove her to do what she did then, she would never know. "I ain't—I ain't Maggie. I'm P-S-Y-C-H-E."

The tittering of the class rose and swelled around her, beating in her ears like a flood-tide in which she wished she could drown, in which she could sink down and down, never to be seen again. Wave upon wave it rose, battering, suffocating, hurting as nothing had ever hurt before. When it receded, and finally died away, she was numb, cast up only half-conscious on a beach where nothing mattered any more, where a name that was not hers was no longer important.

A voice she did not recognize as her own, said, "Here, ma'am." And Maggie Moran sat down, insulated by shock from all further barbs.

She was graded by age, regardless of the fact that she knew less than most of the kindergarten children. She was twelve, and therefore she belonged in the eighth grade. No other yardstick was employed. It was a perfidious system, but it would have been difficult to improve on it under the conditions that existed in the rural schools in that part of the world. The law of the land stipulated that all children must attend school with a fair degree of regularity until they reached the age of sixteen. The law did not, however, insist that they learn anything, nor did it make provision for enough funds to underwrite its own enforcements in a proper manner. The result was overcrowded, understaffed schools in which a teacher must attempt both to instruct and control as many as four or five grades in a single room. Split age groups, with the increased restlessness this would encourage, could not be tolerated, and individual attention was, of course, out of the question.

No one ever failed a year. In order to make room at the bottom for the six-year-olds whom the law insisted must be taken in, classes moved up *en masse* every September with the heavy irresistibility of a steam-roller. Since everyone automatically "graduated" at sixteen if he so desired—and only a very few were ever undesirous of this distinction as soon as it became available—it actually mattered very little from what grade they graduated.

In a community that recognized the mines as the East to which all faces turned, advanced learning, or, for that matter, learning of any kind, was a luxury unnecessary in the essential business of making a living. Neither the War of 1812 nor the Einstein theory were of any interest or intrinsic value to a man destined to spend the greater portion of his waking hours a hundred feet or more underground. That the rock wall at which he hacked was half as old as time meant nothing to him, made the quartz no less hard, his job no less back-breaking.

Psyche, her ignorance mistaken for stupidity, was almost immediately classified as mentally retarded. Her burning anxiety to learn thwarted from the start, she withdrew into an impassive unresponsiveness.

Her term reports were awful, but since neither Butch nor Mag could read the teacher's handwriting, they got nothing from them other than the fact that she had passed. Unaware that everybody always passed, they were very pleased.

"Good for you, kid," Mag would say.

And Butch's comment was always the same. "The kid's real smart, ain't she?"

Psyche never told them how unhappy she was at school. She

never allowed them to guess that the boys and girls to whom she referred were not her friends, that she had no friends at all. For, her natural gaiety and friendliness disguised by her initial shyness, she was as great a social failure as an intellectual one. Eventually she got over the shyness, but by then it was too late to make successful advances to a group who had reached the uneasy, intuitive conclusion that she was, in some way they could not quite define, 'different'. This very difference, for which she might have been persecuted, was fortunately it itself a protection. The clear blue eyes under the straight dark eyebrows were capable of communicating such cool contempt that most of the class, although they would never have admitted it, were more than a little afraid of her. Aloof and lonely, taking care never again to make a fool of herself in public, she somehow managed to create the impression that she ignored the others, rather than they her.

They talked about her, but not to her.

"That Maggie! I ain't never seen nobody so stuck-up."

"Yeah, an' what's she got to be stuck-up about? Nothin'."

"You can say that again. Why, she ain't even smart at her books."

"I bet that hair ain't natural."

"An' them airs she puts on, like she was the queen, or somethin'."

They said the same things over and over again, but they were never able to convince themselves of their truth. The blonde hair was natural, and they knew it. The straight, graceful carriage, and quiet refusal to be drawn into arguments where weight of numbers alone would defeat her, were not airs, but also natural, and they knew this too. With more insight than the teacher, they guessed at an intelligence far superior to their own.

Baffled, irritated, made unsure of themselves by something beyond their comprehension, they kept their distance from a changeling who would gladly have given everything she possessed for a single friend—for someone, anyone, with whom she could share the lonely lunch hours, with whom she could exchange sandwiches, and gossip, and little jokes which would not need to be very funny. Someone who would smile at her when she came into the crowded, untidy cloak-room, who would linger to talk with her at the front door before she set out on her long walk home through the deserted slag hills.

Without realizing that the protective wall she had built around herself was already unscalable, she went on hoping for a whole year that some miracle would produce this friend for whom she so longed. When she came back to school in September of her second year, she had given up any such hope, and, in so doing, became, if possible, even more unapproachable than before. Tall, unsmiling, and to all appearances offensively self-sufficient, she became accepted as a familiar part of the scene if in no other way.

She learned to write, after a fashion, forming her words with a pathetic, cramped attempt at neatness. She picked up the rudiments of simple arithmetic, and some fragments of history which, with no basis of previous knowledge, she soon forgot. The one thing she learned to do well was to read, and this she did entirely on her own.

Coincidence one day led her to open her book of Short Stories and Essays at a page from which the seniors were reading aloud. Mag had taught her just enough, combined with the little she had absorbed in the school, to enable her to follow what was being read, at first with great difficulty, and then with increasing ease. Shaping phrases and sentences under her breath, concentrating as she had never done before, in the space of a few months she became, and was aware of it, a better reader than any of the fifteen-year-olds to whom she listened so intently. The teacher failed to discover this accomplishment because she had long ago given up asking Psyche any questions at all, and no proof of it appeared in the poor written work which she was from time to time required to hand in. Certainly it produced no change in her way of speaking, for she never saw any real connection between the words she read and the distorted version of the King's English which she was accustomed to using; they were, to her, simply two different languages.

Excluded from active participation in either work or play, she fell back on the only thing left to her—the role of spectator. Sitting quietly in the back corner of the room to which she had been more or less permanently relegated, she watched—except when the top class was reading—all the time. It became an absorbing pastime, and, judge and jury both, she developed a calm, detached contempt for the weaknesses unconsciously displayed by nearly every one of her sixty-odd classmates.

She learned to detect a lie almost before it was spoken. She soon could distinguish the difference between a genuine desire to learn and the slick imitation of the show-off who wanted only to be thought knowledgeable. When one of the boys began paying attention to one of the girls, she knew, almost at once, not only the exact nature of his intentions, but also the measure of success he would achieve. Although the bruises were invisible to her, she knew instinctively when a child had been whipped the night before. She saw friendships formed solely to gain an advantage, perhaps social advancement, perhaps protection, perhaps nothing more than the sharing of a lunch-box more appetizing than the general run. She saw girls scream when pinched by the boys, and fail to run away. She knew, but never said, where most 'missing' articles could have been brought to light. With cool, disillusioned eyes, she saw the sins of an adult world in embryo.

From all these things she drew conclusions, one-sided, but basically sound. However, if she had been called upon to state them in even the simplest language, she could not have done it. They became, for the time being, things she knew which must wait for additional maturity before they could be fully useful.

That nearly all her observations were adverse was her unrecognized retaliation for being made an outcast. Her normal tendency to like people she satisfied by evolving the naïve theory that God put mostly bad people, and mostly good, in separate groupings so that they might be with their own kind. She pictured, in the fairy-tale 'outside', large concentrations of human beings activated at all times by only the highest ideals of thought and behaviour. In this way she comforted herself, and saved herself from bitterness, while continuing to dislike the school and every living thing in it. God, she reasoned, had not originally intended her to pass her life amongst these people, and, when He was less occupied, would undoubtedly put right the mistake. Meanwhile it was up to her to be patient.

Two events alone broke the steady monotony of her second year at the school, both of them purely personal, and neither of them happy.

The first occurred in late January when heavy snows made the slag impassable except for a narrow path beaten between the shack and the highway. Psyche, forced, as Butch was, to follow the open road and a route much longer than she usually took, dressed by lamplight, and set out while morning was still no more than a vague promise in the east, her lunch pail frozen to her mitten before the shack was out of sight. Warmly, if untidily, bundled up in thick layers of mismatched clothing, her feet protected by heavy fleece-lined boots, she never minded the cold no matter how low the thermometer dropped.

When she arrived at the school, instead of at once seeking the warmth of one of the big stoves inside, she would stop to watch the skaters on the rink that the older boys kept flooded in a playground now an otherwise unbroken expanse of white. Wistfully she thought that this was something that, if she but had skates, she could do and do well. Moreover, unlike the games that were played in the spring and fall, it was something that could be done alone. The smooth, rhythmic movements, as she watched them, found a rhythmic response within her that cried out to be allowed expression. It was, she thought, like music you couldn't quite hear, like clouds racing before a high wind, like flying.

Psyche never asked Butch and Mag for anything, and she did not consciously ask for skates. But when she arrived home later than usual one cold winter's afternoon, Mag asked what had kept her.

"Did Teacher make you stay in, kid?"

Psyche, hanging up her snowy jacket to thaw out by the stove, shook her head. "No, she don't never do that. I was watchin' the skatin'."

"I was scairt you was into trouble."

"I'm sorry, Mag. I ain't noticed the time."

"They got a rink right there at the school?"

"Yeah, an' it's that beautiful to watch. Like dancin'. I ain't never seen nothin' quite like it. It's sort of as if a person was free when they's skatin'."

Mag looked at her thoughtfully. "You wisht you could do it too, kid?"

"Yeah. Kind of."

"But you ain't got no skates?"

Psyche's voice expressed regret without complaint. "No. But it don't matter."

Laying aside her knitting, Mag heaved herself up from the couch. "Come with me, kid."

Psyche followed her into the storeroom, and then, at her request, went back to the main room for a lamp.

"I want to get at that there trunk," said Mag, pointing to the only visible corner of a mouldering steamer trunk buried beneath an avalanche of cartons, crates, and broken bits of furniture. Ever since Psyche had come to the shack, Mag had been saying that she was going to clean up the storeroom, but somehow it always got put off until tomorrow, and tomorrow never came. Now, displaying a rare energy, she began, with Psyche's help, to unearth the trunk which, at the bottom of the heap, had rested undisturbed for more years than she could remember.

An unpleasant musty odour rose around them with the opening of a lid, which all but came off, and the dress Mag lifted aside fell apart in her hands. Muttering to herself, she delved deep into the trunk, and a moment later gave a grunt of satisfaction.

"There you are, kid!" she said triumphantly, and dragged forth a pair of old skates.

"For me?"

Beaming, Mag nodded. "They're all yours, kid. Now you can have as good a time as them others."

Psyche spent more than an hour polishing the cracked black boots with loving care. The rotted laces were replaced with heavy string. The scratched blades were shone, all trace of rust removed with repeated sandings.

"You think they look all right now?" Psyche asked eagerly.

"Good as new," Mag told her.

"You want I should sharpen 'em for you, kid?" Butch asked, anxious to make a contribution.

"You think they need it?"

Butch took the skates from her, ran a callused thumb over the edges, pursed his lips, and did his best to look wise. "Yeah, they could do with it."

Finally, when there was nothing further that any of the three of them could think of doing to the skates, they were hung on a nail by the front door, and no Christmas stocking was ever hung up with higher hopes for the morrow.

The following morning Psyche was up and away while it was still dark. The stars, glittering, cold, immeasurably remote in a navy-blue sky, drew a pale radiance from snow that crunched harshly beneath her boots, a sharp, dry tearing of a frozen silence broken by no other sound.

Her breath making small frosty clouds that crystallized along the edge of the parka-hood framing her face, she thought, "I'll have a whole hour before the others get there. I'll have learned to do it good by then."

The beautiful, smooth coordination of muscle that was responsible for the way she walked and stood promised her a perfect balance in this new medium, gave her an instinctive certainty that she would be able to glide, and swoop, and circle as well, or better, than any of them.

She knew just how it would feel. She would fly like a bird, her red mittens brilliant wing-tips.

The school was still locked, the sky still dark, when she reached the rink. Even if she had wished she could not have gone in to change from boots to skates beside the stove. Warmed by her own excitement, trembling with anticipation, she did not think of such a thing. Putting down her lunch pail, she unhooked the skates from around her neck, and, sitting down in the snow, drew them on and carefully laced and tightened the strings, oblivious of frost that nipped at fingers momentarily bare.

If she had ever in her life had a pair of shoes that had fitted properly, or had had any understanding of the mechanics of skating, she would have known before she stood up that to attempt to skate in boots not only sizes too wide for her, but also painfully short, would be to attempt the completely impossible.

While she was still on the snow, the blades cut into the surface, and, in effect, she walked on the soles of the boots. At the edge of the ice she paused, took a deep breath, raised her arms—her red-tipped wings—and launched herself fearlessly into flight. For an ecstatic instant she kept her balance, then her feet shot out from under her and she came down heavily on her back.

At first, although she fell, and fell, and fell again, she was not really discouraged. "It's like everythin' else," she told herself. "You gotta learn. There ain't really nothin' to it, you just gotta learn."

Even when she began to realize that neither the next effort, nor the one after that, was going to be any more successful than all the others which had preceded it, she refused to give up. Bruised and aching, her teeth biting into her lower lip, with terrible persistence she went on picking herself up, falling, and getting up to try again.

Her disappointment an agony far sharper than her physical aches and pains, she was unaware that at some time during her desperate, losing battle, morning had superseded night and brought with it an audience she did not know was there until she heard a hoarse boy's voice.

"Will you lookit Maggie! Jees, this is a scream! Hey, Jack, come on over an' see somethin' funnier than a dead cat!"

Sprawled on the ice, Psyche momentarily wished she were dead. Then anger, cold and hard as the glassy surface on which she lay, came to her rescue. Luck was with her, at least to the extent that she was close against the snow bank bordering the rink. Giving herself a sharp push with her hands, she reached the edge, and got to her feet clear of the treacherous ice. Her head up, her back straight, completely ignoring the small boy still watching her but no longer laughing, she picked up her boots and lunch pail and walked away toward the school.

The second small boy, joining the first, said, "I don't see nothin' funny."

"It was Maggie. She was tryin' to skate, and she fell down."

The second boy looked after Psyche's retreating figure. Maggie was not a person whom he could imagine falling down. "You sure?"

"Course I am! I seen her."

"Well—gee, everyone falls down sometime, don't they?"

Psyche, their words carrying clearly to her on the still air, knew a sick relief that she had been caught by only such a negligible advance-guard of her enemies. Fighting against tears, she took off her skates on the steps of the school, and, finding the door now unlocked, carried them to the cloak-room where she hid them under her jacket.

When school was over that afternoon, she stayed at her desk until all the others had left the building. Then, slipping into the cloak-room, she put on her things, and again hung the skates around her neck as she had when starting out from the shack that morning. Hugging them close to her sides with her elbows in order to hide them, she went out, and turned toward the highway without even a glance at the rink where laughing figures glided, and swooped, and circled.

Trudging miserably homeward, she wondered how she was to tell Butch and Mag. Their disappointment on top of her own would be more than she could stand.

"I can't do it," she said under her breath. "I just can't. They was so happy."

Would God strike her down, she wondered, if she were to lie to them? It wouldn't be a bad kind of lie. She could put the skates under the step outside the shack, and later, when nobody was looking, bring them in and replace them at the bottom of the trunk. Mag would think they were at the school and that she was using them, and in that way both she and Butch could go on being pleased about it.

Mag heard her stamping the snow from her feet, and opened the door for her.

"Come on in quick, kid, so's not to let the cold in."

Psyche, pretending to look at the clear, thin red of an early, winter sunset, replied with her face averted. "I'm comin' quick's I can."

When the door was closed behind her, she immediately became very busy taking off her gloves and parka.

"Well, kid, how did it go?" Mag's hearty voice said plainly that the question was no more than a formality.

Holding her cold hands over the stove, keeping her back turned, Psyche said steadily, "It went good, Mag. I—I was like a bird."

The second event occurred in the late spring not long before the end of the school year. In itself it was an outstanding triumph for Psyche in a place where she had never dreamed of achieving an open victory of any kind. Its result, however, was to turn her hours in the crowded class-room for a time from passive to active misery.

The announcement, made by the teacher one morning after the roll had been called, that the school inspector was coming in a week's time, meant nothing to Psyche. She did not know what an inspector was, and she did not care. Nothing that happened in the school ever had anything directly to do with her, and she had long since given up paying any attention to announcements. The rest of the class, however, were galvanized into a feverish and quite unnatural activity. Even the most apathetic cleaned out their desks, scraping out old wads of gum, spitballs, and other bits of equally unsavoury garbage.

Psyche, whose almost empty desk was always scrupulously neat, divided her time between watching this miracle with cool curiosity, and staring out of the open window beside her. Although the slag knew no blooming in the spring, it was still the pleasantest season of the year. The sky was a soft, pale blue when the sun shone, and the air, washed by frequent rains, was at once fresh and warm. Looking at gossamer clouds drifting gently across the serene face of heaven, she could, and did, escape into idle daydreams undisturbed by the inspector's impending visit. It was not until the day before he was due to arrive that any of the general fever communicated itself to her, and this was only because a dictum was issued which, for once, apparently included her. When she got home, she told Mag, "I gotta wash my hair to-night, an' have a bath, an' wear a dress to-morrow mornin'. None of the girls is allowed to wear pants."

Mag frowned. This was a tall order. "Who says you gotta?"

"Teacher."

"It ain't none of her damn business to say when you washes."

Psyche shrugged. "A inspector is comin'. What's a inspector, Mag?"

"He's a guy what comes to see that the school is run right, and that the kids is learnin' their books the way they oughtta."

Psyche ran slender fingers through a mane of hair that was more than a little sticky to the touch. "Then the way I sees it, it's Teacher who is gonna be inspected more'n anyone else. Why ain't it enough if she washes?"

Mag's attitude had undergone a complete reversal now that she knew the reason behind what had at first appeared to be an unreasonable demand, and she was not in sympathy with what was, actually, a very acute observation.

"That ain't no proper way for you to be talkin'," she said severely. "You better get on out to the well an' start drawin' a heap of water."

"Oh, hell!" said Psyche pleasantly, and, kicking off her shoes, went out to do as she was told.

That evening the round iron tub, which was both laundry and bath tub, was filled and emptied three times. Psyche, although she was almost as tall as Mag, could still, by jack-knifing her long legs, get right into the tub. It was not a performance she enjoyed, for the corrugated surface was decidedly uncomfortable and the water was always either too hot or too cold. It was very hard water, making soap almost as difficult to remove as dirt; and rinsing her thick hair was an onerous task, but she would not let Mag cut it shorter than shoulder length.

In the morning Mag looked her over more critically than she had ever done before, straightening the blue bow which partially controlled hair transformed into an unmanageable golden aureole, pulling the short skirt of a faded blue cotton dress, and completely overlooking ragged finger-nails and a high-water mark just visible beneath a pointed chin.

"I ain't goin' to no party," Psyche said plaintively. "Leave me be."

"Like Butch said last night, Teacher always asks the best kids to answer questions, an' you gotta look right."

Calm in the knowledge that she would be the last one to be brought to the inspector's attention on this account, Psyche made no comment. She was pleased with her own appearance, and that was enough. Nobody else was going to notice her.

The inspector noticed her as soon as he came into the class-room. He thought she looked like a highly intelligent young Valkyrie, and had difficulty in keeping his eyes off her.

He was a young man, new to his job, conscientious, and still not so disillusioned as to believe that he could not, single-handed if necessary, remould a school system which he regarded as little short of criminal. Almost as poorly paid as the teachers within his jurisdiction, he was not prepared to accept low salaries as an excuse for laxity or inefficiency. Believing, as he did, that proper education was the answer to nearly all the country's ills, and that most children, given the opportunity, wanted to learn, his sympathies at this stage in his career were with the students rather than the teachers.

Having been introduced to the class, he seated himself at a table placed beside the teacher's desk, and, provided with a chart of the class-room that showed names and grades, proceeded to observe and make notes.

The morning wore on with the teacher, whose angular form had blossomed out in bright silk print, asking questions on all the subjects which had supposedly been covered during the year, and picking, apparently at random, boys and girls across the various grades to give the required answers.

Psyche, a cynical witness to a performance she had seen rehearsed word for word on the previous day, began to think that the inspector, although he did not look it, was a fool.

It was after the morning break that the pattern changed.

The inspector held a low-voiced colloquy with a teacher whose thin, acid face turned bright red as she found herself relegated to the table while the inspector appropriated the desk.

His voice was deep, his diction clear and forceful, and his rapid cross-fire of questions fell around the room like buckshot, leaving devastation in their wake.

Jimmy Grant, who had earlier been asked the date of the Fall of Quebec, and had glibly supplied it, was proved never to have heard of either Wolfe or Montcalm. Helga Tapper, who had known what twenty-three times twenty-three made, failed to get beyond six times six with a repetition of the multiplication table. Rosie Hall, who had named the capital of Finland without hesitation, stated that New York was the capital of the United States. And so it went. A few, but only a very few, managed to make a reasonable showing, and even they, entirely unprepared for an uncoached quiz, were flustered and uncertain.

Finished with this part of his program, the inspector turned his attention to those who had not been previously questioned at all, and settled down to a quiet but methodical plumbing of the depths of their ignorance.

Psyche, entrenched behind an invisible wall in her accustomed role of spectator, was taken completely by surprise when her name was called.

Slowly she slid out from behind her desk, and stood up. Shaking her hair from her shoulders, she moved backwards until her hands were flat against the north and east walls where they met at the back of the room.

The others had said "Yes, sir" when called. Psyche said nothing.

The inspector's curiosity about her had been rising steadily all morning. He had expected that she would play a prominent part in the wholesale bluff to which he had been exposed. When the hours had passed without her being called even once, he had wondered why, had asked himself if the intelligence he saw in her wide-spaced blue eyes, and pure, broad sweep of forehead, was no more than an illusion compounded of beauty and an honesty he could not doubt. The others had quailed before his unexpected attack. This girl was braced, ready to fight back. Why?

"Will you tell me, Maggie, something about the Battle of Hastings."

Psyche's face and voice were absolutely expressionless. "I don't know nothin' about it."

"You must know something."

"I don't."

The man bit his lip. "Will you have the goodness to think about it."

"It wouldn't do no good."

His voice was curt. "Do you know what a simple fraction is?"

"No."

"Why don't you know?"

"I ain't been taught."

He swung round to the teacher, disappointment he would not admit to himself making his tone sharper than it had been. "Why is this girl in the ninth grade when she appears to know less than one of the beginners?"

The teacher, feeling, in this instance at least, on firm ground, said, "She's retarded. We move the retarded ones up as a matter of form so they won't feel too inferior."

Psyche, forgetting the defensive caution which had governed her every move since the horrible blunder of her first day, conscious of nothing but pure, blinding rage, broke out of her shell with the force of an explosion.

Stamping her foot, her eyes flashing, she cried, "I ain't retarded! I ain't inferior! Do you hear me—I ain't inferior to no one!"

A sigh, like a gust of wind, swept across the room as all eyes turned to this self-elected scapegoat.

"Sit down, Maggie!" The teacher's voice echoed the cruel relief on more than sixty faces. By comparison their faults were now negligible. They were safe again.

"Not till he knows I ain't retarded!"

"Maggie! Do as I say. At once."

"No!"

The inspector, on the verge of reinforcing the teacher's command, paused, and, thick eyebrows frowning above piercing eyes, looked slowly around the room. He was an imaginative man, and for a moment he felt as if he stood on the edge of a dark wood watching a pack of wolves close in on a young doe at bay.

"Maggie." He spoke to her, and to her alone.

Psyche, meeting his direct, enquiring gaze, knew that if she could justify herself she had found a friend. Her knees suddenly weak, she supported herself against the wall, and waited mutely for him to go on.

"Maggie—is there anything you've learned that you can tell me about? Anything at all. It doesn't matter what it is."

"I—I can read—real good."

There was an audible snort from one of the boys. Psyche, hearing it, stopped trembling. "I can read better nor anybody in this school," she said decisively.

"This is absurd!" the teacher put in furiously. "She can't read at all. I tell you the girl's simple."

The inspector ignored her. "I would like you to get out your book, choose a story, and read it to me, if you will, Maggie."

Psyche leaned forward, lifted the lid of her desk with steady hands, and took out a book. The pages were thick and dog-eared from much handling, but she leafed through them swiftly, knowing just what she sought for. Then, looking up with an astonishing, gamin smile, she said, "You don't need to be scairt. I can do it. I've chose *The Doll's House* by Katherine Mansfield. It ain't the hardest story in the book, but I likes it the best."

When he was a tired old man, with few illusions left, the inspector would still be able to recall the sound of a husky young voice that mourned the lot of the Kelvey children shunned by their playmates; that comprehended the magic of a single, stolen glimpse at a small doll's lamp; that saved itself from what might have been a wooden parroting of words and phrases by its sympathy with a theme only too well understood.

Although it was obvious to him that she did not know the meaning of much that she was reading, she was still, as she herself had said, a better reader than anyone else in the school. He let his glance rove over a class whose frozen immobility made it plain that they thought themselves exposed to something very close to witchcraft, and knew he was witnessing a Pyrrhic victory.

When she had finished, he said, "You did that very well, Maggie." He spoke quietly, and without emphasis. Still quietly, he said, "The class is dismissed for the rest of the day."

Briefly a thick silence held, then, with a clatter and scramble, they escaped, crowding each other at the doorway, their voices rising in a shrill babble of comment as soon as they cleared the threshold. Only a few of the smallest and slowest noticed that Psyche had been called up to the desk, for she was, as always, the last to leave the room.

The inspector turned to the teacher. "I would like to see you here after lunch. Would two o'clock suit you?"

The teacher, dismissed almost as summarily as her pupils had been, rose stiffly. Suppressing her outrage and anger as well as she could, she said shortly, "I shall be here at two precisely."

After she had gone, the inspector looked up at Psyche with dark eyes which, though unsmiling, were very kind. "How old are you, Maggie?"

"Fourteen, goin' on fifteen next fall."

"How long have you been going to school?"

"I begun last year."

"Why didn't you begin sooner?"

"I dunno. I guess my folks didn't give it no thought afore then."

The inspector tapped the desk absently with the pencil he held. "You want to learn, don't you?"

"More'n anythin' in the world," Psyche told him simply.

"Yes, I think you've given proof of that." He looked out of the window at slag hills bathed in noon-day sunlight, and knew bitterly that there was little or nothing he could do for her. He could, and would, recommend that the teacher be replaced, but it was unlikely any change could be made under a year, and even a really conscientious teacher would be too heavily burdened to have much time to spare for a girl who would, by local standards, be almost ready to 'graduate'.

"Look," he said abruptly, "I can't help you as I would like to. All I can do is to give you two pieces of advice. The first is to get away from this place as soon as you are old enough. The second is to read, meanwhile, anything you can lay your hands on, but you must do this intelligently. To-day you gave evidence of a good ear, and an excellent memory, but half the time you didn't know what you were saying, did you?"

"Well—mebbe not exactly."

The man smiled. "In future you must see that you know exactly. Don't ever read anything again without a dictionary beside you. Look up every single word, and if the meaning is explained in words you don't fully understand, then look up those words too."

Psyche dropped her eyes, and slowly pleating and unpleating a fold in the skirt of her dress, said, "I—I ain't got no dictionary."

"Isn't there one here in the classroom?"

"Yeah, but I ain't allowed to use it. Only the kids what Teacher thinks is bright is allowed to use it for fear it'll get worn out."

"Good God!" Pulling a heavy briefcase across the desk, he opened it, searched its contents, and produced a small green-bound volume which he held out to her. "My father gave me this on my twelfth birthday. It is now yours."

"Oh—no!" Psyche said, swiftly putting her hands behind her back. "No—I can't. Thank you, thank you—but I can't——"

"On the contrary," the man said, "you can't refuse it. And all the thanks I want is the certainty that you will use it, and use it often." Getting up, he came around the desk, and, disengaging her hands, placed the dictionary in them. "Run along now. And—good luck."

That night Psyche slept with the small green book under her pillow, and even after she had blown out her candle she could still see, as plainly as when she had had it in front of her, a fly-leaf with two names on it; one written in ink, a dark, forceful script; the other inscribed with pencil in awkward block letters—Psyche.

It became, in the following weeks, a talisman without which she might not have been able to endure the vindictive persecution of a teacher who, knowing her days were numbered, chose her as an object on which to vent her fear and malice.

Whenever anyone failed to answer a question, Psyche would be called upon. "Perhaps Maggie can give us the answer. Maggie!"

A dozen times a day she was forced to stand up and underline her own ignorance with the only answer possible. "I dunno."

Bearing it with stoic composure, keeping her temper, she eventually found herself left alone again in her corner, free to read and scrawl out words which she would look up later in a dictionary she never took the risk of bringing to school.

*Sharon pulled her grey-squirrel coat more closely around her. On this sunless November afternoon the streets were cold, and she had already three times passed the shop that she could not quite find courage enough to enter. The pattern of the thing she was forcing herself to do was not a new one, but repetition made it no easier. Across the years the shops had varied, as had her purchases, but it had always been in November because a birthday inevitably falls on the same date.*

*Circling the block again, she told herself: "I won't think about what I am doing until I am inside and it's too late to run away. I'll think about Dwight, about going south after Christmas—about anything else, until a saleswoman is beside me, asking me what I want."*

*"Has madam been waited on?"*

*The hot, scented atmosphere, after the sharp outside air, made Sharon feel a little sick. "No," she said, "no one is waiting on me."*

*"Were you looking for something for yourself?"*

*"I want a party dress for a fifteen-year-old girl," Sharon said steadily. "Blue, or perhaps rose colour, but not too unsophisticated. Size fourteen."*

*"Would you please come this way, madam."*

*Passing a wall of mirrors, Sharon saw her own reflection, and thought, I look perfectly natural.*

*The saleswoman paused before a glass case. "I have something here which I think might be just what you are looking for, madam, if she's at all like you. Does she resemble you?"*

*"I don't know," Sharon said bleakly. Then, catching sight of the woman's blank expression, she added coolly, "It's difficult to see oneself in one's daughter."*

*Twenty minutes later she sat in her car, a grey-and-silver dress box beside her, and knew that she was not fit to drive home at once. With shaking fingers she lit a cigarette, and stared through the windshield at a busy downtown street that she did not see at all. Instead she saw a fair-haired girl, tall and slender, dancing with partner after eager partner, her cheeks, flushed with happiness, almost the same colour as the dress that had pleased her so much.*

### 5

IT was a sunless November afternoon when Psyche turned her back on the dirty red-brick schoolhouse for—although she did not know it—the last time. Heavy clouds formed a grey Gothic arch across the sky from horizon to horizon, creating a false twilight that had nothing of night in it, yet that seemed to have severed any true relation with day. And all across the colourless, devastated landscape there lay a windless hush as complete as any that might prevail in the frozen tundras further to the north.

When the last mean fringes of the town dropped away behind her, she quickened her pace, and shivering a little with the cold, pulled her worn jacket more closely around her.

Normally she found nothing to alarm her in the lonely walk through the slag hills; rather she drew assurance from the thought that the very emptiness of the route she travelled robbed it of any personal threat, made unlikely an encounter of any kind. But to-day a vague sense of apprehension caused her to hesitate at the place where she was accustomed to leave the road for the trackless desolation of the slag. She could, she knew, continue to follow the highway to within two hundred yards of the shack as she did in the wintertime, but this would mean adding nearly two miles to the distance she must cover.

"I ain't got nothin' to worry me," she murmured to herself, and, resolutely turning away from the road, set off across the tarnished undulations of a desert in its own way as remote as the central wastes of the Sahara. Like any nomad Bedouin, born and bred amongst uncharted sands, she went into the arid sameness of slopes and gullies, endlessly repeated, without need of direction from sun, or moon, or stars.

Before the road was lost from sight entirely, she paused at the crest of a bare rise to glance back over her shoulder, and suddenly her nebulous uneasiness became a solid core of raw terror.

They had already turned off the road in her wake, two tall, strong-muscled youths, moving at an easy lope just short of running.

Psyche, good vision enabling her to recognize them instantly, knew as instantly what their purpose was in following her, and the exact manner in which they would carry it out. Whispers overheard in a dingy cloak-room; a girl who had left school without warning, and had not returned; her own acute, long-term observation of these two—all these things combined to give her knowledge that was no less terrifying because it lacked any real understanding.

Nausea, born of her own overwhelming fear, held her rigid on the summit of the blackened hillock, a slender, defenseless figure sharply silhouetted against a leaden sky. Then, as though released from an invisible catapult, she wheeled and threw herself head-long down the farther side of the slope toward a depression which, angling off to the right, led into a winding trough more than a mile long. At the end of this trough there was a series of haphazard climbs and descents where, if she could only outdistance them on the level, she might hope to shake them off just long enough to reach the shack and safety.

Her breath coming in short, harsh gasps, she ran for perhaps a quarter of a mile before she dared to look back. A single, rasping sob broke from her. Running side by side, in a silence more deadly than any uttered sound could have been, her pursuers were closing in on her with terrible rapidity. She forced herself to a spurt of speed which turned her whole body into a fiery lance of pain. Bright sparks jumped before her eyes, and her teeth, cutting into her lower lip, brought the warm taste of blood onto her dry tongue.

She was no more than half-way along the length of the trough when she stumbled. She scarcely felt the sharp impact of her knees on the rough ground. Struggling to her feet, she tried to run again while she muttered incoherently. "They ain't gonna touch me—ain't gonna touch—they ain't——"

The strong jerk of cruel fingers bit into her shoulder, almost lifting her off her feet. Swung round on her own momentum, she sensed rather than saw a hulking figure which seemed to tower over her, blotting out the grey ugliness of the slag with its own far uglier intent. Beyond thought or reason, for the moment scarcely sane, she kicked out with all the strength she had, while scream after scream, shrill and inhuman, tore from her restricted throat.

The youth who had caught her doubled up and dropped to the ground, writhing in agony. The other lunged too fast for her to kick again, and she was borne down, fighting like a wildcat, under a weight almost twice as great as her own. Clawing and spitting, primitive in her savage resistence, she heard neither the groans of one, nor the grating voice of the other, saying, "Shut up, you little bitch, or, by Jesus, I'll kill you!" All she heard was the high, piercing rhythm of her own screams, vibrating through her skull, drowning out everything but their own soul-shattering echoes.

Butch, a leviathan forging steadily toward its home port on a course where no other craft ever challenged its right of way, came to a sudden ponderous anchorage in a spot where he had never previously found cause to halt before. All around him rose dark ramparts, lifeless and cold, but from close at hand there came to his ears a sound so anguished in its pain and terror that the sweat sprang out on his low forehead, and his great barrel of a chest swelled with the furious intake of his breath. Turning in his tracks, he plunged forward with a wordless roar in the direction from which the sound came.

To the two youths—one in the act of pulling himself groggily upright, murder in his small eyes; the other tearing Psyche's skirt from her while he brought an open hand down over her mouth with brutal force—the big man was an appalling sight as he appeared over the ridge above them. A giant resurrected from the past, his huge arms already reaching out to crush them, his deep voice thundering his terrible wrath, he bore down upon them as if his sole thought was their utter annihilation.

The first of the attackers, forgetful of pain which was still excruciating, turned and fled. The second, scrambling to his feet, tripping clumsily over the girl in his awful haste, was too slow to escape. Even as he started to run, he was picked up bodily and hurled through the air, landing more than ten feet away with a sickening thud, to lie where he fell until nightfall when, one arm dangling from a smashed shoulder, he staggered away after the companion who had deserted him.

That he did not die, trampled to death under the enormous boots of an avenger who had no mercy, was a debt he owed to Psyche.

Butch, rage a red mist before his eyes, swayed for a full minute between finishing the job he had begun, and going to Psyche who, screaming no longer, crouched on the ground, twitching convulsively. His anxiety overcoming his fury, he went to her, and, dropping to his knees beside her, put an immense arm around her shaking shoulders.

"You're all right, kid. Butch is here. They won't try to hurt you no more. You hear me, kid? Butch got to you in time. You're all right. You don't need to worry no more."

Over and over again he repeated his inarticulate reassurances until, at last, Psyche raised her white, bruised face from her hands, and looked up at him.

Butch, telling Mag about it later, made no effort to keep the pride and wonder out of his voice when he reached this point in his recital. "An' you know what the kid did then, Mag? She smiled, an honest-to-God smile, an' she says, 'Butch,' she says, 'you don't need to worry none over me. I'm okay now.' An' comin' home she wouldn't let me carry her nor nothin'. I'm tellin' you, Mag, that's the best an' bravest kid I ever seen."

"You're right about that. But it wouldn't have done her no good if you hadn't of come along," Mag said soberly.

"Why do you reckon they picked on our kid? She ain't even growed proper."

The wisdom of the ages was in Mag's slow reply. "She may be kinda skinny-like, but the kid's got somethin'—somethin' that ain't gonna bring her all joy."

Mag sat up that night by Psyche's bedside.

"She won't sleep the night out," she told Butch. "She'll wake an' mebbe need somebody."

Wrapped in an old cotton quilt, her untidy masses of red hair pushed up into a torn hairnet, she established herself in a derelict wicker chair, lifted her feet onto an unopened case of beer, and settled down to her vigil in darkness broken only by the glimmer of the one star hung in the corner of the window.

An hour passed, and then another. Psyche turned over again and again, and twice cried out, unintelligible sounds which died down to troubled mutterings which, in their turn, gave way to abnormally heavy breathing. It was after two oclock when she woke up.

"Mag——!"

"I'm right here, kid," the big woman said softly.

Reaching out a hot hand, Psyche searched for, and found, the comfort of a firm, large clasp.

"Are you hungry, kid?"

"No."

"You didn't have no dinner. I could fix you some soup."

"No, I ain't hungry. Mag—I don't want to go back to school no more. I don't want to go never again."

Mag had been ready for this. "You don't need to," she said quietly. "Butch an' me, we don't want that you should, an' if any busybody comes around lookin' for you we'll say you're sixteen. Nobody can prove no different. You can read real good, an' you can write some. I reckon you got enough learnin'. From now on you can just stay to home where you won't have no troubles."

"No troubles——" Psyche murmured, and, relieved not only of immediate physical fear, but also of all the secret burdens of the past two years, fell into a deep, quiet sleep.

On an evening a few days later, Butch hitched his chair closer to the stove, cleared his throat noisily, and said, "I been thinkin'."

Mag, easing her unruly curves into a more comfortable juxtaposition with the lumpy surface of the couch, sniffed derisively. "You're kiddin'."

Unmoved, Butch repeated weightily, "I been thinkin'—supposin' them two bastards was to come here while I was away to the mines."

Mag spared a glance toward the motionless curtain of the storeroom. Then, looking at Butch with more respect than she was in the habit of granting him, she said, "Yeah? You reckon it wouldn't be so good?"

"They're the meanest two bastards I ever come across," Butch told her simply. "I seen 'em, an' I knows. They was bloody scairt, but—I dunno. I been thinkin' it ain't awful safe for you an' the kid out here all alone like. Well, you knows that gun I bought when I left the force——"

"I ain't totin' no gun!" Mag interrupted flatly.

"I wasn't thinkin' of you," Butch said. "I was wonderin' if mebbe the kid could get so's she could use it some."

In the yellow lamplight Mag's broad, perpetually flushed face was a study in conflicting emotions. "You aim to teach shootin' to the kid?"

There was regret but no uncertainty in Butch's heavy voice. "I reckon I gotta. Things ain't the way they used to be. Seems as if there ain't no law an' order no more."

A rough target was chalked on a plank which Butch set up at a little distance from the shack, and after that, on Sunday mornings while the garbage was being burnt, Psyche learned how to handle a heavy-duty Colt revolver. It was to be a long time before she made practical and, in some ways, disastrous use of the art of self-defense as taught to her, and both she and Butch, enjoying these sessions, almost forgot that there was any purpose in them other than amusement. She proved an apt pupil, and was soon winning a fair proportion of the small bets they made between them.

"She's a natural for it," Butch told Mag with great satisfaction.

"I can see that. She's gonna be better'n you afore long if you don't look out. But I don't see no need for her to be carryin' that thing week-days as well's Sundays."

"Leave her be. She's just playin', an' she ain't got much to amuse her."

This last was a truth which could not be very well denied, and from time to time it worried Mag that Psyche should be so much alone.

"It's a lousy shame there's no kids close for you to see," she said to Psyche one day.

"I don't want none."

"How's about that Polack kid a piece back from here? You musta knowed him at school."

Psyche had known him. He was a boy with a liberally indulged penchant for lifting the girls' skirts, and a congenital dislike of the truth in any form. "I'd sooner be seen with a dead rat."

Mag shrugged. She had done her duty. "Well, just as you say, kid. His folks don't speak English so good, so mebbe it's just as well. I don't want you for to get no furrin' way of talkin'."

"I'd get me more'n that with that two-bit bastard," Psyche remarked absently, and, lifting the gun holster down from a nail on the wall, buckled it firmly around her slender hips. "Think I'll go an' practice shootin' for a time. Butch an' me's havin' a competition come Sunday."

"Mind you don't go out of the valley with that thing!"

"I won't."

The slamming of the door, as Psyche went out, was not unlike a pistol shot. The sound still ringing in her ears, Mag looked at Feather Duster, lying forgotten on a shelf behind the stove, and sighed heavily without quite knowing why she should do so.

# 6

THE next three years of Psyche's life, cradled between her unhappy schooldays and the stormy night when she was to leave
the slag for good, were peaceful and relatively contented.
The seasons flowed over the tarpaper shack in an orderly pro-
gression, effecting remarkably few visible changes in it. Late
autumn winds scraped fresh rents in its vulnerable sides; wounds
which Butch, in due course, transmuted into patches very soon
indistinguishable from the scores of others that had preceded
them. The deep, bitter frosts of winter heaved the unproductive,
slate-hued ground, altering the slope of the shack's uneven floor,
changing rather than sharpening the angle at which the shabby
furniture leaned. Spring, when the snow melted from the sides of
the slag hills to form transient lakes and waterways on the floor
of the little valley, was, on the whole, kind to it; bringing nothing
in the way of renewal, it yet took nothing away. And the molten
disc of the summer sun no longer noticeably affected window-
frames and a door bleached to the colour and texture of dried
driftwood.

Butch and Mag suffered some change during this period, but
they had reached a middle age where the mere passing of time
simply served to make them more truly and wholly themselves.
Small habits became more deeply ingrained, physical attributes
more marked.

Butch's stubble field of hair was touched with grey, and he
scratched it oftener. His round, brown eyes retreated further into

caves of friendly wrinkles, and his great shoulders strained more obviously at the seams of shirts which were never quite large enough for him.

Mag simply grew fatter, a state of affairs which led her into discarding any pretense at dressing properly. Equipping herself with an assortment of initially bright-coloured garments which she referred to as 'wrappers', she was rarely seen in anything else. This concession to her vast size resulted in an almost complete cessation of the sporadic trips to town in which she had indulged in former years. A four-mile walk in, and consequently a four-mile walk back, was now too high a price to pay for what invariably turned out to be a poor movie, and a bottle of beer which she could drink more cheaply and comfortably at home. Although the supply was years in excess of the demand, she still knitted enormous vari-coloured socks for Butch; her only real occupation of any kind, she liked it for itself rather than for the dubious results achieved.

Psyche changed greatly, although it would have been difficult to assess that change in so many words, to notice any particular difference at any given time. She put on a little more weight, but not much. Her hair turned a darker gold, but she was still strikingly fair. The clean planes of her face grew firmer, less childish, but, except when she smiled, there was an innocence in her expression that was extraordinarily appealing. Her smile, amused, tolerant, and faintly challenging, was entirely adult.

The chief difference in her was that whereas formerly she had acted first and thought afterwards, now she had a considered purpose in nearly everything she did. However much she had disliked the school, it had nevertheless given her some idea of her potentialities, had made it impossible to return to the aimless existence she had led before she went there. On her own initiative she discovered three new fields to conquer in a place where previously she had thought she had explored every possibility.

They were an odd combination, Psyche's major interests between fifteen and eighteen. She read anything and everything she could lay her hands on, from the bloodied fragments of newsprint in which meat had been delivered, to the Bible. She found she had a real flair for cooking, and developed it to the full. And, quietly and unobtrusively, she learned to play first-class poker.

When she first started hovering behind Butch on Saturday nights while he was playing cards with his three cronies, he did not like it. "Go away, kid," he would rumble, "you give me the jumps."

Later, because she never withdrew very far or for very long, he got used to her being there, and she would sit beside him on the scarred wooden bench, silent, but alert and observant. Eventually he would not play without her, and, if she were not there when he sat down to the table, would bellow, "Where's my little rabbit's foot?"

She never officially sat in on a game. The other men would have been as shocked as Butch himself at the idea of playing with anything that even remotely resembled a woman. In their lexicon, poker was a man's game, and it was a poor imitation of a man who thought otherwise. Nevertheless Psyche, in time, not only played with them regularly, but beat them consistently. It came about so naturally and gradually that Psyche herself was the only one consciously aware of what was happening, and she was very careful to keep it from becoming obvious, for she now looked forward to Saturday night, perhaps even more than Butch did.

The three miners with whom Butch consorted in this manner always came punctually at seven o'clock. Although they travelled different routes across the slag to reach their destination, they rarely arrived more than a minute or two apart from one another. Unwashed dishes were immediately removed from one end of the table, and the clutter of the day—or possibly several days —from the other end. Butch then fetched the cards from a drawer in the golden-oak dresser, while Psyche took four heavy glass tumblers and a bottle of whiskey from the shelf above the sink. Two cracked saucers were produced as ashtrays, and with no further preparation, and no time wasted on idle social interchanges, the game would begin.

Bert, Ed, and Norman were none of them mental giants, and Butch, during the earlier part of an evening, was able, by virtue of painful concentration, to pit his limited wits against them with some success. As time wore on, however, and the level of the whiskey dropped lower and lower in the bottle, the effort would become too much for him, and his winnings would begin to trickle away, at first slowly, and then with alarming rapidity.

Decidedly fuddled, he would stare at his cards and mutter to himself while trying to make up his mind what to do.

Bert, a small gnome of a man with quick brown eyes in a brown nut-cracker face, was the brightest of the quartet, and always ready to prick the big man into rash action. "Come on, come on, Butch. You scairt to raise again?"

At this point a quiet voice would say, "Butch ain't scairt. Why would he be with cards like he's got?" And a slim hand would push a terrifyingly large bet into the centre of the table. "Any of you guys wanna see?"

Three faces would look first at Butch, who would fail to betray a pair of nines because he no longer knew what was going on, and then at Psyche, whose face would reflect a calm certainty of victory they could not believe induced by anything less than four of a kind.

When Butch held a really good hand, she never pushed the betting so far that it was not called and shown. There had to be occasional visible proof of his apparently extraordinary luck.

Refilling their glasses for them, rolling home-made cigarettes for Butch and herself, she played her rôle of audience as expertly as she played Butch's cards for him. She never actually picked up and sorted a hand, and she did not deal for him, but, speaking always through him, she did all his thinking.

Although she knew nothing about psychology or mathematics as sciences, she became more and more fascinated by the inter-locking patterns of personalities and arithmetical probabilities which she seemed able to comprehend and manipulate with such ease. Exhilarated, wide awake, her mind working with a beauti-ful, satisfying precision, she would have liked to play every night and all night.

Mag, who went to bed early on Saturdays, often protested against the hours they kept. "You didn't ought to let the kid stay up so late," she would scold Butch. "It ain't good for a kid to be up in the night, smokin' and losin' sleep."

"It don't hurt her none," Butch would reply, while jingling the amazing amount of coinage he had found in his pants pocket on getting up in the morning.

This was difficult to contradict, because Psyche was as fresh on a Sunday morning as she was on any other morning during the week—in part because she was naturally resilient, and in part because she never drank with the men. They had given her a drink of Scotch one night, and she had immediately been very sick. Like a young coyote, who has once tasted poison and, protected by nature, survived in a similar fashion, she never touched whiskey again.

Although Mag did not know it, Psyche, in the summertime, lost as much sleep through the week as she did on Saturdays.

On warm summer nights, drawn by a restlessness she made no attempt to analyze, she often got up and slipped quietly out of the shack, to wander around the perimeter of the small valley, or climb the slag to watch a rising moon cut a luminous orange arc out of a silver-grey sky. On a moonlit night it was a land bewitched, removed from all reality, its silence so absolute it became a thing in itself, palpable, peaceful as death. Inarticulately one with the universe, feeling in herself the sum of everything that ever had been, or ever would be, she would linger sometimes until the moon set. For on such a night the "outside" drew very close, and the time when she would go out into it seemed close at hand.

Psyche's one great loss, in leaving school, was the loss of ready access to fresh reading matter. Although Butch and Mag could both read after a fashion, it was hard going at the best of times, so neither newspapers nor magazines found their way to the shack with any degree of frequency. The only book in evidence being *Fanny Farmer's Boston Cook Book*. Psyche read that.

After the second time through it, she told Mag, "This is kinda dull, when you just read it like. You want I should make some of these here cakes an' things?"

"It ain't as easy as it looks."

"I can try. If it don't work out—well, it don't work out."

It did work out. Mag might be too lazy to cook, but eating, if somebody else prepared the food, was one of her favourite pastimes, and she was ready enough to impart her skill to a willing neophyte.

If Psyche had had any natural tendency toward excess weight, she would have given evidence of it in the first months of this new activity. With energy to burn, and a tireless curiosity, she kept the big stove roaring from morning until night, producing cakes, muffins, soufflés, pies, and meat dishes which she and Mag sampled as fast as they came out of the oven. As neat in practical matters as she was orderly in mind, she in time rearranged and cleaned up the untidy shelves surrounding stove and sink. From there it was a short step to taking over the entire household, a development which did not particularly please Mag.

"For the luvva Mike, kid," she complained, her lethargic peace disturbed by shifted furniture and clouds of dust, "you done it all yestidday. What's the matter with you that you gotta always be rushin' around?"

"I ain't tired, an' there ain't nothin' else to do."

"Why don't you take a walk?"

"I've a'ready did that."

"Couldn't you bake somethin'?"

Having by this time mastered that trade, Psyche was no longer interested in producing beyond capacity. "I've fixed enough for three days."

"You could read. Where's that magazine I seen you with?"

"It's wore out. Anyway, it wasn't very interestin'."

Mag, knowing that in a matter of minutes she was going to be ordered to remove herself from the couch, was getting desperate. "If I was to find you somethin' new to read, would you quit messin' around an' leave good enough alone?"

Broom in hand, Psyche paused. "Sure, but you ain't got nothin', have you?"

"I dunno for sure, but I useta have a old Bible."

A shadow passed over Psyche's expressive face. Without being told, she knew that the only possible place where she might find the Bible was in the trunk to which she had returned skates she had hoped never to see again. "I'll go look for it," she said abruptly.

At first glance, the torn segment that was apparently all that remained of Mag's Bible did not seem sufficient reward for the reopening of an old wound and the necessity to handle blades still burnished after four years.

She took it in to Mag. "Is this it?"

"Yeah, that's it."

Psyche eyed it with disfavour. "It don't look like much. How did it get tore?"

"I dunno. Perhaps a unbeliever done it."

"It don't look very fascinatin'."

Mag looked at the discarded broom, and said firmly. "It don't do for a kid to grow up without no Bible readin'. I don't know why I ain't thought of it afore, but it ain't never too late. You can start right now, kid."

Psyche opened the partial Bible at the first page. When she was small Mag had taught her simple bedtime prayers, and had created for her a God so unquestionable that when He was referred to it was as if He had just stepped out of the room and might be back at any moment; but she had never before held a Bible in her hands.

"In the beginning God created the heaven and the earth."

She read the first verse twice, and then, without taking her eyes from the page, slowly sat down on the floor and went on reading. A great deal of what she read she understood only in part, even after she had fetched and consulted her dictionary, but much of it was crystal clear.

"And God called the light day, and the darkness he called night."

There was an elemental simplicity in this easily comprehended in the empty world of slag.

Twilight had crept into the room when Psyche looked up, and said, "Mag, is this all supposed to be true what I read in here?"

Mag was more than half asleep. She fumbled for the knitting

which had fallen from her slack hands, and yawned. "Does it matter?"

"No," Psyche replied, after some thought, "I guess it don't. It's the idea what counts."


*Twilight had crept into the long living-room when Sharon closed her book. She had read it twice, and she would read it again.*

*Lighting a cigarette, she knew that she was more at peace with herself than she had been for a long time. While still following her obsession, she had now found something for her mind to bite on, could feel that she was playing an active part in re-discovering her child—if not literally, at least metaphorically.*

*She unlocked the single, shallow drawer of a small inlaid desk, and placed a sheet of writing paper on top of a sheaf of similar sheets. Then, instead of immediately closing the drawer, she read over the notes she had just made in handwriting clear and legible even in the failing light.*

*'—adaptation to environment always qualified by hereditary factors.—If environment is static, the intelligent individual becomes restless: requires change and activity.—Imaginative individual will tend to place a higher value on both actual and moral law than the unimaginative——'*

*For more than six months, Sharon had been reading everything and anything she could find which concerned itself with instinct, memory, and heredity, in the hope that she could put together behaviour patterns which could reasonably be those of her long-lost daughter. That she could be entirely wrong in any conclusions she might draw, she knew quite well. But from what she had read so far, there did seem to be definite evidence in favour of what she so desperately wanted to believe—that her child could have shaped her environment to her own inherent needs, rather than allowing her environment to be the principal factor in determining the kind of person she would be.*

*I will have to read them all again, Sharon thought, all the books*

*I have read so far. I will have to search through them once more, without prejudice if possible, before I go any further. And I must not, must not confuse hope with truth.*

*I can hope that—wherever she is—she will always be all right.*

*I can know—perhaps—that her chances are better than even.*

*No more than that.*

# 5 | THE ARTIST

I

HE came to the mines in the spring in search of material that was 'stark'; a lean young man, prematurely grey, with brilliant hazel eyes, a hard ambition, and a talent not far removed from genius.

The product of a wealthy and consciously sophisticated background, he made no personal concessions to a bohemian profession. Affectations such as silk shirts, over-long hair, and flowing black ties, disgusted him. Immorality for immorality's sake he considered puerile. And to either live or work in a garret, when there was no necessity to do so, would have seemed to him an open confession of imbecility. Nevertheless, he was temperamentally a true bohemian in that he was a law unto himself. Possessed of great charm and few scruples, he acted always in his own best interests, the drive and imagination which were to make him a really great painter unallied with any sympathy for the needs of others. A supreme egotist, he believed in neither god nor devil; had he worshipped anything it would have been his own talent.

His plan to paint in the mining country was one of long standing, and he had so arranged his affairs that he was free from commitments of any kind for five months; free to concentrate wholly on the work which was his mainspring, the *raison d'être* to which everything else in his life was subsidiary.

Installing himself in the one hotel the town boasted, making no secret of his distaste for it, he proceeded at once to devote all his time and attention to the world of slag, which, once discovered, stirred him profoundly. The barren, inhospitable grey mounds and purple-shadowed gullies excited his imagination as no other landscape had ever done before. For two days he roamed across a terrain as primitive as any released by receding Jurassic seas, absorbing its mood, searching a composition that would require no artificial rearrangement on paper. Finding at last exactly what he wanted, he set up easel and camp stool at the base of a triangular valley half a mile from the shack.

It was here that Psyche chanced across him.

Wandering idly amongst the queerly stunted hills, she saw him a fraction of a second before he saw her. When he raised his eyes from his canvas it was as if her slim figure, poised for flight, as immobile as the slag itself, was an hallucination materialized from the copper-coloured haze. For a long moment they regarded one another with equal curiosity. Then Psyche, as keen an observer in her own way as the artist in his, having assured herself that he presented no threat, moved slowly toward him.

Fascinated, he watched her as she approached, seeing an untidy-headed girl, a cigarette in the corner of her mouth, who walked with all the proud, indifferent grace of a young pagan princess; a bare-footed princess, with a shock of heavy golden hair, clad in faded dungarees and a shapeless black sweater.

She came to a halt out of arm's reach, but where she had an unobstructed view of his canvas, and her first words astonished him as much as the deep, vibrant timbre of her voice.

"You seen all the colours! Like me—you seen the colours. Butch an' Mag don't never see nothin' but grey."

He smiled. If his aim was to please, he usually smiled when he spoke. "You like my picture?"

To Psyche, who had never before seen anything other than indifferent magazine and calendar art, his harshly beautiful interpretation was a revelation, but all she said was, "I like it right well."

Anxious not to frighten her, adept at getting on with people when he chose to, he picked up his brush and began to paint, while saying conversationally, "You live near here?"

"Back a piece. What you goin' to call it?"

"My painting? 'Mountains of the Moon'."

"You nuts, by any chance?" Psyche's blue eyes regarded him with clinical detachment. "This ain't the moon, an' them's not mountains."

Resisting a strong desire to laugh, he asked, "What would you call it?" and, deeming it safe to look at her again, laid down his brush.

Psyche pushed her hair back from her forehead and regarded the broken nails of her slender, high-arched feet, while she thought about this.

The artist, trained eyes discarding non-essentials, judged her to be one of the most paintable human beings he had ever seen. The beautiful balance of figure, fine bone structure, and haunting loveliness of face in repose, added up to his conception of the perfect subject. Where in the name of Satan and all his devils had she come from? No untutored miner's child, this. An illegitimate, almost certainly. From a purely aesthetic point of view he would have liked to see her better washed and combed, but first he wanted to paint her—must paint her—just as she was.

Psyche looked up, tossed away the frayed butt of her cigarette, and said quietly, "I would call it—'Mountains of the Moon'." Already moving off, she added, "Well, I gotta be goin'."

A man with less judgement would have tried to detain her. The artist, although he wished he could shackle her to his easel there and then, let her go with a wave of the hand and a casual good-bye.

Convinced as he was that curiosity, if nothing else, would bring her back, he yet found it impossible to concentrate properly on his work after she had gone, and that night slept more fitfully then was customary for him.

Psyche, for reasons that she could not fully fathom, did not tell Mag about this first meeting with him. Disturbed and uneasy, she mentally reviewed the brief encounter over and over again. That his interest in her was as impersonal as it was obvious, she knew instinctively, and yet she was afraid to go back. It was as though she stood on the threshold of a room whose contents, although of compelling interest, might, in their very impersonality, prove inimical to her.

Twice, the following morning, she left the shack, and twice turned back. Seeing its shabby lack of inspiration, its poverty of colour and comfort, more clearly than she had ever done before, she yet found it dearer than ever before.

"What's the matter with you, kid?" Mag asked her curiously. "I ain't never seen you so fidgety."

"Nothin's the matter."

"It must be spring," Mag said sagely. "Folks, specially young ones, tends to get restless come spring."

Psyche did not go back until late afternoon, by which time the artist's impatience was bordering on ill-concealed fury.

His first intimation that she was there was an apparently non-chalant "Hello!" from somewhere behind him.

Swinging round, he saw her sitting on the summit of a small rise about fifty feet away from him. Annoyance, mixed with a relief he resented, got the better of his discretion. "What the devil are you doing up there?" he shouted.

"Watchin' you," replied Psyche, too used to Butch's harmless rages to be perturbed by this greeting.

"Why do it from there, for God's sake?"

"You was busy."

"Well, I'm not busy now. Come on down."

Rising in one fluid movement, Psyche descended the precipitous slope with a graceful ease requiring neither forethought nor any particular attention. "Hot, ain't it? You done a lot since yester-day, ain't you? You near finished?"

The man looked at his painting, and was surprised to find that, in spite of his preoccupation, he had accomplished something. "No," he said, "it's not nearly finished, but I need a rest from it. How would it be if I painted you for a change?"

"That wouldn't be no rest."

"It would, for me. Do you think you could stay still for—say, ten minutes?"

"I guess. You a real artist?"

He mimicked her. "I guess."

Psyche smiled. It was the first time he had seen her smile, and his desire to paint her, not once but many times, was redoubled. Smiling, she had an allure he had not recognized in her before; she became more woman, less child.

"What's your name?" she asked.

"Nick."

"Nick? I ain't never known nobody with that name before."

Setting up a fresh canvas, he asked, without much interest, "What's yours?"

Hesitantly Psyche searched his sharply handsome profile. If she told him, and he laughed as those others had done—— Her breathing a little uneven, her hands thrust belligerently into her trouser pockets, she spelled out the name that was hers, the name that she could not, to her infinite shame, pronounce.

A flicker of surprise showed in narrowed hazel eyes as he glanced up at her. "Psyche?" he said, with some interrogation but no mockery.

Transfixed, Psyche let the two softly crisp syllables sink deep into her consciousness, and the artist, looking at her radiant face, thought with astonishment, my God—she looks as though she has seen the Holy Grail. Then, the urge which was always his primary moving force banishing all curiosity, he said quietly, "Don't move. Stay just as you are—for as long as you can manage it. I'm going to paint you now, just like that." Before he had finished speaking, his brush was moving across the clean canvas with swift, sure strokes.

Psyche, automatically doing what he asked, scarcely heard him. Her eyes lifted to the muted blue of the sky, she gave thanks to an Old Testament God for the gift He had just bestowed upon her. At last she was a person, a real person like everybody else, a person with a name. Psyche—Psyche—Psyche—this was herself, a self to whom anything was now possible. With quick excitement she knew that far horizons were miraculously closer than they had been, and that given the opportunity she was at last fully prepared to explore them.

The rays of the setting sun were slanting arrows that no longer struck the floor of the darkening gully when the artist's fierce absorbtion was disturbed by a quiet but definite voice, saying, "You almost through? I'm gettin' bloody awful stiff."

"Couldn't you just——" he began, and then, catching sight of his watch, said, "Lord, I'd no idea! Sit down. That's enough for to-day. You've been marvelous, really marvelous."

Slowly Psyche drew her hands from her pockets, raised numbed arms above her head, and gently massaged the back of her aching neck.

Nick was beside her at once. "Here, let me do that."

Psyche jerked away from him. "I don't like nobody touchin' me!"

"Don't be a damn fool. With a stiff neck you might be useless to me for days."

The curt objectivity of his concern was so unmistakable that Psyche allowed him to push aside her thick hair and manipulate the muscles of her neck with probing fingers that brought her an immediate relief.

"That better? Good. Now, about to-morrow. Can you be here in the morning? I'll pay you for the time you spend posing."

Irritated by his calm assurance that she would come back again, Psyche stared at him; the lines of his face and hard, lean body were clearly limned, forceful in an integration that openly disclaimed any pressures except from within himself. She was not at all sure that she liked him, but she knew now that her meeting with him was the most important thing that had happened to her within her memory. His speech, so different from that to which she was accustomed, fascinated her. The authority and precision with which he moved and worked were already changing her whole conception of what a man—or a woman—could be, and ought to be. Above all, he represented the outside world, and therefore, in some inexplicable way, seemed to form the first tangible link with her own long-lost beginnings. This, more than anything else, was what had drawn her back to him, and would continue to bring her back.

"I don't want no money," she told him quietly.

"You're a funny girl. Isn't there anything you want that you haven't got?"

"Nothin' that money can buy."

He looked at her in surprise; both her answer, and the manner in which it had been given, were unexpected. She was to continue to surprise him from time to time because he never took the trouble to know her as an individual, as a human being with something more to offer than a lovely face and figure. In due course he learned her story, as much of it as she herself knew, and briefly he was to be attracted to her as a woman, but at no time did he ever credit her with a heart and mind worthy of recognition.

On this occasion it was typical of him that he asked for no explanation of her reply. All he cared about was that she come. Her reasons were of no interest to him.

"What time can you be here?"

" 'Bout nine."

"Good. Don't be late."

When he arrived at the gully the following morning it was to find Psyche there ahead of him.

"Good morning!" he called out.

Psyche did not return his greeting. Instead, she said woodenly, "I can't stay, an' I can't come no more, because Mag don't know you."

Nick carefully deposited easel, camp stool, paint box, and case of canvasses on the unyielding slag. "And who is Mag?" he asked levelly.

"Butch an' Mag's my folks."

"She let you come yesterday."

"I didn't tell her nothin' about you till last night."

Suppressing a strong desire to curse Butch, Mag, all their antecedents, and the universe which encompassed them, Nick considered how he was to deal with this idiotic obstruction. Something in the way in which she had spoken seemed to indicate that these people were not her parents, but her obedience to their wishes was, he guessed, the habit of many years. To suggest rebellion would probably be worse than useless. Greatly as it irritated him, there appeared to be only one thing to do.

"She—Mag—must be persuaded to change her mind."

Psyche shrugged. "I told her you don't make no passes nor nothin' like that, but it didn't make no difference."

He took out a package of cigarettes, and offered one to her. "Since the chief obstacle seems to be that she hasn't met me, she must do so, and at once."

Psyche's wooden mask slipped, and hope and doubt chased each other across her usually expressive face. "I dunno—do you think?"

"Let's not waste time thinking. Which way do we go?"

"Thissaway."

The artist traversed the tortuous route to the shack with a long, fast stride, oblivious of the increasing heat of the day. Psyche, keeping up with him without difficulty, became, the closer they drew to their destination, more and more nervous about the impending meeting. She had not accepted Mag's dictum without argument; argument hotter and more sustained than she had produced in any cause since coming to the shack. Mag, however, suspicious not only of artists, but of strangers in general, had remained adamant. Psyche, conscious of all she owed to the big woman, had at last given in, but with a sense of loss no less bitter because, even to herself, it seemed unreasonable in its intensity.

An innate wisdom cautioning her against letting the artist know that her desire to prolong their association was, for very different reasons, as strong as his own, she walked beside him in silence, speaking only when it was necessary to give brief instructions.

They topped a sharp rise, and the shack lay below them.

Nick stood stock-still. "Is that it?"

Psyche nodded.

"It's marvelous."

Psyche refrained from comment because she had already realized that they spoke, more often than not, an entirely different language, and that this outrageous falsehood had for some incomprehensible reason been uttered in good faith.

"Is that Mag?" He indicated the billowing shape which at that moment appeared in the open doorway.

"Yeah, that's her."

"Excellent. We shall proceed to storm the citadel. And it would be wiser, my slag-born Venus, if you left the negotiations entirely to me."

Psyche's blue eyes questioned him. "You mean for me not to talk?"

He bestowed on her the brilliance of his glancing smile. "I am not always kind, am I, Venus? Yes, it would be better if I did the talking. Introduce us, and then leave it to me."

Mag, arrayed as usual in a faded wrapper, accepted the introductions with hostile majesty, but she was not proof for long against a calculated charm that had melted resistence much stiffer than hers.

Nick, with quiet modesty, presented himself in the simplest language as a respectable craftsman intent only on earning his bread and butter, his sole interest in Psyche a paternally business-like one. He solemnly congratulated Mag on her excellent supervision of her ward, and made passing, but reverent mention of his own parents, omitting to add that they, divorced when he was in his teens, had been on speaking terms neither with each other nor with himself since that time. He admired the shack, something no one else had previously found cause to do, and stated—this with truth—that he would like to paint both it and, if she would be gracious enough to permit it, herself. Privately, he envisaged a Rabelaisian portrait designed to invoke humour and sympathy in equal proportions.

Psyche, a silent audience to this performance, was never to forget a syllable of it. It was her first introduction to the theatre, and her first intimation of the power of the spoken word when used softly rather than explosively.

The final upshot of the conversation was that Nick stayed to lunch at the shack, while marveling inwardly that any human being could find such a milieu supportable, and obtained permission for Psyche to pose for him as often as he wished.

He was preparing to return to work with his now accredited model, when Mag was struck by an after-thought.

"No takin' off of clothes, nor nothin' like that, when you paints the kid, like some of them artist fellows does."

Nick contrived to look extremely shocked. "I wouldn't dream of such a thing!"

"Well, just so's you know the kid's been brung up right," Mag amended almost apologetically.

During the following three weeks the sun rose and set, day after day, a changeless copper ball in a cloudless, burning sky, while Nick, demanding even more of himself than he did of Psyche, made four studies of her and finished "Mountains of the Moon". This was a period when they learned very little about one another, for in his utter absorption in his work he cut all conversation to a minimum. Psyche, however, studying him all the time, began, as the days passed, to form a very clear impression of a stratum of society, hitherto absolutely unknown to her, in which money, because it was plentiful, was relatively unimportant; in which artistic and intellectual achievement ranked above any other endeavour; in which cleanliness was more important than godliness; in which words were used to conceal rather than express feeling.

One day, while resting from a pose, she asked thoughtfully, "You're a gentleman, ain't you, Nick?"

"Oh, my God, Venus! Where did you ever pick up such an obscene word?"

Psyche frowned. "You're bein' clever, ain't you? What do you mean?"

"I mean that there are men and women, and that I find no other distinction admissible."

"Why?"

Nick looked up from his painting, and his hazel eyes were both quizzical and amused. "Damned if I know."

"Supposin' I had said you ain't no gentleman?"

"I would have been flattered."

"Honestly?"

"Must you always be so precise, Venus? All right, let us qualify the statement, and say that my composure would have remained undisturbed, my male vanity unscarred."

Sighing, Psyche said, "You say things just to say them, don't you, Nick? You just like hearin' yourself talk. I wisht I could talk like you."

"A very laudable ambition. I wisht you could, too."

"Couldn't you tell me when I was makin' mistakes? Kind of learn me some?"

He was busy cleaning brushes in a can of turpentine made uncomfortably warm by the heat. "Later, perhaps," he said absently. And they both knew that there was unlikely to be any "later".

That night Psyche sat cross-legged on her bed, and by the light of a guttering stub of candle searched her dictionary for the word "obscene". Since she had no idea how to spell it, she could not find it for some time. When she did, it took her an even longer time to appreciate its use in the context in which she had heard it used. That she finally should understand was proof that, although he did not know it, she had already learned a great deal from Nick.

2

THE cave-in which occurred at the mine on the last day of May of that year was a relatively unimportant disaster, but it killed three men.

Butch came home in the middle of the afternoon, his lumbering gait more awkward than it usually was. His arms hung stiffly by his sides, and his great hands opened and shut spasmodically.

Mag was bringing in a grey batch of laundry, and two ragged towels dropped unheeded to the ground when she saw his face. "Butch—what is it—what happened?"

He looked at her blankly, and then said hoarsely, "It's Bert. He's gone, Mag. He won't be comin' no more on Sattiday nights." In silence they stared at one another, sharing without word or action a dumb animal grief. And for once there was nothing even faintly ludicrous about these two grotesque people who asked so little from life and received even less.

That night the dull roar of rain on the roof muffled the small familiar sounds to which the shack was usually host, and Psyche, lying sleepless in the thick darkness of the storeroom, faced an adult loneliness unlike anything she had known before. The knowledge that nowhere was there anybody who truly needed her, to whom she was bound by any real bonds, was more crystal-clear than it had ever been. Butch and Mag, mortally afraid of any open demonstration, had, in their inarticulate misery, for a time shut her away from them as effectively as if they had slammed a door in her face. Their unawareness that they had done so made it worse, served to underline sharply the basic temperamental differences between them and herself.

With her aching sympathy bottled up inside her, her longing for someone with whom she could really communicate was almost unbearable. Earlier she had wept for the little man with the nut-cracker face, the little man whose bright squirrel's eyes would never again peer at her over a close-held poker hand. Now, feeling slow, warm tears on her cheeks, ashamed because she knew that this time she wept for herself alone, she prayed in silent desperation, "Dear God—don't let it be like this always! Somewhere, some day—someone like me. Dear God, take me back where I comed from!"

*Moving very gently, lest she disturb Dwight, Sharon pushed aside the blankets on her own side of the bed, and swung slender bare feet out on to the carpet. Steady rain covering the small sounds of her going, she crossed in the darkness to the door, and quietly let herself out into the upper hall. A moment later another door opened and closed, and she was alone in the room that no one but herself ever entered.*

*The night-light sprang on under a hand that had known exactly where to find it, and she stood, motionless, her blue eyes returning the unwinking regard of a small brown teddy-bear.*

*Suddenly, the rigid control that she usually imposed on herself broke, and with a choking sob she fell to her knees, frantic fingers torturing white lambs that gambolled across a small, blue bedspread. "Our Father which art in heaven, Hallowed be thy— Oh, God, bring her back—give her back to me—it has been so long——"*

The triple funeral service was held toward the close of a rainy afternoon two days after the cave-in.

It took Butch, and Mag, and Psyche more than an hour and a half to make the wet pilgrimage to the church, for Mag, so long unaccustomed to walking at all, needed to come to a wheezing halt every few minutes in order to catch her breath.

When they finally climbed the short flight of steps to the church door, the knell for the dead was already being tolled, an overtone of mourning which followed them into the undemonstrative, apathetic grief within the church itself.

Psyche, wedged between Butch and Mag in a back pew, stifled by the humid warmth of too many people crowded into too small a space, thought at first that she was going to be sick. Sensitive to atmosphere of any kind, her sickness was not all physical. The defeated hopelessness around her seemed to seep through the pores of her skin like a dark, invisible liquid, sticky but saturating, and she, who had never been in a church before, found herself hoping that she need never enter one again. In vain her eyes sought for even a vestige of the spiritual splendour she had naïvely imagined would illuminate such a place with a radiance born of something other than the sun. But there was only a grey light struggling through narrow windows to mingle with the murky glow of naked bulbs that failed to draw fire from a brass cross on the altar; that discovered no beauty in cramped bunches of flowers already wilting, symbol in themselves of the mortality of all living things.

Her hands knotted tightly together in her lap, her head bowed, she shut eyes, ears, and mind to her surroundings, and concentrated on a mental image of the Garden of Eden.

When the service was over, a service conducted by a man incapable of producing any real hope of an after-life; when the three simple coffins had been borne away; when there was at last no reason to linger longer in that most dreary of God's houses, the people filed silently out into the empty square, there to stand in small, huddled groups, unwilling to remove themselves at once from their only present comfort, the comfort of the herd.

Psyche, although thoroughly depressed, was yet, as always, to some extent set apart from those around her by her unwavering conviction that this was not truly her way of life, that the mines would not forever govern her future, her fate. She felt a very real compassion for the shrunken little woman in black who was Bert's widow, but she could not identify herself with her in any way. Tall, fair, vital, she was certain that she would never wear widow's weeds beside an unsung miner's grave.

Standing on the edge of a group, a few feet away from Butch and Mag, she became gradually aware that she was being watched. It was an uncomfortable feeling, and one to which she was peculiarly unused. For a time she resisted the temptation to turn and find the source of her growing unease. Drawing her old blue coat more closely to her, she put on, and then took off again, the darned cotton gloves, too small for her long hands, which Mag had given her just before leaving the shack. At last, unable to stand it any longer, she swung round, and her searching eyes found, and locked with, a hot blue stare, insolent and unwavering, which seemed to strip her of more than coat and gloves.

He was a young man, dark and sleekly handsome. Better dressed than any man she had ever seen before, he wore a grey suit smoothly fitted to broad shoulders and narrow hips. Lounging negligently against a rickety porch across the square, contemptuous of his surroundings, he contrived to insult the occasion in a manner as offensive as his appraisal of herself.

When he straightened up and started to walk toward her, Psyche knew that, in any other place or at any other time, she would have run from him. Instinctively her hand went to her hip where for so long she had carried Butch's service Colt. The man, mistaking the nature and purpose of the gesture, smiled, regular teeth flashing white against his brown skin. This, he thought, was going to be easier than he had anticipated. A pity, really, because he did not like them easy.

When he stood beside her, he said softly, "Hello, beautiful—doing anything special to-night?"

At the sound of his low voice, as sensual as his bold blue eyes, Psyche experienced a sensation so entirely new to her, and so unexpected, that her voice, shaking in spite of her every effort to control it, carried little or no conviction. "Not with you, I ain't."

"We could take a ride, and talk it over?" He pointed casually to the red convertible on the other side of the road, a startling bird of paradise aloof from the dusty flock of sparrows clustering closer to the church. It was a bait which had often been a sufficient lure in itself.

Psyche scarcely looked at it, which annoyed him. He was still further annoyed when she repeated her refusal, this time no more than a blunt, "No."

"Why not?"

"I don't want to."

He smiled again. He was very sure of himself. "Come on, beautiful, don't be like that. We're wasting time."

Trembling visibly now, hating herself as much as she hated him, Psyche cast wildly around for a refusal as wounding as it was positive. And then she thought of Nick who was everything that this handsome, self-satisfied animal was not. Suddenly calm, she lifted her pointed chin, narrowed her eyes, and said with quiet viciousness, "I ain't goin' nowhere with you never, because you—ain't—no—gentleman!"

The arrow had been too well chosen.

A dark flush appearing in his cheeks, he replied to it with soft-spoken but terrifying violence. "You'll pay for that, you little bitch, and in the way I most want you to. That's a promise."

"Hey, kid!"

Mag's hoarse summons was more than welcome, and turning abruptly, Psyche went to her side. "You want somethin'?"

Mag peered at her suspiciously. "What was you talkin' to that big bastard about?"

"Nothin' much."

"You know who he is?"

"No, an' I don't care."

"He's the super's son."

Psyche shrugged. "So what?"

"So what did he want with you?"

"He wanted for me to go somewheres with him."

"You ain't goin', I hope?"

Psyche's reply was more than emphatic. "I ain't."

Mag nodded her approval, her one and only hat, a strange concoction of bedraggled black feathers, wobbling precariously on its red perch. "You're a good kid. I don't really worry none over you. Look, Butch an' me's goin' over to sit a while with Bert's old woman. You might's well go on home an' get supper goin'."

"You want I should take the lantern out to the road for you? It's likely goin' to get dark right early."

Mag looked up at the lowering sky, and sighed her weariness at the prospect of having to take the longer route back. "Guess you better had. You don't mind goin' back by yourself, kid?"

Psyche noticed that the church door had been closed, and that the small quiet knots of people had nearly all dispersed. Surreptitiously glancing behind her, she saw that the big convertible had gone, too. "Who, me? Why should I mind?"

"No reason—no reason at all," Mag told her, but the same memory was in both their minds.

It was not actually raining when Psyche started out along the road, and for a time there were others going in the same direction. But when she turned off into the slag she was completely alone, and a rising wind and leaden-coloured clouds gave warning of an approaching storm. Walking swiftly, her head held high, she covered the remaining distance to the shack in half an hour, but it was one of the longest half-hours she had ever known, and when at last she saw the shack itself, bleak and unlit in its shallow depression, she broke into a run.

It was not quite seven o'clock, yet when she closed the door behind her, she was in virtual darkness.

"I'll fix the stove an' the lamps afore takin' out the lantern," she said to herself, and the sound of her own voice was an assurance of normalcy which she found very comforting.

Once the two oil lamps were lit, one set on the golden-oak dresser, the other on the table, she stoked up the still-warm embers in the big stove, adding a few twists of paper and fresh coal. This done, she turned her attention to a dishpan piled high with not only lunch but breakfast dishes. When these were finally finished; when the potatoes had been peeled, and ground beef and onions made ready in a frying pan; when even the table had been cleared and scrubbed and three places neatly set, she could find no other reasonable excuse for deferring her short journey out to the highway.

Taking down a lantern from one of the shelves above the sink, she hesitated, and then reached for a second for her own use although she could have found her way blindfolded across the slag from any direction.

Once definitely committed to a course of action, she was not in the habit of either reconsidering or turning back, and now she worked with a swift efficiency far more characteristic than her behaviour of the previous hour. Quickly she checked the oil in the two lanterns, trimmed wicks, and wiped off clouded glass.

Lightning was flickering across the western sky, and the first heavy drops of a fresh rainfall were beginning to spatter against the still-wet ground, when she stepped out of the shack, the lanterns one in either hand and Butch's old oilskin raincape around her shoulders.

Her mind a determined blank, her two-fold shadow a distorted alter ego in the premature darkness, she climbed and then descended, walked for a space on the level, climbed and descended again, and came to a halt only when she stood beside the wet, black ribbon of the highway. Setting one of the lanterns down, she stood there for a moment, the motionless, drunken mail-box her sole companion in the windy night.

It was as she turned to retrace her steps that she heard the steady hum of an approaching car. If her fears had been concrete fears, rather than those of association, she would have fled instead of lingering to be caught in the full radiance of powerful headlights.

Her vague hope, that by some miracle, Butch and Mag might have found transportation with a passing stranger, vanished as the car swept by without stopping. Briefly blinded by the lights, she turned away again without having really seen it at all. And when, now guided only by a single fog lamp, it drew up beside the mail-box a few minutes later, she had already forgotten it, was utterly unaware that the lantern she carried to protect her from the ghosts of yesterday was to be her betrayal as she topped the last slope between the highway and the shack. For, without that fleeting signpost, the man, in spite of his vengeful desire for her, might not have attempted a search for the shack on such a night.

Psyche, hanging up the raincape on the back of the door after having carefully hooked the inadequate catch, felt the vibration of thunder rolling close overhead. Rain, suddenly descending in torrents, hissed through the rusty iron chimney into the stove, and darkened a brown stain in cardboard which replaced a broken window-pane.

With nothing to do but wait, she sat down in an old rocker beside the stove, realizing for the first time how much she had come to depend on Mag's constant presence at all times. Mag's large form, flowing over a couch whose springs now almost touched the floor, had been such a fixture there for so many years that the shabby room seemed bare and denuded without her, and the shack itself, unanchored by her great weight, became a flimsy structure likely to disintegrate with each fresh peal of thunder.

Rubbing her hands up and down her arms, although she was not cold, she listened, tense and lonely, to the increasing fury of the storm : the soft menacing rush of water in flood, as the rain channeled through a cleft beneath the worn board floor; the heavy beat of thunder as it echoed and re-echoed against the low-slung vault of the night; the chattering rattle of ill-fitting casements; the sharp slapping of loose tarpaper as the wind clawed at it. And inside, a false vortex, a small bright square that was too quiet, too static, too empty.

She saw, rather than heard, the door-knob turning. And the tiny click, as the door itself, opening fractionally, caught against the hook, would have been inaudible if she had not known it was coming.

For an instant she did not stir, but rested frozen as she had been when she saw that first, stealthy movement where no movement should have been. Then, almost as if she had been waiting for this thing to happen, she moved with all the split-second swiftness of a young panther, so that when the cheap hook was torn screaming from its socket and the door crashed open against the wall, she was crouched in the far angle of the room behind the stove, a blue-black metal object held steadily in her right hand.

The man, half falling as he burst into the shack, found his balance again with an ease possible only to a trained fighter. And there was something so savagely beautiful in the cruel dark face and the perfectly co-ordinated muscles rippling visibly beneath shirt and trousers rain-plastered against them, that Psyche, if he had rushed her then, would have been physically incapable of shooting him.

Eyes slitted against the sudden light, he paused long enough to get his bearings, and in so doing lost his one opportunity of getting, possibly without even a struggle, what he had come for.

When his eyes did focus directly on her, Psyche, although breathing unevenly, had all her defenses in order again, and the cold barrel of the revolver showed no more promise of wavering than did the stony purity of the set face behind it.

The man smiled, although amusement, in the ordinary sense, was no part of his thoughts. "You little hell-cat—who let you loose with a gun? Put it down before you hurt somebody." And, as he spoke, he began to edge smoothly, almost imperceptibly, across the room.

The rain, slanting in through the open doorway behind him,

formed an ever-widening pool, and jagged yellow lightning framed his sleek dark head with a fleeting, infernal halo.

Pysche would see him again in dreams as he was then, dreams from which she would wake with reluctance, but her voice when she spoke was cool and emotionless. "You keep on comin', the way you're doin', an' it's you who will get hurt—an' hurt bad."

In spite of the way she handled her weapon, he did not believe that she really knew how to use it, and her slim apparent fragility coupled with his own conceit led him to the conviction that she would not, when it came to the showdown, have either the courage or the will to fire it.

Without further warning, without any visible preparation or tensing of muscles, he sprang forward and sideways in one incredible leap which, if completed, would have brought him into the gap between stove and wall within reach of her. The bullet smashed into his shoulder before he was midway there. While the explosion still lingered on the shattered air, he crashed to the floor, his head striking the wall as he fell; and the red blood spurted through his shirt.

Moving like an automaton, her face as white as the man's blood-stained shirt, Psyche came out from behind the stove, laid the revolver with precise care on the table, and knelt down beside him. Expressionless, neither regret nor compassion in her remote blue eyes, she turned him over, with some effort for he was heavy, and, without flinching, unbuttoned his shirt and examined the wound. She noted that the free bleeding was already lessening, and that his breathing, though fast, was neither shallow nor noticeably uneven. It was all exactly as Butch had told her it would be if she aimed straight and found her mark; and she had hit this man precisely where she had intended to.

It had not been real when Butch had been teaching her, and it was still not real. A marionette, its strings manipulated by an invisible hand, she continued to go through the well-taught motions of a lesson she no longer comprehended.

She rose, closed the open door, and, going to the dresser, took from the bottom drawer the one piece of cloth in the shack which she knew to be absolutely clean, Mag's highly valued damask tea cloth. Tearing it into strips, she went back to the wounded man, sat down on the floor, and, making a pad out of the torn linen, placed it gently but firmly over the round, blackened hole where the bullet had gone in. Holding the pad in place with the flat of her hand, she became as still as the sprawled figure beside her.

The storm passed away, leaving in its wake a gentle, persistent rain, but Pysche was unaware of its passing. From time to time the stove contracted audibly as the fire died down, but she did not hear it. The lamp on the dresser flickered uncertainly for several minutes, and then went out, but Psyche, her face a cameo now half in shadow, never moved.

It was thus that Butch and Mag found her nearly an hour later.

Strife, and with it bloodshed, was not new to either of them, but they had already that day gone through what was for them a considerable strain, and so it was Psyche who spoke first, answering the unspoken questions on those two dazed faces.

"He ain't dead," she said evenly, "an' he ain't gonna die." A crack appearing in her unnatural composure, she added piteously, "I hadda do it! He bust in here, an' I hadda do it. He was goin' to make me—to—to——"

"You don't have to say no more, kid," Mag broke in, the story now as clear to her as though it had been explained at length. "You done quite right. Don't never think you didn't." Crossing the room, dropping her coat on the floor as she came, she helped Psyche, now shaking violently, to her feet. "Butch, you big ape, don't just stand there doin' nothin'! Get some whiskey for the kid, and get it quick!"

"I don't want—any——" Psyche began, her teeth chattering.

"You gotta have somethin'," Mag told her firmly, "an' we ain't got nothin' else. I'll fix you some tea soon's I've looked at him." She jerked her massive head in the general direction of the man to whom she had so far given no more than a cursory glance. If he had died where he lay, she would have considered it no more than he deserved, but her shrewd mind was already beginning to grasp implications in the situation which neither Psyche, in a state of shock, nor Butch, in his simplicity, as yet understood. When the doctor came, and he would have to come, it would only be the start of questions which would finally be asked in a court of law. Her face suddenly drawn and grey, she turned her back on Psyche where she sat, still shaking, on the couch, and spoke to Butch. "We gotta get the kid away from here," she said heavily. "She's gotta go right away."

Butch looked at her in blank astonishment. "The kid didn't do nothin' wrong, Mag. It was, like you might say, self-defense."

All the defeated acceptance of injustice of her kind was in Mag's voice when she replied. "The kid's nobody, an' we ain't nobody neither. He's somebody. They'll take her away an' put her in one of them reform schools, as sure as Christ is the livin' God. Anythin'—anythin' at all—is better'n that. She ain't eighteen yet, far's we know or can prove, an' we ain't got no papers for her. We couldn't do nothin' for her once they got her away from us. Why, she ain't even got a proper name."

Butch, his low forehead creased in great ridges, repeated stubbornly, "But she ain't really done nothin' wrong."

"That ain't the point. If he'd done her harm afore she plugged him, mebbe she'd have a better chance. Mebbe they'd take her away anyway. I dunno. All's I know is I ain't goin' to let nobody put our kid in one of them stinkin' reform schools. I'd as soon see her dead. Go take a look at him, an' see he ain't cold nor bleedin' —rot him—an' gimme a chance to think some."

She sat down beside Psyche, and put a big, warm arm around her shoulder; something she had not done since Psyche was a small child. In this, the greatest crisis she had ever faced, she felt miserably inadequate. The kid was already lost to her, of that she was quite certain. It was for the kid herself that she must think now. With so little time in which to do this, a matter of a few hours only, how was she to find a place for the kid to go to, a place where she would have at least a fighting chance of a decent life?

"Oh God," she prayed mutely, "what can I do? She's a good kid, God, You know that. I ain't got nobody nowheres I can send her to, an' how can she go alone, God, without no real learnin', nor trainin', nor nothin'? We ain't got enough cash, Butch an' me, for her to eat an' sleep proper for more'n a month, God, an' she's got to go a long ways from here, an' go quick. If we was to take her out to the road, God, would You send someone decent to give her a ride—would You see that she landed up somewheres where she had a chance?"

"Kid——" She shook Psyche gently to get her attention. "Kid, you gotta—gotta go away for a spell. It ain't noways fair, but what you done to-night—well, I'm feared you might get into bad trouble if you was to stay here."

Reform school was an ugly threat which Psyche had heard used many times over when she was at school, and her actual ignorance of what such a place might be like made her fear of it no less than it would have been if she had known precisely. That it was infinitely worse than an ordinary school, she did realize, and that was enough in itself.

Although the words had come from what seemed to be a long way off, she had both heard and understood what Butch and Mag had said earlier, so now she asked only one question. "Where can I go, Mag?"

"You gotta be brave, kid, because you gotta——" A mental picture of the kid, whom she had come to think of almost as her own, alone and friendless on the dark highway, was for the moment too much for her. Her throat harsh and dry, she began again. "You ain't got nowheres exactly, kid. But you're growed, an' you can cook real good, an' if you starts out now——"

"Mag," Psyche interrupted urgently, "I can't go without I tell Nick first."

The artist fellow! It was almost as if a sky-rocket had gone off inside Mag's head. He had said—what had he said about the kid that day he had come to the shack? Something about wishing she could always work for him. He had laughed when he had said it, but he had sounded as if he meant it just the same. He had said—frantically she searched her memory, and suddenly it was as if he were beside her, saying again, "You ask me if she's a good model. She is so good I wish I could carry her off to work for me indefinitely."

Getting to her feet with an agility she had not known she still possessed, her face ten years younger than it had been a moment before, she cried, "Butch—Butch! You hear that? The artist fellow. The kid can go with him!"

"Where's he goin'?" asked Butch, looking up from a not altogether unhappy examination of the result of his own teachings.

"Don't ask no stoopid questions. There ain't time."

"This here bastard mebbe ain't goin' to come to 'til mornin'. He's hit his head on somethin' as well's gettin' plugged."

"If we don't do nothin' about the doctor for——" Mag calculated rapidly, "—'bout two hours, is he gonna be all right?"

Butch, perhaps because his limited mental capacities had been taxed with little else since, remembered most of what he had learned as a member of the police force, and a rough and ready first-aid was still one of his few accomplishments. "Sure, he ain't gonna die, not to-night, nor any time soon."

"Can we move him? He's in the road there."

Slowly Butch shook his head. He had seen men, in worse condition than this, hauled ungently into a police wagon and survive, but it was not treatment he felt he could recommend. "Better leave him lay. I'll get a blanket to put on him. He's gotta he kep' warm."

By the time he had done this, Mag was seated at the table using a stub of pencil and a piece of lined paper torn from an old exercise book. "Light t'other lamp, will you. I can't see so good as I useta."

"What you doin'?"

Mag did not reply. A few minutes later she reread her own painful scrawl, was far from satisfied with what she had written, but decided it would do. Folding the paper twice, she levered herself up from the bench and addressed Butch. "Take this here letter to the hotel an' find the artist fellow an' give it to him. Don't give it to no one else."

Butch scratched his head in slow perplexity. Events were moving far too fast for him. "What you want for me to say to him?"

Psyche spoke then. "Mag wants for me to go with Nick, Butch, an' I guess this here letter's to tell him so. You see——" her voice broke, and she steadied it with an effort, "—you see I can't stay here no more, else they—they'd get me sure."

Butch's big, hairy hand closed over the letter. He put it carefully in the pocket of his worn blue serge jacket. He took his hat from its hook, walked to the door, opened it, and then stood stock still. Without looking back, he said, "Mag—Mag, you mean the kid ain't gonna rest with us no more?"

Mag tried to swallow the sharp lump in her throat, but it would not go down. "That's right," she said hoarsely. "Now don't go awastin' no more time."

Butch stepped out into the darkness, and the door, which he usually slammed with careless violence, closed behind him without a sound.

### 3

PATIENCE was not one of Nick's virtues. The evening of the second day of rain found him pacing up and down a room he considered supremely unattractive, the while he cursed the weather and wished himself anywhere else but in a stinking hole where, he had by now convinced himself, it rained from year's end to year's end. He had tried sitting in the hotel lobby, but had retired in disgust from its brass cuspidors, dusty palms, and odour of damp linoleum.

When Butch knocked on his door he had reached a stage where any kind of intrusion on his solitary frustration was a relief. Flinging the door open, confronted with an individual whom he had never seen before, he nevertheless said, "Come in."

Butch came in, and there matters might have rested indefinitely if Nick had not said, "Did you want something?"

Butch's life, like that of an old grizzly bear, ran in grooves, in trails of habit worn so deep it was surprising they were not there to be seen. Deflected, without sufficient warning, from his usual paths, his thinking was even more laboured than it normally was. This direct question, coupled with the cool self-sufficiency of the stranger who asked it, upset him, and he could find nothing to say.

Nick, already bored with an encounter which promised to be entirely unproductive, said again, somewhat impatiently, "Did you want something?"

Still unable to frame a suitable verbal reply, Butch simply drew the letter from his pocket and handed it over.

Mag's illiterate note was not easy to read, but its content, once deciphered, was clear and to the point. Nick read it through three times before absently crumpling it up in his hand. Biting his lip, keen eyes looking straight through the bulk of Butch who stood fumbling awkwardly with his old felt hat, he saw Psyche in one pose after another while he weighed the pros and cons of a situation which affected him more vitally than Mag could possibly have guessed.

If he did not, as the note suggested, take the girl away at once, his chances of ever painting her again appeared to be nil. He had two sketches of her unfinished, and it was unthinkable that he fail to complete them, impossible that they represent his last opportunity to work with a model whose equal he might never find again. If he did take her, could he keep her at the studio without advertising her presence there? Yes, that could probably be managed—and, Lord, what an opportunity! If he could have her there under ideal working conditions twenty-four hours a day, he could accomplish in months what it might otherwise take years to do. Alice—could this thing be done without his wife's knowledge? He would give his right—he mentally corrected himself—his left arm before he would wilfully lose Alice. But Alice was three thousand miles away from the converted barn in its secluded valley. She would be away until September—and this was only the beginning of June——

Suddenly he made up his mind. If the note contained truth, if the man were only injured, then he would take her. It was highly unlikely that an intensive search would be made for her if the man recovered. No charge more severe than juvenile delinquency could be made to stick, and taxpayers' money was not usually thrown away on a widespread hunt for a juvenile with no previous record.

His eyes finding a shorter perspective again, he looked directly at Butch, and said decisively, "I'll come." He nodded toward a bottle of whiskey on the night-table. "Pour yourself a drink. I'll be ready in twenty minutes."

He was ready in less time than that, the straps of his case of canvasses checked with care, his clothes and few personal belongings stuffed into a single suitcase.

"Did you see anyone you knew on your way here?" he asked Butch.

"Don't remember none."

"What about the man at the desk downstairs?"

"I ain't never seen him afore to-night," Butch told him stolidly, and then, slowly beginning to realize the purpose behind this interrogation, added, for further clarification, "I don't never come here at night."

"Good. Now you go down the back stairs—they're on the left at the end of the corridor—and out the service entrance to the parking space. You'll find my car there, a black Buick, license number 4DB624. It isn't locked. Get in, and wait for me while I check out."

These were the kind of concise instructions which Butch had been used to receiving and carrying out in a dim and distant past, and, rather than resenting the curt manner in which they were delivered, he was reassured. Almost but not quite saluting as he left the room, he lumbered down the corridor, curiously comforted.

Nick, meanwhile, overlooking no way in which he could protect himself in so far as was possible, went down to the lobby to play, with some flair, the part of an inebriated artist intent on searching out the morning in its lair, and this without delay.

When he left, staggering very slightly, he was quite satisfied that the smirking young man behind the desk would not, if subsequently questioned, in any way connect his abrupt departure with Psyche's flight from the shack.

He arrived with Butch at the shack a half-hour later, having left the Buick parked beside the highway close to a red convertible that had caused him to raise his eyebrows and whistle softly under his breath.

They found Mag alone with the owner of the red car. Although still prostrate, he was showing signs of returning consciousness, groaning and stirring restlessly under the blanket which had been laid over him.

Nick looked around the room. "Where is she?"

Mag nodded toward one of the two limp curtains at the back of the shack. "She's layin' down. She's been sick."

"She's better now?"

"Yeah she'll be okay. It done her good, really. You goin' to take the kid?"

Nick went over to the man on the floor, looked at him for a moment, felt his pulse, and then turned to Mag, and said quietly, "Yes. And we'd better leave at once. This man is going to come to soon. It's important that he doesn't see me. Are her things packed?"

Silently Mag pointed to a cardboard carton, tied with oddments of string, which stood beside the door.

Butch cleared his throat. "You better go get the kid, Mag," he said thickly.

Mag's hand was already on the curtain when she said, "You understand that the kid can't never come back?"

Nick nodded. "I understand."

A terrible, urgent appeal appeared in the big woman's voice and eyes. "You'll treat her decent, won't you? She's—she's a good kid."

Nick nodded again, and because he believed what he was saying for at least as long as it took him to say it, there was both sincerity and conviction in his reply. "I'll take good care of her."

"God bless you," Mag whispered, and went into the little storeroom to her kid for the last time.

# 4

THE long night drive through darkness into a grey dawn was, although neither Nick nor Psyche knew it, not unlike a film being run in reverse. For Psyche was going back to the city in which she had been born, following a road, again by night, and again in haste, over which she had travelled for the first time nearly fifteen years earlier.

Nick drove, as he did everything else that he enjoyed doing, with a concentration that allowed no unnecessary distractions. Lean brown hands close together on top of the wheel, intent eyes never wavering from the outer rim of the white path cut by the headlights, he kept the speedometer needle hovering just under eighty on the straightaway, and took the curves for the most part without dropping below fifty. The small towns through which they passed were silent, deserted islands, apparently as untenanted as the black oceans of forest that surrounded them on all sides —forests that began to give way reluctantly to the greyer darkness of fields and pastureland only after they had been on the road for something over three hours.

During the earlier stages of the journey Psyche, a waxen figure with a waxen face, sat rigidly clutching the tattered portion of the ancient Bible that Mag had at the last moment thrust into her hands. Her sole tangible link with the shack, she held on to it as if she never meant to let go of it again. Yet, as mile after mile dropped away behind them, with darkness producing only further darkness, the tight fingers gradually relaxed their frantic grip, and the golden head began to loll and jerk with the motion of the fast-moving car.

For a time fatigue blotted out all thought, conscious or unconscious, and her awkward sleep was that of utter exhaustion.

Her nightmare began as a pleasant dream. Warm and happy, she drifted through space in a bed encircled by white bars which, rather than imprisoning, gave a wonderful sense of security. And just out of sight someone was singing a song whose words would not come through clearly to her, but whose musical cadences were achingly familiar.

"Mmmm—Mmmm——" she murmured.

Nick, glancing sideways, and seeing that she slept, did not disturb her.

Below her there spread away, it seemed to infinity, a great field of pale-blue grass, while above her she could see a cloudless pink sky. Slowly, the pink sky began to darken; a chill wind whined between bars no longer white but black as the slag at night; and the soft blue blanket, under which she lay, began to creep of its own volition over her face, a stifling weight forcing the breath back into a throat choked with screams that died before they found utterance. Wildly, hopelessly, she thrashed out at a faceless, formless horror that attacked her now in a chaotic, bruising turmoil of darkness.

Nick was caught completely off guard by her piercing scream. The car swerved dangerously. Then he had it under control again, and slowed to a stop at the side of the empty highway.

When he was free to turn to her, she was awake, her eyes clouded with fear and uncertainty. "Nick—what was it? I heard somethin'—I dunno what."

He laid a hand over both of hers, and finding them ice-cold, began to chafe them. "You cried out, Venus. That's all. You were asleep, and must have been dreaming. Don't you remember now?"

Psyche shook her head. She did not want to remember. "I remember nothin'."

"We've just passed over a very rough piece of road. I'll fix you up on the back seat and you can sleep properly."

"I don't think I want to sleep no more."

"You need it. You can at least try."

He rolled up his trench-coat as a pillow for her, made her take off her scuffed shoes, and wrapped her in a motor-rug.

As he was closing the door, Psyche lifted her head from the improvised pillow. "You're bein' very good to me, Nick."

"You didn't expect that?"

"Not for sure."

When he saw no need for pretense, Nick attempted none. "We are, at the moment, a mutual-benefit society, Venus. It would be stupid not to protect each other's interests with as much grace as the situation allows."

It was a different brand of honesty from Psyche's own, but it was, nevertheless, honesty, and as such more reassuring than any gentle evasion. It established in words, and without equivocation, the only possible relationship that could for long be satisfactory to both of them.

They had moved out of the storm area, and Psyche, as the car again travelled southwards, lay watching an ever-changing pattern of stars and tree-tops. After the static horizons of the world in which she had lived for so long, this simple night-time panorama held a breathless fascination for her. Knowing that at last she had been caught up in the current of a moving stream, conscious of a deep, wordless satisfaction that this should be so, she went tranquilly to sleep.

They stopped for breakfast, with more than five hundred miles of highway unrolled behind them, on the outskirts of a large city; a city whose widening spokes reached out from a lakeside hub still eleven miles distant.

It was scarcely eight o'clock, but the restaurant was almost full. Nick led Psyche past the crowded confusion of the counter to an empty booth at the back. Amongst a clientele at that hour composed mainly of truckers they passed unnoticed, the tall, shabby girl, and the poised man in the paint-stained flannels and leather windbreaker.

Nick ordered orange juice, eggs, and coffee, and when they

were served they ate in silence, occupied with thoughts they had no wish to communicate to one another.

Nick was concerned with purely practical problems. Situated as the studio was, he saw no real reason why Psyche's presence there should become known. He had at no time encouraged visitors, and moreover was expected to remain in the north country until Alice's return and the reopening of the city house in the fall. If he could contrive to do the necessary shopping on his own, and did not, by some foul chance, run into anyone he knew, he would spare himself endless complications and a tedious tissue of lies. The buying of food would be relatively simple. Clothes for Psyche presented greater difficulties, but she could not be left in her present disreputable state.

"What size are you?" he asked.

Psyche looked at him in surprise, as she answered automatically, "Fourteen, Tall."

"You don't know your exact measurements, do you?"

All the clothes she had ever owned had been bought by mail, and so she did know. She told him.

"The Greeks had a word for it," Nick murmured, and without further comment or explanation retired again into silent preoccupation.

Psyche, meanwhile, had been realizing with painful clarity how entirely dependent she was on a virtual stranger, and how little claim she had on him. In the isolation of the slag she had thought of him as an old friend. She knew now that this was not true. Studying, unobserved, the sharp, well-modelled planes of his face, the thin mobile mouth, high intelligent forehead beneath curling grey hair, and startling hazel eyes, she knew that she could safely depend on this man only for as long as she was of real use to him. From what she already knew of him, it seemed to her highly unlikely that he would make any personal demands on her, but in every other way he would probably expect absolute compliance with his wishes. His work, his hours, and his habits would control all her waking hours. Any consideration she received from him would be in direct proportion to her willingness to work with and for him. That she was valuable to him, he had proved. Until she could determine exactly how great that value was, she saw that she would be very foolish to display any initiative, to ask for anything he did not offer voluntarily. To be looked upon in the light in which he obviously regarded her, as a more or less mindless chattel, both irritated and dismayed her, but it really frightened her to think of what her situation might have been without him.

She broke the silence with a single question. "I can't never go back, can I?"

"No, Venus, one can't ever go back. One always has to go on. That's life."

It was the answer she had expected, and she accepted it without argument. It would be a long time before it would be safe for her to return to the shack. During that time the space which she had occupied would close over, would cease to exist. They would miss her at first, Butch and Mag, in a multitude of ways, as she—tears pricking her eyelids—already missed them. Later on they would, if not forget her, at least accept her absence without active regret, for in spite of their affection for her they had never had any real need of her, and her need of them existed only for as long as she dwelt with them. Dimly she caught a glimpse of the beautiful, elemental simplicity of her long relationship with them; the caring for the young and weak by the mature and strong until, but only until, the young could stand alone. She had left them too suddenly, but it had been time to leave.

Nick was right. She could never go back to the shack. But he was not entirely right, for she was going back somewhere else, somewhere she could not even remember. This she neither could nor would doubt.

"Are you ready to move on?" Nick asked.

"I'm ready."

The tumult of sound and confusion of movement that assailed her as they drove into the city proper were, at first, almost more than she could bear. Before long, however, excitement and curiosity overcame her initial recoil, and she began to besiege the artist with questions.

He stood it as long as he could, displaying a patience which those who knew him well would have found it difficult to credit. He told her how street-cars were operated. He explained the use of traffic signals. He concurred in her belief that the parks were attractive. He did not agree with her that the people were also attractive. He said, yes, the street lights were left on all night. He told her that there were more than a million inhabitants of this city. He commented on the number of denominations represented by what were, to her, a surprising number of churches, and told her cynically that if she counted the movie houses she would find there were even more of them. He explained that dogs were kept on leads so that they would neither get lost nor bite people.

"Do they often bite people here, Nick?"

"For God's sake, Venus, shut up! I can't drive in heavy traffic and talk at the same time."

Psyche thoughtfully regarded the crowds thronging a main intersection at which they had stopped for a red light. Morning sunlight flooded brick canyons across whose concrete floors there flowed an unceasing tide of humanity.

"It must be awful tough to be alone here," she said slowly. "I mean with perhaps nowhere to go, with no folks like." Almost as if she had a premonition of her own future, she continued, with real urgency: "A person wouldn't rightly know what to do, Nick, what would a person do if they was alone here?"

The light turned green, and they shot forward on the crest of a mechanized wave. Nick, absorbed with the problem of a present, rather than a future survival, did not reply.

They made three stops, and each time he parked on a side street and left Psyche in the car. Content to wait for him, once for nearly an hour, she watched a parade that was to her a department-store catalogue come to life. Here were the wonderful clothes, the matching shoes and handbags, the feathered hats and white gloves, that she had always so much admired. And, if they had all been smiling, even the painted faces might have been lifted complete from those glossy, much-thumbed pages. The absence of the never-failing smiles disturbed her profoundly.

That these fortunate mortals should not be as carefree as she had always supposed them to be necessitated a rescaling of values that upset most of her preconceived notions. Watching the expressions of the passers-by she found them shuttered, possessed of a studied indifference to others both chilling and new to her. Did one have to look like this? she wondered. Was this expression something one put on for the street along with suitable clothes, or did it go deeper, representing an actual indifference to everything outside of purely private concerns? Could she, Psyche, look this way, if she chose to?

Reaching up, she turned the rear-view mirror to an angle where she could regard her own reflection. Her eyes betrayed her. But when she lowered her long lashes until her eyes were shadowed, partially hidden, she saw a self as cool and apparently uninterested as any she had seen that morning.

She returned the mirror to the precise position in which it had been, and let her glance travel downward over her cheap, creased blouse, threadbare coat, and long-unpolished shoes, and knew that she was ashamed of them not because they were old and worn, but because they were not clean. Catching sight of her dirty, ragged nails, she felt her face go hot, and thrust them out of sight beneath the folds of her coat.

Once more watching the people walking past, her regard was now subjective instead of objective, prepared to discard for the moment anything that could not be turned to a useful personal application.

It was nearly noon before Nick headed the big car towards the northern suburbs again.

Pysche rarely suffered from headaches, but her forehead was throbbing painfully by the time she realized, with unqualified relief, that their eventual destination was to be outside the city.

Although she was to know every tree, every bush, almost every blade of grass in the gentle valley surrounding the converted barn, she never forgot her first sight of it. If she had entered into paradise itself, she could not have been more enchanted.

Here was a place in its own way as remote from the world as the shack had been; but this was a soft seclusion without harshness of any kind, a seclusion protected and tranquil, with no memory of past upheaval or threat of future dissolution. The valley was composed of an immense field thickly sown with wild flowers, its lush green grass patterned with the shadows of a few tall elms, its boundaries wooded hills sloping gradually backward toward the calm inverted bowl of the summer sky. The barn, approached only by a footpath, stood in the middle of the field, its weathered brown timbers, red roof faded by many summer suns, and solid field-stone foundations as integral a part of the landscape as the pines and maples on the hillsides.

The car in low gear, they wound slowly down the steep gradient of a narrow, rutted track that disappeared entirely where long grass and woods met to give way one to another. Here Nick turned the car, backed it under the shelter of a huge maple, and cut the ignition.

Gazing upon such beauty as she had previously only dreamed about, Psyche gave a deep sigh. "The flowers," she said softly. "They's so beautiful."

"They're beautiful."

"They're beautiful," Psyche repeated, unconscious that she had been corrected, or that she had accepted the correction. "They yours, Nick?"

"They're anybody's. They're wild."

This was what Mag had told her about. Incredibly, here was tangible proof of a truth she had never quite been able to accept. Although later she was to fill the studio with fresh flowers every day, she was not ready for it yet. Stepping out of the car, she dropped on her knees and contented herself with breathing in the fragrance all around her while gently touching a single petal of a single white daisy.

Nick, watching her, saw a classical shepherdess in a field of asphodels, and, in seeing her thus, failed to see her at all. His fingers itching for brush and palette, he looked at his watch. "Come on, Venus, we've still a lot to do to-day."

Both of them burdened with the purchases he had made that morning, they followed the path single file across the field to the barn and a small green door let into the stone foundations.

As Psyche discovered on the following day, when she went

exploring on her own, there was a door on the other side of the barn that gave access to a dim world of empty stalls, mounds of dusty hay, and the disintegrating remnants of a long-disused farm wagon. But the door that Nick now unlocked opened on nothing but an enclosed staircase, up which they mounted.

No one who had ever been to Nick's studio had failed to stop at the head of the stairs and pay immediate tribute to the striking beauty of its proportions. The cathedral vault of the beamed roof, finding an apex in a single mighty roof-tree, framed, at the far end of the room, an immense triangular window that was in itself almost the entire north wall. The east and west walls, against which were clustered groupings of well-proportioned modern furniture, were lined with brilliant canvasses. And, supported by the wide pine planking of a floor sanded and waxed to a clean, pale beige, were an easel, work-table, and model's stand which, close to the great north window, made up a still-life study oddly attractive in that setting.

"This must be the most beautiful room in the world," Psyche said quietly.

Nick looked around him with the pleasure he always felt when he returned to this place after any absence from it, but he was not given to exposing his feelings, even in so unimportant an instance as this.

"It will do. Take a look at the rest of the place, and then we'll eat. I'm hungry as the devil. Kitchen, bedroom, and bath are behind you. The bedroom will be yours for as long as you stay. I'll use one of the couches out here."

Turning to face the south end of the studio, Psyche saw a wall, broken by three doors, that rose to a height of about eight feet, at which point a false ceiling ran back to the outside wall. Raising her eyes to this high isosceles section of the outer wall, she saw sunlight striking through the rich colours of a circular stained-glass window, the single eccentricity that Nick had allowed himself when he had had the old barn made over. Fascinated, as she always was, by any harmony of colour, she did not at once look away. And, as her gaze lingered, a memory, buried so deep within her it could scarcely be termed a memory, stirred, and the multi-coloured pattern of the window seemed to resolve itself into symmetrical bits and pieces, each one a tiny rainbow in itself. Behind these shimmering splinters of light she saw a different set of shapes, mounting one upon another in a spiral curve that she must, must—must see clearly.

She struggled to bring the memory into focus, her whole being concentrated in an effort so terrible that when it faded instead of clarifying, leaving her with a reality that now reminded her of nothing at all, she felt faint and ill.

"Nick——"

"What is it, Venus?"

Her face paper-white, swaying on her feet, she said, "I feel sick."

He came quickly across the room to her, and led her to a deep chair facing the north window. "The drive was probably too much for you. You aren't used to that sort of thing. Sit here, and stay still. I'll make some coffee."

Psyche heard him, but she made no effort to reply. Her eyes fixed on a green sweep of field, a rise of wooded hill, and a segment of blue sky, she faced the knowledge that it was neither the drive, nor the unpremeditated wrenching asunder of her life, that had so upset her, but something else that, though suggested in some way by these events, yet had nothing to do with them. In the night and morning just past she had brushed close against a long-closed door, not once but twice, and had twice sheered away from it in spite of herself. One can remember a dream on waking, draw it piece by piece from the subconscious. She knew this, because she had so often successfully done it. And, if one wants to, one can usually retrieve an elusive memory. Why then had she not remembered whatever it was that had hovered so near to her, when she had tried so hard to do so? Was it because there was something that she did not want to recall, or simply because it was so very long ago? And why should she have been frightened? For she had been frightened, very.

"Here's your coffee. Feel better now?"

She looked up to see Nick standing beside her, and knew that she was glad he was there.

"Nick—is it possible for a person to remember anythin' that ever happened to them?"

"Possible, but not probable."

"You mean that it's all there like, but you can't get to it."

"That's right. Old memories have to be properly cued."

"Cued?"

"Eat while you talk, or you're wasting time." He gestured toward a plate of sandwiches that he had put down, without her noticing it, on a small table beside her. "A cue is a thing, person, spoken word, or situation that reminds one of something else through an association of ideas. Memory is usually aroused by some present similarity to the past."

"I see," Psyche said slowly. "As if, for instance, you had once seen an odd-lookin' house with a dog in front of it. If you saw the house again, you would remember the dog even though he wasn't there no longer."

Nick's lean face creased in a smile part humorous, part derisive. "There's fish in those sandwiches. Keep eating. They say it's brain food."

Psyche's thoughtful expression changed briefly to one of mockery that more than matched his. "You eat. It's your brains I'm pickin'."

Nick's spontaneous laughter echoed against the high, beamed roof. "I think we will get on well together, you and I, Venus. You go on surprising me. Can you cook, too?"

"Well enough. Can a person remember as far back as when they was three?"

"Sometimes. Not usually."

"Could you do it just by tryin' hard enough?"

"Unlikely, without a psychiatrist's help. Even then you might not."

"What's a psychiatrist?"

"A doctor who specializes in the study of the mind."

Getting up from the edge of the model's stand where he had been sitting. Nick lit a cigarette, and began to pace restlessly around the studio.

"Psychiatrist—psychiatrist," Psyche repeated under her breath.

Always before she had thought of going forward, to come at last full circle. She had never thought of looking backward down the valley of the years. Now that the possibility had occurred to her, she was not at all sure she liked the idea, and was painfully puzzled by her own instinctive withdrawal from it.

"If you've finished, go and sit over there," Nick said, and pointed to the model's stand.

"Then what do I do?"

"Nothing. Just sit. And don't talk."

"Can I smoke?"

"If you like."

"I ain't got no cigarettes."

Taking a package of cigarettes from his pocket, he tossed them to her. "Tell me when you want more. Now be a good girl, and keep quiet. I want to think."

"What about?"

"You. How I'm going to paint you."

For perhaps twenty minutes he circled her, studying her from every angle, his eyes narrowed in a frowning face. Then, without warning, he came to a halt in front of her, and said abruptly, "Go and have a bath, wash your hair, and put on one of the blouses and skirts you'll find in the bedroom. A white blouse. I can't even see you, the way you are."

A crimson flush stained Psyche's cheeks. Biting her lip, she looked down at her telltale hands. She had meant to wash them as soon as she arrived at the studio. With no habit of cleanliness of this kind to guide her, she had entirely forgotten her intention. Getting up without any of her usual grace, she walked stiffly toward the bedroom.

Nick, watching her go, was well aware of her embarrassment, but made no move to alleviate it.

That Psyche should revel in being clean, and that he should spend a good part of the next few days hammering on the bathroom door while she luxuriated in hot, and at first over-perfumed, baths, was something that he had not anticipated. He had thought he would probably have to wash at least her neck for her, and in all likelihood be scratched for his pains.

When she finally emerged, nearly an hour and a half later, he greeted her with a long, low whistle, and a smile for once completely free of irony.

"Can you see me now?"

If he had had any lingering doubts as to the wisdom of bringing her to the studio, they were discarded there and then. For in her he now saw clearly what he might have searched for in vain for the rest of his life, an unselfconscious beauty with no trace of sophistication; a beauty in no way childish, yet unmarred by any worldliness.

"I can see you, Venus."

And as the sound of his own voice died on the warm quiet of the afternoon, he knew how he most wanted to paint her. He had called her Venus half in tribute and half in jest, but the picture already taking shape before his mind's eye would be tribute alone —to a young Venus, a young goddess of the love of which the poets sang, the untouchable personification of an unattainable ideal.

He saw her against a background of swirling grey mist touched by golden dawnlight, her figure moulded by the flowing simplicity of classical white drapery. Mist that obscured the arms; the Milo Venus echoed but not duplicated. A dawn that reflected the gold of her hair, but did not compete with it. In spite of the classical pose, the painting that he now saw, as vividly as though he had already completed it, was that of a comparatively well-clad, essentially modern Venus. A twentieth-century Venus with slim hips, long legs, and shoulder-length hair.

## 5

AN ability to live in the moment was a talent that Psyche had developed to the full during years when uncurbed restlessness would have led only to frustration bordering on madness. Now she used this talent to put behind her the knowledge that the studio could never be more than a temporary shelter, while at the same time making use of every possible opportunity to prepare herself for a future in which she was unlikely to have even such an uncertain protector as Nick.

Like a plant buried by accident too deep in the soil, she had grown up with her potentialities for the most part latent, her patient hopes for the future based simply on the inevitable passage of time. That her insatiable thirst for knowledge had made her at all times an active participant in the patterning of her life, she had not seen at all. Now, as the days went by, she realized more and more clearly how much she could do for herself, and the realization was as heady as wine, sharpening her already quick perception, stimulating her powers of observation and assimilation.

Understanding that at this stage Nick would help her to learn only in so far as that learning made her a more acceptable companion, she allowed him to initiate ideas that, if she had proposed them herself, he would probably have ignored.

Accustomed to a solitary life, she in no way resented, was scarcely even aware of, the fact that she was almost as cut off from the world as she had been at the shack. Accepting without question Nick's statement that she must for her own protection stay away from people for a time, sensing no ulterior motive on his part, she explored with an inexhaustible interest and curiosity that limited but beautiful corner of the universe in which she found herself.

Nick, unhurried by time or weather, was, once his preliminary sketches were finished, more relaxed than she would have thought possible. His demands on her time and endurances were reasonable, and, although he was as profane as ever, his sardonic smile was proof that he felt no irritation. Working steadily on a full-length canvas that promised, even in its inception, to be the best work he had ever done, he treated her with the tolerant kindness he might have shown to an amusingly precocious child.

The correcting of her grammar was something that he undertook, not on her behalf, but because he found it an increasing offense to himself. To have his idealized Venus, after an enforced silence, step down from the model's stand and abominate his conception of her the moment she opened her mouth was more than he could bear. That she should prove as apt a pupil in this as in everything else failed to surprise him only because of his absolute lack of interest in her as a person. He had wanted her to be clean because, fastidious himself, he refused to live under the same roof with anyone who was not. That cleanliness should become, almost overnight, a fetish with her, he regarded as his own good luck. The satisfaction and sense of well-being that she derived from it meant nothing to him. In the same way he accepted her willingness to improve her English as a fortunate accident, without once marveling at the mind that so quickly and easily absorbed all it was taught. Only in the realm of the purely physical did he question the stamp of the environment in which he had discovered her.

One day, laying down his brush and flexing cramped fingers, he said, "Venus, yours it not, thank God, the kind of face that wins beauty contests. Nevertheless, one of your parents must have been something quite out of the ordinary."

Psyche's husky voice was almost harsh. "Why not the both of them!"

"The both! That excruciating grammar of yours is tearing my sensitivities to shreds. How can anyone look so lovely and sound so terrible?"

"You're tryin' to put me off by makin' me mad, ain'—aren't you? Why couldn't the—I mean, why not both of them?"

"Just couldn't be, Venus. You wouldn't be here if they had been."

"You think they—weren't married?"

Nick looked at her curiously. "I wasn't actually thinking of that. Would it matter?"

"Of course."

"Why?"

There was a setness to her expression that he had not seen before, and her voice was positive. She seemed daring him to contradict her. "Decent folks who have children always are married. Mag said so. And not you nor nobody else is goin' to say my parents aren't decent people."

"Don't drop your g's," he said absently, while he absorbed her use of the present tense and all that it implied. "This is something you have apparently thought about a great deal, Venus?"

"Yes, I have."

"Then how do you explain——" He allowed the sentence to go unfinished.

Psyche's troubled eyes sought the window and the sunlit green of the summer afternoon, and her mouth was no longer set but vulnerable with an old hurt. "I must have got lost. I'm just lost—that's all."

Briefly Nick had some inkling of just how lost she was, and an unusual compassion moved him to say, "You might be right, Venus. Perhaps you did just get lost, who knows how, and so I should have said——" He paused, and smiled, "—the both of them."

"You mean that, Nick? Mag didn't never really believe it. About me gettin'—getting lost, I mean. But kids, kids near on to three, as I was, do sometimes get lost and not found, don't they?"

He would have been prepared to wager a large sum of money that she had been left on the doorstep of the shack by a mother who had known briefly, but not briefly enough, a man with more quality than conscience. However, when he replied, he did not betray his thoughts. "It could quite easily have happened that way, Venus."

It was the first time Psyche's inner belief, that she had not been cast off deliberately, had ever been supported from outside, and from that moment on she never allowed it to waver again.

Seeing the brilliance of her smile, Nick knew a fleeting compunction. Then, with a mental shrug, he decided that if she needed a fiction of this sort to sustain her, there was no harm in her having one. That he had given her, instead of a temporary reassurance, something of lasting consequence, he did not know then, and never did know.

"Well," he said, "are you ready to pose again?"

Psyche nodded. "I'm not at all tired now."

"Good. On two counts. You said that like a lady who wouldn't recognize an 'ain't' if she tripped over one."

"I know it," Psyche said demurely. She knew too, as she again took up the pose that was becoming almost second nature to her, that she now really liked this man. Without moving her head even a fraction of an inch, her glance slid sideways to watch him as he set to work again, and she thought, "I would go on liking him even if I didn't like him"—and knew exactly what she meant by the apparent contradiction.

Later, when the day's work was ended, when the mellow light of sunset muted the gaudy fresco of colours on Nick's palette, she turned from the model's stand toward the great north window. Her elbows resting on the edge of an open section, her chin cupped in her hands, she knew that she was happier, more at peace with herself, than she had ever been.

Watching the summer evening close in over a scene that, though now familiar, still seemed scarcely believable, she knew that she would remember it oftenest as it was just then, with the first star glowing above the dark lace of tree-tops sharply outlined against a cloudless, slowly darkening sky.

"Venus."

Psyche did not turn her head. "Yes, Nick?"

"Have we any more rags anywhere?"

Laughter threaded itself through her reply. "Plenty. In a drawer in the kitchen."

"What the devil's so amusing?"

Looking around, seeing his frowning face, she said, still laughing, "Sunset. Rags. Nothin' at all."

Contemplating her, he said slowly, "You've changed since you came here. How long is it? Three weeks—four?"

"I'll get your rags for you," Psyche told him, no longer even smiling.

Every other day Nick left the studio to go into a neighbouring village to buy food. Psyche, while he was gone, would wash dishes and prepare the meals for the day.

The first time he left her alone, he paused at the top of the staircase, and said, "You won't run away while I'm gone, Venus?"

"Where would I run to?"

The hazel eyes smiled. "You have a point there. I won't be gone long."

On these occasions he never was away long, but later on he quite often left her alone in the evenings, and twice he was away all night. He offered neither excuse nor explanation for these absences, and Psyche asked for none. She missed him, but not acutely, and the studio was a place in which she never felt lonely, where she had no cause to be uneasy, and where she could occupy herself for any given length of time.

She would clean house, enjoying the texture as well as the sight of objects that all had quality. She would study and re-study an art gallery of which she never tired. And she would carefully press and sponge any article in her wardrobe that she had worn even once. That she had as many clothes as she did was due not to over-generosity on Nick's part, but to the fact that on rainy days—when the light was not right for work on what he now called *The American Venus*—he did sketches of her to be incorporated later in magazine illustrations. He never asked her to pose in the nude because he considered nude paintings to be as devoid of personality as they were of clothing, and it was the individuality of her beauty that made her so valuable to him.

On the evenings when he stayed at the studio, and this was oftener than not, he insisted that they each turn into their respective beds as soon as it was fully dark.

"A Venus with blue circles under her eyes is not—although there are those who would undoubtedly find this pleasantly suggestive—what I have in mind at the moment," he told her.

In the twilit hours between dinner and dusk, more content in each other's company than either of them realized, they rarely did anything at all constructive. Sometimes they merely sat in chairs pushed back from the gate-leg table at which they had eaten, smoking and making desultory conversation; a way of putting in time for Nick; a further exploration of the English language for Psyche. Sometimes they strolled around the perimeter of the big field, the twin glow of their cigarettes not dissimilar to the fireflies that haunted the long, dew-soaked grass. Very often these walks would bring them eventually to the car, where Nick would turn on the radio. Then, he lounging in the front seat and Psyche stretched on a rug on the ground so that she might look up at the stars, they would listen to music that, no matter what its tempo, seemed to her to emanate from some heavenly rather than earthly source; music that, though fuller and clearer in tone, yet seemed in many ways as remote as the long-lost melodies of an ancient gramophone whose loss she still, on occasion, regretted.

In this way a warm June drifted into a warmer July, and Nick and Psyche drifted closer to a moment that neither of them anticipated.

The rich green of the field became yellowed by the summer suns; daisies and buttercups gave way to goldenrod and everlasting; and "The American Venus" emerged, an almost living perfection, from a once dead canvas.

Cynic and unbeliever though he was, Nick felt, as he worked, something very like reverence, for he knew beyond a shadow of a doubt that what he was doing with eye and hand, brush and palette, was destined to become immortal.

Psyche realized that he was satisfied with the painting, but she had no conception of the depth of that satisfaction; for, although he often talked while he painted, a running monologue more colourful than the colours on his palette, he never at any time touched on anything personal to himself.

"Now you take Van Gogh——" he would begin, and a well-informed commentary on the times, works, and idiosyncrasies of the painter would consume anything from ten minutes to an hour.

Or it might be artists in general who were the subject of his dissertation. "Free Souls we're called by a proletariat wallowing in its own abysmal ignorance. Free! My God, an artist's body and soul are in fetters from the day he is born until the day he dies. He lives for his work, nothing else ever counts. Not wine, women, or song. Look at us, Venus. How many of the damn fools would believe that I am interested only in painting you? None of them. Your head is down a quarter of an inch. Because they're fleshly nincompoops themselves, they believe everyone else is. They have no comprehension of art for art's sake. They credit us with all the sins in the decalogue, with orgies that would make your beautiful hair stand on end."

"What are orgies, Nick?"

"Don't ask me. I'm just a hard-working artist who wouldn't have the slightest idea. How many times do I have to tell you not to talk while you're posing?"

"It ain't easy when you——"

"Look, Venus, I'll throw something at you if you don't keep quiet. And, for the love of God, don't ever say 'ain't' again in my hearing. I thought you had learned better by now."

A day arrived when Psyche judged her position strong enough to rebel against the injustice of being eternally on the receiving end of a one-sided conversation.

A not sufficiently silent audience to an uninhibited lecture on the private life of Toulouse-Lautrec, she had been told twice, and in no uncertain terms, to hold her tongue, when, to Nick's utter astonishment, she simply stepped down from the stand and walked away from it.

"You're damned unfair," she said coolly. Then, without another word, she took her old, dismembered Bible from the bookcase where she kept it, sank with unconscious grace onto a low hassock, and calmly began to read.

For once rendered speechless, Nick looked at her partially averted face, and seeing no more emotion than he had read in her voice, realized that he had received a reproof requiring more than a temporary apology. Suppressing an impulse to swear at her, he felt in his pockets for cigarettes, while an at first unwilling smile erased the dark frown that had preceded it.

"Well—well," he murmured.

Psyche paid no attention to him. Her soft white draperies, falling from bare shoulders, remained unstirred by any movement. She was reading Joshua. When "the sun stood still" she never failed to find it a credible phenomenon. There had been times, with midsummer heat trapped in the slag hills, when she had almost believed the sun stood still again, so gradually had it moved beyond the heavy copper haze.

"Can't you find something more topical to read than that?"

Psyche, wise enough to recognize an olive branch when offered, looked up. "I have nothing else."

Nick's reply was a sweeping gesture that encompassed three well-filled bookcases. "You are fasting in the midst of plenty."

"But they're yours."

"I don't glue them to the shelves. Help yourself."

Unwilling to ask him for anything he did not offer, Psyche, much as she had wanted to, had never at any time touched his books. Now, laying aside her Bible, she began to examine the contents of the bookcase within her reach at the moment.

Without further comment, Nick waited for her reaction.

The sixth book into which she had looked open on her lap, she said with obvious disappointment. "But they're all artists and pictures. Nothing else."

"That doesn't mean they'll poison you, does it?"

"They just don't mean anything to me, that's all. For instance, who's this Rubbins? Do you like his stuff? Is it any good?"

Running his hands through his hair, Nick looked down at the

top of her blonde head with amused exasperation. "Rubbins—
Rubbins! What in hell are you blithering about, my impossibly
ignorant young Venus?"

"It says Rubbins right here. Look for yourself, if you don't believe me."

Leaning over, Nick said, "Ah—yes, Rubens. *Susannah and the
Elders.* A masterpiece."

"You mean it's good? All I see is a nasty old guy peering
through some leaves at a fat girl with nothin' on."

"Heaven help me! I suppose it would be too much to expect
you to refer to him as a lecherous old gentleman, but surely,
surely you can manage to say noth*ing.*"

Psyche smiled. "You're teasing me."

"Never."

"Honestly—do you really like this picture?"

"Since you specifically ask for honesty, I am compelled to say
that I do not. But I admire it. Enormously."

"Why?"

"You ask a devil of a lot of questions, Venus. Must I have a
stated reason?"

"There's a reason for everything, isn't there?"

"Oh wise young judge! The technique is flawless, and the skin
tones reminiscent of the work of the incomparable Titian."

"Tech-nique," Psyche repeated faithfully. "What does that
mean? And who is Titian?"

Nick looked at his painted Venus, and then back to the living
counterpart who was causing him so much more trouble. Forcing
continued patience upon himself, he said mildly, "It will be noon
in another half-hour, Venus. Don't you think you could call a halt,
to your barrage of questions until after lunch?"

Psyche's sceptical eyes, and the tilt of her head, told him before
she spoke that she recognized the evasion for what it was. "You
mean that you will be ready to answer questions after lunch?"

Nick's nod was a promise, but an ungracious one.

Inwardly Psyche knew an intense satisfaction. To have allowed
this to become apparent would have been a mistake. "Please—

Nick. I have to learn something sometime. You know so much, and I—well, I have to know things, too."

"Do you? Perhaps you do. Though I can assure you that with what you've got you won't find advanced education essential to your success in life."

Psyche did something then that she had never done before in her life. Of her own initiative, she put her hand on someone. "Please. I'm serious."

The slender hand resting lightly on his bare forearm, and the wistful, husky voice, together made an appeal that he suddenly found it impossible to resist. "All right, Venus," he said gently, "we'll make a gentleman's agreement, you and I. In future I will devote one precious, irreplacable hour of every mortal day to answering all questions, suitable or unsuitable, on or pertaining to my own particular field. In return you will contract to keep your lovely trap shut while you are posing."

Her hand increased its pressure for an instant before its warmth was withdrawn. "Thank you, Nick."

For the rest of the morning Psyche stood in the exact position that she had held for four or five hours a day for what was now more than six weeks, and Nick concentrated with his customary fervour on the work that he loved more than anything else the world could offer him. Outwardly nothing had changed. Nevertheless, their battle of wills, and the manner in which Psyche had won it, marked a subtle but very definite change in their relationship. Nick continued to treat her for the most part with an amused tolerance, but it was no longer the kind of tolerance he might have shown to a child. Psyche, on her part, made an even greater effort than before to conform to the standards of speech and manners which he represented, without realizing, however, that she was now doing it to please him as well as herself.

The siesta hour, as Nick ironically called it, became a part of the day to which she looked forward from the moment she got up in the morning. Receptive to fresh knowledge of any kind, she became for the time being almost as interested as Nick himself in the subject that he never really tired of talking about.

Velasquez, Goya, Frans Hals, Tintoretto, Sir Joshua Reynolds,

Titian, Rembrandt—at one time and another he talked to her at length about all of them, gave her demonstrations of their various brush strokes, and explained and analyzed colour plates of their works. To Psyche, these painters and many others became personalities never to be forgotten, their individual styles usually recognizable at a glance.

Rembrandt's work she admired above all, and Nick congratulated her on her taste.

"He must have been one of the rich ones, surely, Nick?"

"No. He died in abject poverty."

"But why? Why should so many of them have been poor when they didn't really need to be?"

A shadow seemed to fall briefly across the lean, alert face. "An artist is a complex piece of machinery, Venus. He is not like other people. You cannot judge him as a man and as an artist at one and the same time. To do so is a mistake. A mistake made too often by too many people." Then, deliberately changing the subject, he said, "Let's take a look at some of the moderns. We've been neglecting them."

In this way Psyche, who had never heard of the Battle of Hastings, and who had difficulty with the multiplication table, became unusually well informed in a highly specialized field. For she not only listened to him with fierce attention, but also spent the greater part of her evenings, when alone in the studio, poring over books he had used to illustrate points that, when he made them, were never dull.

Inexperienced in human relationships, unaware of how insidiously propinquity can impair normal judgement, she became, as the summer waned, as fascinated by the teacher as by his teachings. Her initial clear-eyed appraisal of him blurred by a gently moving stream of days undisturbed by any interruption from the outside world, she began to see virtues in him that he did not have, and never had had. Reason, if she had consulted it, would have told her that she was no closer to being a part of Nick's private life than at the moment when she first laid eyes on him, that this desert-island existence could not possibly represent his pattern of behaviour either past or future.

That she did not betray her altered attitude to him was due chiefly to the fact that she did not herself know consciously how much it was changing. She had gloried in the realization that she was growing up. That there was more than one way of doing this, and that it could be a painful process, she had yet to learn.

Without knowing why she did so, she took even more trouble than usual with the combing and arranging of her hair, with the manicuring of long, immaculate nails. And when she looked in her mirror she was pleased to see that she was far from plain.

Her sleep disturbed more and more often by dreams in which she again saw lightning and a cruelly handsome face, she failed to see that these dreams had any significance in relation to a present from which they seemed far removed.

One evening when they walked, she and Nick, around the field in the short dusk of late August, she stumbled, and, catching her hand to steady her, he did not afterwards let go of it.

Nick scarcely noticed that they were, as they had never done before, walking hand in hand.

Psyche, who usually disliked being touched, was sharply aware of it.

6

IT was on an evening towards the middle of September that Nick finished "The American Venus", and on the evening of the same day that he destroyed a measure of the unsophistication that had made it possible.

When he laid down his brush with the knowledge that it would be a desecration to lift it again to that particular canvas, it was also with the knowledge that he had created a masterpiece. For some minutes he studied every detail of a goddess at whose shrine the world would in all probability worship for generations to come. Then, his inner exultation tempered by an undefined regret, he turned his back on his easel to look out at a countryside, sultry beneath a hot blue sky, as motionless as any painted landscape would have been.

"Nick! Aren't you going to work any more to-day?"

"It's finished, Venus. You can step down from your pedestal for good."

Psyche's protest was completely involuntary. "No!"

"You feel as I do? I hadn't expected that. Odd, isn't it? We should be toasting our achievement in vintage champagne and throwing paper streamers at one another. Instead——"

It was the closest he had ever come, or ever would come, to offering her his friendship. Later Psyche was to look back at that moment and recognize it for what it was—the end, rather than the beginning, of an idyl. An idyl remarkable enough in itself, yet chiefly remarkable because it had lasted as long as it had. During the long, warm days of a summer that had seemed as if it might never end, they had been an indissoluble trinity, she, and Nick, and the painted Venus. With the completion of the work that had bound them to a common aim, a single ambition, they had lost the ingredient that had held them together.

Sufficient unto herself, the Venus withdrew into an ethereal world of her own, leaving Nick and Psyche alone as they had not been since their first twenty-four hours in the studio nearly four months earlier.

Silently Psyche watched while Nick lifted the picture from his easel and set it up against the wall close to the window. It was as if a piece of herself were being detached, taken away without warning, leaving her incomplete, temporarily unsure of her own identity.

She looked down at the revealing white costume that she would never wear again. "I'll go and change."

"Don't!" Nick said abruptly.

"But——"

"I like you the way you are."

"But, Nick, I don't feel properly dressed."

His brilliant eyes caught and held hers from across the room. "Does that matter?"

Actually it had not mattered before. Now it did. Psyche, opening her mouth to protest again, closed it without having uttered a sound.

Still watching her, an unreadable expression on his face, he said slowly, "Why shouldn't we celebrate, Venus, you and I? Caviar and champagne and—you and I, Venus. The idea appeals to me, and there will never be another occasion as suitable. Pygmalion—and a Galatea who, bare-footed, will vanish at midnight unable to leave a slipper behind her. If I mix my allusions, forgive me. I find no exact parallel, nor wish to."

He is seeing me, really seeing me for the first time, Psyche thought, and her voice, when she spoke, was unsteady. "Must you always talk in riddles?"

"Have I? Do I? Perhaps I do. Forgive me again. In simpler terms, we are going to have a party that neither of us, I think, will ever forget. I am going out now. I will be back before dark. While I am gone prepare a feast fit for the goddess that, pro tem., you still are."

Psyche, when she was alone, wondered where he had gone and why. Beyond that she did not think. A Grecian goddess tending a modern electric stove, she moved in a trance, doing her share toward setting the stage for a one-act play in which she did not consciously want to take a part.

He came back when a purple dusk had isolated the old barn from hills and woods and sky, setting it adrift on the quiet, dark tides of the approaching night.

Hearing his step on the stairs, she had an instant of lucidity in which panic, cold and sharp, set her free from the spell he had cast upon her. Then he was beside her, his timing, his actions, perfect.

"For you, Venus."

Psyche, looking at the great armful of golden roses he held out to her, felt the coldness recede before a warmth such as she had never known. Her cheeks flushed with pleasure, she gathered them to her, heedless of thorns, and buried her face in these, the first flowers any man had ever given her.

When, at last, she looked up, it was to find that he had turned out the lamps and that the studio was now lit only by two tall candles.

"Nick—I——"

"Don't thank me, Venus," he said gently. "It wouldn't be right."

He had found both caviar and champagne, and with them, it seemed, a reckless gaiety that carried them throughout dinner on the crest of a wave of laughter.

The candles were guttering low in the candlesticks when Nick rose from the table, circled it, and lifted her to her feet.

"Nick—don't. Please."

His face against her soft hair, he murmured, "Don't run away from me, Venus. Not yet. Not to-night."

"Please—no, Nick."

"Look at me, Venus. Look at me and tell me—if you can with truth—that you don't need me now as much as I need you. Tell me this, Venus, then leave me—if you must."

If his hand at her waist had increased its pressure then, if the firm fingers that slowly turned her face up to his had used anything other than the gentlest coercion, she would have broken free from him while she still could, would have shaken off the warm languor induced by that deep, persuasive voice.

When her eyes met his, it was too late to run from him or from herself.

His first kisses were as tender, as undemanding as his embrace, his lips lightly tracing the contours of her face, while his arms drew her gradually closer. Unresisting now, Psyche allowed him to make love to her, becoming as passionate in her submissiveness as he was in the steadily increasing passion and variety of his lovemaking. And when he carried her to the couch where all summer long he had slept alone, she clung to him, the heavy pulse of her blood telling her what her mind no longer tried to deny, that this was everything she had ever sought, that this was love. For he was an expert in his way, an expert at creating illusions, not only on canvas, but also on the more delicate fabric of the emotions.

And he talked all the time, his usually staccato diction softened to a whisper as gentle as his sensitive, caressing hands.

Psyche, caught beyond hope of recall, lulled to a false sense of security by the hypnotic rhythm of that voice that promised so much with such effortless beauty of word and phrase, gave herself to him and—as she thought then—to a love which would enfold and keep her not just for that night, but for all the days and nights to come.

How long she slept, before waking to find the candles dead and the studio invaded by the first grey light of dawn, she did not know. For an instant, seeing the beamed roof high above her, feeling the unexpected texture of the couch, she thought she must be dreaming still, and then memory returned—Nick. But where was he? Why was he no longer beside her? Raising herself on one elbow, pulling the rug he must have laid over her more closely around her shoulders, her eyes searched the studio with an unformulated apprehension that turned to immediate relief when she saw him, his sleeping face toward her, stretched out on another couch that stood against the opposite wall.

For several minutes she stayed where she was, revelling in a sense of complete well-being, at first refusing to think in any really concrete manner of anything at all.

Where her doubts came from, she could not have said, but suddenly her sensuous pleasure was gone, and she was alone with a desperate need for reassurance, for Nick's arms again holding her, his voice again telling her—ice closed slowly around a heart that seemed to stand still—what he had not told her, what he had not said even once, that he loved her.

Her mind, that beautifully precise instrument that was as much a part of her as her warm blood, reviewed with cold clarity every word he had said to her at a time when she was scarcely aware that she heard him at all, and she could find nothing that could be interpreted as other than endearments without lasting value of any kind. If he had been naturally inarticulate, she might still have hoped. Her mouth curling in a smile as bitter and unamused as her unsmiling eyes, she did not delude herself. If there were ever occasions when Nick did not say exactly what he intended to say, no more and no less, she had yet to encounter one.

Pain and humiliation made her feel literally ill, and the knowledge that she had been a very stupid, very young fool, left an acrid taste in her mouth.

Briefly she had glimpsed a paradise in which she walked side by side with someone who cared only for her, who would be with her both in joy and sorrow. She had offered heart and mind and body to a man who had wanted only the least part of the gift. The giving of herself physically was, because she had done this in good faith, of little importance beside the searing hurt of not being wanted as a person. That she should be desired as a woman was to her, because she was entirely without vanity, no compliment; rather it constituted an insult to her real person—to Psyche, the individual.

It was an insult, she vowed silently, that she would not endure again from Nick, or from any other man. Somewhere, some time, she would meet and love a man who did not want to leave her when the sun rose, who would want to be with her always, who would need her as she needed him. And until she met that man, she would walk alone, sleep alone, and, in any way that really counted, live alone.

But Nick—what was she to say to him when he woke? Nick—whom she had thought she knew so well, how could he have done this thing to her, how been so wilfully cruel, unless he had thought it would mean as little to her as she was now sure it had meant to him. Had he, in his own way, been as mistaken as she in hers?

Noiselessly she gathered the rug around her, and rising, tiptoed across the room until she was standing within less than three feet of him. Scarcely breathing, she studied his face, stripped in sleep of his usual half-humorous cynicism, defenseless as that of a young boy. Could this be Nick, this stranger who must, she knew without question, at times be in need of outside support, of close companionship of some kind? Had this man, in part really understood for the first time, lived by and for himself alone for thirty years or more? Her gaze never leaving his face, she thought not;

and a hundred details, noticed from time to time but not fitted together, presented her with a staggering truth. This man whom she now realized she had never known at all, was not in any real sense at home when he lived at the studio. The artist might be at home there, but the man was not. And when he was at home, did he live alone? It seemed highly unlikely.

Suppressing a wild, hysterical desire to laugh, she saw that she had been more than half in love with a myth as unreal as the Venus who had stood silent watch over their lovemaking.

For a moment longer she lingered, and then fled silently to her room where, the door locked behind her, she fell to her knees beside the bed and wept for something she had lost without ever really having it, for a dream that had been no more than that. And when at last she dried her eyes, she remembered the fierce pleasure of a man's mouth against her own, the aching delight of a man's arms holding her close, and wept again.

It was after eight o'clock, and a blanket of heat had already banished the dew from the long grass of the valley, when she returned from a walk that had taken her far from the barn, along hedged lanes she had never seen before and would not recognize if she were to see them again.

When she had slipped out through the green door at sunrise, it had been with the confused idea that she would not return to it. The fact that she had taken nothing with her was proof that she had seen the complete impracticality of such an idea even while pretending to entertain it. If she had had any money at all, she would have packed her few possessions and left for good. Because Nick had said he would pay her for posing, she had refused the small savings Butch and Mag had been only too eager to give her. As yet Nick had paid for nothing, and she wondered now whether this was because she had no present opportunity to spend money, or because he had wished to make quite sure that she would not leave until he was ready to let her go. With a new-found cynicism she thought that the latter supposition was in all probability the correct one. There was no longer any need for her to remain in hiding, of that she was certain. Yet, as she followed the winding path across the field to the barn, she knew that, even now, she did not really want to leave this place that she had grown to love so much, this quiet refuge where until to-day she had been so completely content.

It required courage to mount the narrow staircase, but, since it was something she had to do, she did it with decision and outward assurance. Before she reached the top she could hear Nick whistling quietly. When she emerged into the studio it was to find him busy with brushes and turpentine, another canvas already set up on the easel.

When he saw her, his words were as casual as though this morning were no different from any other. "Morning, Venus. Breakfast be ready soon?"

"Ten minutes," Psyche told him evenly, while she experienced an overpowering relief. He had not, apparently, guessed her secret. That he should even surmise she had imagined herself in love with, and loved by him, would have been more than she could have endured.

Nick, whistling again, interrupted himself long enough to say, "If you have time while the coffee water is heating, see if you can dig up that extraordinary outfit you were wearing the first time I saw you. I want to finish off one of those early sketches."

All day Psyche posed, her hair once more an uncombed mop of gold, in the old dungarees and shapeless black sweater in which she had once been so comfortably unselfconscious. Nick, talking as usual while he painted, calmly avoided even a glancing reference to what had passed between them.

It was not until nightfall that he put his hand on her arm as she turned toward her room. "Stay with me, Venus."

Psyche had thought herself fully prepared for an invitation that she had been morally certain would be forthcoming, if not that night, then the next—or the one after that. To find herself wavering for even an instant was something that she had not expected. Unable to trust her voice, she shook off his hand with an abruptness that in itself betrayed her weakness.

"Do I have to plead a cause in which we are both equally interested, Venus?"

Psyche backed across the room until she stood in the bedroom doorway. "Have you any intention of marrying me, Nick?"

"Good God! What has that got to do with anything?"

"You haven't answered my question."

"You know the answer well enough, Venus."

"Then you know mine," Psyche said levelly, and closed the door between them, the subsequent click of the lock a sharp period to her sentence.

She hoped that her refusal of him would be accepted in the same way her surrender had been, without comment. The following morning, however, she discovered that it was to be a primary topic of conversation.

He waited until she was already posing, the clear north light showing small lines of strain around her eyes, before embarking on a discourse that he obviously expected to be less one-sided than usual. Psyche, recognizing his attempt to provoke her into talking, at first refused to do so.

"The lady known as Mag must have said a good deal to you on the subject of holy matrimony, Venus. Did she, I wonder, amongst other misconceptions, implant in you the conviction that love can be found only in a legalized union? Love is a dream, evanescent, fleeting, to be caught and then released, unpolluted by mundane considerations. You seek, Venus, in your untutored simplicity, to chain down something that cannot be chained. Love has many guises, and——"

"I am not in love with you!" Psyche interrupted violently.

"Nor I with you, in the sense in which you seem to be interpreting the word. Nevertheless, what I offer you is a rare enough gift in itself, call it what you will. In spurning it, you rob yourself to no advantage, for I mean you no harm. More than that, I have done you no harm."

"No?" The monosyllable, as she employed it, borrowed his own brand of cool irony.

He continued to work without pausing. "Venus, it had to happen to you sometime, as surely as the sun rises each morning. It might have been bad, very bad. With me it was good. We both know that. Take it where you find it, Venus, and thank whatever

Gods there be, for you will not find it often. In marriage, that bourgeois custom that seems to have such an unnatural appeal for you, it can be—and too often is—a complete failure. A ring on your third finger will be no guarantee of happiness, physical or otherwise. What I offer you, on the other hand, is guaranteed. We have proved that once already. Next time you will find it equally true."

"There isn't going to be a next time, Nick."

"You don't dislike me, do you?"

It was difficult for Psyche to be anything other than honest. "No, I don't dislike you," she replied slowly. "I should—but I don't."

"Then stop talking and behaving like a little fool."

He was no longer painting, but Psyche, her hands thrust deep into the pockets of her faded dungarees, held her pose. This was how she had once stood, and in these same clothes, in a world which, though arid and harsh, was one in which she had never needed to compromise. Unconsciously she reverted to the language which had been hers until so very recently. "There ain't goin' to be no next time."

He knew then that she meant what she said, and knew also that it was not, and never had been, in his nature to force compliance on any woman. His face expressionless, he began to paint again. "Have it your own way," he told her curtly, "though what tortuous and ill-informed logic produces this decision of yours, I cannot guess. Perhaps you will at least satisfy my curiosity, if nothing else, by telling me why there was nobody else before me?"

He has no heart, he has no conscience, Psyche thought bleakly. I was clever enough to know these things about him in the beginning. How could I have forgotten so easily? And now he, who has talked so often of sensitivity, asks me a question like this. I ought not to answer it, but I will, because it is time he learned—as I have—that one can't judge people by how often they wash, by whether they say "isn't" or "ain't".

"There wasn't anyone clean enough," she replied slowly.

"What in hell do you mean by that?"

"Just what I say."

"I presume that I am, for example, clean enough?"

Psyche hesitated for a fraction of a second, and then said distinctly, "I thought you were."

Nick stepped away from his easel, and his voice was as cutting as a winter wind. "Will you have the goodness to explain that remark?"

This was a side of him that Psyche had never seen, but she stood her ground with a question which was in itself an oblique reply. "You're married, aren't you, Nick?"

"How did you know that?"

"I didn't, really."

"But now you do?"

"Yes," Psyche said without emphasis, "now I do."

His eyes as cold as his icy voice, he said, "My private life is none of your business, Venus, and never will be." With which, he turned and strode toward the stairs.

Psyche heard the slamming of the door below, and, soon after that, the coughing roar of the car engine. Depression held her to the model's stand. A tired, and temporarily shabby Venus, burdened with doubts she could not resolve, as apathetic as the noonday silence that closed in around her, she asked herself where she was going and why. Travelling a road with few decipherable signposts, her own untried judgement her only rod and staff, she wondered dully how she would ever find her way. She had deliberately angered the one person who had any interest in her, had perhaps forfeited his good-will entirely—and for what?

Sitting down, she covered her face with her hands, and rocking slowly to and fro, whispered, "I don't know—I don't know. Oh, God, I just don't know."

## 7

NICK had left the studio without a considered destination, and it was habit rather than anything else that took him to the village post office.

Drawing in to the curb, he heard the dry crackle of fallen leaves beneath the tires, and was aware as he had not been before that summer had given way to autumn.

Inside the small post office, he received his mail with an indifference that evaporated instantly when he saw the conspicuous colour of a telegraph envelope. Putting aside a bundle of newspapers, he ripped it open and took in its contents in a single comprehensive glance. 'Boat reservation canceled stop flying home stop arrive sixteenth flight 407 stop love Alice.'

His first reaction was one of unqualified pleasure, for he was, within his own limitations, genuinely fond of his wife. Then, computing dates, his dismay more than equalled his pleasure. He had exactly twenty-four hours in which to get rid of a girl who was at the moment his entire responsibility. By the following afternoon no trace of her presence must remain to be discovered by Alice who would, he was sure, insist on seeing his summer's work as soon as she stepped off the plane. Alice was a very sophisticated young woman, but she would not, he knew, accept any such greeting as "I have been faithful in my fashion". Once he had disposed of the actual Venus, it would not be too difficult to imply that *The American Venus* had been painted in the north country where he had found the model for it—an untruth well substantiated by the paintings he had done of her against the background of the slag.

His car as good a place as any in which to consider his problem, he went back to it, and getting in, sat absently tapping on the steering-wheel with the long, paint-stained fingers of his left hand.

What he should have done, he saw quite clearly, was to find her another job long before this, and he cursed the procrastination that had allowed him to drift without making any plans for her future. The one kind of work he could have arranged for her on short notice, modelling for another artist, he calmly set aside as impossible. He thought, as it happened quite correctly, that such an idea would not occur to her because she did not think of herself as a professional model, and, as long as he himself had anything to do with it, his Venus was going to remain uniquely his own.

It took him some time to find a solution to his difficulties, and, when he did, he had to rationalize it considerably before even his conscience would tolerate it. He was irritated that his conscience should bother him at all, and to disguise from himself the brutality of his intention he decided to pay her more generously than he might otherwise have done.

It was not until he returned to the converted barn toward nightfall, having amongst other things cashed a cheque and made arrangements with the local taxi, that he recalled the circumstances of his departure from it, so completely had he already severed himself from the dream-like quality of the preceding summer months.

"Bloody hell," he muttered, but he was smiling when he came into the studio.

Psyche, rising quickly from the chair in which she had been sitting, braced for she did not quite know what, saw his smile and had one of her sudden flashes of insight: as a model he would always remember her; as a person he would remember her only very occasionally; as a woman he had already forgotten her.

"Venus, come and sit down here for a few minutes. I want to talk to you."

When he handed her the telegram she needed to read it once

only to appreciate its exact implications as far as she herself was concerned.

She had realized from the beginning that, in one form or another, this moment was inevitable. Even more precisely, she had known that the first snows of winter were unlikely to find her still at the studio. In spite of this foreknowledge, and in spite of her mixed feelings, the shock was so numbing that she could not find her voice, and the flimsy sheet of paper fluttered between hands which briefly trembled uncontrollably.

Nick, repressing any pity he might have felt, trusting qualities in her that he did not consciously attribute to her, waited for her to speak first, to set the tone of a conversation he wished already over and done with.

He is cruel, Psyche thought passionately, and he is selfish beyond belief. Why should I make this easy for him? Why shouldn't I scream and spit at him? What do I owe him—nothing, nothing, nothing!

And what, asked a voice deep within her, does he owe you? And she knew, growing calmer, that the answer was the same—nothing. She had fled with him because she needed a refuge and had none. He had taken her because she could be of use to him. They were quits, she and Nick.

When she spoke her voice was steady, and her hands no longer shook. "Where am I to go?"

That she should make it quite so simple for him was more than he had had any right to hope. To have thanked her would have been to put himself in the wrong, which he was not prepared to do. Instead, he outlined his plan for her.

Chain-smoking, watching his lean expressive face through a shifting curtain of cigarette smoke, Psyche saw that she was again in danger of being partially hypnotized by a voice and personality capable of investing even the drabbest of prospects with glamour and colour.

When he had finished, she said, "This place you want to send me to, this Community Shelter, it sounds to me like one of those schools."

Genuinely taken aback, because he had been at some pains to make the Shelter seem a great deal more attractive than it actually was, he said, "A reform school! Don't be idiotic, Venus. It's nothing of the kind. As I have already explained at some length, it's a place designed to help girls like yourself who need guidance and a temporary roof over their heads. You will be free to walk out at any time. It's entirely a matter of choice whether you stay or not."

"You're quite, quite sure of that?"

"Would I send you there, if I weren't?"

Psyche's blue eyes were unfathomable. "You might."

"Good God, Venus, what do you take me for?"

"I don't know, Nick. They'll find me a job, will they, and a place to live in?"

"That's what they're there for. Now, I've arranged for a taxi to be here at four tomorrow afternoon. Do you think you can be ready by then?"

"I can be ready," Psyche said evenly. "I have to be, don't I?"

"I wish you wouldn't put it like that, Venus."

"What other way is there to put it?"

Her glance wandered from him to embrace slowly, item by item, the contents of the big room, the things she knew so well by sight and touch that they might have been her own. Even the stars, imprisoned in the frame of the great north window, seemed personal to her, a gift given only to be taken away, never to be seen again in that same pattern.

Hiding tears she did not want seen, she got up abruptly, and, without any further attempt to speak, went to her room. But when the door was closed behind her, and she leaned against it in a darkness which should have been protective, it was as if she had stepped instead into a black void, too immense, too terrifying in its limitless immensity for tears to be of any avail.

With panicky fingers she sought the light-switch, found it, and turned on the light. But the darkness remained. The darkness of a slowly wheeling universe where the tiny harbour of the known, in which she stood, was threatened on all sides by the great tides of the unknown.

Dwight stared at the bill which, by some error, had found its way to his office desk.

'One pair of silver sandals. Size 8AA. $32.00.'

Lines of unutterable weariness etched themselves in his face, and sorrow dwelt in the keen, grey eyes. He had too often bought extravagant bits of fur and brocade for a 7 triple A to be able to persuade himself that he was making any mistake.

More than six years now since Sharon had, to his knowledge, done anything like this. He saw again in retrospect another bill, and it was as shocking as it had been when first seen and comprehended. 'One doll's carriage. Grey leather. $24.95.'

On that occasion he had been a coward: had told himself it was a present, even while knowing instinctively that it was not.

This time he would have to face her with it. She must not be allowed to go on with a secret life which he could not but regard as extremely harmful to her, which might—he forced himself to think it in so many words—end by affecting her sanity.

He waited until they were sitting on the terrace with cocktails in the late afternoon. Then he simply put the bill in her hand, and said, "This is something we must talk about, my darling."

With only the most casual glance at the piece of paper which had upset him so much, Sharon put it aside and laid a quick, reassuring hand on his arm. "I've wanted to talk about it for a very long time, but was afraid it might worry you." With a small smile, her blue eyes faintly quizzical, she added, "I was right, wasn't I? It would have—in fact, does worry you, doesn't it, darling?"

"It isn't—healthy," he told her slowly.

Sharon's husky voice was quiet but decisive. "I am no more neurotic than you are, if that's what you mean, and yet in one particular instance we are neither of us entirely normal. We can't be. The door to her room is never locked, but you have not been into that room since the night when she was taken away, have you? I know you haven't.

"We are two different people, Dwight, dealing with a common problem as best we can to suit our different temperaments. You believe that we will never see her again. Don't deny it, dearest—this once let us be completely honest. And so, believing this, you try to put your hurt away where you can't see it, sealing all doors which might lead to it as tightly as possible.

"I, on the other hand, believe that someday we will find her again. I can give you no reason for this, but nevertheless I believe it utterly. It would be impossible for me to go on with my life and believe otherwise, given no cause to think her dead."

"But, Sharon——"

"You are going to say that there is still no excuse for buying skates, and prams, and dolls, and clothes, and push-toys and pull-toys—oh, yes, I've bought all that, and a good deal more—for a daughter whose very face is unknown to me."

Sliding to the ground at his feet, she clasped her hands across his knees, and looked up at him.

"You must try to understand this thing I do, Dwight. It is terribly important that you understand, and find me, if not reasonable according to your lights, at least entirely sane. A great many people, I quite agree, would not.

"I am essentially a realist, and I know that the odds are against my hopes coming true. But it's not impossible, and so I—being me—can not remain inactive, doing nothing as the years slip by.

"We lost a child, at the time scarcely more than a baby, who might return to us a girl, perhaps a young woman, or even—if God could be so cruel—a middle-aged woman. I am preparing myself for her. It isn't enough to say to myself, 'She is eleven, she is fifteen, she is nineteen.' It has no meaning. So I provide myself with tangible proof that I have, somewhere, a daughter who is now almost nineteen years old. I must, of necessity, guess at her size, her colouring, and her likes and dislikes, but, because I have now read so much on heredity and because she did look so much like me when she was small, I think my guesses must be very close to the truth about her."

"And what do they add up to?" Dwight asked gently.

"With any luck—the best of you and the best of me," Sharon told him, and a brief smile touched her lips and eyes, a smile that mocked herself for a conclusion so obviously tailored to her wishes.

"I won't pretend," she went on, "that it doesn't hurt, and hurt intolerably, to go into a shop, and consider, and finally purchase —perhaps a coat—from a saleswoman who says, 'Your daughter will look a dream in this blue, if she is as fair as you are, madam.' Sometimes I've wanted to scream, 'You fool, you idiot—don't you know I have no daughter now!' But it helps so much more than it hurts, because it makes her real to me, a believable individual, not a baby who no longer exists anywhere." Her steady voice broken by a trace of urgency, she asked, "Does this make any sense to you, Dwight?"

It would not have been his way of doing things, but he realized now that it was, for her, an outlet which it would have been difficult to find in any other way. To be completely reassured, however, he had to know one more thing; so instead of answering her question, he asked, apparently without much interest, "What do you do with these things you buy, my darling?"

"I give them away, of course. What else would I do with them? When she was little, when the things were toys and so on, I gave them to the Neighbourhood Workers. Now I take them to the Community Shelter. Dwight—darling, you haven't answered me, haven't told me that you understand."

Pulling her closer to him, he said, with deep tenderness, "It's all right, my dearest. I do understand."

He not only understood, but was almost grateful that she ease her longing by identifying her child with the surroundings and way of life that should by rights have been the background of her growing up. For, although he had long since given up any hope that they might recover her, he could not bring himself to accept the fact that she might be dead. It was for this reason, more than any other, that he thought of her as rarely as possible, because, whenever that particular door in his mind blew open, he saw things he would much rather not have seen.

Lost in thought, he suddenly became aware that Sharon had raised her head and was smiling in a manner that she reserved for him alone.

"Dwight," she said, "do you think you are capable of being excessively, recklessly, and indecorously gay? Have you the initiative to don white tie and tails in order to escort me to a place, sinful and glittering, where you might wine me, and dine me, and dance me off my feet?"

The gravity of his dark, good-looking face melted into an expression that made Sharon catch her breath.

"If I ever understood you half as well as you understand me, you would be a very lucky woman. Ten dollars says I will be dressed and waiting at the door while you are still looking for the right lipstick and those preposterous silver ear-rings I hope you are planning to wear."

# THE SOCIAL WORKER | 6

PSYCHE'S second entry into the city lacked much of the impact of her first visit with Nick nearly four months earlier. This was not only because she had seen it before, but also because all summer long she had been aware of its proximity. On cloudy nights there had been a glow in the southern sky, the diffuse reflection of an earthbound constellation close-packed with myriads of ersatz stars. And when a south wind blew, it had brought with it the muted, unaccentuated echo of a ceaseless maelstrom of sound. Although she had kept the idea far in the back of her mind, not wishing to examine it sooner than was necessary, she had known that her logical next step would in some manner take her into this never entirely quiescent stream of life.

Thus it was with some sense of pre-identification to support her that she found herself being carried by taxi deeper and ever deeper into the heart of a precisely laid-out warren of streets and cross-streets.

She would have liked to question the driver about the place for which she was bound, but glimpses, caught from time to time in the rear-view mirror, of a dour, tight-lipped face, did not encourage her to break through a barrier of silence that obviously suited him better than conversation.

Any hope she might have entertained that the Community

Shelter would be clothed in at least an outward semblance of beauty was slowly dissipated as they continued to penerate increasingly narrow and congested thoroughfares.

Shrugging off her coat, feeling beads of moisture on her forehead, she became aware of heat that, drowsily pleasant in the valley surrounding the old barn, here was almost insufferable. Discovering, after some experiment, how to open the window beside her, she closed it again immediately, recoiling from the unaccustomed fumes of gasoline and oil, smoke and hot asphalt; from the concentrated odours of a place in which nature, as represented by anything other than humanity, maintained only the most precarious foothold.

One of Psyche's greatest strengths was a natural optimism, an instinctive refusal to believe that any situation, no matter how bad, would not in time improve. In spite of this, her heart began to sink as she observed the shabbiness and poverty of the neighbourhood they had reached. The houses, standing close against the sidewalks, were joined one to another in long dismal rows. Window-sills boasted greyed pieces of household linen, and doorsteps were adorned with souring bottles of milk. Sharp-eyed children, unreprimanded by slatternly women gossiping before their own or a neighbour's front door, played in the centre of the road and hurled epithets at the taxi as they reluctantly made way for it.

Up to this point they had been moving, both literally and metaphorically, downhill. But now, crossing a street-car line, they entered a district where the houses, although they showed no promise of affluence, yet clung to remnants of decayed grandeur. Gaunt, mid-Victorian structures with narrow windows, steep roofs, and discoloured brick walls, they seemed to brood over the passing of better days, casting an almost palpable aura of depression over the iron-railed park that they flanked.

There was no hint of squalor here, and poverty, if it existed, was well camouflaged; but Psyche experienced no lifting of the spirit, for not only were the houses old, but even the great oaks scattered across the park seemed, in spite of their heavy green foliage, to have lived too long, to have lingered to throw lengthening shadows over a century to which they did not belong.

When the taxi came to a stop in front of one of these houses, she knew, looking at the blank inhospitality of the face it turned toward her, that if she had had anywhere else at all to go to, she would have gone there.

"That'll be four-sixty, lady."

Unused to handling money, Psyche was nervous and uncertain. "I'm sorry. How much?"

"It's right there on the meter."

She did not know what a meter was, and, if he had not pointed with an unclean finger, would not have understood what he was talking about. As it was, all she really comprehended was that the figures represented what he expected her to pay. Opening her purse, fumbling with increased nervousness amongst its contents, she found her money and carefully counted out the precise amount. Tipping being entirely outside her experience, she added nothing to the fare, which might or might not have been the reason why the disgruntled driver, when he saw she had left her purse on the back seat, drove off without returning it to her.

Psyche, standing on the pavement, unaware of her loss, was only too glad to see the last of his scowling face.

Setting down her suitcase, she put on her gloves. Then, with her coat over her arm, she picked the suitcase up again, and walked up to a door above which she could see the faded legend 'Community Shelter'.

Neither the shack nor the studio had had either door-bell or knocker. Here she was confronted with both. After a moment's hesitation, she chose the brass door-knocker, and finding it immobile, nailed fast to the door, pushed the bell with peremptory force.

The door was opened by a girl in a limp green dress; a girl with mouse-brown hair and defeated brown eyes.

"I have come——" Psyche began.

The girl in green interrupted her without emphasis or interest. "I know. Come in."

Walking in, Psyche saw a large, ill-lit hall, innocent of carpeting, or of furniture other than a single wooden bench. Her glance encompassed a circle of closed doors and a staircase that mounted to a landing before disappearing in a further upward climb. Nowhere was there any visible movement, but she received an impression of hidden, subdued activity more oppressive than reassuring.

The girl opened a door on the left. "Wait in here. I'll go and find somebody."

Still carrying her suitcase, Psyche went into the room thus discovered, and, hearing the door close behind her, fought an almost ungovernable impulse to wrench it open again, to escape from what, to her troubled mind, seemed little better than a prison.

The room was small, and a yellow blind, drawn nearly to the bottom of the single window, threw an unhealthy saffron light over walls badly in need of repapering. Worn brown linoleum covered the floor; a brown repeated in a scarred desk, a monumental filing cabinet, and a regimentation of wooden chairs. On the high ceiling an uneasy conference of house-flies clustered, from time to time dispatching emissaries to explore the room below.

Sitting down on the edge of one of the chairs facing the desk, Psyche thought, "I should hate Nick for this." Then, her mind a determined blank, her eyes fixed on the exact centre of the yellow blind, she waited.

Miss Smith, an unwilling member of the underpaid, overworked permanent staff of the Community Shelter, was, when informed that still another stray needed her attention, in what was even for her a very bad frame of mind. The volunteer who ought to have relieved her at tea-time had failed to put in an appearance. Two of the homeless girls who should, in her opinion, have fawned upon her in grateful humility, had chosen instead to be insolent. And the unseasonal heat, added to these annoyances, was producing behind her narrow, lined forehead the initial symptoms of what she was wont to refer to as a sick headache.

An embittered spinster, the dreams she might once have nourished long since turned to gall and wormwood by her own unfortunate disposition, her sole qualification for the job she held was the fact that her father had been a Presbyterian minister. A man who had, when he died, taken his pension with him, leaving his ageing daughter with nothing to offer the world other than a familiarity with—and presumed interest in—charitable undertakings. Actually, the only charity connected with her work as she practised it was the mistaken impulse that had prompted someone to bestow it upon her. She had accepted the position without gratitude, looking upon the necessity to do so as simply a further injustice in a life made up of injustices. That she was, and always had been, more handicapped by selfishness than by lack of money or plainness of appearance, she neither could nor would see. Unconsciously hating herself for being physically unattractive, she hated all women in degrees determined almost entirely by the extent to which they compared favourably with herself.

Descending the stairs on her way to the office and the more stagnant warmth of the lower floor, she felt as if she were progressing downward through suffocating layers of injustice. And the soft, even slap of her large, rubber-soled shoes on the bare treads found a rhythm with her slow pulsing dislike of this existence, this place, this moment, and the immediate task ahead of her.

Wishing to startle, to seize and keep the upper hand in an interview which had robbed her of the solace of solitary self-pity, she opened and closed the door of the small, stuffy office in one sharp movement, and was already seated behind the desk by the time Psyche had risen to her feet.

For a moment they faced one another without speaking, the lovely young girl, and the sour, thin-mouthed spinster, and an instant mutual dislike was born of that moment.

"Sit down." Miss Smith's voice was dry without being crisp; harsh without being forceful.

Slowly Psyche sat down again, but her chin remained tilted upwards, and her straight, supple back was unrelaxed.

Without introducing herself, or making any pretense of welcome, Miss Smith drew a block of printed forms toward her. "You have no home?"

"No," Psyche told her.

"Any relations?"

"No."

"How old are you?"

Psyche hesitated. Was she eighteen or nineteen? This was the time of year when she could not state her age with even passable certainty.

Watching her, Miss Smith found her beauty a personal affront, and her pride of carriage a deliberate insult. "Please don't lie."

With an extraordinary effort of will, Psyche kept her temper. "I'm nineteen," she said evenly.

"Your name?"

"Psyche."

Miss Smith's prim lips drew together in a hard, tight line. She had been exposed to such unlegalized fancies as Rosalind, Juanita, and Marigold. And most of Hollywood's first names had, at one time or another, been paraded before her acid disbelief. This, however, was an apparent affectation which, to her somewhat confused way of thinking, bordered on the blasphemous.

"Your last name. And have the goodness to make it a little more credible."

"You mean?" Psyche asked, and her voice was not as even as it had been.

"I mean I want your last name."

Again Psyche hesitated. She had borne the name Moran long enough to get used to it, to feel that since Butch and Mag had willingly given it to her, she had some right to it. Yet as Maggie Moran she had never felt she was herself, and here and now she knew it was intensely important to be herself, Psyche, and no one else.

"I don't know my last name."

Miss Smith, evaluating her direct blue gaze, and the intelligent clean-drawn contours of her face with the bright hair waving back from it, could not help knowing that there was some quite unusual discrepancy in the situation before her. Deliberately refusing this knowledge and the opportunity it offered, her conscience the vassal of a mind small in every way, she continued to hew the strict line of bureaucratic procedure.

Her small eyes flickering from Psyche to the form in front of her, she both wrote, and said, "Illegitimate."

"What does that mean?"

It had been quite unnecessary to say the word aloud. In doing so, she had not expected the added, and venomous pleasure of elucidating. "It means that your mother and your father were not married."

Psyche's anger brought fresh colour to cheeks already flushed by the heat. "You have no damned right to say that!"

Miss Smith felt almost happy. "You will either go, or apologize at once for speaking so rudely."

Alarm cooled Psyche's fury, and then as quickly faded, leaving her quiet and emotionless. She looked at the woman opposite her, at the mean mouth and antagonistic eyes. She looked around the depressingly ugly room. She looked up at the ceaselessly circling flies. And she knew that it was not here, whatever it was she needed; that there was nothing for her here, and never would be. That she had been maliciously steered toward this conclusion, she realized quite clearly, but this did not matter, for it was, she knew, a conclusion she would inevitably have reached by herself. In one sense she had never been independent; in another, and more important sense, she had always been entirely independent, and she intended to remain so.

With a sweep of her arm, she gathered her belongings together, and getting up, walked swiftly to the door. On the threshold she paused, turned, and said distinctly, "You bitch!"

Then she was crossing the still empty, still oppressive hall; was opening, undetained, the door with the false knocker on it; was going down the walk to the street and a future that was, as the sun sank toward a western horizon serrated by a cubist pattern of chimney-pots, now without signposts of any kind at all.

# 7 | THE PROSTITUTE

I

Bel was, in spite of her lack of height, a noticeable figure as she walked through the southern entrance of the park at sunset. Horizontal bars of sunlight struck ruddy sparks from the black curls beneath her wide-brimmed black hat, and turned her red dress, tightly moulded onto a plump well-corseted shape, to flame colour. Even her face, beneath a thick coat of make-up that disguised neither her age nor her hard-bitten good humour, was transiently ruddier than artifice had made it, more alive than those of the loungers who watched her make her way along the gravelled paths.

Walking slowly in fabulously high-heeled pumps, she exchanged greetings, a casual word or a flick of a short carmine-tipped hand, with the men who still sprawled at the day's end on the wooden benches or on the short, scorched grass. Mentally she classified them, and quite correctly, as bums, but they were familiar to her by sight as she was to them, and Bel was no snob.

Psyche's was the only head that did not turn, even when Bel seated herself on the other end of the bench on which she was sitting. Her gaze travelling between the gnarled trunks of two huge oaks, between the straight spears of a tall iron fence, and across the street beyond, she kept her eyes rivetted—as she had for more than an hour—on the front door of the Community Shelter.

She had never known, and would never know again, a despair equal to that which overwhelmed her in the moment when she discovered the loss of her purse.

When she had walked away from the Shelter, she had begun at once to marshal her thoughts. She felt remarkably self-assured, strengthened rather than the reverse by her passage-at-arms with the social worker. Her first consideration, she knew, must be a roof over her head, and in order to find this she must get a newspaper. Very few newspapers had ever penetrated as far as the shack, but she had read these few over and over again, the classified advertisements in their own way as interesting to her as the usually out-of-date news. Pleased with herself that she should know what to do in this present crisis, she decided that room and board were what she wanted, and that, ignorant as she was of the city, it would pay her to use a taxi. Did cities have maps? They must have. She would buy one, if she could, when she bought a newspaper. Automatically, scarcely conscious that she was doing so, she felt for the shoulder-bag containing the money which would make these things possible.

The knowledge that she no longer had it, and a precise memory of exactly where she had left it, smote her almost simultaneously. She had put it down after paying the taxi-driver—and had not picked it up again. As if it were there in front of her, she saw it lying on the worn leather upholstery, and unconsciously reached out in front of her in a vain attempt to pluck it back out of time already three-quarters of an hour distant, while she thought frantically, "Oh, God—oh, God help me, what will I do now!"

All the spreading noise and movement of the city, held in abeyance by her previous preoccupation, seemed to strike her then, to batter her with the manifold fists of a menace against which she was no longer capable of defending herself.

Shackled by her own awful helplessness, she stood, as if in the middle of a living nightmare, unaware of the passers-by, of the shape and form of the street scene around her, of anything beyond the fact that when she moved away from the small piece of public pavement she occupied she would be moving to nowhere. Ahead of her there was nothing. And behind her? She saw a long corridor divided into compartments by locked and bolted doors. What lay behind the first door she did not even know. And the second—if she were to beg food, sleep in fields, and finally find her way back to the shack, it would not be to the shack but to a reform school. The green door to the studio was shut fast by her own fierce pride as much as by Nick's probable refusal to reopen it to her. And the last, with its charity as false as its tarnished knocker—she would die on the street before she would attempt to open that one again.

She pictured herself walking, walking, walking, along streets whose names she did not know, streets which led endlessly into still more streets; walking through the alternate light and darkness of day and night, a black-and-white chequer-board laid across increasing exhaustion : walking amongst crowds whose faces were turned always away from her, the unknown and unwanted; walking until, at last unable to go on, she fell, to be ground to dust by regiments of hurrying feet that found her so slight an obstacle they noticed her no more than the fallen leaves.

Was there anything she could do to help herself? Any positive step she could take in any direction? Trying to think clearly, she saw a sliver of hope to which she might cling for a time at least. The taxi-driver, when he found her purse, might bring it back to the place where he had left her. Remembering his unlovely face and disposition, she knew that he probably would not. But he might, and as long as there was this possibility she could act upon it.

Turning quickly, she went back the way she had come.

For a time she stood against the fence of the park on the opposite side of the street from the Shelter. Then, disliking the curious glances she was beginning to attract, and realizing that she could continue to keep her vigil from inside the park itself, she moved to the bench on which she was still sitting when Bel sat down beside her.

Bel was always interested in people. They were, in effect, her business. At first sight she had taken Psyche for one of the art students who, coming to the art gallery on the north side of the park, introduced an element otherwise out of place in that district. However, as she seated herself, her quick dark eyes told her that this original estimate was a mistaken one. Appraising the simple but good clothes, the old suitcase, and the clean decided profile, she was both curious and puzzled.

"Hot, isn't it?" she remarked casually.

Psyche looked around, but her eyes scarcely focused on the woman in red before swinging back to the only centre of vision which at the moment meant anything to her. "Yes," she said, and no more.

Startled by the open desperation in the blue eyes which had met hers so briefly, Bel did not immediately speak again. She was by nature sympathetic, but she had grown up in a hard school, and minding her own business as she expected others to mind theirs was a basic principle of her existence. Looking up at a sky striated with clouds fast turning from rose to grey, she knew that it was almost time to return to an establishment which, belonging to her, required her presence after nightfall. Yet, compelled by something in the taut figure beside her, she lingered where she was, hesitating between a renewed attempt at conversation, and, as she phrased it to herself, letting well enough alone. Just why she should have given way to an impulse of which she disapproved she could not have said.

Opening a black purse, she pulled out a package of cigarettes and held it out. "Smoke?"

Looking at Bel again, this time Psyche did not turn away, and, in failing to do so, admitted that a hope which had been at best apocryphal was now no hope at all. If the taxi-driver had intended to come back, he would have done it before this.

Butch had once told her that a condemned man was always granted a last wish.

She had asked, "Would a person care? Would they want anythin'?"

"They cares, all right," Butch had said heavily. "Nearly always they wants a cigarette."

There seemed to her now to be something symbolical in Bel's offer, coming as it did at the darkening close of the darkest day of her life, and she understood Butch's reply to her long-ago question as she had not understood it at the time. She should by rights have wanted food, a shoulder to weep on, many things, but all she wanted was a cigarette. And this she wanted very badly. Yet so great was the apathy of her hopelessness that she did not at once make any move toward accepting it.

Bel's red lips hardened. "You thinking Mrs. Astor should of introduced us?"

"I wasn't thinking anything—except that you are kind."

"Then for the love of Mike take one! My arm's getting tired."

Giving her a light, Bell did not miss the quick, deep inhalation which gave her away as a smoker who would not have been without cigarettes if she had had any choice in the matter.

"You from out of town?"

"Yes," Psyche said.

"Ever been in this burg before?"

"Yes."

Bel could usually place people with astonishing accuracy, and it bothered her that she should be unable to bracket Psyche anywhere within her wide experience. What's the matter with the kid that she can't say anything but 'yes', she wondered. And what's the matter with me that I stay here talking to her? I'm getting the hell on home before I talk myself into something.

Snapping the clasp of her purse, she got up abruptly. "Well, I've got to be going. Nice to have known you, baby. Happy landings."

"Good-bye," Psyche said, and she essayed a smile which did not reach her eyes.

She had not expected Bel to stay, to mean anything to her beyond that brief encounter, and so was not disappointed when she went. She did not even watch her go, but unconsciously she listened to the sound of high heels, picking their way over loose gravel, until they could no longer be heard.

Remotely she considered moving on herself, but with nowhere to go it seemed an illogical thing to do, so she simply stayed where she was in the centre of a vacuum in which outside sights and sounds, though recorded by her eyes and ears, had no significance for her.

She saw the street lights come on, sudden pools of yellow light accentuating the darkness outside their individual orbits; saw the men who had loafed in the park get up and drift away, one by one: saw a tall, blue-uniformed figure begin a measured circuit of the now deserted paths. She heard a dog barking; was aware of car doors slamming, of car horns blaring; heard a woman's voice calling a child in to bed; heard the distant strains of a radio playing a popular tune that tried to be gay, and was not; heard the soft rustle of leaves above her head, stirred by a breeze that promised to relieve the heavy heat, and then died before fulfilling its promise.

Bel, standing by the open casement of one of the two bay windows in the large, ornately furnished living-room of her second-storey apartment, saw and heard these same things. A prey to memories she had thought buried for good, unable to dismiss a mental image of the face that brought these memories to the surface of her mind, she had been standing there since she came in.

Now, speaking over her shoulder, she said, "The cop's doing his rounds."

Kathie, looking up from a book, considered it fortunate she should be the sole witness to a state of nervous indecision entirely at variance with Bel's normal, and necessarily tough realism. During the four years she had been at Bel's place she had never seen her other than decisive and sure of herself.

She laid aside her book. "Why are you so concerned about this particular girl, Bel?"

"I don't know," Bel said evasively. "There was something about her that got me, that's all."

"She's probably gone by now."

"Maybe. But I don't think she has. The kid's got no place to go, that's my guess."

Kathie did not like the trend of this conversation. She, more than any of the other girls, stood to lose too much if Bel did anything foolish. "She'll be all right," she said evenly. "You said yourself that she was well dressed. You're letting your imagination run away with you."

Bel scarcely seemed to hear her. "It can be kind of a turning point in a girl's life—having no place to go."

Kathie, by virtue of the extraordinary combination of professions that she practised, exercised a freedom of speech that no one else in Bel's house would have dared to imitate. "Pull yourself together, Bel," she said quietly. "You're being sentimental, and you can't afford to be."

She's right, Bel thought, I'm being a damned fool. And just because that kid reminds me of somebody, I'm going to be an even bigger damned fool.

She looked all of her forty-seven years as she swung round to face the girl behind her. "I'm going to take her in," she said, and her tone was warning that she would brook no argument. "Go on out to the park, and bring her back with you."

Kathie rose to her feet. "Are you sure you'll be doing her a favour?"

Bel's expression was grim. "I said I was taking her in, not taking her on. There'll be no mistake about that."

Shrugging, Kathie gave up. "All right. I'll get her."

"Go quickly, will you? That cop isn't going to leave her be if she stays there much longer. He'll have the wrong idea about her."

Kathie's smile was as cynical as her parting thrust. "Don't blame him. At this rate he won't be much ahead of events."

When Kathie said she would do a thing, she did it. She had no sympathy with the errand on which she had been dispatched, but she went swiftly, even though it meant adding an additional hazard to the precarious tight-rope of her own Jekyll and Hyde existence.

She saw Psyche as soon as she entered the park, a motionless, fair-haired statuette in the pale periphery of light cast by a street lamp outside the iron fencing. A figure which, in spite of its immobility, conveyed no feeling of relaxation.

"Damn," she murmured under her breath. But when she approached Psyche, and spoke to her, there was no hostility in her manner.

"Bel sent me. If you have nowhere to go to-night, you can come back to her place with me."

Looking up, Psyche saw a plain, dark girl in a plain, dark dress; a thin girl of twenty-eight or nine, with a straight fall of dark hair, and a white triangular face saved from mediocrity by enormous eyes and a bitterly beautiful mouth.

"I don't know anyone called Bel," she said tonelessly.

Kathie was unmoved by beauty, and she was not old enough herself for youth to have any appeal for her, but intellect, even in its feeblest manifestations, never failed to command her interest. Recognizing in Psyche the possibility of real intelligence, she curbed a rising impatience, and said quietly, "Bel sat beside you, and talked to you, here, earlier this evening."

The woman in red who had given her a cigarette. Now she was offering her a refuge. It was too completely unexpected, this lifeline held out to her without any reason that she could fathom.

"She—Bel, is sure she wants me?"

"She is," Kathie replied briefly.

"I would be foolish not to go, wouldn't I?"

Kathie's expression was enigmatic. "That's for you to judge."

"I'll come," Psyche said, but she did not move.

"Do you expect me to carry you, or are you going to get up and walk?" Kathie asked ironically. Then, her voice sharpening, she said, "Come on. Get up now, will you. The law is bearing down on us, and I, for one, have no desire to stay and converse with it."

This time Psyche really saw the policeman approaching, and, suddenly free of the lethargy that had bound her, grasped some of the factual implications of her situation. Rational as she had not been since discovering that she had lost her money, she realized that a prison cell on a vagrancy charge would have been her fate rather than any gradual, anonymous annihilation.

"I'm sorry," she said. "I've been a bit confused. Let's go."

2

ALTHOUGH Psyche was not entirely ignorant, she was still in many ways an innocent, and it was two or three days before she fully understood the purpose and nature of Bel's establishment.

One of the chief reasons for Bel's success was her refusal to allow anyone at any time to place any particular emphasis on the one factor in her business without which it would have ceased to exist. A very shrewd woman, she took a leaf from the book of the preceding century, and operated on the principle that a good time was an intangible, some of whose many facets must, of necessity, reflect a social and communal base. Working carefully over a long period of time, she had created a façade so apparently blameless that she had never at any time had any trouble with the police; and, within her four walls, an atmosphere so comfortably gay that many of the men who came there almost forgot their original reason for coming. With infinite patience, always taking the long view, she had built up a steady rather than a casual clientele, looking for more than a well-lined purse before she granted the freedom of her premises.

She was well rewarded for her pains, and not only with money. Six evenings a week the big living-room, with its rose-shaded lamps and well-cushioned furniture, had the aura of a pleasantly informal club.

The club, although fully licensed in certain respects, nevertheless had a few strictly enforced ground rules. The girls were allowed to accept presents, over and above their proper share in the membership fees, but never cash as such. Bel had two reasons for this, both of them good : large sums of money, if they were ever unfortunate enough to be visited by the police, would be difficult, if not impossible, to explain satisfactorily; secondly, she had the acumen to see that the kind of illusions she worked to achieve would not stand up for long before the harsh wind of a too obvious commercialism. That the presents that some of the girls, particularly May, managed to extract from their admirers, were extremely valuable, did not matter to her.

The rules that governed behaviour were never expressed in so many words. They simply became obvious, and, supported by custom, were observed without protest.

The club opened around eight o'clock, and closed ostensibly at two-thirty. Between eleven and twelve o'clock the serving of whiskey was discontinued, strong coffee being provided in its place; and food, too attractive to be ignored, was on hand at all times. Thus, steering clear of specific individual pressures, Bel avoided any awkwardness that drinking might have precipitated.

Her greatest strategic triumph, however, was in her handling of the poker game that was in session every evening and all evening. A less clever woman might have been tempted to make this a personally lucrative side-line. Not Bel. The game was always absolutely on the level, and the players could sit in or drop out on their own terms.

An evening at Bel's was much like going to a private party, with the minor difference that one could, from the start, be honest with oneself about one's intentions.

During the daytime Bel's place resembled nothing so much as a well-furnished girls' boarding-house—an impression strengthened by the fact that all the girls left the house for a number of hours every day, their times of departure determined by the part-time, outside jobs without which Bel would not accept them.

As she explained to Psyche later, "I can't have the responsibility of keeping them when they go off, and I wouldn't have the heart to turn them out on the street. I tell them they got to have something to fall back on, and besides you can't expect anybody to have any respect for a girl who lies around all day doing nothing."

Although she was entirely honest in this expression of her feelings, Bel might have added that her insistence on a secondary occupation for her girls was a not unimportant part of the front she showed to the world, a front so cleverly stage-managed it would have been almost impossible to improve upon it.

Her establishment consisted of the second and third stories of two semi-detached houses that she had at first rented, and later, prospering, bought outright. The two houses, in effect one building, were situated on a side street running south from the square encircling the park and art gallery, but close enough to the corner for an oblique view of the park to be possible from all the windows that faced the street. It was a location calculated to a nicety. She was sufficiently near to the faded grandeur surrounding the park to make the presence of cars outside her place unremarkable, yet not so near that the people inhabiting this section would be likely to evince any interest in her. Further south, the district, deteriorating rapidly, housed a class that fully appreciated the reciprocal value of leaving other people alone.

From outside, the size of the quarters she occupied could not be guessed at, for, although the upper two stories had been converted into one unit, the ground floor with its two separate entrances had been left more or less untouched. On the south, all access to the upper floors had been cut off, and she rented the independent apartment thus formed to a Lithuanian family who, not at all fortuitously, were unable to converse intelligibly with anyone other than fellow Lithuanians. A large and boisterous family, apparently perfectly happy in their linguistic isolation, they unwittingly created—particularly of a summer's evening when gathered en masse around their front doorstep—the impression that they must, of necessity, occupy much more of the house than was actually the case. Later on, Psyche, becoming fond of the fat and smiling baby, was often a part of this group, her blonde head a startling contrast to the dark ones around her.

Bel's disposition of the ground floor on the north side was somewhat different, but equally well-considered. Inside the front door one found an enclosed stairway blocked by a door that was always kept locked; this was the real entrance to Bel's own domain. At the back of a narrow hall was another door. This led to Kathie's quarters, for Kathie did not, at least for the record, 'live in'. The three remaining ground-floor rooms were let to an old lady who was, conveniently, almost blind; an old lady whose name had been one to conjure with in the society of the early nineteen-hundreds. A severely straight figure, clad all in black, her patrician features waxen clear behind a fine black veil, she could be seen, morning and afternoon the year round, walking slowly up and down in front of the great house on the square that had once been hers. Seeing her thus, one saw again, if at all imaginative, the gracious leisure of the turn of the century; saw carriages with liveried footmen; saw plumed hats and trailing pastel-tinted skirts; saw, as she still saw, all the images of a once bright yesterday.

Bel had used her head, rather than her heart, when she had given this tenant her small niche on the edge of the only world she would ever again see clearly. However, as was so often the case with Bel, her sympathy involved her as she had not anticipated in advance, and, as living costs rose, on one pretext or another she continued to reduce a rental already disproportionately low.

When Kathie, who often audited her accounts for her, had questioned her about this, she had made no attempt to rationalize her generosity, simply saying tartly, "That old dame stays there as long as I have a bean to my name."

To Psyche, therefore, as she followed Kathie up the walk to Bel's on the evening when she first came there, was unfolded a montage of impressions specifically designed to mislead people a great deal less innocent than she was.

They were met by vocal greetings from the Lithuanian family, a dimly seen cluster in the dusk—greetings in broken English difficult to interpret, but unmistakably friendly, irrepressibly cheerful. And as this welcome subsided into carefree, private laughter, she saw on her right—a three-dimensional portrait framed in darkness—the old lady sitting by her open window, her white head resting against the sombre tapestry of a wing chair, her delicate blue-veined hands folded tranquilly in a black silken lap.

The inside hall was dimly lit, but when Kathie unlocked the door to the stairway they entered at once into the rosy reflected light of a big room which, as Psyche stepped into it, seemed not unlike a rose-coloured heaven, the core of its warmth and brightness the plump woman in red who came forward to welcome her.

"Come right on in, baby, and make yourself at home."

Her voice unsteady, Psyche said, "I don't know why you have done this. I—I don't know how to thank you."

"Think nothing of it, baby. I once had it tough, myself. Here, Kathie, take the kid's things up to that little room you used to have." Then, turning and addressing a man standing behind her, she said, "This is her, Joe. The kid I was just telling you about."

Psyche saw a swarthy, heavy-set man in his fifties, with eyes, beneath thick dark eyebrows, as shrewd and friendly as Bel's own. A large diamond winked on the little finger of the hand he extended to her, and, although there were many who would have deplored his presence in that place, his firm clasp and genial self-assurance added a note of permanence and stability to the scene that would have been lacking without him.

"Joe's a special friend of mine, baby," Bel said. "If you stick around, you'll be seeing a lot of him, so you better decide to like him."

For the first time in twenty-four hours, Psyche smiled. "I don't have to decide."

There was triumph in Bel's voice. "There you are, Joe! What did I say? I told you she was a nice kid, and I wasn't born yesterday."

The man stroked a chin which would always, even after he had just shaved, betray a blue shadow. "You've made a good friend, girlie. You're lucky."

"You don't need to tell me that," Psyche said quietly. "I know it."

It was Joe's turn to smile, a smile which showed even white teeth, gold-stopped in two places. "Okay, Bel. You were right. I guess you and the girlie here will work things out between you."

The light that had transiently come into Psyche's face faded, and even the warm glow of the lamp failed to cover up her drained whiteness.

Bel, watching her, said quickly, "You're dead beat, aren't you, baby? Look, I'm going to take you up to your room pronto, and one of the girls will bring you supper on a tray."

"I'm sorry. You see, I lost my purse, and I——"

But Bel would not let her go on. "You can tell me all about it in the morning, baby. Right now, you're going to bed. My God, she's got beautiful hair, hasn't she, Joe? Come on, baby, it's this way."

It was not one of the girls, but Bel, herself, who brought a tray up to the third floor room under the eaves which Psyche was to like better, in many ways, than any other room she ever had.

"There you are," Bel said, putting the tray down on a table beside the bed. "Just set it outside the door when you're finished, and someone will chase it later on. Sleep as late as you want, and don't worry about a thing. Just sleep tight, don't let 'em bite, and we'll have a real good talk tomorrow."

Listening to the sound of small pumps descending the stairs, Psyche knew that the tap of high heels would always remind her of Bel as long as she lived.

She looked around the little room, at the blue curtains, at the window-seat from which one could see out over the tops of the trees in the park, at the frilled dressing-table, at the soft grey carpet, at the reproduction of Gainsborough's Blue Boy hanging against a clean grey wall—and knew that, hungry as she was, she must cry before she could eat.

When she woke in the morning, she realized that the house and her room both faced east, for direct sunlight poured in across the window-seat. It was this, as much as anything else, that oriented her immediately, that told her as soon as she opened her eyes that she was no longer at Nick's. The intermingled sounds of traffic, voices, and all the machinery of a great city at that hour in high gear, were a secondary impression, and one that she was in a mood to like. Silence, at that moment, would have been disconcerting.

Lying there, not quite ready to move physically into this strange new day, she found it almost impossible to believe that she had left the studio only the previous afternoon. Nick, the red-roofed barn, and the long, warm hours of the past summer seemed like an interlude already dimmed by the passing of much time. Curiously it was the shack that seemed close to her just then, closer and more real than it had been since the night on which she had fled from it. Briefly she knew a painful nostalgia for something that could never be hers again, for the uncomplicated existence—actually so far removed from what she really wanted—that she had known with the two big, simple people who had never been other than kind to her.

When she was dressed, she went downstairs and retraced her steps along the corridor flanked by closed doors through which Bel had led her on the previous evening. Entering the living-room, she found it deserted, but from an open doorway at the far end she heard a radio playing and Bel's slightly hoarse voice raised above it.

She approached this door, and saw a large, streamlined red-and-white kitchen, divided by a counter into two parts, the nearer section furnished with chrome-fitted red tables and chairs. Bel was partial to red.

Bel, in a dressing-gown, sat at one of these tables, an empty coffee cup in front of her, talking to a girl whose back was to the door.

"Hello," Psyche said uncertainly.

Bel's response, on seeing her, was just right. Casual, friendly, it was as if she had been used to having her around for a long time. "Hello, baby. Come on in and have something to eat. You sleep well?"

"I had a wonderful sleep."

"You don't know Monique, do you?"

Monique was, surprisingly, as French as her name. Bilingual, she had no need to speak French, but it was something she did anyway. "Bonjour, chèrie."

Psyche looked blankly at the pert face, under a lacquered cap of black hair, that smiled up at her.

Her eyes sparkling between incredible lashes that Psyche was to learn were put on and off with her clothing, Monique rose to display a slight but beautifully neat figure. "*C'est à dire*—good morning, honey. Glad to know you. See you later. *Maintenant, il me faut partir tout de suite. Je suis déjà en retard.*"

With which, her hips swinging to the music of a radio that at Bel's place was never turned off, she walked out of the kitchen.

Bel lit a cigarette from the stub of another one. "She's a show-off, that girl, but you'll like her, baby, when you get to know her better."

Psyche found Bel's calm assumption that she was going to stay very comforting, but she could not accept it without protest. "I can't stay here. You don't understand. I haven't any money—any job—anything."

"You want cream and sugar, baby? Now relax, and take it easy. You wouldn't be here if I didn't understand that much."

"But I can't pay my way like the other girls who live here."

"For God's sake, baby, you don't think——" Bel began, and then stopped abruptly, her small pointed teeth catching her full underlip. That she should have to explain her mode of living to this clear-eyed girl was something that had not even occurred to her. Now, faced with the necessity, she knew that she could not do it, knew that she was going to refuse to recognize it as a necessity.

Psyche, completely misinterpreting the expression on Bel's face, said quickly, "You are so kind, I know it doesn't matter to you about the money, but don't you see it matters to me—terribly."

Yeah, Bel though wryly, but it isn't going to matter as much as something else. Maybe Kathie was right, and Joe too. Maybe I've been a damn fool.

If Psyche had known then what Bel could have told her and did not she would almost certainly have left. By the time she discovered it for herself, she already had all the assurance of personal freedom she needed, and was so passionately grateful to Bel she would have done almost anything other than condemn her in favour of a society that had put her out on the street from which Bel had taken her in.

She talked with Bel that morning, uninterrupted, for nearly two hours. She told her story from the beginning, omitting neither fact nor conjecture, finding, in the dark eyes fixed intently on her, a sympathy and comprehension such as she had never met with before.

When she had finished, Bel was silent for a moment, and then remarked, almost to herself, "It's like I said. Having no place to go can be kind of a turning-point in a girl's life." Then she went on briskly, "Seems as if there isn't too much you can do to earn pay, baby, not good pay. But there are lots of ways you could be real useful to me here, if you wanted to. You stick around a while, helping me out, while we figure something better for you."

"Give me something to do right now," Psyche said quietly. "I'll never be able to repay you properly, but I can try."

### 3

ACROSS the succeeding weeks Psyche became more useful to Bel than either of them had anticipated in advance, not the least of her usefulness being the manner in which, without premeditation, she became an accepted and welcome part of the life of the street. An advantage, from Bel's point of view, that by this time was not lost on Psyche.

Bel, letting it be generally known that Psyche was her niece, found it a pleasant relief to have one member of her household about whom she need have no concern at any time. And the persistent feeling that she was doing, by proxy, what she had once hoped to do for a blue-eyed, fair-haired child, now long since dead, brought her a comfort she had never admitted to herself that she wanted.

The girls, given their instructions by Bel, were friendly enough from the beginning, but it was not until they were convinced that Psyche herself had no intention of undercutting them that they fully accepted her anomalous position in the house. As time went on, perhaps because she was from their point of view so unsophisticated, so amusingly inexperienced, they developed a protective attitude toward her, seeing her as a symbol of what—without regret—they could never themselves hope to be again. Regarding her as very young, failing to recognize her as an already forceful and well-integrated person capable of making her own decisions, they gave themselves individual credit for keeping her at least as unsullied as when she came amongst them.

Psyche, for her part, was secretly sorry for all of them, because she could foresee nothing but the bleakest future ahead of them. Happiness, as she so firmly envisaged it, was not, and never would be, their lot. She did not judge them on moral grounds, in spite of Mag's teachings and her own innate recoil from the life they led, because to do so would be to judge Bel, and this she could not do.

She was destined to forget Ruth, and Joan, and Violet almost completely, remembering little more than that Ruth and Joan were sisters sharing an undistinguished prettiness and an ability to giggle, and that Violet sometimes cried in the night. Though whether she cried because she was alone on these occasions, or because she so rarely was, Psyche did not discover, for her strange violet eyes, as unrevealing as pale amethysts, never gave anything away.

Monique she remembered only because Monique taught her to dance.

But May and Kathie were memorable.

May missed real beauty because she had too much of everything. Her baby-blue eyes were too large, her wealth of curls too golden, her mouth too brilliantly full, and her figure, though well-proportioned, too extravagantly opulent. On the other side of the footlights she would have been magnificent. At close quarters she was somewhat overpowering.

She ate little, seeming to subsist for the most part on a diet of chocolates. Good-natured, always smiling, she yawned often, displaying unabashed a healthy pink cavern lined with flawless white teeth.

As Bel put it, "May is an easy girl."

Being with May was certainly restful, particularly if one closed one's eyes.

She dressed in pinks and blues, owned a squirrel coat dyed blue, and had a passion for jewellery curbed only by the limitations of her purse and the number of places on her anatomy where she might properly—or improperly—display it.

At one and the same time practical and romantic, men were to her divided into two simple categories, cheapskates and "the handsomest thing you ever saw". What amused Psyche was that the two so often became interchangeable overnight, "the handsomest thing you ever saw" being summarily demoted to swell the already crowded ranks of the cheapskates.

May, originally a beauty-parlour operator, under protest put in three hours a day at this vocation, although, judging from the results, it seemed likely that she spent a great deal more time on beautifying herself than she vouchsafed to the customers.

"I don't know how she holds that job," Bel said one day. "I guess it's just because she can get away with things. I never met a girl who could get more for less. She's clever, in her own way, May is."

May was the epitome of what one might have expected of someone in her profession. Kathie, on the other hand, was, in all respects but one, the absolute antithesis. For Kathie, with her Puritan face, and tortured mouth reflecting an incessant warfare between mind and body, was a full-time dedicated teacher who ought, by rights, to have taught at a ranking university.

Outwardly denying in every way possible the curse set upon her in adolescence, she wore neither make-up nor jewellery, and her clothes were plain to the point of severity. In so far as she was able, she looked what she was, a poorly paid public-school teacher. But she could do nothing about her eyes; deep-set and dark, they had but to look at a man to glow with an unholy magnetism as powerful as any sorcery of old. Even the glasses she affected when teaching did not entirely disguise this flame or the horror of self that accompanied it. Judith, with the head of Holofernes at her feet, might have looked as Kathie often did when she came from her room in the mornings.

It was impossible for Psyche to think of Kathie as one of the girls. She stood alone, apart from any known social grouping. Yet it was because Kathie was there that Psyche stayed at Bel's place as long as she did.

At first Psyche was contented enough with days each one of which added something to her general knowledge, served to fill in the startling hiatuses in her practical education.

Learning how to shop, both by telephone and in person, she gradually relieved Bel of all the household marketing. As often as was expedient, she went to the shops, rather than telephoning, because she liked being one of a crowd and took a real pleasure in her growing competence as a city dweller. Street-cars ceased to terrify her, and, threading her way in and out amongst heavy traffic on foot, she soon forgot that at one time it had required all her courage to step off the pavement.

She took over more than her share of the cooking, but Bel would not allow her, as she suggested, to do it all.

"That wouldn't be good, baby," she said. "The girls would get to thinking of you as a kind of servant, and then they'd push you around."

There was a good deal of wisdom in this, so Psyche concentrated on those things that Bel herself had previously had to do unaided, leaving the girls to press their own clothes and take their proper turns with cooking and dish-washing.

The only servant the establishment boasted was a taciturn old woman with a seamed face, dyed hair, and work-coarsened hands, who came in during the daytime to clean. Psyche avoided her because the old woman watched her with such a hungry mixture of envy and admiration, often mumbling under her breath, "Just like you—just like you, dearie."

There was no mistaking her natural assumption that Psyche's rôle in the house was the same as that of the other girls, and that she herself had once followed a similar course and also been lovely to look at. The horrible part of this was that it was believable, for the ghost of a long-lost beauty still peered forth from the rheumy old eyes.

Psyche, repelled afresh whenever she encountered her, wondered how the others could continue to see that living example and go on as they were doing.

The task that she most enjoyed was that of attending to some of the wants of the old lady in the apartment downstairs.

The first time she went down, Bel cautioned her, "Just act as if you had dropped in for a visit. That old dame's got a lot of pride. If she seems to like you, you can do like I've been doing, and sort of pick up a few things and tidy up a bit for her. Because she can't see so good, she loses things if they aren't in their right places."

Open affection in her eyes, Psyche said, "You are so nice, Bel."

"The hell with that. I'm just human. Go on down, baby, and see how you make out."

Psyche was able to make friends with all classes and distinctions of people without too much effort. The friendship that sprang up between herself and the reserved, aristocratic old lady, however, required no effort at all. Recognizing almost immediately qualities in each other that both possessed, they spanned the incalculable difference in their two backgrounds as if it did not exist.

Psyche had never before had any close contact with anyone on a purely voluntary basis, and the freedom from any necessity to proffer confidences that this gave her was one that she accepted with unqualified relief. Even when they knew each other very well, she did not talk about herself, and it was not at first-hand that she finally learned the story behind the tragic descent in the world of this cultivated and once wealthy lady. In the long talks they had together they discussed manners and modes, attitudes, and human behaviour. Since both of them were, by force of circumstances, remarkably unworldly, there was a delightful simplicity about these conversations; a simplicity saved from banality by two quick minds starved for an opportunity to think aloud.

Psyche, always observant, realized that there was much she could learn in niceties of behaviour from her new friend, and when observation alone was not sufficient to provide her with the answers she sought, made no secret of her ignorance. The occasion on which she first had tea in the small apartment cluttered with treasures of another era found her completely at a loss.

Having been instructed where to find a heavy silver tea service, and finding it somewhere else, she said, "I'm sorry, I don't know exactly how to arrange things."

"The tea-pot on your right, my dear. The hot water jug beside it. The cream and sugar on your left, and the cups in front of you. It is customary to serve lemon, but I am afraid I have been rather remiss and there are no lemons in the house."

After that Psyche took it upon herself to see that there were always "lemons in the house". In time she not only dropped in on the old lady but also accompanied her on at least one of her two daily promenades up and down in front of the big house facing the park. On days when the weather made walking impossible, she served tea—with an elegance that both pleased and amused her—and read aloud from one of the many leather-bound volumes arranged precisely in a glass-fronted bookcase. Here her lack of any proper education showed up only too clearly, and she was at times painfully embarrassed by her inability to pronounce words properly, or to give to poetry the easy flow it demanded.

She would stumble, and, glad that the still beautiful but dim blue eyes could not see her flushed face, say, "I'm so sorry—I'm doing it very badly."

"Not at all, my dear. You have a lovely voice. You are simply not accustomed to reading aloud. Perhaps I remember—'The splendour falls on castle walls, and——' Do go on, my dear, I am enjoying it so much."

Psyche realized how gracefully and tactfully she was being helped, but she did not understand until long afterwards that their reading matter had been chosen far more on her account than her hearer's; that a debt was being quietly repayed even while it was being incurred.

That another debt was to be discharged at a time when she and the old lady would be all that stood between Bel and the toppling of the structure she had so carefully built up, she could not, of course, foresee.

She never brought the manners and freedom of speech of Bel's place downstairs with her, but she derived a mischievous pleasure from unobtrusively practising a few of the airs of the drawing-room upstairs. She could have laughed openly when she discovered, in an argument with Monique, how effective were slightly raised eyebrows, and a cool, "I would rather you didn't——"

Bel was very pleased with the merging of her two altruistic interests. "Seems like you can hit it off with anybody, baby," she told Psyche. "It saves me a lot not to have to be going up and down like I was before. I'd like to see the person you couldn't hit it off with any time and all the time."

"You're asking to meet Nick, though you mayn't know it."

"Him! He doesn't count. He was just a louse."

"He wasn't just that," Psyche said slowly. "That was the trouble. He wasn't just a louse."

Bel shrugged. "Have it your own way, baby. I can't agree with you, but you should know."

Psyche found Bel almost always like that, pleasant and agreeable. During the nine months she stayed at Bel's they had only one open difference of opinion, and that was about money. Accepting her board and lodging gratefully, feeling she more or less earned that, she flatly refused to take any money.

"For God's sake, be reasonable, can't you, baby? You can't live with no cash at all."

"Maybe not, but I won't take it from you."

"Why in hell not when I want to give it to you?"

"I haven't earned it."

"It's my money. Can't I do what I please with it?"

Psyche's face and voice were equally implacable. "Not this time."

"How are you going to buy anything for yourself?"

"I don't know. I'll figure it out."

Tossing a mangled cigarette into an enormous brass ash-tray, Bel tried coaxing. "Take a little something, just to go on with. To please me."

"Bel—I can't. Don't you see that?"

"I see that you won't," Bel told her crossly.

Very occasionally, when she was either excited or upset, or both, Psyche lost her careful grip on the mode of speech Nick had taught her. Now, shaking her shining hair back from her face with a sharp toss of her head, she said fiercely, "Leave me be, can't you, Bel! I wouldn't have nothin' if I was just to take, take, take!"

It was Psyche who eventually solved the impasse, and in a manner which at first shocked Bel, so different were the standards she applied to Psyche from those which she set up for herself and her girls.

On an afternoon a few days later Psyche came down from the little room which she could not think of as having ever belonged to anyone else, and found Monique dancing alone in the living-room. When Monique had nothing else to do, she always danced. Her small, vivacious face wiped clean for the moment of any expression, her eyes opaque, she would become one with the music of the never silent radio. But in spite of, perhaps even because of, the immobility of her face, tomtoms beat in the heart of an unknown jungle when Monique danced.

Responding to rhythms more primitive than she knew, Psyche said involuntarily, "How I wish I could do that!"

Monique seemed scarcely aware of her presence, and she did not break her step. "*Quoi?* The rumba?"

"Any of it."

"*Vous ne pouvez pas danser? Mais, c'est incroyable! Venez ici, et je vous montrerai comment le faire.* Come on, honey, I'll give you a lesson *tout de suite.* Why, there should be a law against letting girls grow up in such ignorance. *Maintenant, faîtes comme moi, mais lentement au commencement.* Do just as I do, but take it easy at first."

Talking to Monique was like listening to the introductory music of a song: you waited patiently for the words, and then you knew where you were. It might have been annoying. For some reason it was not.

It was the first of many casual lessons, and at the end of it Monique said, "*Bien*, you're going to be good, honey. Damn good. *Et maintenant, regardez ce que j'ai acheté aujourd'hui.* Look what I bought with the little nest egg I found on the poker table last night. *C'est beau, n'est-ce-pas?*"

Psyche, looking at the very beautiful gold bracelet on Monique's slender arm, said thoughtfully, "It's lovely. You mean you won enough in one night to buy something like that?"

"*Oui, et pourquoi non?* The boys don't play for chicken feed, you know."

Psyche was on easy terms with all "the boys", and it was a tribute both to her and to Bel that all but one of them had left her strictly alone. The one who had attempted to overstep his privileges had done so only once. Bel had seen to that.

Wandering around in the earlier part of most evenings, emptying ash-trays, refilling glasses, and laughing at well-meant pleasantries, Psyche had enjoyed the party atmosphere without ever really becoming a part of it. Now, after thinking it over carefully, she could see no reason why she should not join in the principal public activity indulged in at Bel's place, and some very good reasons why she should.

She spoke to Bel after dinner that night.

Bel was in her room struggling into a black satin dress that allowed very little leeway for anything other than existing in it. "That you, baby? Here, help me get into this damn thing, will you?"

"You should either have this dress let out, or have your foundation taken in," Psyche remarked frankly. "Bel, will you do me a favour? Lend me ten dollars."

Bel's face, a somewhat overblown rose, emerged from the neck of her dress. "That's more like it, baby. You're almost talking sense now. But I'm not lending it. I'm giving it."

Psyche hesitated momentarily, and then gave in. "All right. Thank you very much, Bel."

Something in her manner caused Bel to look at her more closely. "What are you aiming to do with this ten bucks, baby? Not that I wouldn't give you a hundred and mind my own business, if that was the way you wanted it."

"I'm going to get into the game to-night, if it's all the same to you."

"You're kidding me!"

"No."

"But it wouldn't be proper!" Bel said, and saw nothing laughable in what she was saying.

Psyche had been smiling, but she became suddenly serious. "Look, Bel, don't let's be silly about this. I'm not a child, you know."

"Ladies don't play poker," Bel said stubbornly.

"For heaven's sake, Bel, I'm not a lady either!"

All the hardness, the shrewd smart veneer of a woman who had fought her way up out of the gutter, seemed to drain away from Bel's face, leaving her pretty features soft and vulnerable. "You were meant to be a lady, baby, and though maybe you don't know it, in lots of ways you are one now. I was never meant to be any better than I am, but you've got class, and you're going to have something better. Just how it will come, I don't know, but it will. If you got into any kind of trouble through me, I'd want to go out and cut my own throat."

Though really touched, Psyche was not to be deflected from her purpose. "I won't get into any trouble, I promise you," she said quietly. "After all, there isn't so much difference between playing and watching the others play. I'm there, in either case."

"You'll just lose your money."

"If I do, then that settles it. I won't play again."

Psyche suspected, and quite rightly, that Bel gave in at this juncture only because she was positive that the money would be lost very quickly.

The boys were beginning to arrive when Psyche went up to her room to change into her one dress. A blue cotton, it was not particularly suitable for a late November evening, but she knew that in it she looked even younger than her nineteen years.

Naturally straightforward, she nevertheless saw nothing un-ethical in using every weapon at her command when entering lists of this kind. She looked on poker as a game of wits, and felt that anyone foolish enough to risk his money in such a way deserved to lose it. This was a point of view she never changed throughout her lifetime.

When she slipped into an empty chair next to Joe, there were already six in the game, May and five men.

May, flowing forth from blue satin, supporting a weight of jewellery that it must have been a task to carry around, stared at her with pale blue eyes wide and astonished. "Hon, are you sure you know what you're doing?"

Psyche looked around with a hesitant smile. "Does anybody mind? It looks like such fun."

It was exactly the right approach. The men were all over forty, and hard-headed business men, but no girl as young and fresh as Psyche appeared just then could have failed to appeal to their more sentimental side. With wicked satisfaction she saw winks exchanged, and smiles grow paternal. It would not last long, she knew, this advantage she had seized, for these men were not like Butch and his cronies. Still, it should last just long enough for her to get a reasonable stake. After that, she was more than prepared to meet them on even terms.

"You know how to play, baby?" Joe asked doubtfully.

"Oh, yes." While telling the exact truth, Psyche managed to make it appear that she probably did not know.

May, who had as keen a nose for money as she had for French perfume, and who hated to see anyone wilfully throw it away, was genuinely upset. "You'll be just giving your candy away, hon. Whyn't you watch instead?"

"But I would like to play—so much."

"Well, I guess it's your funeral, hon, but I sure hate to see you do it."

Trustingly, Psyche looked from one face to another. "I don't have to lose, do I? I might win, mightn't I?"

"How much dough have you got, honey?" Joe asked gruffly.

"Ten dollars."

It was a pittance, compared with the sums that crossed that table every night of the week, as Psyche well knew. But if she had started with fifty, or even twenty-five, she would not have won their sympathy or nearly as much of their money.

It was two hours before they really began to credit what was being done to them, and by then Psyche had won more than three hundred dollars. Cashing in her chips from time to time so that she never had too obvious a stack in front of her, her tactics were perfect from start to finish. In addition to this, she played in phenomenal luck. It was her luck that helped to blind them.

"The girlie's sure got beginner's luck," they told one another.

It was Joe who first recognized her for the expert she was. "I thought you said you couldn't play this game, honey?" he said softly.

Psyche's smile was no longer *jeune fille*. "On the contrary. I said I could."

"And you can."

"I can," Psyche told him calmly. "You raising me, Joe, or seeing?"

They were not angry, any of them. Instead, they took it as a wonderful joke on themselves, as Psyche had hoped they would.

"That's a smart little cookie, that kid of yours, Bel," they said, chuckling.

"She's a good kid, too, and don't you go forgetting it," Bel told them defensively. Far from pleased with the result of the experiment, it was some time before she could accustom herself to the idea of seeing Psyche at the poker table nearly every evening. Her definition of a "nice girl" was even more rigid than had been Mag's conception of a "bad girl".

A cold wind was rattling bare branches in the park, and grey skies were heavy with a promise of snow soon to come, when Psyche asked Bel if she would help her to buy some warmer clothes.

"I'm used to the little shops now," she told her, "but in a department store, buying something like a coat, I wouldn't know quite what to do."

Bel was only too glad to go with her, and for the occasion wore her best black coat, a small black hat with a two-foot red quill in it, and a pair of colossal silver fox furs. In a red purse that could have passed for a small suitcase she put some extra money to assist with purchases she suspected would stagger Psyche by their cost. She was quite right in thinking that Psyche was ignorant of the price of good clothes, but she had erred in another direction.

They had already threaded their way through the main floor aisles of the big store to which she had chosen to go, and were waiting for the elevator, when she asked casually, "How are you fixed for money, baby?"

"I have thirteen hundred dollars," Psyche replied without hesitation.

Bel almost fainted. "Come again!" she gasped.

Psyche repeated what she had said. It had taken her a long time to count it all, but she had done so twice, and was quite sure of the amount.

"My God!" Bel whispered. "And to think that I worry about the girls keeping too much cash in the place. Have you won all that from the boys?"

"I must have. It hasn't come from anywhere else."

Recovering from the initial shock, Bel looked at her with mingled respect and exasperation. "You sure know what you're doing, don't you, baby? Well, when we're through here, you're going to put what you've got left in a bank. Didn't you ever think of what the cops would say if they found all that dough in your room?"

"No," Psyche said slowly. "No, I didn't." It was the kind of thing she did not think about if she could help it. In so far as was possible she kept her eyes shut to the interpretation that the law would undoubtedly read into her presence at Bel's place.

Although refusing to look at the practical hazards of her position, she had begun to worry more and more about the effect that the kind of life she was leading might have on her as a person. The gambling in the evenings, the idle thread of gossip that ran through the days as the girls drifted in and out, the smiling don't-give-a-damn cynicism that characterized all of them but Kathie

—these things would be bound to leave their mark on her if she stayed with them too long.

Abruptly, waiting for an elevator that was slow in coming, she saw that she could not, must not let herself be stamped in a manner that she knew instinctively was all wrong for her. Hers was a tough, combative spirit, but she was not hard. If she were to become even a little hard, to lose sight even briefly of the vague goal toward which she had been striving for so long, she would be lost, would have taken a turning from which there was no going back. And, as she stepped into the crowded elevator after Bel, she came to two lightning decisions: she would play no more poker with the boys, and she would leave Bel's place as soon after Christmas as she could. Bel had had some justification for being disturbed about her. Bel had been right, and she had been wrong.

Thank God, she thought to herself, thank God for whatever it is that makes me see these things in time.

The discreetly dressed saleswoman, who came across a discreet beige carpet towards Psyche and Bel, noticed Psyche first and for a moment thought she recognized her. But she had only waited on Sharon once, and that some months earlier, so the memory was not clear, and, when she took a good look at Bel, vanished entirely before a train of thought that led anywhere but back to Sharon.

"Are you being waited on?"

"No, just waiting," Bel replied pointedly.

There were occasions when this particular saleswoman regretted the polite servility that her job imposed upon her. "What may I show you?"

"Coat, hat, suit, wool dresses, size fourteen," Bel said succinctly.

"We don't usually show hats in this department, but if you wish one to go with a coat or suit it can be arranged. Take a seat, please, while I see what we have."

Psyche, sitting down with Bel on a beige velvet loveseat, looked around at floor-length mirrors, subdued lighting, and artificial flowers almost more beautiful than the real thing, and was impressed. "It's nice, isn't it, Bel?"

"A real sucker's layout," said Bel, tapping a cigarette on a red thumbnail before lighting it. "But they've got good things if you know how to choose them."

The saleswoman came back with a bright blue fitted coat, and a small blue hat garnished with pink feathers. Psyche, putting these on, saw in the mirror a self she had never seen before, and hesitated between being very pleased and equally displeased. The pink feathers, lying close to her cheek, made her clear skin appear slightly flushed, and the blue accentuated the rich gold of her hair.

She turned toward Bel. "What do you think?"

"What do you?"

"I—I don't know. They're a little——"

"They're more than a little, baby," Bel said shortly, and addressed the saleswoman. "Do you think the kid looks good in those duds?"

"Well, madam, I——"

"Be your age, sister."

"I was only trying to dress her to please you, madam," the saleswoman replied stiffly.

"Then you're doing a bum job of it," returned Bel equably. "Just forget about me. Take a good look at the kid, and start all over again. Pretend she lives on the hill, and is going to say 'Charge it!' and maybe you'll do better."

An hour later Psyche was in possession of a new wardrobe, and very happy with the choices they had made, all of them good, all of them plain.

"The plainer it is, the more they'll soak you for it," Bel told her while the saleswoman was making up the bill, "but you'll get style for your dough."

"The feathers were pretty, though weren't they, Bel?" Psyche asked, a little wistfully.

"Real pretty. They would have looked just fine on May."

Psyche suddenly felt no regret, only gratitude to Bel for having recognized clearly what she herself had merely sensed. Impulsively she put her arm around Bel's plump shoulders, and gave her a quick hug. "How and where did you learn to be so wise, Bel?"

Bel never forgot that spontaneous, affectionate gesture. It was as if her own illegitimate but passionately loved child had, instead of dying of slow starvation, grown up to find her, in some ways at least, more than adequate. "Who, me?" she said, reddening. "I'm just a dope."

"No, Bel, you're not. And you'll be glad to know that I'm not going to play cards with the boys any more."

Having voiced her decision, it became final, and that evening, instead of sitting in the bright, hot living-room, with a cigarette between her lips and a mounting stack of coloured chips in front of her, she went for the first of the long walks that were to become a habit with her.

Wrapped in the fleecy warmth of the loose grey coat she had bought that day, she walked down the corridor toward the living-room in time to hear a man's voice ask, "Where's the girlie to-night?"

For an instant it was as if time had rolled back, and she heard again Butch's deep, bull-like roar, "Where's my little rabbit's foot?"

Her eyes smarting with unexpected tears, she turned and, contrary to her original intention, sought the back stairs and the rarely used back entry. Mag had told her not to write for six months, and when she did, to enclose no return address. The six months were not quite up, but she knew as she came out into the crisp, cold night air, that she would write before going to bed. There would be no reply, but that would not matter. Her own letter would in itself be a small link forged with a past which seemed destined to be cut away from her, segment by segment, leaving her with nothing but the insufficient comfort of an immediate present.

Psyche liked walking, as she liked any kind of physical movement in which there was a definite rhythm, but it is doubtful if she would have walked as often or as far as she did during that winter had she not found a purpose in so doing.

Striking northward, unconsciously rejecting the dingy neighbourhood to the south, she noticed almost at once how carelessly some people exposed their private lives to the passer-by. Many of the houses were curtained against intrusion, all evidence of activity within reduced to opaque squares of light; but an almost equal number displayed small theatre sets without sound track, flashing on the sight as one drew level with them, and extinguished by one's own forward progress.

Psyche's interest in these often static, often unoccupied stages was at first no more than the casual interest of anyone whose eye is drawn out of darkness into light. But after a time, with nothing else to think about, she began to speculate about the people inhabiting the houses into which she was allowed this partial admittance. Putting together what clues she could, she guessed at professions and hobbies, at degrees of success and the lack of it, at family content and discontent. There was no exact moment at which she added the question that was to turn this pastime from an idle amusement into an absorbing pursuit. She simply found herself thinking, "Would I fit in here? Is this a place where I would feel I belonged?"

It was a short step from there to a definite and purposeful search for a scene into which she felt she could move without the necessity for change or confession on either side. Merging her ideas of what she herself wanted to be with a wishfully perfect projection of her original home, she rejected one setting after another. And as these rejections mounted, so did the excitement that drew her on toward the next possibility, and the next.

It was late when she came back to Bel's place on that first evening, but as the winter progressed and she searched further afield, there were times when she did not return until after midnight.

Bel, ignorant of the purpose behind these long, solitary walks, sensed that somehow, in a way she could not fathom, they were part of a drawing away which, although she saw it as inevitable, nevertheless hurt her.

Watching for Psyche's return, she would greet her, and ask almost anxiously, "Everything okay, baby?"

And Psyche, perhaps shaking glistening particles of snow from her glistening hair, would reply quietly, "Yes, Bel, everything's okay."

Then, after talking with the boys for a few minutes, she would go up to her room to sleep and dream of a life as far removed from the life at Bel's as any life could be.

4

Psyche stayed on at Bel's throughout that winter as a result of a conference at which she herself was not present.

Her own intention to leave unweakened, she had had several unproductive talks with Bel on the subject of what she could, or should, do, before the Sunday morning after Christmas when Bel sought the advice—for what it might be worth—of the girls.

Sunday morning, toward noon, always found all of them, in various degrees of dress and undress, sitting around the living-room drinking coffee, Kathie, in tailored shirt and slacks, would have been up for some hours correcting homework and laying out schedules for the coming school week. May, in a pink or a blue satin négligé, would have only just got out of bed. The others might or might not have been up earlier. Bel, who at one time had slept as late as any of them, had fallen into the habit of break-fasting with Psyche at ten, after which Psyche would go down-stairs to spend the balance of the morning with the old lady.

"The kid wants to get herself a job," Bel told them without preface.

"She must be nuts," May remarked, yawning.

"What kind of a job?" Kathie asked curiously.

"That's the trouble," Bel said, "she doesn't know, and no more do I. I thought maybe some of you girls might have an idea or two, seeing you all work at something."

Monique, having searched the radio dial for dance music, and finding none, was making the best of a bad job by jerking her hips in time to a hymn. "*Elle sait déjà bien danser.* With some more lessons maybe she could be an instructress."

Bel snorted. "The kid's got brains as well as feet. She can do better than that."

"I like that! *J'ai aussi——*"

"We're not talking about you, hon," May put in pacifically. May liked peace. She also liked the small jewelled hand mirror in which she was regarding herself. That the jewels were synthetic, she had yet to discover, and for the moment both the donor and his gift were enjoying her highest regard.

Ruth and her sister Joan giggled, for no apparent reason.

"She could look for a job in a store, maybe," Ruth said.

"And where would that get her?" Violet asked acidly. "At best into a two-room hole in a wall filled with squalling brats and a man without enough take-home pay to bury himself decently."

"She wouldn't get anywhere," Kathie said slowly. "She's never been taught any arithmetic. She couldn't handle the money end of a job like that."

"She does all the shopping," Bel reminded her.

"When you're buying, people will wait. When you're selling—they won't," Kathie replied. "It takes her several minutes to add two and two and arrive at a satisfactory four."

"She's bright. She could learn," Bel persisted.

Kathie got up and walked restlessly over to the window. "You have to learn first. That is the difficulty, Bel."

"Maybe she could go to school a while," Joan put in brightly.

It was Kathie's turn to snort. "And sit in the eighth grade—if she could qualify for it—with little children! Don't be a fool."

Violet looked at no one in particular, and her blank amethyst eyes were as unrevealing as always. "She hasn't really got a chance. When you're down, you're down, and you don't ever get up again. You don't get any second chance."

Monique's shrug was expressive. "Speak for yourself, *chèrie. Moi*—I'm going places."

May yawned, but she was not bored. She had been thinking. "With her looks, and being—well, you know—not really experienced, as you might say, I could probably get her as nice a set-up as a girl could want. Place of her own, real good address, and just the one guy to put up with. Real respectable——"

Bel turned on her like a she-wolf. "You don't know what respectable is! You keep any ideas like that to yourself, you hear me?"

May's good humour remained undisturbed. "Just a suggestion," she said lazily, and yawned again.

They went on discussing the problem for some time, but no matter what they said they always ended up against the same stumbling block. Psyche was not only untrained, but also basically untaught in any way which could be of practical use to her.

Bel's worried frown deepened. "She's got to learn things, things in books, that's the hell of it. She just don't fit in anywhere, the way she is. The trouble is the kid was meant to be a lady. Not one of your la-li-dah fakes that are only skin-deep, but a real honest-to-God lady. The kind that goes to church in her second-best duds, and doesn't kick a girl when she's down."

Kathie, who had said nothing for a time, turned abruptly from the window, and spoke to Bel as if they two were alone in the room. "This means a lot to you, doesn't it, Bel?"

"Yeah. It does."

"Does she want to learn?"

"She's crazy to."

"If that's the case, I'll teach her," Kathie said evenly. "If she's prepared to work, and work like the devil, I can teach her enough in four or five months that she will have a chance to make something of herself. Whether she does or not will be up to her."

That evening after supper Kathie went up to Psyche's room, a thing she had never done before, and never did again.

Sitting down on the edge of the bed, she let her glance travel around the room. Her thin face pensive, her eyes shadowed, she remarked absently, "This was my room when I first came here. I suppose you know that. It hasn't changed. Five years—five years. Dear God, is it possible?"

Psyche was not always at ease with Kathie. Her brooding expression, lit by the sometimes shocking brilliance of her eyes, and her lovely unhappy mouth, were compelling, but disturbingly so. Kathie's was a face that, while refusing sympathy, seemed overcast by foreknowledge of something so dreadful that one looked away for fear one might see it as clearly as she so evidently did herself.

Unable to divine the reason behind this unexpected visit, Psyche did not know quite what to say. "Did you hang 'The Blue Boy' there?" she asked, remaining on her feet.

A glimmer of real interest showed in Kathie's face. "Yes. Who told you what it was?"

"Nobody. I knew. I mean I recognized it, naturally."

"It doesn't seem very natural to me, all things considered. How did you know?"

"Nick taught me about pictures."

"Nick?"

"He is an artist," Psyche said quietly. "I lived with him for——"

Kathie interrupted her. "I'm not asking for any girlish confidences. Look, sit down, for heaven's sake, and relax. Find yourself a cigarette and give me one. I'm going to be here for some time. Now, how much do you know about paintings?"

Seating herself on the window-seat, a cigarette in her hand, Psyche regained her self-assurance. Smiling, she said, "It would take me several days to answer that question."

"You think you know so much?"

"I know I do."

"Name half a dozen of the Renaissance painters, and give me some of their principal works."

"I can, but why should I?" Psyche asked.

Kathie pushed a curtain of dark hair back from her forehead. It was an impatient gesture. "I'm here to help you. I've been talking to Bel. I want to know what kind of material I have to work with."

Grasping the unspoken implication, Psyche's defensiveness dropped away from her at once. "You mean—you'll teach me?"

"Of course. Why do you think I'm here?"

"I didn't know. You didn't say."

"Sorry, I thought Bel would have told you. She says you want to learn. Do you?"

And Psyche, although she was not aware of it, answered with the exact words she had chosen when answering a similar question put to her years earlier by a man whose gift of a small dictionary she still used and prized. "More than anything else in the world."

The pattern of their days established itself very quickly.

Kathie was a hard taskmaster, and Psyche had to rise at six in order to satisfy the increasing pressure of her demands and at the same time do as much for Bel as she had previously done. She had also to fit in two luxuries that she could not bring herself to give up—her walks in the late evening, and the hours she spent with a courageous old lady who never failed to treat her daily visits as unplanned and delightful surprises.

Handling the marketing and housework she had assumed with an ever greater efficiency, she spent less and less time actually in Bel's place, passing most of each day downstairs, either in the apartment that echoed to the whispers of a past magnificence, or in Kathie's large back room.

In spite of its size, and its pleasant furnishings, by day Kathie's room was not nearly as attractive as her own. For, when the curtains were open, one saw a weedy back yard, walled in by a broken board fence, and given over to garbage cans and scabrous cats. But she found she could work in this room with a far greater degree of concentration than she could in the room under the eaves. Even when Kathie was not there, some lingering trace of her presence remained to encourage her when she became depressed, to spur her on when she was tired. For Kathie, very soon recognizing in Psyche a pupil to complement her own so far more or less wasted talents as a teacher, drove them both to the limit of their endurance.

Although she often told Psyche to relax, she never did herself.

For a time she would sit beside her at the desk in front of the window; then she would get up and pace the room, pausing to lean over her shoulder and mark the work with sharp, strong pencil strokes.

Arithmetic and spelling were the only two specific subjects, and for the most part Psyche laboured over them alone. "It's a pity," Kathie remarked, "that so much of your time and any of mine should be wasted on anything so elementary, but these are gaps that must be filled in."

On the first afternoon that Psyche spent with her, a stormy Saturday afternoon with heavy snow obliterating the dismal view, Kathie outlined briefly her general approach to the task she had undertaken. "I agree with you that the sooner you leave this house the better, and so our time together will be short. I cannot teach you individual facts as such. I don't even want to. But I can and will teach you how to think, how to reason clearly. When I am finished with you, you may not know Archimedes' Principle, the date of the Spanish Armada, or who invented the telephone. What you will know is how to find these things out for yourself, how to place them in relation to the rest of man's development and history, and how to retain the knowledge thus gained if you find it of sufficient interest to do so. In short, you will be in a position to make full use of your greatest gift—your mind. I've watched you, and you think before you speak, always. You are thinking of the words you will employ as much as of the sense of what you are going to say, aren't you?"

"Yes. How did you know that? Do I make mistakes?"

"Rarely, if ever. That is, in part, how I knew. Chiefly it is because you think quickly, and it would be more natural for you to speak quickly. As a matter of purely academic interest, and I use the word in its true sense, how long did you stay with this artist you mentioned?"

"Four months, more or less."

"Between you, you achieved a miracle," Kathie commented. "But it isn't good enough. You are going to have to concentrate on the English language more than anything else. Words are your tools. They must not only be infinite in number, but as brightly burnished as any blade ever forged in Damascus. You don't know where Damascus is, do you? Well, I am not going to tell you. Later you can look it up for yourself, and copy out those things about it that you find most interesting. To-morrow we will discuss the maturity—or lack of it—of what you have written. You don't know what infinite means, do you? Well, that you will learn at once."

When she saw Psyche's first piece of written work, she groaned. "My God! Do I have to teach you how to write, too!"

She taught her a beautiful copper-plate. Much later Psyche learned that such writing was taught exclusively in private schools, and another stone of regret was laid on the cairn of sorrow that by then stood above her memories of Kathie.

Her life now full to overflowing, Psyche became a confirmed clock-watcher. Joe had given her a small gold watch at Christmas, and she wondered how she had ever lived without one. She was grateful to him during every minute that it ticked off during days that never seemed quite long enough. Bel would have clawed his eyes out if he had given so much as a dead geranium to any of the other girls, but she was immediately pleased that he should have done this for Psyche. It was a palpably seal of approval on what she herself had done, and was doing.

"That's real nice of you, Joe," she had said, when he presented it. "Put it on, baby. It's real pretty on her, isn't it, Joe?"

Although Kathie, and to a lesser extent the old lady, were contributing toward the consummation of the dream Psyche pursued, it was to Bel that she continued to give her greatest measure of affection. And as the winter wore on she began to worry about Bel as much as Bel worried about her. To live forever on the alert, forever in danger of having one's livelihood taken from one, seemed terrible, regardless of how that livelihood was obtained. Certainly it did not seem right for anyone with a heart as warm and generous as Bel's.

"Bel," she said one day, "aren't you afraid sometimes?"

"Afraid of what, baby?"

"Oh, afraid you'll make a mistake. That something will happen."

Bel, looking sombrely down on a street where steady rain was turning the last of the winter's snow to slush, said flatly, "Something may happen, baby, but if it does it won't be my fault. I don't make mistakes. Only once. I did the wrong thing the day I let Joe into the dump."

Psyche was completely taken aback. "But Joe's the only one with you, Bel! I thought you liked him a lot."

"I do, baby. I do. That's where I make the mistake. It don't pay for a dame like me to get too soft about any one guy. It makes you think too much. Too damned much."

"There isn't any way——" Psyche began hesitantly.

"None, baby. No way at all. Go pour me a drink, will you, there's a good girl. This weather sure gives me the pip."

When Psyche came back to the living-room with Bel's rye and water, it was to find the curtains pulled, the lamps lit, and Bel herself as bright and gay as her red dress.

"That's better, isn't it? When it's lousy outside, you can always make your own weather, can't you? Tell me, baby, are you still learning as fast as you want?"

Psyche smiled, and made a small grimace. "Even faster!"

It was true. Kathie was forcing the pace as if each day might be their last. Spending very little time on anything else, she now carried the lessons with Psyche over into the evenings, something she had not done previously.

One evening, after they had picked up and closed the books that were scattered half across the room, Kathie paused midway between desk and door. Psyche, looking at her, realized that she was even thinner than she had been, and that her strained face was more haunted than ever.

"Kathie," she said softly. "Kathie, you're doing too much for me. You're making yourself sick."

"It's the only worth-while thing I do. It's all I've got left," Kathie replied harshly. Then, her voice tight and unnatural, she said, "If you'll give up that damned walking for one night, I—I'll stay down here, and we can go on."

Psyche rubbed the back of a slender hand across her aching eyes. "It wouldn't be any good. I can't think straight any longer."

"All right," Kathie told her quietly. "Good night." And turning she went swiftly to the door.

Psyche's coat lay across the bed, but she did not at once make any move toward it. Leaning against the edge of the desk, she stared at her reflection in the long mirror above Kathie's bare-topped maple dressing-table. Seeing herself more objectively than she usually did, she saw that she had changed in appearance. The planes of her face were sharper than they had been, and she had lost the golden tan which had been her skin colour summer and winter at a shack where the brilliance of sunlight on snow had been as strong as that of the midsummer sun. But the change went deeper than that. The blue eyes looking back at her were more thoughtful than they had been, the clear-cut mouth was firmer, and there was something faintly questioning in the lift of the dark eyebrows. I am not as pretty as I was, she thought dispassionately, but I am more me—and I am glad. Thinking this, she remembered a time when she had been mortally afraid of losing herself in a mirror, and smiled at the child she had once been.

Still smiling, she rose, put on her coat, and went out.

Spring was late in coming that year, and it was not until the end of April that crocuses bloomed in the park, and the naked skeletons of the trees began to veil themselves in delicate cobwebs of soft green. But, if it was late, when it did come it was benign, the lengthening days warm and sunny. The birds came back from the south, flock after flock, to mingle with sparrows that knew no other compulsion than a year-round search for bread crumbs on a familiar asphalt heath. The loungers reappeared on the park benches. The Lithuanians emerged from a crowded hibernation. And Bel resumed her regal, late-afternoon sorties to the park.

Psyche, made lazy by the season, by a gentle breeze and golden sunlight, deserted her books one day in favour of strolling with Bel and sitting with her once again on, as it happened, the same park bench where she had met her some eight months earlier.

"It doesn't seem long, does it, baby?"

"No, it doesn't." Not long in time, certainly, but in every other way a small lifetime. A little lifetime in which she had acquired friends, confidence in herself, some money, and, above all, the varied knowledge that would make it henceforth possible for her to at least support herself.

Watching a small boy follow a pigeon across the gravel path onto fresh green grass, she knew, contrary to what anyone else might think, that her meeting with Bel was one of the most fortunate encounters of her life, past, present, or future. Never, as long as she lived, would she ever deny Bel.

She would have liked to.say this, but it was not possible. It came too close to something that they had never talked about in so many words, she and Bel.

Her eyes still following a perplexed little boy who was discovering that he could not narrow the distance between himself and a pigeon apparently unaware of his existence, she asked idly, "Who goes into the gallery on the other side of the park, Bel?"

"Folks who are interested in pictures, I guess," Bel replied indifferently.

"I wish I belonged."

"What do you mean, baby?"

"I wish I were a member, or whatever you have to be to get in."

"Far as I know, all you have to do is pay your way."

Psyche's attention no longer wandered. "You mean anyone can go in there? You and me, for example?"

"Far as I know."

Psyche was on her feet in one swift, graceful movement. "Come on, Bel, we're going to go and find out, right now."

"Who, me? Have a heart, baby! I'm not a great one for art."

"Come on," Psyche said firmly. "I'm not going alone. Bel, think of it, paintings! Perhaps I'll see something I know, something I saw in one of Nick's books."

In the face of her vivid excitement, Bel ceased to resist, but she made no secret of her reluctance. "I don't belong in that type place," she said, straightening her brief skirt as she rose, and taking a firmer grip on her capacious handbag.

They were alone as they mounted a short flight of stone steps to revolving glass doors.

"Maybe it's closed," Bel remarked hopefully.

Psyche, looking at a framed notice beside the doors, said, "No, it will be open for another hour. It's the middle of the week, and late in the day, that's all."

Bel, exploring the depths of her handbag for a change purse as they went through the turnstile inside, did not look up until they were approaching the Sculpture Court, a sunken square lit from above by a single enormous skylight. When she did look, all she could do was stare in stunned disbelief, her coat a brilliant splash of colour against the austerity of tall pillars, marble floors, and plaster and bronze figures cast in a fluid but everlasting immobility. An opulent scarlet statue, momentarily as motionless as those others on which she gazed, she scarcely seemed to breathe.

Then, expelling a long breath, she said in a hushed voice, "Well —call me a dirty name! And they'll throw a girl into the clink for showing her navel at fifty paces."

Psyche, who had moved on toward the arched entrance to a long gallery, said, over her shoulder, "Exhibition of Contemporary Art. Bel, what exactly does contemporary mean?"

"Search me," Bel replied, but her answer was automatic. Turning, she walked back to the attendant near the door. "Tell me, Mac, do they let kids into this joint?"

"Yes, madam, of course. And on Saturday mornings there are classes which——"

But Bel was no longer listening. Staring blankly out across the Sculpture Court, she was muttering, "It don't make sense. It just don't make sense."

Psyche's call was soft, but it echoed in the empty vastness of the great entrance hall. "Bel, we haven't much time!"

Catching up with her, Bel followed her in frowning silence.

The gallery which Psyche had chosen to start with was a large one, and Bel, after looking, for the most part with open disapproval, at a few of the pictures, retired to a couch in the middle of the room. Failing to see an ash-tray, she sat back with her hands in her lap, her lips compressed as primly as those of any country school-teacher exposed against her will to a burlesque show. "Little kids. Little innocent kids. It don't make sense."

Psyche, meanwhile, utterly engrossed, moved slowly from one

canvas to another, missing nothing of brush stroke, colour, or composition. All that Nick had let fall in the course of his many monologues came back to her, and his crisp, ironic voice cut so clearly across her memory she almost expected to find him standing beside her. If she had, she knew she would have been unreservedly glad to see him, for she no longer thought of him as anything other than an artist. If she dreamed at all, it was not of Nick.

"Why haven't I come here before?" she wondered. "Why was I so long in discovering this place? I must come again with Kathie." And, thinking this, she could not know that it would be a long time before she came back, and that she would never come with Kathie.

Reaching the end of the wall she had been following, she hesitated between circling the gallery in which she was, and moving on through another arch into the next. Looking at her watch, realizing that closing time would make it impossible for her to see much more that day, she decided to take a quick look into the room beyond.

She saw the *Venus* immediately. With an entire wall to itself, individually lit, it would have been impossible to miss it.

'Bel——" she gasped, and this time her voice was high and clear. "Bel—look! There's me!"

The sharp tap of Bel's high heels on the marble floor was the rapid tattoo of soldiery called to arms. Arriving in the second gallery, she had no need to ask questions. *The American Venus*, aloof and beautiful, was in herself a wordless answer to any question she might have posed.

Colour suffusing her cheeks, dimming bright patches of rouge, she said in a tight voice, "The dirty louse! Why the hell couldn't he have had the decency to be satisfied with making love to you!"

"That was only once," Psyche told her, her eyes fixed on the painting.

Bel stared at her. "What do you mean, baby? You said you stayed at that studio place four months."

"Yes."

"Then I didn't hear you right, did I?"

"Yes, Bel, you did, but I'm not asking you to believe me."

Bel's eyes swung from the lightly clad Venus to Psyche's face. She was more confused than she would admit even to herself, but on one point there could be neither doubt nor confusion. "I believe you, baby. It beats me, but, so help me, I believe you. I always said you were a good kid, right from the beginning. You've learned the hard way, haven't you, baby? That punk must have meant a lot to you for you to have said yes and no like that. But at least you learned." She sighed, scarcely aware of the fact that she did so, so she added, "Me—I guess I was just too dumb to learn."

"Don't say things like that about yourself, Bel."

"I don't often. To be honest with you, baby, I don't even think them. But I'm certainly too damn dumb to understand this place. Let's get out of here. It gives me the creeps."

"Just a second. This painting of Nick's. It's really terribly good, isn't it? Compared with all the others—well, you just can't compare it, can you?"

There was no reply. Looking around, she saw Bel walking away down a long perspective of arches, her back uncompromisingly stiff and straight. Watching her for a moment without moving, Psyche's lips parted in a ghost of a smile that had something protective, almost maternal in it. Then, with a last glance at the *Venus*, she ran lightly, silently after the receding figure in scarlet.

Sharon sat at the grand piano idly playing selections from pieces she had once known well. She was not a good player, and was aware of it, but she had been good enough in another incarnation to play the Lord's Prayer each night before a nursery door was shut, to play it, and sing it in a husky, liquid voice. Against her volition, she found her fingers searching for the opening chords, and it was with relief that she heard the telephone breaking across a spell she had no real wish to weave.

The kitchen door opened as she reached the hall. "I'll take it myself," she told the maid, her hand already on the receiver.

"Hello? . . . Hannah, how nice. How are you?" She was glad it was Hannah. With her acrid wit and ultra-sophistication, Hannah was an ideal antidote for nostalgia.

"You busy, darling? Anyone with you?"

"No, I'm alone," Sharon replied.

"Darling, the most curious thing——" Hannah's usually decisive voice was uncertain, not easy to hear.

"Go on. You're being very intriguing."

"Are you sitting down, Sharon?"

"Of all the silly questions!"

"Are you?"

"Yes. Is this some new kind of game?"

"No. I was at the art gallery this afternoon. I saw an exhibit by this man they're all talking about."

"Well?

"He has one picture I think you should see, darling."

Sharon injected an interest into her voice that she did not feel. "Why? Is it so very good?"

"It's marvellous. He calls it 'The American Venus.' But it isn't its excellence as a painting that will interest you. It's something else."

"Well, go on, Hannah, for heaven's sake!" Sharon said, laughing. "You probably don't realize it, but you're being irritatingly mysterious."

The telephone crackled. Then Hannah's voice came through, shocking in its sudden force and clarity. "Sharon—the Venus—is you."

## 5

DEATH had always been, to Psyche, quite unreal, a fate too far removed from herself and those she knew well to merit either fear or speculation.

This made Kathie's death an emotional shock, apart entirely from the personal loss involved, from which she did not recover easily. For, some time in the early hours of a rainy May morning, Kathie hanged herself.

Alone, in darkness, driven by devils she no longer had the will to fight, she climbed on a chair under the light fixture in her room, tied a black silk dressing-gown cord around her slender neck, and ended for all time the strife that had torn her apart since adolescence.

It was Bel who found her; Bel who, unaided, cut her down in the dismal twilight that passed for daylight at nine that morning, and laid her on a bed that had not been slept in. Bel who, her face leaden and her feet dragging, quietly searched the room for anything that might connect it in any way with her own establishment, and then locked the door and went slowly, heavily upstairs.

It was a Sunday, and she woke and talked with May first. After that, for the moment doggedly shelving the appalling crisis facing her, she climbed a further flight of stairs to Psyche's room.

Psyche, waking to a weight pressing down on her shoulder, tried ineffectively to shake it off while burying her head deeper in her pillow. Then the urgency of that pressure, and the quiet voice accompanying it, cut through the remnants of a deep sleep, and she opened startled blue eyes.

"Bel!" she exclaimed in alarm. "Bel—you've been crying!"

Bel sank to the edge of the bed, and took one of Psyche's hands in both her own. "This is going to be hard to take, baby."

Pulling herself upright, Psyche whispered, "What is it? Tell me quickly, what is it?"

"It's Kathie, baby. She's dead."

"Kathie! Oh, no, no—not Kathie! Oh, no, Bel—not Kathie!"

"It's true, baby. We can't change it."

Driving the knuckles of her free hand into her forehead, Psyche asked, "How did she die?"

As gently as she could, Bel told her.

Listening to words that could not be other than bald, Psyche lived with Kathie through a night that had ended in death; thought her thoughts, suffered her agonies, fought her last losing battle with her, and knew that she herself had unwittingly helped to upset the precarious balance that had been maintained between two ways of life.

Her throat rasped with sobs, she said wildly, "I didn't help her. Bel, I should have helped her! Oh, God—oh, Kathie—oh, what have I done!"

Bel's voice was as sharp as a slap in the face. "Stop that! And pull yourself together! Nobody could have done anything, ever. She was never at peace. She is now."

"But I feel——"

"How do you think *I* feel?"

Staring at Bel's ravaged face through a hot blur of tears, Psyche slowly began to realize what this thing meant to Bel, and with the realization a little of her sense of proportion returned to her. "I'm sorry," she said unevenly. "Forgive me. I—I didn't help her, but I can—I must help you now. Give me a few minutes alone, Bel, and I—I'll be all right."

"There's nothing for you to do, baby," Bel told her gently. "I don't want you mixed up in this."

"But I am in it. You can't keep me out!"

"Take it easy, baby. I've got to go now. Don't come down until you feel like it."

Psyche turned her face away. "A few minutes. Just—a few minutes."

"You're sure you're all right, baby?"

"Yes, Bel, I'm all right. In a few minutes I'll be ready to help you. In a few minutes, Bel."

Bel hesitated at the door. The rigid back, and averted face hidden from her by an uncombed mass of hair, worried her, but she had no choice, she had to go. For her there was no more time for tears, for sentiment of any kind. Later, but not now. Now she must face her responsibility to the living, and she did not know what she was going to do. Deep inside herself she knew she was frightened, but it was knowledge that she would not allow to rise to the surface of her mind. She had come through tight places before, and, she told herself, she'd do it again. The difficulty was that she could not see how.

Going down the stairs, she decided to telephone to Joe at once. Joe could help her to figure out something if anyone could. A projection of Kathie's face, as she had seen it little more than half an hour earlier, seemed to be hung against the drab morning light. Wherever she looked she saw it.

"You've got to get a hold of yourself, Bel," she muttered, and when she went to the telephone she carried a half-tumbler of straight rye.

It was easy to talk to Joe. He had a mind like a steel trap, and did not waste precious time on sympathy.

"We've got to call the doc, Bel," he said when she had finished. "There's no way around that. He's got to see her, and the sooner the better."

"Would he cover for a thing like this, Joe?"

"I don't know. Leave it with me. I'll see him right away, and we'll figure things. Have you talked to the girls yet?"

"May only."

"Yeah, you can count on her. The others still asleep?"

Bel hesitated, and then said slowly, "All but the kid."

"How did she take it?"

"It's hit her hard, Joe."

Joe had been thinking while he talked. "It may be that young kid could do a lot for you now, Bel, if she has the guts."

"She's got them, but I'm not asking her to do a thing. She's going to be kept out of this, Joe."

He had no comment. "I'll be over as soon as I can," he said, and rang off.

Psyche and May were alone in the living-room when he came. Bel, who had been with them until a few minutes before his arrival, had gone to her room to dress.

His heavy face grave, the blue shadows on chin and cheekbones more noticeable than usual, he looked at Psyche, and said, "I want to talk to you, honey, alone."

May, for once shorn of all jewellery, all make-up, her full face oddly innocent, said, "I'll scram."

"Better if the kid and I do the scramming, May. It's Bel I don't want around when I talk with her. We'll be maybe fifteen minutes. Tell Bel the Doc will be here in less than an hour."

Kathie—Psyche thought, as, without a word, she followed the big man down the front stairs and out of the front door. Kathie—Kathie—Kathie. Dear God if there were only something I could do for her even now. Kathie——

They went to the park; a park gentle with the tender green of a spring that was Kathie's last.

"We could have sat in my car round the corner," Joe said. "This is better. Nobody will notice us here."

Psyche did not reply. No reply seemed necessary. Kathie——

Bel's wrong this time, the man thought, glancing sideways at the girl on the bench beside him, assessing a white face in which only the blue eyes seemed alive. She's dead wrong. This kid needs to do something for somebody, for her own sake.

"How good are you at putting on an act, honey?"

This was a direct question. It required an answer. "I don't know."

"Can you lie with a straight face?"

"I don't know."

"Bel helped you when you needed it. Now it's your turn to help her. Will you do it, any way you can?"

"Yes," Psyche said evenly. "Any way I can."

"You'll have to do it in spite of her, which may make it tough. She doesn't want you in this."

"She has no choice."

A heavy hand touched her shoulder briefly, a diamond ring flashing in sunlight which would never warm Kathie again. The clouds were breaking up. It was going to be a nice day. Kathie——

"Well, listen carefully to what I'm going to say. Are you listening, honey?"

"Yes, I'm listening."

He knew she was not, but he was good with people, he understood them. "If you help Bel the way I want you to, you'll be helping Kathie, too," he told her quietly.

"Kathie——" Psyche turned to him with vital, painful eagerness, and did not know that in saying that name aloud she had thrown off the first numbing effects of shock.

Satisfied that he now had her complete attention, he outlined what he wanted her to do. He was a shrewd man, used to dealing with emergencies, and he had seen, almost at once, that there was only one way of saving Bel without taking risks that might put the lot of them, temporarily at least, behind bars.

"We could try to hush this thing up completely. Call it heart attack. It would cost a packet, but it could be done. It's a damn dangerous thing to do, though, and it might come unstuck. If it did, everyone who ever knew that girl would be for it. As I figure it, there's only one other way we can keep the heat off Bel's place. Keep the whole thing clean. Keep that girl's name clean for her."

"Go on," Psyche said impatiently.

"It can be done through you and one other."

"Who?"

"The old lady in the apartment downstairs."

Psyche frowned her disbelief. "But she can't do anything, Joe. Why, she doesn't even know about Bel!"

"She is going to help simply by living where she does, and by being what she is—or was. The doc is on our side. He can satisfy the police because what they'll be interested in is all there for them to see. They will want solid fact. They'll find it. That the girl was unhappy and committed suicide will be enough for them. It won't be enough for the newspapers, and the only way we can keep those bloody newshounds from sniffing out the whole story is to give them something else to sniff at. The old lady is the story they've got to be given, and you, honey, are the only one who could give it to them and stand a chance of getting away with it."

"But I don't see—what story?"

"The old lady's never told you?" He looked genuinely surprised. He then sketched in a background so fabulous it took Psyche's breath away; eventually so disastrous she would have wept if she had had any tears left. He finished by saying, "How many millions Sir James threw away in the last two years before he died, God only knows. Enough to ruin him, anyway. She should have had him shut up, of course. Too much pride, I suppose."

Psyche thought of the quiet, patrician face, the lovely almost blind eyes, and kind mouth. "Or too much love," she said soberly. "What happened to her then?"

"She dropped out of sight. In time she was forgotten. Most people believe she went to Europe and died there. She did go to Europe. She came back seven years ago. That was when she took the place at Bel's. Without the handle nobody recognized her name. You can see what a story it would make, can't you, honey? Any newsman would. All they have to do is go back into their files thirty years or more to find enough material to write a book. Tie those gilt-edged days in with the present set-up, and you've got a front-page sob story with a dozen different angles to it."

"I don't like it, Joe."

"I didn't expect you would. Bel won't either. But we're going to play it like that, just the same."

"They won't need to see her, will they, Joe?" she asked urgently. "It should be enough just to know she's there, shouldn't it?"

"That will be up to you, honey. If you're good enough, if you play it right, you can keep them out of everyone's hair but your own. They'll want pictures, but they can get those on the street without her ever knowing they're doing it."

"And she can't see well enough to read a newspaper," Psyche said slowly. Without further elaboration she saw exactly what he wanted her to do. She was to stand, literally and metaphorically, in front of both Bel and the old lady, shielding the first completely and delivering the second into the hands of the enemy even while attempting to protect her. It would not be easy, but Joe was right—she, because she need not pretend to be anything other than she was, because she had no personal secrets to hide, was the only one who might conceivably put it over.

"You've never met any newsmen, have you, honey? Well, some of them may seem sloppy and not too intelligent, but don't make any mistake, in their own way they're as smart as they come. Each time you tangle with one you'll be playing a pair of deuces against a full house. Your one advantage will be that you know it, and they don't."

Psyche looked down at her sandaled feet, and saw that unconsciously she had been making a pattern in the gravel: a pattern not unlike an angel with wings outspread. Was it her own guardian angel? Or Kathie's? Or no more than a meaningless smear in gravel warmed by a hot spring sun?

Her eyes narrowed, she said thoughtfully, "It will be like a poker game, won't it? If I think of it that way, I can do it."

Joe pulled a long black cigar from his pocket, bit off the end, spat it out, and got to his feet. "We'd better be getting back, honey. The doc should be there by now, and it won't do for me to be around these parts once this thing breaks."

As they left the park, church bells were ringing, a first requiem, it seemed, for Kathie. And it came to Psyche that Bel had said the only really sensible thing that had been said since a sombre dawn that now seemed a long way back in time.

Bel had said, "She was never at peace. She is now."

Kathie——

BEL was not easily persuaded.

"You want me to throw that old dame to the wolves!" she said violently. "I won't do it, Joe."

"Have you any better ideas?"

Bel stared moodily at a row of geraniums, usually in the front windows, now lining the kitchen counter. The geraniums were the all-clear to the boys, the signal that Bel's place was ready to welcome them. May had removed them without prompting. As Joe had said, you could count on May.

Psyche turned a coffee cup, refilled three times, round and round in its saucer. "You've got to think of the girls, too, Bel."

"They'll make out."

"Yeah. In the clink, most likely," May contributed without rancour.

"I won't have the kid mixed up in this," Bel said, as she had already said several times before.

May did not usually smoke at all. This morning she was chain-smoking. "She'll be kind of mixed up when they lock her in."

Bel's head jerked back, and her face, beneath make-up she had applied automatically, was old and haggard. "What do you mean?"

"She'll go in with the rest of us, Bel," May said quietly. "Maybe she'll get loose sooner, but you won't be able to stop them taking her in."

"Is that right, Joe?"

He nodded. "That's right."

"You haven't any choice, Bel," Psyche told her gently. "You really haven't any choice at all. If it works, good. If it doesn't—well, we won't be any worse off, and I will have done something for you and for Kathie. Don't you go on trying to take that away from me."

"Give me a cigarette, somebody," Bel said hoarsely. "Joe, how have you figured it? The other girls will be waking up soon. We better have it all straight before any of them bust in here."

The police arrived just before noon. The doctor came back with them. They accepted his story, that he had been called in toward mid-morning and had himself cut the dead girl down. They talked briefly and politely with an old lady who could tell them nothing. They talked briefly and politely with the owner of the premises who also told them nothing. They talked at slightly greater length but still politely with the owner's niece who, it appeared, had been the only one in the house to know the dead girl at all intimately.

"How long had you been taking these private lessons with her, Miss Moran?"

"Since early in January," Psyche said.

"And you noticed a difference in her behaviour recently?"

"She was highly nervous. Very restless."

"Could you give us any reason for this?"

"No," Psyche replied steadily. "She—she was a very reserved person."

"Would you have known if there was any man?"

For you—Kathie. "There was no man."

They went away quite satisfied that there was nothing further to be learned at the girl's lodgings. Enquiries would be made at the school, but they did not expect to find much there. It was, after all, a very ordinary story. A friendless school-teacher, plain and unloved, lonely and underpaid, who had not found life worth living. They came to the city, girls like this, from all over the country, their hearts set on a career or marriage, or both. They met, only too often, with nothing but disappointment.

It was a depressing, but nevertheless very ordinary story.

When the two black cruisers no longer stood against the curb, Bel lifted her tiny feet out of brogues two sizes too large for her, shed a black cardigan in the middle of the living-room floor, and went to her room and locked the door. Violet continued to stare woodenly at a finger-nail bitten to the quick. Ruth and Joan cried quietly on each other's shoulders. May, lifting the pillow she had held over Monique's head, left her to continue her hysterics uninterrupted. And Psyche was sicker than she had ever been in her life.

After that initial ordeal Psyche was able to handle the reporters without much difficulty. Disliking their mission, contemptuous of anyone who made a vocation of prying into other people's affairs, she even took a certain grim pleasure in misleading them. That they were, as Joe had warned her, far from stupid, helped rather than the reverse, for it turned what might have been a series of dreary evasions into a sharp game of wits.

There were four of them who came and went on the Monday and Tuesday of that week.

All through Monday and Tuesday Psyche, in her blue dress, her hair tied back with a blue ribbon, sat in the living-room near the top of the stairs, a shopping-bag and a light coat on the floor beside her. The girls, in their plainest clothes, went out to work as usual, all except May. May and Bel took turns watching the street through a carefully drawn lace curtain.

"This looks like one of them, honey," May would say. "Get into your routine."

And a reporter, reaching the front door, would meet a tall, pretty girl on her way out to do the daily marketing. A very appealing girl, wistful and grave, who would reluctantly allow herself to be drawn into conversation, and who, having said something she obviously wished she had not, would try to insist that he go in and talk to her aunt instead.

Perhaps twenty minutes later he would depart, feeling like a bit of a louse but none the less jubilant because he had come across a very nice story where he had had no real reason to expect one. It had, after all, been nothing but a routine assignment.

Psyche, successful but unbearably depressed, would climb the stairs again to sit and leaf through love story magazines May had thrust upon her, and which she had not had the will to resist. There was nothing in these purple pulp stories which even remotely resembled love as she envisaged it, and as she was quite certain that somewhere, sometime she would find it. That she *would* find it was something she was as sure of as she had once been sure that that she would never stand, a widow, beside an unsung miner's grave.

At the moment, however, this was a certainty which gave her little or no comfort, for its realization seemed to her then to be a long way off.

By Wednesday afternoon, it was apparent that they had seen the last of the reporters, for no more had come, and the papers had all by that time carried, in one form or another, the story which had been given to them. Kathie, in every case, had rated no more than a brief paragraph on an inside page.

Bel turned slowly away from a window at which she had spent most of her time for three days. A sigh of relief and fatigue escaped her. "Well, I guess we've seen the last of them. You've done a good job, baby. There isn't any way I can thank you. You'll just have to take it as read, baby."

"Let's not talk about it, Bel."

"I wish we could have gone to the funeral, you and me," Bel said. "That part of it—well, it just wasn't right."

"It didn't matter, not really," Psyche said.

But it had mattered, terribly. Regret, that Kathie should have gone to her last resting place alone, was a leaden weight within her.

She stood up. "If there's nothing you want just now, Bel, I think I'll go up to my room for a while."

"Go right ahead, baby," Bel said. "Have yourself a sleep. You deserve it. I'll call you when supper's ready."

When she reached her room, Psyche did not lie down. Instead, she sat on the edge of the window-seat, chain-smoking, and staring blankly at the *Blue Boy* that Kathie had hung up at a time when some hope must still have remained alive amongst the ashes of her growing despair.

Bel's voice, when she raised it, had real carrying quality. "You still sleeping, baby? Supper's on!"

If I don't answer, Psyche thought, she will come upstairs, so I must answer.

"I'm coming!" she called, without hearing the sharp note of hysteria behind her words. And when she went to the mirror to comb her hair she saw nothing in her reflection to warn her that she was very close to the breaking-point.

She had eaten neither breakfast nor lunch, but it was not until she reached the living-room and saw the geraniums once more in place in the window, that she realized it would be quite impossible for her to face even the thought of dinner. She would go out, she decided swiftly, and she would go now. Bel would not want her to leave, might even want her to remain in all evening. But she could not stay to watch it all begin all over again as if nothing had happened.

She wasted no time while fetching her coat and gloves, but it was slowly, and with a reluctance she could not have explained to herself, that she approached the kitchen door.

They were all in the kitchen, Bel and her girls, sitting on red-and-chrome chairs around a red-and-chrome table.

It was like a tableau in red and black and silver, briefly without movement, posed, as all faces turned toward her where she stood, equally still, in the doorway. Bel's red dress and black curls, May's flashing silver ear-rings and black satin, Monique's lacquer-black head and silver blouse, Violet's heavy silver bracelets and barbaric red finger-nails, Ruth's and Joan's red lips parted in smiles without meaning. There were other colours there, but they were momentarily obliterated by a three-colour process that screened out all but the dominant red and black and silver—red lipstick—black mascara—silver tinsel.

Bel was the first to speak, and because Psyche had known in effect what she would say, it was like a prepared speech, rehearsed, inevitable. "You're not going out, baby! Not tonight."

"Yes, Bel."

"But you haven't had anything to eat."

"I'm not hungry." I wish they would move, Psyche thought. I wish somebody else would say something.

"It's going to rain, baby," Bel said, and her voice was an entreaty. "You won't be gone too long, will you?"

"No," Psyche said. "I won't be gone—too long."

There was still some light in the sky when she let herself out of the front door.

She had meant to close the door quietly, but a draught from the empty hall behind her forced it shut with a sharp, unintended finality. Unbidden, the picture of her life as a long corridor of closed doors sprang to her mind again, and she was visited by an urgent impulse to re-open this particular door at once, simply to prove that it could be done.

She lifted her hand toward the knob; then, deriding herself silently for her foolishness, let it fall again and turned away from Bel's place.

7

WALKING northward from Bel's, Psyche knew almost at once that if she continued to walk in the evenings she would now do it without direction or objective. The will-o'-the-wisp she had chased all winter had ceased to beckon her, the far past drawing away, to vanish cloaked in dreams she was unlikely to dream again. They had not been purposeless or futile, those dreams, because they had helped across the years to shape her, to give her guidance of a kind that her environment had not provided. She would continue to believe that she had not been cast off deliberately, and that her origin, unknown though it might remain, was such that she need not be ashamed of it, for she saw in herself some factual proof of this. But to go on thinking that she might stumble across a road that would lead her back to a real place, to real people, was to be a child playing hide-and-seek in a dark wood, hunting for something she would not recognize even if she found it.

In the autumn, on a day unmarked on any calendar she had ever seen, she would be twenty. Seventeen years since Mag had discovered her on the doorstep of the shack. To stare back across a gulf as wide as that was to stare at nothing. Even so short a time ago as the previous day, this knowledge would have hurt and depressed her. Now it was simply a fact to be accepted. I am an adult, she thought, and it is up to me to see that this is not an end but a beginning.

She came to a stop on a corner where neon lights burned, multi-coloured, against brick buildings flowing one into another, all individuality lost in the waning light. I must have somewhere to go, she thought. Where can I go with any good reason?

She drew back against an unlit shop front to avoid being jostled by the passers-by, and looked up at a sky shuttered by heavy clouds that refused any possibility of an afterglow. It was unlikely to rain soon, but when it did, it would rain hard.

She did not see the gaunt grey wolf of a man who, furtive even in a crowd, passed in front of her, his eyes fixed on the pavement beneath his feet, his left hand massaging a twitching muscle in his cheek.

There will be no moon tonight, she thought, as there was no sun today. And, thinking this, she knew suddenly where she would go.

A dark wind from the west caught at her open coat, causing her to shiver involuntarily as she turned and set off swiftly toward the east, her eyes sombre blue pools in an expressionless face. She had no wish to do what she was doing, but, in an instant, it had become something she must do before she could feel free to re-route her life into what would be, for the first time, a channel of her own choosing.

Ordered echelons of street lights admitted the defeat of another day when Psyche reached a high stone wall beyond which spread unilluminated acres with no defense against the night; a no-man's land shrouded in thick twilight, enfolded in a silence more compelling than the stir of the living world from which it had been isolated.

Skirting the wall in search of the gate that must break it at some point, she was alone on a street undisturbed by anything other than the sound of her own footsteps and the quiet whimpering of the gusty wind.

The black iron scroll-work gates were locked. Rising to more than twice her height, broad enough when open to permit the passing of a funeral cortège, they stood a barrier, until the sun should rise again, against any pretense of communication between life and death.

She lifted her hands in order to hold on to iron as cold and insensate as those it guarded, scarcely realizing that she did so because she needed the physical support. I should never have come to this place, she thought. To have imagined even for a moment that by so doing she could re-establish some ephemeral connection between herself and Kathie was to have allied herself with the ignorance and superstition of the dark ages. Kathie's body might be buried here, but Kathie herself was not here, and never had been.

Psyche knew that she would have felt this even more strongly if she had been able to enter amongst white tombstones and black clipped cedar and yew. Yet she clung to the gates without the strength or will to tear herself away.

"Though I walk through the valley of the shadow of death——"

Faint, suddenly dizzy, she stared down dark aisles where white marble and black foliage were now diffused and blurred as if by the shadow of death itself. And it was several minutes before she realized that her vision was being tricked by sheets of rain.

I must find some shelter, she thought confusedly.

Her hands still held out in front of her, she turned away from the cemetery gates, afraid that at any moment she would actually faint.

She saw the sign on the opposite side of the street when she was a little less than half a block from the locked iron gates. Lit by a yellow light, bold black letters offered her the sanctuary she so badly needed—"Strangers Welcomed".

As she stepped off the curb on to the road, the wet slur of her shoes sounded as she imagined a tide must sound, running out fast, sucking futilely at the insecurity of constantly shifting sands. She never saw the heavy truck, even when it loomed above her, when its brakes screamed a warning too late for her to hear.

*Nick's wife, Alice, opening her own front door, recognized Sharon at once, although she had never seen her before.*

*"He has come back, hasn't he?" Sharon asked, and she had difficulty in keeping her voice even. "He isn't still away?"*

*Alice, in full possession of the story in so far as Sharon herself knew it, and knowing also as much as Nick had seen fit to tell her, said gently, "Yes, he's back."*

*"Can I see him now?" Now—this minute—sooner. I have waited a week, a week in which I have scarcely slept. Don't, for the love of God, keep me waiting any longer!*

*Alice, looking at the face so like the one she had seen in Nick's paintings, recognizing the desperate anxiety in blue eyes oddly familiar, was suddenly really angry with Nick for having refused to wait at the house, for having gone to the studio.*

*"I'm sorry," she said, even more gently. "He is at the studio. Come in while I sketch out the route for you. It isn't easy to find."*

*Sharon managed a travesty of a smile. "Thank you. He didn't say anything?"*

*"I think you had better wait and talk to him."*

*Less than an hour later Sharon was walking rapidly across a daisy-strewn field toward a red-roofed barn.*

*Still later that day she slammed behind her, with uncharacter-*

istic fury, a door bearing a false door-knocker beneath a faded legend that read "Community Shelter". "Bitch!" she murmured, sick and white with anger and frustration.

The following morning, Dwight at her side, her hand close held in his, she descended a tarnished, treeless slope toward a weatherbeaten tar-paper shack.

# 8 | THE DOCTOR AND HIS WIFE

I

THE eyes, dark, brilliant, compelling, seemed to hang disembodied against a grey mist that surged without dissipating. Eyes like twin lancets, sharp as the keenest scalpel, that probed mercilessly into her bare and unprotected brain.

Psyche, twisting her head to and fro on the pillow, could hear her own voice answering questions, but the questions themselves were inaudible to her conscious mind. It was as if those hypnotic eyes were capable of making their own demands without recourse to words, of dragging forth things she did not even know about herself.

My head hurts, she thought. Why should my head hurt? A name—a name—you are asking me for a name now, but this time I will be too clever for you. A name—you want Bel's name. Bel said never to give her name to anybody—ever—ever—ever.

"Ever—ever—ever," she whispered.

Didn't you hear me? I gave you your answer. Now leave me alone.

But the question was repeated, and repeated again, until she knew that the response she had made was not adequate, that she would have to find a more acceptable one. A name, she must give a name. Not Bel's name. Not the name of anyone she had ever known—a name belonging to nobody.

"Sharon!" she cried out in anguish, and slipped back into the unconsciousness that had claimed her off and on for over five weeks.

The doctor, his eyes still fixed on her face, continued to lean across the end of the high hospital bed for some time. Then, taking a gold pencil and a note-book from the pocket of his suit, he wrote steadily, filling three pages with small precise hand-writing. Not until this was done did he move around to the side of the bed to lay his hand first on Psyche's forehead and then on her wrist. Satisfied, he rang for a nurse, and, while waiting for one to come, whistled softly under his breath as he looked with clinical detachment at a patient who was of extraordinary interest to him.

He was a handsome man, but a cold one, the brilliance of his intellect shedding no warmth over his manner or his long, ascetic face. Tall and spare, at forty-five he stood securely on the summit of his own particular mountain peak, from which vantage point he looked down, not without contempt, on the mental, emotional, and nervous aberrations he made it his business to dissect. His success pleased but in no way surprised him. Ambitious, unhampered by sympathy, he had climbed to the top of his profession with a minimum of waste effort, combining brain surgery, for its greater material gains, with the psycho-physiology that was his ruling passion. Seeing his own mind as a perfectly equipped operating table on which to take apart lesser minds, he expected to leave a lasting mark on research in the fields of memory and heredity.

"You rang, Doctor?" The nurse sounded breathless, for she was more than a little afraid of this man whose large, deep-set eyes could impale one like a butterfly on a pin.

"Your patient will regain normal consciousness within the next twenty-four hours. When this happens, you are to advise me at once. Please see that the nurse on night duty is given the same instructions."

"Yes, Doctor," she said, and found that she was speaking to a distinguished back that was already halfway across the room.

She closed the door after him, something that he did not expect to have to do for himself, and went over to the bed. Looking down at a strained white face and tangled blonde hair, she thought rebelliously, "Why can't he leave her alone until she's feeling better. It's a wonder he hasn't killed her instead of curing her." But even as she thought this, she knew that no other man on the continent could have lifted the depressed area at the back of Psyche's skull with the same delicate skill and precision.

Going to the bathroom for a wash-cloth, absently pausing before the mirror to straighten a white cap on thick auburn curls, she considered the story that, in bits and pieces, had emerged from a long delirium, and was forced to admit that she herself was intensely curious to know the whole of it. Her curiosity, however, was offset by sympathy that caused her to align herself, in this case, with patient rather than doctor. To study, and attempt to question, someone who did not know this was being done, seemed to her utterly unfair, if not actually dishonest, and she was secretly pleased that so far, to the best of her knowledge, the doctor had been unable to unearth anything as factual as names and places. He had discovered the girl's own name, now written on her chart, and that was all. Odd, how she had guarded these things, almost as if she had prepared herself in advance for an inquisition before which they must under no circumstances be disclosed. She might have dropped from Mars for all they knew about her that could be put to any practical use. She had been brought in without a purse, without identification of any kind, and every Moran in the telephone book had denied all knowledge of her. Lucky for her that there had been witnesses to her accident, that the trucking company, because the truck had been running without lights, had been made to accept full responsibility. Otherwise she would have landed in a public ward, rather than in Private Patients with a private nurse who—she grinned at herself in the mirror—should be getting back to her job.

Very gently wiping perspiration from a damp white forehead, she allowed her glance to wander to the chart on the table beside the bed, and small teeth bit the underlip of a pretty mouth. It just doesn't seem right, she thought. It was not, however, the chart itself, with its temperature graph descending to normal, that bothered her, but the name at the top. Maggie Moran. I suppose I'm silly about names, she thought, but they usually do fit somehow, and this one doesn't. She isn't one bit like a Maggie Moran. I wonder if there can be some mistake about it.

Psyche's wide-open eyes, fastened on her face in steady inquiry, startled her so much that she jumped visibly. She had seen the blue eyes open before, but not like this, not with depths in them.

"I've been sick?"

The young nurse had herself in hand again. Professional, competent, she said quietly, "Yes. Quite sick. You are almost better. Now don't talk. Just lie there without talking, and I'll call the doctor."

I must have been partly conscious before this, Psyche thought rapidly, because I know I am in a hospital and I am not surprised. When did I come here? Yesterday, or the day before?

"Don't call him yet—not for a minute."

Her hand hovering just above the bell, the nurse hesitated. "I have orders——"

The perspiration was breaking out on Psyche's forehead again. "Give me just a moment first."

The nurse looked at the open window, at a patch of sky reflecting late afternoon light, and then at her watch. Nearly six o'clock. In three minutes she would be going off duty. "All right," she said, "but don't ever tell anyone. If Svengali finds out that someone even said boo to you before he did, it will be the end."

"Svengali?"

The nurse's cheeks were pink. "That slipped out. Forget it. You're sure you feel strong enough to talk now, Miss Moran?"

Psyche's flicker of surprise at being addressed by name, and by that name, was so slight that the nurse, if she had not been expecting it, would have missed it. I was right, she thought triumphantly, it isn't her name. She isn't sufficiently oriented yet to have been surprised simply because we knew her name.

"I seem to have rather a headache," Psyche said, "but otherwise I feel all right. Tell me, how long have I been here? What happened?"

"You were in a traffic accident, and you've been here just over five weeks."

"Five weeks!"

"I know. It doesn't seem possible, does it? You were hit by a truck, and you've been more or less unconscious ever since. But don't worry. You're perfectly all right now. A few weeks' convalescence and you'll be as good as new."

Lifting her hand to her head, Psyche thought, it doesn't look like my hand; it's too thin, too colourless. "Does—does anyone know I'm here?"

"You mean your family?"

Again there was a flicker in the blue eyes, but this time the nurse could not interpret it. "No. My friends."

"I'm afraid not. You had no purse. No address."

Thank God for that, anyway, Psyche said to herself. At least I haven't involved Bel in anything. But five weeks—she must be wild with anxiety.

"How did it happen?"

"You walked in front of a truck that had no lights. It was at night, just after ten o'clock, and it was raining."

"Do you know where I was?"

The young nurse did know, and, with a quick glance at her watch, told her.

"But I don't live——" Psyche began, and stopped abruptly. A long way from Bel's—she must have been walking as she usually did. No slightest memory of her pilgrimage to the cemetery returned to dispel this conviction.

"Where do you live?" the nurse asked gently.

"Do I have to live anywhere?" Psyche asked, and there was both confusion and a hint of desperation in her face.

The nurse bent to straighten the sheets and smooth out the pillow. "No," she said, in a voice little more than a whisper, "there's no law that says you must. Do what you want. Tell the doctor that you can't remember, but be careful, he's not easy to fool."

Mists that had parted were gathering again. It was difficult to see through them, to think through them. "Thank you——" she murmured. "Thank you. I won't forget. I won't let him know that you—that you——"

The nurse, a quick hand searching for the pulse in a blue-veined wrist, thought, she's asleep this time. I shouldn't have done it. I don't know whatever possessed me. But I'm glad, just the same. In the morning, after a normal sleep, she won't be so defenceless.

Pressing the bell for her relief, her rounded chin was both very stubborn and very young.

The night nurse came in with a rustle of starched skirts. Her starched manner was soundless. "No change?"

"No change."

### 2

WHEN Psyche woke, early morning sunlight was tracing bars of gold on a pale green wall, and she knew, even before she looked around the small, bare room, that she was alone.

Her watch, the watch Joe had given her, lay on the table by the bed. Reaching for it, acutely conscious of her own weakness, she saw that it was not quite seven. Her eyes moving on to the telephone, she thought, they will all be asleep, but the extension in Bel's room will wake her, and this may be my only chance. Five weeks—I have lost five whole weeks out of my life. What have they been thinking all this time? That I ran away from them without even a good-bye? Would Bel think that of me?

To lift the receiver was a real effort, and when she had accomplished it, she cradled it on the pillow beside her head.

"Number please?"

She gave Bel's number, and waited, her heart beating so heavily she wondered if the operator on the hospital switchboard could hear it. For what seemed a long time she listened to the evenly spaced ringing of a bell that brought no response.

"The party does not answer."

"Try it again, will you, please." Bel—wake up! It's me, Psyche. You must wake up!

"Hello!" The man's voice, angry, thick with sleep, was so unexpected that for a moment Psyche could not reply.

"Hello, who is it? What do you want?"

"I want to speak to Bel. At once, please."

"She don't live here no more."

"Wait! Don't go! Where can I reach her?"

"I don't know, lady. She didn't leave no address."

Slowly, automatically, Psyche replaced a receiver that now conducted nothing but the singing silence of an abruptly broken connection. She knew well enough what must have happened, if not in detail, at least in its rough outlines. The geraniums were gone for good this time. For a reason she might never know, Bel had been forced to move out, to fold her tents and disappear. As Bel might have put it herself, she had taken a powder, and heaven only knew where she might be, she and her girls. They would not be together, but scattered to the four winds.

It must have been something to do with one of the boys, Psyche thought dully. That would be the one avenue that Joe might not have been able to barricade. Joe would stand by Bel. In a way she would still be all right, but she would no longer be independent, and Bel, to be truly Bel, had to be her own mistress before she was anyone else's.

The door opened quietly, and the nurse, seeing that she was awake, came at once to her bedside. "Good morning, Miss Moran. How are you feeling?"

"Fine, thank you." I have just lost all my friends. I own one set of clothing which may or may not be wearable, and one wrist-watch, and one name. I feel like the devil, thank you.

"I will call the doctor at once."

This was not a nurse Psyche was aware of having seen before, and she remembered her obligation to the smiling young redhead of the previous evening. "Where am I?" she asked mechanically. "What happened?"

"Don't try to talk yet. The doctor doesn't want you to talk until he comes. Just lie quietly. You are doing very well."

A heavy apathy settling on her, Psyche had no desire to do anything other than lie quietly. To stay where she was forever would be easy, so much easier than resuming a struggle that never seemed to lead anywhere, that finished up in one blind alley after another.

I just don't care any more about anything, she thought bitterly. I am doing very well.

The doctor, called from his bed, was shaved, dressed and ready to leave for the hospital in twenty minutes. He was a vain man, but his vanity did not reach to externals when he was in a hurry.

He left a message for his wife, who would in all probability sleep until noon, and drank a cup of coffee, standing, in the front hall. His glance roved over waxed oak panelling, polished Jacobean furniture, and an Aubusson carpet rich in subdued colour. Nora had extremely good taste. In some respects, he thought acidly, she had made him an excellent wife.

He put his empty cup down on a narrow refectory table, took his bag, hat, and gloves from the maid who had stood, holding these things, waiting to open the door for him, and went out to his car.

The door of his car was opened and shut by a chauffeur who, liking neither his employers nor the uncertainty of his hours, stayed with the job because he was unlikely to find another that paid him so well. Wooden-faced, he got in behind the wheel. Bought, that's what I am, he thought. Bought, just like this ruddy big limousine. The bastard. Never a "good morning" or a "good night". Doesn't even call a guy by his name. Just orders, like he was the Almighty's right-hand man.

"Where to, sir?"

"The hospital."

Some day I'll paste him one and teach him some manners.
"Very good, sir."

The doctor had first employed a chauffeur in order to make full use of hours otherwise, from his point of view, wasted. Sitting in the back of the big car, undisturbed by pedestrians, traffic lights, or other vehicles, he was able to explore neat mental files, and with the material thus conveniently at hand weigh and consider the manifold eccentricities of the human animal. This morning his thoughts ran in the groove that interested him above all others. Believing as he did that heredity was a stronger factor than environment in the formation of any given individual, and determined to prove this, he faced a challenge that he found coldly exhilarating. That he should have to produce not only tangible proof, but an enormous weight of it, in support of anything so obvious, at times irritated him profoundly: so much so, that he had even considered abandoning surgery entirely in favour of devoting all his energies to research. That he did not do this revealed an Achilles heel that he did his best to conceal. Contemptuous of other people, he was yet driven by a need to impress them in every way possible. Childless, he had no need of a large house, but he could not give it up. The constant parties given in that house bored him, but without them his possessions would have had no audience. His household staff was too large, but he added to it rather than cutting it down, and his chauffeur had become a sign of status without which he would have felt naked in the eyes of the multitude.

Arriving at the hospital, he got out of the car without a word, and, his long legs taking him quickly but without loss of dignity up a flight of broad steps, disappeared through doors manipulated for him by a doorman who touched his cap in silent respect.

Expressionless, the chauffeur watched him go. There was a coffee stand half a block from the wide avenue on which the hospital faced, but with no indication as to when his services would next be required, he knew that he would not dare go to it.

The doctor, when he reached Psyche's room, dismissed the nurse with a curt nod, and drew a chair up beside the bed of this, one of the most interesting guinea pigs he had ever had the good fortune to run across.

"Do you remember me?" he asked.

Turning her head on the pillow, Psyche said, without enthusiasm, "I remember your eyes."

"Do you know how you got here?"

Psyche remained silent.

Now that she was fully conscious he wanted her co-operation. His manner underwent a subtle but definite change, and his brilliant eyes, instead of probing, asked for her trust and confidence.

"You were struck by a large truck, and were brought here with concussion and a skull fracture. I am the doctor who operated on you, and I can assure you that you will suffer no future ill effects. Do you remember any of this?"

"No."

"That is quite normal. Don't let it disturb you. Would you tell me what you last remember?"

"I went out for a walk."

"At what time did you leave home that evening?"

The question was very casually put, but Psyche recognized it for a leading one.

"I went out after dinner. About seven," she replied, and volunteered no further information.

He did not press her further. Diagnosing her defensive lassitude as a natural concomittant of her weakened condition, he decided it would be best to leave her alone for the time being. Later he would elicit a consecutive and willing recital of a story he already knew in part.

"Any headache or soreness at the back of the head?"

"Not now."

He nodded his satisfaction. "That is as it should be. The last dressings were removed a week ago. You will find that you have lost some of your hair. Fortunately it's underneath and won't show."

"You think that matters?" Psyche asked flatly.

"It will. To you."

He had found out all he wished to know at present. The crude

English she had used at times while delirious belonged to an earlier stage. To speak well was now natural to her; she had perception; and she gave evidence, both in manner and in facial expression, of a high degree of intelligence. She would be supremely useful to him.

Rising, he said, "I will leave you now. I will be in again tomorrow."

He came in every day, and Psyche, either propped up in bed or sitting listlessly in a big chair by the window, accepted his visits with the same indifference she showed to everyone and everything with which she came in contact.

Any further protection of Bel rendered futile by Bel's disappearance, she told him, bit by bit, almost everything he wanted to know, without bothering to try and fathom his reasons for questions that often seemed haphazard, entirely pointless. She did not, however, tell him her name. To give him that would be to deliver herself into his hands completely, which she was not prepared to do. Guarding this, the one thing she truly possessed, she held it, an amulet, between herself and a powerful modern witchcraft.

Only twice, during the weeks she spent convalescing, was her indifference pierced. Once when she woke in the night to hear a ragged voice screaming broken words and phrases that trailed into silence with the swift, soft passing of a rubber-wheeled stretcher. Chilled through and through, she thought, "Did I perhaps sound like that?"

And again, when the young auburn-haired nurse came into her room with a bouquet of flowers.

"You've made a mistake," Psyche stated, rather than asked.

The girl smiled, and shook her head. "No. No mistake. They're from me and some of the other nurses. Happy middle of July. We thought it terrible that you should be here so long and not have any flowers."

"You shouldn't have—you're too kind."

"Yes, we should. You're a very nice patient. We think you deserve them."

Her smile heartbreaking, Psyche said, "Thank you so much.

Thank them all, and wish them a—happy middle of July from me."

It was the doctor who informed her that she was ready to be discharged from the hospital, and at the same time presented her with a solution to the problem of where she was to go until such time as she would be strong enough to look for work.

"My wife has suggested that I bring you home with me for a few weeks," he told her casually.

Frowning her incredulity, Psyche asked, "Why should she?"

Dr. Scarletti was, several generations back, of Italian origin, and his expression just then was that of a Venetian doge putting poison into the goblet of someone unwise enough to dispute his authority. "Because I guided her to the suggestion," he replied softly.

Shivering a little, Psyche thought, "I do not envy his wife. I wonder what she is like." Aloud she said, "Thank you. I'm afraid I am going to refuse your invitation."

Taking out a cigarette, fitting it into a black holder, he said, "And I think you will change your mind."

"I feel like a bird being hypnotized by a snake," Psyche thought. "I wish he would look away?"

"Why should I?"

"Because with your help I think we may be able to find out who you are, and where you came from originally. That is, always presupposing that you came more or less directly from there to the shack where you were brought up."

"Of course I did!"

He had thought long and carefully as to the best approach to take with her, and was now objectively pleased with the success of his reasoning. One could nearly always anticipate the reactions of an intelligent and well-balanced individual.

"How do you know?"

Badly shaken, faced for the first time with the possibility of more than one hiatus in her life, Psyche said, "I just know."

"You mean you can remember?"

This is what he was like in the beginning, when I didn't really know what I was saying. This is what his eyes looked like. "You know very well I can't remember!" she flared.

"I can help you to, if anyone can. To work together on it would be in both our interests. In mine, because I am engaged in proving certain general theories. In yours, because you wish to know specific facts at present securely locked in the farthest recesses of your memory."

"I was too young," Psyche said uncertainly.

"You were not. Given time we can reach back at least six months into the sealed section of your memory that represents your life before your somewhat dramatic arrival at the shack. I am not, I might say, in the habit of introducing strangers into my household, but I see it as the only way in which we can collaborate satisfactorily. I am an extremely busy man, and what spare time I have is found during the late evening."

"He is doing this for himself, not for me at all. He will make charts and diagrams; he will fill notebook after notebook; he will question me and question me; he will dissect every move I make. If I agree to this idea, I will be haunted by those eyes even when they are not fixed on me. And for what? In all probability nothing of any value to me. Yet—what have I got to lose? And where else can I go?"

"All right," she said. "I'll come."

Dr. Scarletti rose from the chair in which he had been sitting. "I will fetch you when I leave the hospital tomorrow evening."

"You are sure your wife won't mind?"

"Quite sure," he said calmly, and there was no reflection in his brilliant eyes of the scene with which Nora had greeted what had been an ultimatum.

## 3

NORA SCARLETTI was not beautiful, and never had been, but there were few women who could compete successfully with her in any ring she thought worth entering. When she wanted something, material or otherwise, she went after it. When presented with something she did not want, she got rid of it. But whatever she did, she never came out into the open. Smiling, she worked under cover, and her manoeuvres were a sleight-of-hand rarely seen through.

To have married a man whom she could not always deceive had been a cardinal error, one which, when she discovered what she had done, she had at first thought to rectify at once. However, seeing a certain spice in the situation, and realizing that it would be difficult to find a better trophy to hold before the world, she changed her mind. Knowing that he would be unlikely to endanger either his professional or his personal reputation by divorcing her, appreciating the convenience of his sexual coldness, she found it refreshing to be able to unsheathe her claws in private without undue risk. Before any audience at all—even the servants, whom she looked upon as robots rather than human beings—she was charmingly devoted to him, not only because this was one of the unwritten laws in their agreement, but because she was more jealous of him in all ways than she would have been if she had loved him.

She was alone in her bedroom on the evening when he was to bring Psyche home with him. She had been dressed and ready for half an hour, but until she heard the front door open, she intended to stay where she was.

Slowly she walked up and down the length of a pale-green carpet, the reflection of her petite, black-clad figure caught and lost and caught again by gold-framed mirrors, her slim shadow falling in distorted patterns across cream and gold brocade.

It had been a hot day, but the house, its curtains drawn until seven o'clock, had remained cool; and Nora, in her high-necked black silk dress, was coolness personified, sophistication at its most highly polished. She nearly always wore black relieved only by a single striking piece of jewellery, this evening a hand-carved jade clip the colour of her eyes. If you were a woman, you were stabbed immediately by one of two convictions when you met Nora—either that you were almost vulgarly over-dressed, or unforgivably under-dressed. In spite of this, if it were part of her strategy of the moment that you like her, you probably would. Men nearly always liked her. Her smooth dark hair and decep-tively simple clothes appeared to them unstudied, their effective-ness a very attractive natural phenomenon. And her pointed face, with its slightly crooked nose, creamy skin, and smiling green eyes, was a subtle invitation to intimacy.

Pausing before open windows, she looked down on a large garden, the lawn chequered with lengthening shadows. A year earlier she had had roses and delphiniums torn out and replaced with a formal planting of flowering shrubs. A marble fountain, from which a tall column of spray still rose through direct rays of sunlight, had been her latest innovation, and one with which she was objectively pleased. But now, although she looked at it, she was not thinking about it.

Maggie Moran, she thought—princess in beggar-maid's cloth-ing! If it were anyone other than you, my dear doctor, I would consider you out of your mind. And you are out of your mind if you think I am going to put up with this impossible situation meekly. Come into my parlour, Maggie, and see how you like it. My God—what a name! And I have been asked—no, told—to make you at home. Well, I shall. So much at home that you will be more uncomfortable than you have ever been in your life.

Glancing at a small platinum wrist-watch, she saw that it was seven-thirty.

Psyche, looking at her watch as the car came to a noiseless halt, saw that it was seven-thirty. As uninterested in the magnificent, double-fronted stone house as she had been in the big car, she waited while the doctor stepped out on to the sidewalk. Then, climbing out past a chauffeur who stood rigidly to attention, her suitcase in his hand, she fell into line in the small procession that proceeded up the walk to the front door.

Another door, she thought bleakly, and did not care whether this one opened for her or not.

What Nora had expected of Psyche, if she had given it shape and form at all, had been something resembling an uncombed Alice in Wonderland. The tall blonde girl with the almost arrogant pride of carriage, who lifted indifferent blue eyes to her as she came down the stairs, was an extremely unpleasant surprise.

Antagonism licking through her, she came forward, her hand extended, her light, musical voice warm with welcome. "I'm so glad John brought you here. We'll have such a nice time together while he is out brainstorming his other patients."

"Thank you," Psyche replied, and acknowledged Nora Scarletti's charm with a brief smile.

Turning to her husband, Nora laid one finger on his arm, and rising on tiptoe brushed his cheek with her lips. It was a delightful gesture, one that suggested that further demonstration was withheld only because they were not alone. "Tired, darling? Cocktails are ready in the conservatory." Then, addressing the maid who had been waiting unobtrusively in the shadows at the back of the hall, she said crisply, "Marie, take Miss Moran's coat and bag up to her room for her. There's just one bag, is there, Miss—my dear, I'm going to call you Maggie right away. So stupid to be formal. This is all your luggage, isn't it?"

"I think I'll like her," Psyche decided, and wondered why she had been so sure in advance that she would not. "Yes, that's all. I hadn't that much yesterday. One of the nurses went shopping with me this morning."

"On whose money, I would like to know," Nora thought

viciously. "You poor darling. We'll have to do something about that later on."

"I have all I need just now," Psyche told her. The auburn-haired nurse had been right. It was better to have a few really good things in this household than to have quantity. She had, pushed by the young nurse, drawn out all but fifty dollars from her bank account in order to do this. In a different frame of mind, she would probably have refused, have been afraid to strip herself of any of this meagre protection, which she had remembered only that morning.

"Mrs. Scarletti is terribly nice," the girl had said, "but she'll make you feel like something the cat dragged in if you aren't properly dressed."

The conservatory, walled on three sides by glass, was like an extension of the garden, and Psyche, sitting in a comfortable lounge chair, was more off-guard than she had intended to be. The doctor, staring thoughtfully into the single cocktail he allowed himself, left her alone, and Nora, chatting easily, banished any restraint there might have been.

When the dinner gong rang at eight o'clock, the doctor rose, thinking, "Nora is showing good sense for once. She understands that I meant what I said." That Nora's attack was about to commence he did not foresee and because she was clever enough to choose weapons invisible to him, he did not recognize them as such. If the dinner that night had been too casual, he would have remarked the omissions. Accustomed to pomp and circumstance, he did not notice that it was over-elaborate.

Psyche's first sensation, on seeing the long, candle-lit table, was one of pure delight in its perfection and beauty; her second, as she took in the multiplicity of crystal goblets, forks and knives and spoons, that surrounded each of the three places set at it, was one of the most acute dismay.

"Over there, Maggie dear."

Left to herself, Psyche could at least have seated herself gracefully. Taken unawares by a white-coated houseman who drew out her chair for her, she was awkward, and knew it.

"I do hope you like oysters, darling?" Nora's voice was anxious, begged her to say that she did.

Helpless in the face of such an appeal, Psyche replied in the affirmative, while she wondered wildly what she was supposed to do with objects she had never seen before, with crushed ice, lemon, and sauce.

Hers was a poise that was strengthened by direct attack, that accepted an open challenge with confidence. Now, blind to Nora's malice, having taken the first fatal step in a direction from which there seemed to be no retreating, she became mired deeper and deeper in difficulties of which only she appeared to be aware.

Attempting to see what Nora did, which fork she used and how, she found her view obstructed by flowers whose heavy perfume made her a little sick. By evil chance—she never thought of it as design—the same thing applied when she glanced obliquely toward the doctor. Realizing that she was being watched from three directions, from behind as well as from either side, and that seated as she was she could be clearly observed, she felt as an animal might, trapped in the open, its every move followed by eyes concealed in the thick coverts around it.

Three times during a six-course dinner she tried to ask for help, and somehow not only failed to get it but to make it clear that she needed it. "Oh, God," she thought, "I should never have come here. Never. How can anything as simple as eating be made so horribly complicated?"

"The pigeons are very good, aren't they, John?"

"Excellent," the doctor replied. He was enjoying his dinner, and, while he ate, quietly planning the lines on which he would commence a real study of a subject no longer in a position to escape from him until he had finished with her.

Glowing dark eyes. Long green eyes. Bland servant's eyes piercing through the back of her skull. What did one do with a mouthful of tiny, needle-sharp bones?

The finger-bowls were Georgian silver, the mats Alençon lace. "At least I know what to do with these," Psyche thought grimly. And as she carefully lifted them from her dessert plate, she saw again a bare deal table and jelly glasses set on brown paper mats, and heard Butch's great voice saying, "Dee-licious—damned if it ain't!"

A full understanding of homesickness sweeping over her, she thought, "If I could go back there now, this minute, I would never want to leave again."

They had their coffee in the drawing-room, a rose-and-gold symphony that would have been almost too large for fifty people. In spite of its size, Psyche felt that in here things should be better than they had been in the panelled dining-room. For some reason, they were not. Perhaps it was because even Nora fell silent, and they were left without anything to say, two who should have been alone together at the day's end and a third, a stranger who had no excuse for intruding upon them. Thus it appeared to Psyche, and thus Nora meant it to appear.

When they had finished their coffee, the doctor turned to Psyche. "We might make a small beginning to-night, if you are not too tired."

"I *am* too tired," Psyche thought, "but I want to do it because then I will believe that I have some purpose in being here."

"I would like——" she began, but Nora interrupted her.

"She needs to rest to-night, John. She should go to bed right away."

Dr. Scarletti's handsome features were expressionless as he searched his wife's face, but he found nothing there other than a concern in which he did not believe. That she was hindering him deliberately he was almost sure, but her statement was a valid one regardless of its motivation.

"Perhaps you are right," he said coldly.

"Of course I am, darling. Women often know more about other women than even their doctors do. She may be crossed off the sick list, but she still isn't strong. You can perfectly well wait until tomorrow evening to begin your little guessing games."

Fury, which always seized him when Nora disparaged his work in this manner, kept him silent, and Psyche's last impression of him as Nora led her toward the door was of a tall, command-ing figure, frightening in its complete immobility.

At the foot of the staircase she resisted the guiding pressure of Nora's hand. "I think he's annoyed," she said quietly. "Really, I would like to talk with him for an hour or so now."

And regain some of your shattered confidence, my dear Maggie? Oh, no. Perhaps even discover that it was I, not you, who angered him? Oh, no! "Nonsense, darling. In a few minutes he will be deep in some ponderous tome and have forgotten all about you. Come on, I'll take you up to your room. I do hope you like it. It's my favourite room in the house."

When Psyche stood on the threshold of the room that was to be hers, seeing it in detail by the light of lamps controlled from a wall switch, she turned to the small, slim woman in open desperation. "Couldn't you give me something else? Something smaller, simpler? Please!"

Nora's bell-like voice was soft with compassion. "John has told me a little of your story, Maggie dear. So tragic. I could not be happy if you didn't have the very best I had to offer. Now—good night, and sleep well."

Alone, Psyche looked around the enormous bedroom, and knew that she was going to hate it—more, probably, than she would ever again hate any inanimate collection of things. Mutely it defied her to touch any part of it, to sully, even by her presence, its impossibly delicate perfection.

Glancing first at the closed door behind her, she stooped and took off her shoes before walking across a carpet that was not just off-white, but pure white. The whole room was done in white and silver; white damask on the chairs, on the head-board of the bed, on the small stool in front of a dressing-table crowded with fragile china figurines; silver shades on slender silver lamps that seemed poised, ready to fall if one but looked at them; silvery walls, on which hung silver-framed abstractions that started no fresh chain of thought, because there was apparently no thought in, or behind, their meaningless convolutions. The only thing that looked as if it were meant to be touched without gloves was her blue nightgown, laid out on the snowy expanse of the bed.

Nora, when she went downstairs again, found her husband in the library that was also his study. It was where she had expected to find him.

Looking up from the papers spread across his desk, he said curtly, " In future I must ask you not to interfere in any way between myself and Miss Moran. In short, you will be good enough to mind your own business."

Nora smiled. She was in a very good humour. "Haven't you made her my business too, darling?"

"Up to a point only. Which room have you put her in?"

"The west front, darling."

The doctor's eyebrows betrayed his very real surprise. "I thought you reserved that for royalty, my dear Nora."

"You told me to do everything I could for her. I am. Everything I can."

"Almost too much," he returned, but he did not follow the thought through. "What are you doing to-night?"

"Playing bridge."

"Can't you find anything better to do than that?"

"What do you suggest? That I spend an enchanted evening lying on your couch baring my libido?"

The doctor regarded her with acute distaste. "It would be an unwholesome spectacle."

"I could show you something more wholesome if you wished. But you don't wish, do you, darling?"

His eyes fixed on her, he thought, "Some day I will rid myself of this woman. When I have finished my work, when I have placed myself so far above the herd that their loose tongues cannot reach me, she shall go out of my life, and she shall not go unscarred."

Usually quite impervious to those eyes, Nora felt cold to the marrow. But hers was a devil that operated in any climate, and she could not forego the pleasure of a final, wicked mockery. "Don't rape Cinderella while I'm out," she said, and left him.

Motionless, he heard her go up the stairs, and a few minutes later come down again. He listened to the front door closing, to the sound of her car as she backed it out of the double garage. Not until all audible reminder of her had gone did he get up and turn off the overhead lights.

Returning to his desk, he seated himself, shadows obscuring

him save for long, well-manicured hands moving purposefully in the circle of light cast by a heavily shaded desk lamp. Drawing a large pad of lined paper toward him, he wrote at the top of a clean sheet—'Margaret Moran'. In brackets after the name he placed a small question mark. Then, neatly subdividing the sheet with ruler and pen, he added three sub-headings: Heredity—Instinct—Memory.

Somewhere outside in the dusk a single robin was still singing when Psyche sat across the desk from the doctor, twenty-four hours later.

"I have no liking for this man," she thought, "and I don't expect I ever will have, but it is better here than in the rest of the house, though I'm damned if I know why."

"My wife has looked after you satisfactorily to-day?"

Couched in these terms, it was a question she could answer without polite evasion. "She has been very kind. She spent the whole afternoon with me."

"Good. Now we are going to approach our problem from three different angles. This evening we will establish our pattern, little more. I intend to begin with association tests, go on from there to question and answer, and finish up with conversation, the purpose of which will be to supply cause and motivation for your reactions to the earlier parts of the program."

"And if I don't always answer as fully, or as truthfully, as I might?" Psyche asked quietly.

"I hope you will. If you don't, that in itself may be revealing. However, I can give you my absolute assurance that nothing you say to me will be used in any form sufficiently personalized or complete to be recognizable."

"Even so——"

Dr. Scarletti allowed himself a frosty smile. "Even so there are a few things that you might prefer to keep to yourself, if you can. That is quite understandable, but I hope you will have the good judgement to limit your discretion to the immediate past. If it is any satisfaction to you, I might say that you have shown a remarkable degree of success so far in doing exactly that. Yours is an unusually controlled mind, Miss Moran. For that reason I would like to make it quite clear that this is not to be psychoanalysis in the ordinary sense, and that both your time and mine will be wasted if you do not exhibit an interest and initiative at least equal to my own."

He looks like a portrait of himself painted three hundred years ago. "How long do you think it will take?"

"We will have either succeeded or failed in six weeks."

"As long as that!"

"You don't look forward to staying here for that length of time?"

Avoiding a too penetrating gaze, Psyche concentrated on the pale smoke spiral rising from her cigarette. "It's rather a long period in which to mark time, in which to do nothing useful."

"You don't consider that what we will be doing will be useful to you?"

"Yes, in a way, of course, but——"

"I think we had better try to dispose of your 'buts' before we attempt to go any further. You might be interested in some of the tentative conclusions I have already reached."

She watched him pick up a stack of papers, and start leafing through them. At the top of each page she saw a name that was not really her name, and was astonished by her own passionate wish to see 'Psyche' written there, as if this alone would make truth of hypothesis, would in itself illumine to its farthest corners a long darkness. But still she could not bring herself to tell him.

"Does all that concern me?" she asked incredulously. "Have I already told you so much?"

"This is only a very small beginning. Now, having correlated and studied these notes, I think I can safely say that if you did not go direct from your parents' house to the shack, the intervening space of time could be measured in months. When I say 'parents' you must realize that I employ the term as a symbol representing guardianship, and choose it simply because, on a purely mathematical basis, it is the most likely relationship between a child of three years and the adults living under the same roof. Because of the nature and precision of your memories. I think that your friend Mag must have misjudged your age a little. I would say that if you are not already twenty, you are much closer to it than you have assumed."

"But I remember nothing!"

"Although you are not aware of it, you remember a great deal." The doctor turned another page. "Now here, for example, we have your statement of the age at which you first envisaged parents with definite physical attributes, and a description of them as you represented them to yourself. You have described a young man and a young woman, the latter bearing a very close resemblance to yourself as you are now. If these people had been nothing more than a product of your imagination, it would have been much more natural if they had been middle-aged, or at least approaching it. You drew for yourself the picture of a woman so young she could not possibly have been the mother of a ten-year-old child. You were, at ten, remembering what you had seen when you were approximately three. You attempted, and failed, to imagine brothers and sisters as part of your family circle. If the whole conception had been entirely imaginary, you would have had no difficulty in fitting them in—any number that pleased you. My present contention, and we will explore it a great deal more thoroughly, is that your mind refused brothers and sisters for the excellent reason that they did not exist."

"Go on," Psyche said quietly.

Dr. Scarletti had intended to do no more than ensure her co-operation, and this he felt he had already done. She was, however, an exceptionally sympathetic audience, and he decided that it would serve some purpose to talk a little longer.

"Every human being is an infinitely complex puzzle, unique, individual, never exactly duplicated. Each one responds, however, to certain basic physiological and emotional stimuli. Knowing this, rough behaviour patterns can be calculated in advance on the foundation of a known ancestry and heredity. These patterns are blurred, reshaped, and at last moulded into their final form by the onslaught of environmental pressures. There are those who believe that such pressures are greater in their effect on the individual than the original, or hereditary, shaping. I hold, and strongly, to the reverse belief. I consider, therefore, that you at this moment represent far more of your original heredity than might be generally supposed.

"Working in reverse, studying you more carefully and thoroughly than you have possibly realized, I have sketched in the kind of background from which I am virtually positive you must have originated. Yours is, I would judge, a purely Anglo-Saxon heritage for some generations back. Both your inhibitions, and the directions in which you are uninhibited, are representative, quite apart from bone structure and colouring. To come a little closer to the present, I consider it almost a foregone conclusion that not one, but both of your parents are—or were—endowed with a very high degree of intelligence, and were extremely well educated."

As if the words still echoed on, undying, Psyche heard a sentence she had flung at Nick. "Why not the both of them?"

"The rapidity with which you threw off the manners and colloquialisms of speech that were yours for so many years is, I think, proof of this last contention. First, because you have inherited the measure and kind of mental equipment to make such a thing possible. Secondly, because I believe that you were returning, to some extent at least, to remembered standards. With your subconscious memory as my chief instrument, I expect to fill in the details of a provisional history so precisely that its counterpart in reality can be rediscovered. A fascinating experiment, don't you think?"

"Yes," Psyche replied slowly, "it is a fascinating—experiment."

To herself she thought, "He will give me bright fragments that I can cherish as truth; but more than that, no. He is extraordinarily clever, this man who sees so much that is human with so little humanity, but he would have to be a veritable wizard to accomplish what he now proposes." And she knew that whatever else she might or might not be led to believe under the influence of those magnetic eyes, she would not believe in wizardry. The unending winds of time had blown too long, the restless sands shifted too often, for this to be anything other than a glass through which she would see at best darkly.

"Does six weeks still seem like too much of your life to give to such a purpose?"

Psyche's blue gaze rested on the sheaf of papers on the desk between them. Although she could not persuade herself that he would succeed, he would nevertheless give her much of herself that she might otherwise never know. To deny such an opportunity would be to prove herself both a fool and a coward, and she was neither. Even if the days to follow were as wretchedly uncomfortable as to-day had been, six weeks would pass very quickly.

"No, it is not too much," she said.

"Did you have a good time, Hannah?" Sharon asked.

"Does one ever have a good time at a summer resort?"

"You're beautifully tanned."

"I'm glad there's something beautiful about me," Hannah replied crisply. "Well, where is your art exhibit?"

Sharon led her across the hall, past the circular staircase, and through a door that opened into a large library. "There you are," she said quietly.

A tall figure that contrived an angular elegance, Hannah walked past Sharon, to come to a halt at the far end of the room where hung seven paintings. The minutes passed, and then she said, "She's very like you in all ways. She's lucky. If she hadn't been tough——"

"Are you telling me I'm tough?"

Hannah swung round. "Yes. Very. You couldn't have stood up to this, any of it, if you hadn't been. Where is the 'Venus'?"

"In the National Gallery," Sharon told her bitterly. "It was bought the day it was hung. It isn't for sale now at any price. What would you like, tea or a drink?"

"How long have you known me, darling?"

Sharon smiled, which was what the dark woman had intended, and moved toward a mahogany cabinet.

"Did you like the artist?" Hannah asked curiously.

"Yes and no. He's an attractive egotist. Mostly no, I think. Ring for ice, will you, Hannah."

"Why did she leave him?"

Sharon bit her lip. "Apparently because she wanted to."

"But you don't believe him?"

"It's difficult not to believe him. He has a great deal of charm. But—no, I didn't."

Hannah did not speak again until they were seated in two deep chairs near a window through which could be seen the terraced garden.

"Your delphiniums are fantastic, darling."

Sharon leaned forward to light a cigarette. Hannah was her closest friend, but there were a few things she had not told her. "I'm fond of blue," she said quietly.

"And the rustic foster-parents?"

Sharon's smile was spontaneous this time, and her blue eyes were soft and amused. "Butch and Mag? They are incredible, awful, utterly preposterous, both of them—and I loved them."

"And so I suppose you and Dwight have set them up for life?"

"We owed them more than we can ever repay."

"And what are you doing now?"

Sharon's gaze, clouded over, returned to the paintings in front of which she sat for many hours every day. "We are employing an army of detectives—and waiting."

Hannah reached over, and her hand rested for an instant on Sharon's, but, when she spoke, she was characteristically unemotional. "How long can you take it? The waiting?"

"Indefinitely," Sharon said steadily.

Hannah, watching her, knowing the control she was setting upon herself, said slowly, "Mightn't it help to talk to someone now and then? Someone who was in no way personally involved in this?"

"Heaven knows I talk to enough detectives."

"No, I didn't mean anything like that. I meant talk simply as a release. Say what you feel occasionally without restraint. You and Dwight protect each other, and you have too much pride to *have hysterics in front of me. I met a man at dinner last week. A brain surgeon really, but he does a lot of psychiatry. His name's gone for the moment. Extraordinary eyes, but the most impersonal man I ever met."*

Sharon shook bright, loosely waving hair back from her face.

*"No, thank you, darling. If you run across an obstetrician who makes a specialty of producing lost daughters out of his black bag, you might let me know. But I don't need anyone to tell me what to think, or how to think it. Not now—or any time."*

4

AFTER ten days in the Scarlettis' house, Psyche knew that the fragile thread that the doctor was attempting to reconstruct between the past and the present was all that kept her from running as far as she could get, not only from the house itself but from everything it represented.

From the moment when she had stepped into the car on leaving the hospital, she had felt as if she were enclosed in a glass case heavily insulated against contamination from any outside source. A glass case, furnished with treasures which must not be breathed upon by the infidel, and inhabited by individuals who questioned neither their own superiority nor the inferiority of the masses with whom they communicated as little as possible. If there had been any joy in this self-imposed segregation, she could have understood it better. But, standing of a morning in the embrasure of the drawing-room windows, partially concealed by heavy damask curtains, it seemed to her that a Lithuanian family publicly sprawled on their front steps knew more of joy than the length and breadth of the street she now looked at would experience in decades.

The quietness of the tree-lined street, its great houses set well back from the sidewalk, should have been restful; instead, she found it peculiarly oppressive. On windless days the tar-paper shack had been imprisoned in a basin of almost unearthly quiet, had stood removed from the world in an unmoving, static isolation., And Nick's barn, visited only by nesting swallows and an occasional contemplative cow, had been enfolded in a timeless, pastoral lethargy. But both these conditions had owed their lack of stress and strain largely to physical factors. Their quiet had been a natural quiet. This residential quiet was unnatural, was the forced result of man-made strictures that forbade all outward evidence of normal, every-day life.

No children played on this street. No dogs frisked on lawns as lacking in interest as unused squares of green velvet. No laundry desecrated back gardens where even the colours of the flowers seemed suppressed. Delivery vans came and went, but they did so quickly and unobtrusively, as though obscurely ashamed of the prosaic functions they serviced. Sometimes a servant, in a black-and-white uniform, would emerge to polish a brass number plate, to sweep steps and walks with the prim decorum befitting her negligible station in life. Or a fashionably slim lady, made ageless at a distance by her rigid conformity to style, would come out to walk as far as a waiting car. But, more often than not, the street lay deserted and empty under the morning sun, as if a sudden plague had struck down all its occupants, nothing remaining of them but the massive brick and stone shells in which they had hidden their manifold fears and uncertainties while still they lived.

That both fear and uncertainty existed in this milieu, Psyche saw quite clearly, and yet it was knowledge which her conscious mind had the greatest difficulty in accepting. Without ever examining the thesis for flaws, she had automatically assumed that the really privileged, the wealthy and well-educated, would be free from petty competition, would be generous and contented in their security. The cocktail hour in Nora's rose-and-gold drawing-room was enough in itself to disabuse her of this conception, for there she overheard remarks and conversations that, for polished, deliberate malice, shocked her as nothing had ever shocked her before. That those who talked, and those who were talked about, should be interchangeable, should willingly mingle day after day, was beyond her comprehension.

If she had come across failings in another level of society, she would have written them off, ignored them much as she had ignored the practices at Bel's place. Here, she could do no such thing, for here to all outward intents and purposes was the goal toward which most people, herself included, strove. Deeply troubled, experiencing an increasing confusion of mind and spirit, she knew that, rootless and alone though she was, she would not exchange places with any of the people she met here for anything in the world.

Only in the mornings when the doctor had left the house, and Nora was still in bed, did she achieve anything that approached tranquillity, and even this was marred by servants who appeared to find her constantly in the way. The huge drawing-room, the austerely beautiful dining-room, the delicate French morning-room, the library, even the conservatory, were all invaded by duster, mop, waxer, and vacuum-cleaner; for Nora, when she came down at noon, expected to find the lower floor in perfect order. The best thing, Psyche knew, would have been to stay in her own room, but she fled from its impossible purity as soon as she was dressed, feeling that even the rumpled bed was a profanity she should somehow have managed to avoid.

Metaphorically chained to the house by Dr. Scarletti who, contrary to her own opinion, did not consider her well enough as yet to go out, she would wander from room to room, picking up a book or a magazine, and then putting it down again, unable to concentrate on any one thing. And unconsciously, as the morning wore on, she would become more and more tense as she waited for the first sound of a light, well-bred voice that always greeted her in the same way.

"Maggie darling, where are you hiding?"

Immediately *gauche*, feeling as if she actually had been hiding,

Psyche would go to the foot of the stairs to meet Nora, too quickly, obviously uncertain of herself. And even as she went, she would be thinking with near panic, "This is not me—this uneasy creature so often at fault, with two left hands and several left feet. Something is all wrong, terribly wrong. It can't be me—or can it?"

And seeing Nora, fresh and cool in a simple linen dress, she would find it, temporarily at least, impossible to believe that there could be anything to criticize adversely in any life Nora elected to lead.

Nora did not say quite the same thing every morning, but it usually added up to the same thing. She was always warmly solicitous. "Darling, didn't you sleep well? It worries me to see you looking so tired?"

Joint victim of a growing disillusion that she recognized, and of a war of nerves that she had not the slightest idea was being waged against her, Psyche, who had slept very well, would feel fatigue wash over her in heavy waves.

Or it might be, "Darling, you must be terribly pretty when you are well." And Psyche would have a sensation of deep lines imprinting themselves across the clear contours of her face.

Admiring Nora for her chic, her beautiful sophistication, and her adroit social sense, she was yet perpetually ill at ease in her presence. Nora never seemed to find her lacking in any way, was always swift to cover up her blunders, but things constantly went wrong when they were together. Even though Psyche applied all her quick intelligence to the task of not falling into the same error more than once, fresh pitfalls continued to open up before her.

When Nora had suggested that she be introduced to the people who came to the house as a distant connection of the doctor's, rather than as a patient, she had seen this as simply further evidence of Nora's at times overwhelming thoughtfulness on her account, without understanding that the status of "poor relation" was the lowest category into which she could possibly have been put. If she had been presented as a raving lunatic her social rating would have been considerably improved.

Nora, who might have been excused for forgetting her when

there were guests, never did. Nora constantly drew her toward a group, or an individual, and Psyche saw it as entirely her own fault that she would almost at once find herself staring at casually turned backs. What she did not realize was that she wore a mask as cool and composed as those who found her wanting, and that she was rejected not only for failing to belong, but for the unforgivable sin of appearing not to care. Consistently snubbed, she withdrew into the role of observer, as she had done at school, liking what she saw as little as she had then. Given any choice, she would have withdrawn altogether, and taken herself out of range of some of the contradictions that perturbed her. But Nora would not allow this.

"It would be so much easier for you if I weren't around," she told Nora.

Nora's laugh was gently chiding, softly amused. "What would my friends think of me if I were to hide a relation of John's in the attic when they dropped in?"

"I hadn't thought of it like that," Psyche said. "I'm sorry." And thought to herself despairingly, "I am in the wrong again. How did it happen this time?"

One afternoon when a correct, impassive maid had closed the door behind the last of several guests, she turned impulsively to Nora, and said, "Do they really mean all the dreadful things they say?"

Nora, regarding overflowing ash-trays and empty cocktail glasses with distaste, replied, apparently without thinking, "About you, darling? Of course not. How could they? They don't really know you at all."

Psyche stared at her. "Do they talk—about me, too?"

"How clumsy of me, Maggie dear! I misunderstood. They only say nice things about you, of course."

Putting a still too thin hand to her forehead, Psyche pushed back a wave of hair which felt damp and heavy to the touch, and realized as she did so that her head ached. "Of course," she said levelly.

Nora looked thoroughly upset. "Darling, you simply mustn't think—look, this is a horrid conversation. Let's go out and sit by the fountain. The sun is down, and it won't be too hot for you. You can tell me how you and John are getting on with your experiment. I hear so little about it, and I am so interested."

Psyche very much disliked talking about herself to Nora. Seen through Nora's eyes, her life to date appeared as a series of irreparable misfortunes. Although tactful, Nora was so very sympathetic that Psyche sometimes had the unpleasant impression that she was attending her own wake, having in some curious way failed to notice the ultimate disaster that had made such a thing necessary. She even went so far as to wonder once or twice if some part of her had not in truth died under the wheels of a heavy truck—the part that had really cared about living, that had once dreamed dreams of a bright future.

That Psyche should begin to adapt herself in less than a month to an environment previously so foreign to her was something that Nora had not anticipated, but the steadily diminishing number of small, barbed darts with which she could safely prick her was undeniable proof that this was the case.

Psyche, although her original liking for Nora had become considerably tempered, nevertheless believed implicitly in her goodwill, and sought to please her by conforming. She had always held a cigarette between thumb and first finger; she now used her first and second fingers. She learned to conduct herself with assurance at a table as elegant as any at which she could ever imagine sitting. She accepted what the servants did for her with a slight inclination of the head, refraining, at first with the greatest difficulty, from any spoken recognition of service rendered. She left her purse in her bedroom, rather than carrying it wherever she went as the girls at Bel's had done. She sat, even when relaxed, with her feet crossed neatly under her chair. She no longer shook hands with people when introduced, and no longer said she was pleased to meet them; instead, she smiled, and said 'How do you do'. She wore her clothes well and they were basically simple, but she increased their simplicity by removing all trimming that was not functional. No revision of her vocabulary seemed necessary because Nora and her friends, when the occasion demanded, swore easily and fluently.

If she had attempted to ape manners to which she was unaccustomed simply because she was self-conscious and ill at ease, she would in all probability have failed, or, at best, succeeded only in part. Motivated by a desire to please, and building on a firm basis of natural grace and poise, she was extraordinarily successful. Satisfied though she was with this success, it yet contained in itself some component of conditions which she found daily more oppressive.

Only in the evenings did the suffocating atmosphere within the glass cage lighten a little. Shut up in the library, partially mesmerized by Scarletti's forceful personality, she nevertheless regained a foothold on what to her was solid ground. The doctor's interest, because it was not sympathetic, because it was entirely clinical, steadied her, allowed her to see people and events outside the cage without distortion.

During dinner, the intensity of his regard, rarely releasing her for more than a minute at a time, was very close to unbearable. But as soon as they were alone together, like a judge retiring into the vested anonymity of wig and gown, the man as such became subservient to his purpose. And since that purpose was that she walk, with all the ease and naturalness possible, the familiar paths of her own yesterdays, she renewed herself in the course of increasingly long evening sessions. Like Penelope unraveling each day's work between sunset and the next sunrise, she was able to untangle the web of uncertainty and distress which Nora's subtle malice wove around her in the daytime, shaking herself free of invisible strands which, if they had been allowed to accumulate, would have dragged her down as they were intended to do.

Nora, on the other hand, found no relief for the suspicion, jealousy, and outraged vanity that, seeded together, were blossoming in her like some evil, hybrid fungus. If she had thought Psyche unattractive, she would still have fiercely resented her presence in the house. Sensing in her an attraction far more potent than that of mere good looks, her original objective animosity had turned into a vicious dislike that she had more and more difficulty in concealing. The seeking of amusement where and as she pleased, if done discreetly, was one of the rights she had wrested from a marital bargain heavily weighted in her favour. To have freedom thrust upon her, however, was not what she wanted at all, and the soft click of the library door closed against her evening after evening was a fan for fires that scarcely needed fanning. A small, slim cat, its long nails symbolically bloodied, she held a wicked temper on the fraying leash of her own best interests.

It was a leash that snapped on the night when Dr. Scarletti, without thinking, not only closed but locked the library door.

## 5

THE last Friday in August was one of sultry heat that flowed across the day into an oppressive blue-purple twilight.

Sitting deep in a red leather arm-chair to whose contours she now adjusted herself automatically, Psyche looked beyond the desk and its pool of light, beyond the doctor's handsome mediaeval head, and out through open windows to the fountain, a pale wraith dying slowly, unevenly, in the silent grasp of evening. Listening intently, she sought to catch the echo of falling water, but it was a cool whisper too faint to reach her.

"I believe there is going to be a storm," the doctor remarked.

Perversity claimed Psyche. "Do you? I don't."

A long, spatulate finger placed on the book in front of him, Dr. Scarlatti continued as if she had not spoken. "It will break before midnight. And now, I think we are ready to begin."

When you say it will storm, a storm is to be expected, Psyche thought with silent irony. When you are ready, we are ready.

Odd that I should be of such importance to you in one respect, and so completely unimportant in all others. I wonder what you would do if I were to get up, say I was weary of this, that as far as I could see it was leading me nowhere, and that what you were getting out of it was of as little interest to me as my concerns appear to be to you.

Looking up, she found Scarletti's brilliant eyes fixed on her, and, a little taken aback, knew by his next words that he had in this instance read her mind with extreme accuracy.

"You would perhaps like to know one of my most recent deductions," he said smoothly. "It will undoubtedly please and startle you. Yours is, or was, a wealthy family."

"That must be guesswork!"

"Conjecture, if you like. I do not indulge in guesswork."

Neither her face nor her voice betraying how little this idea pleased her, Psyche asked evenly, "What makes you think so?"

"If you don't mind, we will not go into it in detail at present."

And if I do mind? We will still not go into it. He must be guessing. I have told him nothing which could have led him to such a conclusion. Or have I? I cannot see the fountain any more. It must be night. And tomorrow will be another day, and then another night, and a day, and a night and—and I don't think I can stand much more of this.

The doctor, regarding her as he might have regarded a specimen on a dissecting table, knew now that if his conclusions were correct, she could only have been separated from her family in one of two ways, loss or kidnapping. He inclined toward the latter theory because loss without recovery would have been possible only if travelling had been involved, and nothing had turned up to indicate any gap between her hitherto subconscious memories, now shaping into a credible whole, and her known beginnings. He was even prepared to wager that her birthplace was in the same country in which she had been brought up, rather than across the nearby border as it might quite easily have been. With cold exultation, he realized that when his hypothesis was complete, he would in all probability be able to put his hand on immediate, tangible proof of its essential correctness. Another ten days at most and he would be ready to put his theories to the test. A lesser man might have been tempted to jump the gun, but not Scarletti. As a student he had been contemptuous of those who looked up the answers in order to work both ends toward the middle, and he had not changed. To him a solution he could not produce himself was not worth having.

"To-night," he said, "I intend to vary our procedure a little. I want you to look forward rather than backward. It will be useful at this juncture to know what your aims are, what you think you might do with your life."

Psyche did not reply at once, and when she did, it was to say slowly, "I don't know."

A shadow of impatience clouded the doctor's unwavering gaze. "That is not an answer. You have not fought an unfortunate environment for nothing."

Lacing slender hands tightly together, Psyche said evenly, "I didn't think so—once. Now I do."

"Now you do what?"

"Think it was for nothing."

More than a little annoyed, Scarletti continued to question her for some time before he was forced to admit that his hitherto co-operative subject could neither be driven nor led in the particular direction he had chosen. That she was not being deliberately obstructive he knew, and yet at the same time there were elements in her refusal to think of the future that he felt she could have explained had she chosen to do so. Being thwarted in any way at all did not agree with him, and it was much earlier than usual, no more than ten o'clock, when he stood up abruptly, and said, "I think that will be enough for to-night."

Psyche's small sigh of relief was very audible in the ensuing silence. "I can't——" she began, and broke off. "What was that?"

The sound from the front hall had been very faint, but they had both heard it.

Muttering something unintelligible under his breath. Scarletti strode to the door, jerked at it, paused an instant in surprise when it did not give, and then unlocked and opened it. The hall, highly polished woodwork gleaming softly in the light of a single wrought-iron lamp, was empty.

A moment before, Psyche had wanted nothing so much as to escape from the close seclusion of the library, but, as the doctor stood aside for her to pass, she moved forward into the hall with an unaccountable reluctance. She had reached the foot of the stairway, and her hand was already on the broad newel-post when Nora's voice, biting, malevolent, swung her around as suddenly as the lash of a whip might have done.

"Which was it, Maggie darling? Was I locked out—or were you locked in—or both?"

Her black dress melting into the darkness of the drawing-room behind her, emeralds flashing at her bare throat, Nora's head undulated like that of a cobra about to strike. "Was it an anatomy class to-night, Maggie—darling?"

Sick with shock, white to the lips, Psyche clung to the newelpost unable to move or speak, a frozen corner of a triangle completed by the doctor still standing at the entrance to the library.

Scarletti's voice was cold and emotionless, but it was the voice of wrath itself. "This time you have gone too far, Nora."

The swaying figure in black shifted its focus of hate, and a soft hissing seemed to wrap itself around the sentences shaped by a thin red mouth. "I who have gone too far? Stop acting, you selfrighteous hypocrite, if you haven't forgotten how! You think you are God, don't you? A little tin god before whom everyone must bow and scrape, and say yes and no as you dictate, and lick your boots, and pay homage day and night in order to feed your insatiable vanity. You think——"

Livid with anger, Scarletti cut in with such loathing in his voice and hooded eyes that, for a moment, Nora was silenced. "For this, my dear wife, I will see you stripped of all you possess, of every single thing you have taken from me, giving nothing in return. You are a parasite, a leech, from whom I will cut myself loose if it costs me all I have. You, and all your kind—useless, selfish, malice seeping from every over-perfumed pore—should be exterminated at birth. That you should be sterile is the only virtue you possess."

Psyche, paralyzed by an ultimate and complete disillusionment, wished with every fibre of her being to run, and could not. What made her disillusion doubly terrible was the realization that these two had lived together feeling as they did, and might, for purely material reasons, conceivably continue to do so.

Her words no more than a hoarse whisper, she murmured, "No —no!"

Nora's green eyes flicked across her and then back to her husband. "You call yourself a doctor. I call you a vulture, savouring pickings from minds you render even more helpless than when they grope their way to you for succour. You feed on them, lord it over them, think yourself their superior——"

"Will you be quiet!"

"A little tin god with no soul," Nora crooned, "in love with your own profile, stalking the corridors of your empty kingdom."

Scarletti's hypnotic eyes blazed out of a smile that might have been modelled in old ivory. "A kingdom from which you are about to be exiled, my dear Nora. From the outside, looking in, you may think more highly of it. You are, I promise you, going to be poor, and therefore alone, your neuroses patterning your face daily with fresh lines."

"While you become arthritic from kneeling at the altar of your own ego!" Nora flung at him. "And don't mislead yourself into thinking I won't be there to see it. I am not leaving, but your slum-reared patient is! And I tell you now that if you ever again try to bring any of your damned derelicts into this house, I will see you pilloried in every newspaper in the country. When I am through with you, you won't even be accepted as a veterinarian."

Still smiling, Scarletti said softly, "I have evidence collected against such a contingency as this. Evidence on which I can, and will, secure an uncontested divorce, unpleasant though the proceedings will be. I am in a position to get rid of you, my dear Nora, without the necessity of gagging you with so much as a single dollar bill."

Taking one cat-like step forward, Nora almost spat at him. "Uncontested! You fool! Do you imagine that the games you have played here in this house with your—your bedraggled blonde won't provide——"

Psyche, running up the stairs, nausea climbing her throat, stumbled as she reached the top. The silken pile of thick carpeting was against outflung hands, then she was up again, and a moment later reached the white and silver bedroom.

Working with feverish speed, she emptied the contents of cupboards and drawers on to a bed already turned down for the night. Her possessions were too few for their transference to her suitcase to take long, and it was no more than ten minutes after she had fled from a scene grown intolerable past bearing that, coat over her arm and suitcase in hand, she made her way noiselessly down the back stairs to the service entrance.

Out on the street, the summer night heavy and still around her, she did not hesitate, but turned at once toward the north in response to a homing instinct that would not be denied. Somewhere to the north lay the shack. She was not going back to it, but in facing in that direction she underlined her rejection of nearly everything she had known since leaving it.

Three-quarters of an hour later she walked away from the end of a street-car line toward the beginning of the highway she intended to follow.

Behind her she heard thunder, like a muffled roll of drums, and, looking back, saw rose-red lightning flash across the southern horizon. The storm had broken over the city, but overhead, and to the north, the sky was a clear, dark canopy emblazoned with stars.

## 9 | THE TRUCK DRIVER

FOR a time scattered dwellings bordered the highway, some already shrouded in a sleeping darkness, others showing yellow squares of light. Keeping to the shoulder of the road, walking neither slowly nor fast, Psyche was as indifferent to them as she was to the occasional cars that, in passing, touched her with sharp gusts of air and traced her shadow, weirdly distorted, on dusty grass and hedgerows, across road signs and fence-posts.

Unoppressed by any necessity other than that of putting one foot in front of the other, she realized, to her surprise, that disgust and disillusion had given way to a light-hearted satisfaction in simply being alive and entirely on her own.

Listening to the even sound of her footsteps, to the crickets in a nearby field, to an owl in a copse ahead of her, she thought, "I should be afraid; afraid of being alone in the night, in the world; afraid because I am not yet really strong again; afraid of what may happen to me when my small amount of money is gone. Instead—I am afraid of nothing. I am free, and that is enough. To hell with Nora, to hell with the doctor—to hell with everybody."

The big oil truck, when it passed her toward two o'clock in the morning, was doing more than sixty miles an hour. Psyche noticed it, and no more than that, but the harsh grinding of its brakes as it slowed down and came to a halt some hundred yards ahead of her drew her full attention. If she had ever been going to remember another truck, and another night when faulty brakes had been applied too late, it would have been then. But, remembering nothing, she approached now stationary tail-lights with no more than the wariness natural to an encounter which might, or might not, be of use to her.

When she came up beside the high cab on the off side from the driver, the door was already open, and she leaned against it as she looked up at the man clearly picked out by the lights on the dashboard.

"Want a lift, sister?"

She saw a crew cut, a rocky profile, and a sweat-stained T-shirt disclosing muscular arms and a burly chest. The truckers who had stopped at the derelict mail-box in the slag had not been any more beautiful, but they had always been good to her. It was a breed with which she was thoroughly familiar, and in this instance a quick scrutiny was enough to convince her that it would be perfectly safe to accept the offer.

"Thanks," she said, and handing her bag up to him, pulled herself up the steep step.

It was not until the truck was under way again, and she had settled herself as comfortably as possible on the hard seat, that she began to realize how close to physical exhaustion she must have been. Her feet and legs ached, and the hand in which she had been carrying her suitcase jerked with small spasmodic cramps. Flexing her fingers, she opened her purse and took out cigarettes and matches.

"Like a smoke?" she asked.

Without taking his eyes from the road, the trucker said, "Don't mind if I do. Going far?"

Drawing smoke deep into her lungs, exhaling it slowly, Psyche said, "I don't know."

"You out of a job?"

"I suppose you could put it like that."

"Broke?"

"Not quite."

The rhythm of the heavy engine was soothing, and the sameness of the small area trapped in the brilliance of the headlights was pleasantly soporific. Quite content to be where she was,

Psyche let her head rest in the angle made by the door and the back of the seat, and stretched her long legs forward until her feet were braced against the floor where it sloped upwards toward the hood. She might not know where she was going, but for the first time in many weeks she knew what she was doing.

The large, blunt-fingered hand, coming to rest on her knee, was not entirely unexpected. Firmly, but without haste, she removed it. "Nothing personal," she said quietly. "I just don't, that's all."

"Didn't figure you would, but no harm in trying, was there?"

"No," Psyche said, "there's never any harm in trying." No harm in trying anything, ever, as long as one knows when to stop. No harm in dreaming, in straining after the impossible, as long as one knows when to stop.

"You got any folks, sister?"

As long as one knows when to stop. "No."

"What kind of work you figuring on getting?"

"Just about anything anyone will give me, I guess." Shifting her gaze, she glanced sideways at him, and was held, fascinated, by the snake, tattooed around his brawny arm, which writhed and twisted as he handled the wheel.

"That there's Irma," he said conversationally. "T'isn't everyone who falls for Irma, but you can't deny she's a lively little bitch."

As the dash-lights found her, and then lost her again, Irma was like a living serpent seen by the flicker of a jungle camp fire.

"I'm almost afraid she'll get away from you," Psyche said, amused in spite of her recoil from an art form that did not appeal to her at all. "How long have you had her?"

"Let me see. I got out of the navy three years ago Christmas, and Irma and me got together maybe a year before that. Close as I can figure it, four years."

Slowing briefly, they rumbled through a hamlet where a single bulb hanging above a cross street, and one coldly blue neon sign, seemed to emphasize, rather than deny, the apparent absence of any living being. Then, picking up speed, they were again roaring through a countryside empty of buildings other than occasional farm-houses.

"Why did you leave the navy?"

"Too goddam much water. Night driving in these big babies is kind of like being on a ship, only you can get off, if you see what I mean. I like to get off when I want. Another thing, once I pull out, I'm captain of this rig. I sets her on the North Star, and from there on what I says goes."

Studying two signs above the windshield which read, without equivocation, "NO SMOKING"—"NO RIDERS", Psyche asked idly, "The North Star. What is that?"

"That's the one star that don't move. You're setting a course for somewheres, you look for the North Star and you can figure where you are and where you want to go."

What a lot there is that I don't know, Psyche thought soberly. "I don't suppose you could show me where it is?"

Irma stretched and appeared to yawn as her master pointed in front of him. "Sure. You see them pines up ahead on the left?"

Locating a pyramid of darkness denser than the luminous darkness of the summer sky, Psyche said, "Yes."

"Well, now, you look to the left some more and then up and you see the Big Bear. Got it? Now you follow off the side away from the tail and take a line not just straight up to that bright one there, and that's it, sort of off by itself a ways."

Looking at heavens blazing with close-packed galaxies, Psyche wondered how anyone could ever distinguish one star from another, let alone describe one as being "sort of off by itself". Actually, she supposed, they were all very much off by themselves, but they certainly did not appear to be.

Feeling that the greater probably included the less, and recognizing a more specific quest as quite hopeless, she said, "Thanks. I see it."

"You'll find that star useful," he told her, pleased with himself. "I'm stopping to refuel here. Me and the wagon both. Want some coffee?"

As the truck turned off the highway between gas pumps and an all-night lunch counter, Psyche shook her head. "I'll wait for you here."

"What's the matter with you, sister? You running away from something?"

"No, not in the way you mean. But you don't really want me to go in there with you, do you?"

"Why in hell wouldn't I? I'm never ashamed to be seen with a good-looking dame."

Psyche pointed to the sign that so plainly said "NO RIDERS".

"What about that?"

The trucker's square face broke into a grin that took ten years off his possible forty or more. "The bastards that care about that type thing are all snug in their beds, or maybe some person else's. Anyway, they aren't here, you can bet on that."

They sat at a marble-topped counter, where Psyche, eating a thick sandwich served to her on a thick white plate, and drinking coffee from a thick white mug, rejoiced not only in the coarseness of the china but also in the clatter around her. Here was contrast that pushed the Scarlettis' elegant dining-room further into the past, and nothing could have pleased her more.

"Do you know how to use a lobster pick?" she asked her companion.

"Dunno that I do."

"Maybe that's why we get along."

"Do you?"

"Do I what?" asked Psyche, who had begun to work out how long it was since she had seen a sandwich with a crust on it.

"Know how to make out with one of them lobster things?"

"I do now. But don't hold it against me."

"I don't hold nothing against nobody, sister. Live and let live, that's my motto."

A smile touched one corner of Psyche's lovely mouth. "And anyone who doesn't agree with it gets a poke in the nose. Is that right?"

"That's right. You ready to go?"

Outside, a lessening of the darkness was a first intimation that before long the night would begin to give way to daylight. Pausing an instant on the steps of the lunch counter, Psyche yawned and shivered slightly.

The next two hours were a blur in which she dozed, and waked, and dozed again.

"Can you add figures, sister?"

Blinking, surprised to find that the sun was rising, gilding a green countryside with a promise of heat to come, she said, "I'm quite good at it."

"Ever worked as a cashier?"

"No."

Changing to low gear as the big truck lumbered toward the crest of a long gradient, he said, "Well, maybe that won't matter."

Psyche thought in passing that sunshine did not improve Irma. "Is it a job? Do you know of one I might get?"

"Maybe."

With difficulty Psyche kept her voice calm, almost uninterested. "Where?"

"Oliver's. An eatery about fifty miles north of here. We'll hit it soon after six-thirty."

Psyche's first impression of the town in which she was to live for a time was more than favourable, and, even from the outside, Oliver's restaurant attracted her at once. Its imitation-log frontage was in the centre of the single, long block of shops that comprised the commercial life of the little town—a mart bounded on the north by a post office and a hotel, and on the south by a railway crossing. Around this small hub there spread out a lazy pattern of unpaved side-streets lined with white frame houses, and maples that enfolded them in cool, protective shadows.

Situated in the heart of a lake district, summer residents the principal reason for its existence, the town had yet to wake when the truck stopped in front of a restaurant whose plate-glass windows were just beginning to reflect early-morning sunlight.

"This here is a classy dump. We'll go round by the back," the trucker said, without a trace of embarrassment.

The position of cashier at Oliver's was not one that a transient, without references or previous experience, would normally have stood a chance of obtaining, but when Psyche was presented to him, Ollie, with a week of the summer season still ahead of him. was desperately trying to replace a girl who had let him down without notice. Any local girls who might have measured up to the standards he required were already preparing to shake the dust of a small town from their shoes for the winter. Psyche, swimming against the tide, appeared at what was, for her, a most propitious moment.

Ollie was in the kitchen in his shirt-sleeves. Normally he wore coat and tie, but at a quarter to seven he had not yet taken up his public duties. A swarthy, thick-set little man in his early fifties, he reminded Psyche in many ways of Bel's Joe.

"This here's a friend of mine who wants to work for you, Ollie," the trucker said. "She hasn't done the kind of job you want, but she's good with figures, and like you can see for yourself, she's got class."

During the ensuing colloquy Psyche was aware that she was being sized up by shrewd dark eyes well used to judging people, and she was weak with gratitude and relief when she was told she would be given three days' trial.

With a grin and a wink, the trucker said, "Well, I guess you're all set, sister. Be seeing you."

When he had gone, Ollie said briskly, "No time to show you the ropes before we open, honey. I'll do your job for you to-day, and you stay with me and keep your eyes open. That's a nice dress you're wearing, not too fancy. You wear that kind of thing and you'll be exactly right. Now, we better get you fixed up with your name."

Crossing the big kitchen in which a cook and two fresh-faced waitresses were already working, he led her into a small office. Going to a filing cabinet, he opened a drawer, and took out a large box which he placed on one end of a polished oak desk. Looking at it, Psyche's surprise was clearly written on her expressive face.

With a self-satisfied smile, Ollie said, "Look like solid silver, don't they, honey? Nearly a hundred of them, too. All the girls' names you're ever likely to bump into. Now, which one's yours?"

She knew what was coming, but she said it anyway. "Psyche."

Shocked disbelief wiped the smile from his face. "Say that again?"

Psyche said it again.

"You're kidding!"

"I'm sorry. I'm not."

Looking down at the desk where he had already laid out an assortment—Mary, Elizabeth, Ann, Antoinette, Catherine—he rubbed the bald spot on the back of his head, and said unhappily, "This has never happened before. I guess you'll have to use your other name, honey. What's your other name?"

On the verge of breaking the news to him that she had no other name, Psyche changed her mind. The last thing she wanted to do was to appear odd or difficult in any way. Maggie—Margaret. It would do.

"Margaret."

"Oh, my gosh, honey, that won't do. We got a Margaret. One of the girls you saw just now in the kitchen is a Margaret. Look, we got to open in twelve minutes. Isn't there something you always wish you'd been called instead of that outlandish handle you got? Here, take your choice!" Scooping up several fistfuls of nickel-plated brooches, he spread them at random before her.

"Do I have to be called anything?"

"It gives a friendly note. The customers like it."

"I don't——" Psyche began, but Ollie would not let her go on.

"Make up your mind, honey. It's time we were out front. Here, this is a nice one. Simple. Dignified."

He held out a short, square palm, and Psyche saw traced across it in glittering Old English script—Nora.

Drawing in her breath sharply, she exclaimed, "No!" And reaching blindly into the box, said, "I'll take this one."

In time she became used to being called Rosalie, or, depending on who spoke to her, Miss Rosalie; but she never liked it.

Ollie, on the other hand, was entirely satisfied. "That's fine," he said, when he saw what she had chosen. "The customers will like that. Now, I'll make you acquainted with the rest of the staff, and one of the girls will show you where to wash up. Be as quick as you can, honey, and when you're ready you'll find me out front."

Five minutes later Psyche walked through the restaurant proper toward the front entrance and a glass show-case of cigarettes and candies on which rested the cash register over which she was to preside. And even as she approved green leatherette, and fresh flowers, she experienced an odd pang as she realized that the space on the street outside, occupied earlier by the big oil truck, was now empty.

It was Sharon, herself, who had suggested that they read a little longer before going up to bed, but Dwight, watching her, saw that her book had slipped from her hands.

Guessing what she was thinking about, he was aware of familiar pain against which he could erect no effective bulwark. If necessary, he would have laid down his life for her, his good, his beautiful, his passionate wife. That the one thing she most desired should be beyond his power to give her was a stark truth he at times found almost unbearable.

"Sharon——"

She looked up at once, and warmth came back into blue eyes which had been blank, fixed on a fathomless distance. "Yes, my darling?"

"You can share it, you know."

"I was," she said simply. "Nothing, not this endless impotent waiting, not anything, really matters—as long as I have you."

He got up from the chair in which he had been sitting, and crossed to the couch. He sat down beside her, and took both her hands in his. "We might get much further, much faster, if we gave it to the newspapers," he said gently.

"No, darling, no! We discussed that before."

"That was some weeks ago. There is a limit to what you can take, Sharon."

"As long as I have you," Sharon said quietly, "I can take anything. I can wait for the rest of my life—or hers, if I have to. But there must be no publicity."

It was a point that the man had not stressed when they had talked of it previously. He had not wanted her to recognize as clearly as he did himself the infinite number of unpleasant possibilities that seventeen years might contain.

When Sharon spoke again, he realized that he had again discounted her basic realism as he need not have done.

"Because I keep the wishful thinking on top," she told him quietly, "you must not think that I don't see what we may be up against. I know as well as you do that there may be things a reporter could turn up that would smear and twist her whole future. That must not happen. Even if it means that we never find her—still, that must not happen."

# 10 | THE NEWSPAPERMAN

I

DURING the few brief weeks that she worked at Oliver's, Psyche was more wholly contented than she could ever remember being. Deeply satisfied with her own complete independence, thankful to be temporarily rid of all personal claims, she hibernated emotionally while adjusting herself as a free member of a free society.

Grown used to adapting herself to rapidly changing circumstances, she settled into her new routine in a matter of days.

She liked Ollie who, despite his brooches, was an employer with very few quirks. She liked the stir and movement of a day which began at seven o'clock in the morning and did not end until midnight. With Sundays and the middle of every afternoon to herself, she either walked or read as the weather and her mood dictated. If she had chosen, she could have had friends, and from the beginning she could have had dates in as varied and great a number as she wished. For the time being she wanted neither.

The people whom she saw most often were those who lived, as she did herself, in rooms above the restaurant, and who, making a special arrangement with Ollie, ate all their meals in the restaurant. They were a heterogeneous collection, but each in his or her own way contributed something to her growing understanding of, and sympathy with, humanity as a whole. Although she was never intimate with any of these people, as the weeks passed she came to know them very well simply through observation and the closeness of contact obligatory in the circumstances under which they lived. Becoming aware of their problems, seeing the different ways in which they accommodated themselves to conditions as they found them, she began to achieve a perspective with regard to her own life infinitely more mature than it had been previously.

Up until this time she had always found herself within a framework of living unified in itself, making her the exception, setting her apart as unique not only in the minds of others but in her own. Now she began to see herself as unique only in so far as she was individual. Having long considered it a tragedy that she should have no known origin, she recategorized this state of affairs under the heading of misfortune. As for the present, irrespective of the past, she achieved a degree of objectivity that would not permit her to see herself as other than relatively very fortunate.

That the work she was doing would not continue to satisfy her indefinitely, she knew, but for the time being it more than sufficed. And to think, even vaguely, of leaving this peaceful little town, was to relinquish a tranquillity too rare in her experience to be other than precious in itself.

By chance, in this place, she had found not only a job but pleasant acquaintances in whom there had been no necessity to confide. She had not at any time had to say that she was ignorant of her origin, that she did not know who she really was. The relief this brought her was so great that she became daily more determined not to embark on any future course that would implicate her in the telling of a story she would now prefer to forget almost in its entirety.

She would continue to be grateful to Butch and Mag, to Bel and to Kathie—even to Nick, who, through his faults as much as his virtues, had given her a very precise idea of the kind of man who could be of permanent interest to her.

Each of these had contributed toward her present ability to

make a place for herself in an everyday world. But to explain her various relationships with them was, she was convinced, close to impossible.

She wondered how long it would take, in her new life, to build up a personal history—a history she could present to other people as sufficiently complete to need no previous detail, other than that she had come from the north and had no living relations. Even more important than this, how long would it take to prove to herself that she was the kind of person she had always hoped to be, on the basis of an imagined heredity? Two years. Perhaps three. Perhaps longer.

This metaphorical journey would, to be successful, have to be undertaken to all intents and purposes alone. No really close relationship would be safe.

As autumn clothed the town in red and gold and bronze glory, and the summer tourists vanished like migrating birds, what had at first been a tentative decision became, for Psyche, a firm resolve.

She was realistic enough to know that she would probably have to pay some price for this decision. Sensitive, imaginative, she was nevertheless a fighter, and on the late September morning when Steve Ryerson came into the restaurant, she was already prepared to pay that price.

She had found peace of mind. She would retain it, at any cost.

## 2

WHEN Steve Ryerson, at the end of his third college year, had taken a summer job on a newspaper, he had had no prior intention of making this his profession. By the middle of that summer, however, it was as apparent to him as to his managing editor that he was a born newspaperman.

The editor had called him into his office, a week before the university reopened, for a purpose as obvious to both of them as it would not at first have been to an outsider.

A short man, the editor conducted all interviews from the chair behind his large, untidy desk. "You're too goddamn well dressed," he said.

Steve grinned. "Is that all you wanted to say to me?"

"You look like a goddamn gentleman."

"You don't," Steve said pleasantly, "pay me enough to be able to call me names."

"What's your price?"

"Double what I'm getting now."

Commencing with some beautifully balanced blasphemy, the editor told him what he thought of this suggestion.

Steve sat down in a chair near the desk, stretched long legs out in front of him, lit a cigarette, and waited for the recommencement of negotiations whose outcome had at no time been in any doubt. He would not get the salary he had asked for, but he did not care about this. He *would* get the kind of assignments he wanted. He did care about this.

During the next three years, work alone would never have brought Steve Ryerson the brand of success he very quickly achieved—any more than his terse, compelling prose would have done, if it had had to stand unsupported. The core of his success lay, from the beginning, in his unerring instinct for a story.

Under his own by-line, Steve produced news where, previously, no news had been known to exist. The obvious leads he left to others to explore, and human interest as such did not move him. An apparently cynical crusader, his armour bare of any lady's favour, the articles he wrote shook the established order of things where, in his opinion, it most needed shaking. His news stories, when they broke, had both bite and drama while still adhering to unembroidered truth.

That a devotion to truth, as a thing in itself, was not always easy to adhere to in his particular field, he discovered early. With dispassionate realism, he accepted this as entirely human if not entirely admirable, and built the kind of reputation he himself wanted within the terms of reference as he found them. That this should at times prove difficult did not discourage him, for the simple reason that his own self-respect would always mean more to him than the opinions of others.

On the late-September morning when he came into Oliver's, he was, ostensibly, on holiday. A small assignment, actually out of his line, that he had undertaken only because he was to be in the vicinity, did not give the lie to this as much as did his typewriter, already set up in the cabin he maintained on a lake two miles from the town. His fishing tackle was still in the trunk of his car where, with a mixture of regret and amusement, he knew it would probably remain.

Psyche, when she heard the door open, was standing by the cash register while she checked over the accounts from the previous day. It was a time of day when, breakfast over, there were scarcely any customers, and she was responsible for looking after what few there were. So, although she was half-way through a long column of figures, she looked up to face the man who had paused briefly in the open doorway.

Sunlight, shining directly into her eyes, blinded her for the moment to anything more definite than an impression of broad shoulders, and dark hair thick and close against a well-shaped head.

Shaken by coincidence, by the memory of another man in another doorway limned not by sunlight but by sheet lightning, she silently called herself a fool for imagining that some, at least, of the same ingredients might be implicit in this encounter.

This, you idiot, she told herself fiercely, is a complete stranger, and one whom you will probably never see again. He can not possibly present any kind of threat to you. Neither will he be of any interest to you.

Yet, when he came forward to the counter behind which she stood, she needed all the poise she had ever acquired in order to behave naturally.

"Is it too late to get some breakfast?"

Psyche met the gaze of smiling grey eyes, and, tall though she was, she had to look up to do so. "Of course not," she said. "Would you like to sit down and look at a menu, or would you like to give me your order now?"

Steve, who had paused in the doorway because his interest had been stirred by his first sight of her, was still further intrigued by a voice and manner as greatly at variance with her surroundings as was her appearance. But it was not until she had led the way to a booth, and taken his order, that he became convinced he had seen her before. He could, he knew, be mistaken in this, but it was a kind of mistake he rarely made.

As he waited for her to bring his breakfast, he reminded himself that he had left the city at seven that morning in order to enjoy a week of comparative relaxation. To start immediately seeing a mystery where almost certainly none existed, was no way to go about doing this. Yet it annoyed him that he could not pin down the elusive memory that now insisted, not only that he had seen her before, but that the setting had been very far removed from the cashier's desk at Oliver's.

"Hello, Steve. No news still bad news with you?"

Absorbed in thought, Steve had not been aware of Ollie's approach. He laughed at a pleasantry the little man was never able to resist whenever they met, and said, "That's right, Ollie. And it looks as if it's bad news for me this week."

Although he saw him rarely, this was one of Ollie's favourite customers. "That's good," he said. "You don't take enough time off, Steve. You don't relax enough."

"Well," Steve said, "I'm relaxing now. Sit down and tell me what's new."

For a minute or two they talked about inconsequential changes in the district before Steve, watching the door through which she would reappear, asked about Psyche.

"I see you have a new cashier, Ollie."

Ollie, who had forgotten that Psyche had ever had any name other than the one he had quite literally pinned on her, beamed. "You mean Rosalie? She's a lovely girl, isn't she? And smart, too. Not that the others weren't good girls, mind you, but there's never been anyone in the place to compare with Rosalie."

Mentally Steve winced at the repetition of a name that he did not like, and that seemed oddly unsuitable for the girl to whom it was attached. "How did you happen to find her?" he asked casually.

"It's a funny thing you should ask me that," Ollie said. "Because to put it the right way round, she found me."

"How did she do that?"

"Rode into town one morning on one of them big oil trucks," Ollie said simply.

Steve stared at him. But before he could make any spoken comment, he saw the swing-door at the back of the restaurant begin to open.

"You were lucky," he said, and with easy adroitness turned the conversation into a different channel. "You would need someone good with the kind of Labour Day business you must have had."

"Steve," Ollie said, "you wouldn't believe it if I told you how many cars—oh, hello, honey. When you've set that down for Steve here, go rustle a cup of coffee for me, and one for yourself."

That Ollie should be on friendly terms with this man in no way surprised Psyche, because Ollie was on good terms with everyone he had ever met. His suggestion that she join them, however, caught her completely unprepared. It was not without precedent, but in this instance she had not expected it.

"I'll get your coffee right away, Ollie," she said. "But after that, if you'll excuse me, I'll go back to yesterday's accounts."

"What did I tell you, Steve?" the little man said. "Isn't she a wonder? Always working. Now you listen to me, honey. I'm the boss, and I just told you to get yourself some coffee."

So I was not imagining things, Psyche thought swiftly. They were talking about me when I came through from the kitchen. Which is all the more reason why I should not make a fuss about this coffee business. This man is already curious about me. I must do nothing to aggravate that curiosity.

"All right, Ollie," she said, smiling. "Thank you."

Steve, seeing her smile for the first time, discarded any lingering doubts he might have had on one score. She was as out of place at Oliver's as she would be in an oil truck.

After she had gone to get the coffee, he turned to Ollie with no further pretense. "Is she as attractive as she looks?"

Ollie, forgetful that a newspaperman might have an impersonal rather than a personal interest in her, looked smug. "You're interested, aren't you? I thought you might be. That's why I wanted you two to get together. It hit me that you'd maybe be more her type than the guys she gets to meet here most of the time."

"She doesn't go out much on dates?"

"She doesn't go out that way at all. But don't get me wrong, it's not because she couldn't."

"No," Steve said thoughtfully. "It wouldn't be because she couldn't."

Psyche knew in advance that when she came back this time the tall man with the disturbing eyes would stand up, and that she would have no choice but to take the place he offered in the booth beside him.

Because it happened exactly as she had known it would, she slipped into the place against the wall gracefully and without hesitation, but she was more aware of the man beside her than she had ever been of any man in her life.

"You don't take sugar, do you, honey?" Ollie said. "Well, you don't need it."

Steve shifted a little so that he could look directly at Psyche. "I've seen you before, haven't I?"

Her face and voice equally composed, Psyche said, "I don't think so."

"I have an idea it was about three years ago."

"No. That simply isn't possible."

It could not have been three years ago, Psyche knew, because at that time she had been walking barefoot on a slag heap. But if he were not entirely mistaken, if he had seen her somewhere more recently, this could only have happened when she was in the city. On the one occasion when she had gone into the city with Nick, she had stayed in the car. During her time at the Scarlettis she had not left the house. Which left Bel. He might have seen her while she was at Bel's place, either on the street, or in one of the large stores. Either alone, or with Bel.

He was still looking at her. "You were wearing white," he said slowly.

Oh, God, Pysche thought, if I was with Bel, don't let him remember. Don't let him find out anything about me that he can't see for himself. This could be enough, and will have to be enough.

"I really think you're mistaken," she said.

"If Steve says a thing's so, it likely is, honey," Ollie told her.

"He's human, isn't he?" Psyche asked.

"My guess is, yes," the little man said. "But that's something you could maybe tell better than I could, honey."

"Ollie, you're impossible!" Psyche said. Then, because she saw that they were both laughing, she began to laugh, too.

After that, it seemed perfectly natural to be exactly where she was, and with the company she found herself in. She felt as though she had been on her way toward this moment for a long time, as though she had in a sense created it herself. Here and now was her world as she wanted it to remain, in perfect proportion. Even when she learned that the man was in newspaper work, the original unease, which had gone hand in hand with instantaneous physical attraction, did not come back. She could trace no similarity between him and the reporters who had come to Bel's place after Kathie died. There quite simply was no similarity. And he had, apparently, dismissed his earlier idea that this was not the first time he had seen her.

Steve, in the course of easy, casual conversation, attempted to learn something about her. That he should, at the end of nearly an hour, have learned nothing at all, sharpened rather than dulled his interest in her; for he had conducted too many "casual" interviews to interpret her evasions as other than deliberate. Lovely to look at, parrying his oblique inquiries as skilfully as he made them, she presented him with a challenge from which, for a variety of reasons, he no longer had any wish to turn aside.

He looked at his watch. "Ollie," he said, "do you chain your white slaves down, or can they escape occasionally?"

"Steve," Ollie said, "it's not everyone I'd tell this to, but sometimes I even push them out on to the street."

Steve looked at Psyche. "If I were to drive past this afternoon at two o'clock, would I be likely to find you out on the street and in need of rescue?"

Unaccountably afraid to say yes, yet hesitant to say no for fear this might mean the end of something that had not really even begun, Psyche spread her hands helplessly in front of her. "I—I have work to do."

"You've forgotten," Ollie said. "This is your afternoon off, honey."

It was not her afternoon off, and Ollie, Psyche knew, was quite as aware of this as she was herself. He is behaving, she thought with inner amusement, like the mother of an ugly duckling. It had, apparently, really bothered him that she had never gone out with any of the men who had asked her. But then he did not know about Nick. Nobody, if she could help it, was ever going to know about Nick. She had told Bel. That had been in her other life. Nick did not belong, and never would belong, in this new life.

"Even if it wasn't your afternoon off, honey," Ollie said, "there isn't much to do at this time of year." With a sweep of one short arm, he asked her to witness the truth of this in a restaurant empty and quiet in the morning sunlight.

Psyche turned to Steve. "All right," she said quietly. "You'll find me in need of rescue at two o'clock."

With a smile that Psyche knew she would be unlikely to forget, he said, "Good. And, by the way, you had better bring a coat with you."

Psyche's dark eyebrows drew together in a small frown that was a question in itself. "A coat? It's as hot as midsummer today."

Steve stood up. "You're going to help me with my homework. I'm taking you out to the arena."

"Oh, no!" Psyche murmured. But he did not hear her because he was now speaking to Ollie.

### 3

WHEN the man drove up the main street of the little town at two o'clock, it was to find it caught in the doldrums of early afternoon. With the exception of the slim figure in blue standing outside the log front of Oliver's, it was temporarily empty of all other life. A few parked cars stood at the curb. Dead leaves, drifted from the side streets, lay in meaningless patterns across the deserted road. The only thing with any significance at all, in the scene as he saw it, was Psyche. And briefly he thought of her as an actress against the backdrop of a play in which she was palpably miscast, in which she seemed painfully alone, not only at the moment, but in all ways.

If it had been winter, he could have allowed himself the impersonal gesture of putting a rug around her when she got into the car. As it was, there was nothing he could do for her, and he was astonished that he should so much wish that there was.

"I see you didn't forget your coat," he said, as they passed through the quickly reached northern fringe of the town.

"No," Psyche said, "I didn't forget."

"Have you been out to the arena very often?"

"This will be the first time," Psyche told him quietly.

He spared a glance from a road that now ran between sun-soaked fields of yellow stubble interspersed with trees brilliant with colour. "Most people would have been curious, if nothing else."

"I am not most people."

This, he felt, was a truth too self-evident to call for comment. "I think you'll find it interesting," he said.

"I'm sure I will," Psyche said, but only because she wanted to please him.

She had deliberately refused the knowledge that the big wooden arena, where ranking figure-skaters practised during the off-season, was a place to which she could have gone at any time since she started to work at Oliver's. It was not a walk any longer than many others she had taken in other directions. But the memory of a frozen dawn and a small school rink was too painful to be willingly resurrected, even after the passage of more than seven years.

And now, when the man backed his car off the highway and came to a stop beside a sandy path leading to a door in a blank wooden wall, she could feel tension a hard knot within her.

They sat midway up the tiers of wooden benches encircling an oval rink. The spectators were few, and widely scattered. The skaters were equally scattered, each, attended by his or her own private coach, appropriating a section of blue-white artificial ice bounded by invisible but definite limits.

"Cigarette?" Steve asked.

"No thank you," Psyche said. She wanted to smoke very badly, but could not trust herself to hold her hands steady. For here was not only fluid grace beyond anything she had previously imagined, but hurt as fresh as when it had been inflicted on her.

The man lit a cigarette, and put the packet back in the pocket of his trench-coat. And as he did so, he noticed her hands, clasped together so hard that the knuckles were white and a flush of colour had run up under long, unvarnished nails. Without appearing to do so, he glanced at her face, and saw reflected there the same tension he had seen in her hands. He was too good a judge of people to doubt the actuality of an emotion whose source entirely defeated him. In this place there was, as far as he could see, no cause for it at all. Nevertheless he knew that he could not, for the time being, begin again on an attempt to crumble her defenses.

Without premeditation, he laid his hand over hers, and held them until he felt them relax.

For Psyche, the warm, strong pressure of his fingers thawed cold that had been a hidden part of her for longer than she could remember; cold that stretched back a long way beyond the specific unhappiness evoked by her present surroundings.

She looked up at him, with a smile breath-taking in its brilliance, and asked, "Is this the way you always do your homework?"

"Always," he said, his grey eyes teasing her.

This, Psyche thought, is what it feels like to be happy. I've never known before. "What are you really supposed to be doing here?"

"Something that I am not trained to do," he told her, "but that I have been asked to do because I am here. A matter of economic expediency on the part of my newspaper, and weak-mindedness on my own part. I am expected to hazard a guess as to whether any of these skaters are potential Olympic material."

"A year ago," Psyche thought, "I would not have known what he was talking about. If it had not been for Kathie I would never have heard of the Olympic games, much less been made to trace their history, on my own, back across the centuries to Mount Olympus. I would not have known what the word 'potential' meant. Kathie—Kathie, why did it have to end like that for you?"

She stared directly at the man beside her, searching the lean, hard planes of a face whose only open betrayal of sensitivity was in the lines of the mouth. "What would he think if I were to tell him about Kathie?" she wondered. "Would he condemn her? Would he condemn me? It is a risk I can not, and will not, take."

"You are probably much better qualified than you pretend to be," she said.

"A little, perhaps. But not much."

"You must have done some sports reporting?"

"Practically none. Spot the best skater on the rink for me. You'll be doing me a favour."

He had removed his hand from hers, but Psyche had difficulty in concentrating on the rink. Finally, she said, "The girl over there, I think. The one in red. I don't know anything about it, but she seems to me to be the best."

"For someone who doesn't know anything about it, you're doing very well. You've picked last year's national champion from amongst some very close contenders."

"Have I? It's the way she moves. She makes it seem so easy." The boys and girls at the school had made it look easy, too. A delusion. It was not easy at all.

"Change your mind about a cigarette?"

Relaxed now, Psyche nodded. "Yes, thank you. Can you skate?"

"I used to. But not this kind of thing. Hockey."

"You were probably very good," Psyche said, as she leaned toward the light he held for her. He would, she thought, be good at anything he did. If she were to continue to walk the tight-rope of a present with no admissible yesterdays, she would have to be very careful.

"Well, that's it," he said. "They seem to have finished for to-day. We can go now."

Rather than being relieved, Psyche found that she was disappointed, a reaction she could not have credited in advance. Unconsciously wistful, she watched the gaily clad figures glide one by one toward the exit from the ice, as she and the man descended a flight of steps.

They were almost at the rail, when she stopped, and said, "Look, there are more coming on now."

"Locals," Steve told her. "Using the ice for an hour or so before it is flooded again."

"How lucky they are!"

Something in her expression, as she said this, made Steve think of a waif with her face against the glass of a shop filled with toys forever beyond her reach. The impression was so vivid that he spoke almost without thinking. "Would you like to skate for half an hour before we go?"

"I can't skate," Psyche said abruptly.

"Why not?"

"My ankles are too weak."

One of the first things that had struck him about her was the co-ordinated grace with which she walked. "I don't believe it. We'll see if we can rent some skates."

"No! I don't want to!"

If she had not opposed the idea he would have been glad enough to withdraw from it. Now, his curiosity about her again fully aroused by a refusal much too emphatic for its context, he turned to a rink attendant standing near them, and said, "Can we rent skates here?"

"Yes, sir," the man said. "If you'll just come with me, I'll see what I can do for you."

"Steve—please!" Psyche said frantically. "I told you I can't skate!"

"You'll have to convince me," he said calmly.

Psyche, as they walked along a corridor beneath the tiers of seats from which they had just come down, knew without being told that his light clasp on her arm would tighten at once if she tried to pull away from it. In agony, she saw that she had three alternatives.

She could flatly, and if necessary, rudely refuse to go any further with this idea of his. In which case she might never see him again.

She could explain, and it would have to be in detail, why she recoiled from the very thought of putting on a pair of skates. The truth would find him sympathetic, she was certain, but it was the last thing she wanted to tell him.

The final, and it seemed only possible alternative was to suffer a re-enactment of humiliation she had never been able to forget, and live through it as best she could.

Without another word, she allowed herself to be led into a windowless room lined with benches and lockers.

As if from a great distance, she heard Steve talking to the attendant. Then she was sitting down, and her shoes were being gently but deftly removed from her feet.

"You won't have much difficulty in fitting me," the newspaperman said. "The lady, however, as you can see, has a very slender foot."

"I think we can find something for her," the attendant said. "We buy, second-hand, what are originally very expensive boots and skates."

"Good."

"I have an eight triple, sir, that might be just right."

For Psyche the immediate present could no longer be clung to. Only the past remained. It was like a nightmare in which, after having struggled with terrible effort up a steep mountain slope, one begins to slide inexorably backwards and downwards, one's brief glimpse of the mountain top no longer a spur but a symbol in itself of its unattainability.

*The stars, glittering, cold, immeasurably remote in a navy-blue sky, drew a pale radiance from snow that crunched harshly beneath her boots, a sharp, dry tearing of a frozen silence broken by no other sound.*

*Her breath making small frosty clouds that crystallized along the edges of the parka-hood framing her face, she thought, "I'll have a whole hour before the others gets here. I'll have learned to do it good by then."*

Not until she was walking up a wooden ramp, trapped equally by the skates on her feet and the firm hand on her elbow, was she able to make a partial return to the present. That it should be only a partial return was something she was quite unaware of as, a glassy surface directly in front of her, she clung to the rail and refused to let go of it. "I can't not do it—I can't not do it!" she said piteously.

Astounded, Steve heard diction and grammar so at variance with anything with which the husky voice had so far presented him, that he could not at first credit it. The one thing that was quite clear was that he had somehow precipitated an emotional crisis stretching far beyond this moment, and, in doing so, assumed the responsibility of deciding whether it would be better to let her withdraw, or make her go on. Either way he might make a bad mistake. With only instinct and the little he knew of her to guide him, he made his decision.

"You must trust me," he said quietly. "You're not going to fall down. I promise you."

"I ain't afraid of fallin' down. It's just—it's just that it's happenin' all over again!"

He put aside the familiar, sharp excitement he always felt when he first found confirmation of a story whose existence he had previously only suspected, in order to concentrate wholly on the problem at hand.

"What I am objecting to is that nothing is happening at all," he said, and placing his arm securely around her waist, lifted her bodily onto the ice.

Forty-five minutes later, he closed the left-hand door of his car and went around to the driver's seat and got in beside her. "Well," he said casually, "none of your fears were justified, were they? Lord, it's a hot afternoon. They should have a decompression chamber in that place."

He had started the motor, and was reaching into the glove compartment for a fresh packet of cigarettes, when he saw that Psyche, her face in her hands, was weeping uncontrollably.

With only the briefest hesitation, he cut the motor, and drew her to him. "What's troubling you now?" he asked gently.

"I—I—I *was* like a bird, wasn't I?" Psyche said. And, her face hidden against his shoulder, she wept harder than ever.

## 4

STEVE, when he let Psyche out of the car in front of Oliver's at a little before five o'clock, made no reference to any possible future meeting between them.

Although she had told him nothing factual, she had, he knew, betrayed more of herself than she had intended to, or would ever be likely to again. If he were to solve the complex mystery that intrigued him as much as, or more than, any he had ever come across before, his only hope of doing so now lay in staying away from her, and searching, undistracted, for a memory that had yet to come clear.

For he would, he was reasonably sure, know a great deal—if not all—about her past, once he had pinned that memory down. And this was something he intended to do if he had to stay up all night in order to do it.

After a makeshift dinner prepared on a one-burner hot plate, he stretched out in a deck-chair on the verandah of his cabin and lit the first of what was, as the night wore on, to be a long succession of cigarettes. Blind to the black-and-silver enchantment of the moonlit night, he moved slowly backward in time across every lead that he saw as at all pertinent.

The moon had set, and the first light of dawn was sharpening the serrated pattern of pines on the farther shore of the lake, when he came across the clue for which he had searched without any thought of sleep through more than nine hours.

Slowly he stood up, and pulled himself to his full height to ease stiffness from both his shouders and his legs.

That the clue he had finally found should point in a direction that seemed to make no sense at all, perplexed him even while he could not doubt its validity.

His first decision was to get in his car and follow up his lead as fast as possible. On second thoughts, he saw that it would be better to reach his destination toward the close of the working day rather than in the middle of it. This particular quest was one that he very much preferred not to advertise until he had a few of the answers.

When he reached the city in the late afternoon, he drove straight to the towering stone building that housed the offices of his own newspaper. Avoiding the city room, where he would have been forced to stop and talk, he took an elevator directly to the eighth floor and the newspaper's morgue.

He had known and liked the tall, dark-haired woman at the desk inside the door for a long time. "Wyn," he said, without other greeting, "have you got some off-the-record time to spare?"

They were always in a hurry, these men and women who came to her department to look through files that dated back across more than fifty years, who needed yesterday's ashes in order to kindle to-morrow's fires. Quite often they wasted her own time as well as theirs; but when Steve Ryerson came looking for something, the search was rarely fruitless.

"All right," she said. "What are we looking for?"

"Theatre news."

"Who, or what?"

"It's damn vague this time. A picture of a fair-haired girl in a white evening dress."

She looked at him in surprise. "Is that all you can tell me?"

"That's all I can tell you because it's all I know," he said.

"What year?" she asked resignedly.

"We're starting four years back, and working forward."

"Oh, my God!"

It was, Steve felt, farther back than he needed to go, but he was thorough in anything he did.

Four hours later, in the vault-like silence peculiar to a large office building after closing time, he looked up from a table stacked with clippings, ran both hands through his thick hair in a gesture of irritated frustration, and said, "You better get the hell out of here, Wyn. We're arriving nowhere, fast."

She had already given him three hours of unpaid overtime, but she simply shrugged. "I'm staying if you are."

He stubbed a cigarette in an overflowing ash-tray. "All right. But we'll eat before we go on."

They went to a restaurant in the same block, and the pavement under their feet was still warm even thought it was long after sundown.

They were waiting for coffee at the end of a meal during which he had maintained a preoccupied silence, when he brought the flat of his hand down on the table with a force that made the china rattle. "By God, I think I've got it! Right church, wrong pew! Come on, you don't want any of that rotten brew they call coffee here, do you? You can exchange it for a case of the best Scotch whiskey. Name your own brand."

She was too used to newsmen to be particularly surprised, but she said dryly, "You mean a bottle, not a case, don't you, Steve?"

"I said a case, and I mean a case. Don't waste time."

She picked up her purse, and attempted to smooth the wrinkles from a black cotton dress wilted by the unseasonable heat. "This must be quite a story."

"I'm beginning to think it is," Steve told her quietly. He had his elusive memory placed now. All he needed were names to go with it.

Back in the deserted morgue, he was no longer at all vague.

"Three years ago I covered a theatre fire," he said crisply. "It was in early October. A first night, and all the best people out in their glad rags. I don't want the story. I want the full-page spread of pictures that went with it. Think you can find that?"

"What you mean is, do I think I can find it in thirty seconds flat?"

His smile was momentarily devoid of all tension. "You're a bright girl, Wyn. Thirty-five seconds."

Three minutes later she laid, not a full page, but a single clipping in front of him. "This is what you want, isn't it?"

Photographs did not always do Sharon justice, but this flash picture, taken against the background of a soot-blackened brick wall, might have been a studio portrait. Her fur coat lost somewhere inside the theatre, she had stood in the cold October night, composed and quiet, waiting for Dwight to get their car. Her blonde hair framing her face, her white evening dress as unruffled as her manner, she could have been ready to be presented at court.

Steve, staring transfixed at a picture of Psyche that yet could not possibly be Psyche, began to whistle softly under his breath while he fitted guesswork with fact.

Looking up abruptly, he said, "Do you know anything about this woman, Wyn?"

"A little. Not much."

"Would she, and/or her husband, rate a separate file?"

"Quite possibly. I'll go and look."

The file, when he had it in his hands, was not large, and for the most part failed to interest him. He was nearing the last of the items when he came on the one that sent excitement crackling through him. Swiftly computing dates, he saw that it could fit. Looking back at the picture of the lovely woman in white, he knew beyond a shadow of a doubt that it did fit.

Wyn, who had been studying Sharon's picture, said slowly, "It may be just a coincidence, but I think——"

"What do you think?"

"I'm not sure. Just a minute."

Leaving him, she was back almost immediately with still another clipping, which she laid side by side with the one they had been looking at. "Oh," she said, disappointed. "They're very much alike, but they aren't the same, are they?"

Steve, his eyes moving from Sharon to a newspaper reproduction of a National Gallery acquisition of the past year, seeing the extraordinary resemblance between the two, knew that this was additional proof of a conviction that actually needed no further proof. For in looking at "The American Venus" he looked at Psyche.

"There should be a medal struck in your honour, Wyn," he said. "That case of Scotch will be delivered with a bunch of roses tied to it."

"Is this a story that is going to stay off the record?"

"Consider it so until further notice."

It was a story that he could break at once, if he wished; but for reasons that he did not stop to analyze too closely, he wanted to add to it anything he possibly could before doing so.

The following morning he left his downtown apartment early, and drove outside the city limits to circle the drive of a large stone house. Unchallenged, he briefly invaded a privacy hitherto unknown to him. From there he went back into town to enlarge further, through channels of his own, his knowledge of the people who lived in that house.

This part of his program completed, he made it his business to discover as much as could be readily known about the painter of "The American Venus." Using every connection he had, seeing no need here for secrecy, he learned more about Nick in four hours than Psyche had learned in four months. And when, toward evening, he in his turn walked across the big field to the converted barn, he was well armed in advance for an interview that he foresaw might have its difficulties.

Their antagonism was immediate.

Nick, cleaning brushes at the end of a day's work, was caught completely off guard by a visitor as unexpected as he was undesirable. He had been equally surprised by Sharon's visit. On that occasion, however, he had realized at once that discretion was a mutual aim, and that in refusing to tell her what she wanted to know he might unnecessarily create an unpleasant situation. The purpose behind this tall, lazily moving newspaperman's presence in the studio seemed obscurely threatening; for Steve, after debating the advisability of doing so, had decided in favour of making his profession clear, while at the same time intimating that he would not necessarily use what he learned.

Given time, Nick would have been acute enough to see that he could keep his own counsel with impunity. As it was, he gave ground steadily before subtle pressures well known to a man used to extracting information from those unwilling to part with it.

Steve, lounging against the model's stand on which Psyche had once posed, his back to the light, finally rose to his feet, satisfied that he had learned all he needed to know. But when he reached the head of the stairs, he turned to make a sudden stab at something that he neither needed nor really wanted to know.

"How long did she live here?"

Nick, who had not admitted in so many words that she had lived in the studio at all, replied easily, "A little over four months, but I would like it clearly understood that she did so alone. I myself, as you already know, do not live here."

Grey eyes and hazel fought a last silent duel, but this time the brilliant hazel eyes were unrevealing, giving away nothing.

Steve, striding back across a field, now warm with sunset light, thought, "He's lying, damn his soul!"—and cursed himself for caring one way or the other.

In his car again, he did not turn back to the city, but took the road to the north, following at once the only lead that the artist had given him. And when he passed Oliver's close to nine in the evening, he refused to examine his own feelings. But he could not banish an image of Psyche that had gone with him through every step of his search. It was as if she were in the car with him, and all he would have to do to prove this would be to put out his hand and touch her. Both innocent and sophisticated, vulnerable and strong, as appealing in laughter as in tears, she could not be submerged in her story as he would have liked.

After a night spent in a second-rate motel, he spent the greater part of the following day at a shack that, following the artist's reluctant instructions, he found without difficulty.

It was one of his many gifts that he could adapt himself easily and unselfconsciously to almost any surroundings. Perceptive, sensitive to the embarrassments inherent in the mixing of different classes and conditions of humanity, he fitted himself briefly into Butch and Mag's primitive existence as if he had always been a part of it.

His shirt sleeves rolled up, his hands in his trousers pockets, he was audience to Butch's Sunday ritual of garbage disposal. Perfectly seriously, he listened to Butch's somewhat improbable plans for retirement. Sharon and Dwight had made it quite possible for him to retire; but it would take Butch some years to get beyond the planning stage.

Apparently more than comfortable, Steve sat with Mag on the sagging red couch, and listened to the big woman talk on a subject obviously close to her heart—her kid. And as she talked, an ineradicable picture of a thin, lonely, tow-headed child was etched on his memory. A picture all the clearer because of the simplicity of the language with which it was evoked.

Butch and Mag, thinking him an emissary of the kid's parents —an idea he did nothing to contradict—were both friendly and expansive. That they should have any other reason for being hospitable did not occur to him.

When, after having shared two meals with them, he prepared to leave, he was curiously reluctant to bid them what he considered to be a quite final good-bye. And he would, even then, have been torn between chagrin and amusement, if he could have heard the exchange between them after he had turned away from the shack.

Side by side, they watched him until he had disappeared amongst slag hills already merging with a night sky.

"That there's a real man, that is," Butch said weightily.

Contentment was an almost visible mantle around Mag's shoulders. "He wasn't givin' nothin' away, but it was easy to see. The kid's got herself a good man. We'll be seein' the both of them together the next time."

Needing time in which to think, Steve checked in for the night at a commercial hotel in the nearby town—the same hotel, as it happened, where Nick had once paced a dreary room and rebelled against rain that kept him from painting.

Following almost the same trail over which Sharon had travelled three months earlier, he now knew a great deal more than she did, because he knew, as she did not, where the trail might properly be said to end. There were still gaps, it was true, but he no longer judged these to be of any real consequence. Whatever had happened to her between leaving the artist and turning up outside Oliver's in the oil truck, she had profited rather than lost by it. He had, at the shack, been given a convincing portrait of a "good kid". He himself had met a lovely girl. Not just pretty, or attractive, but lovely in every way. Between these two it was quite impossible to credit any aberration in her own pattern of personal behaviour.

His face deep-etched with fatigue, he mixed himself a drink, turned out the lights, and sat down in an old leather arm-chair by the window. Then, and only then, did he admit to himself what he must have known subconsciously through the whole of the preceding forty-eight hours.

He had pursued her back across the years not in order to expose her, but so that he could know how best to help and protect her. If she would let him, he would protect her to the best of his ability across all the years that lay ahead of her. But this was something that would have to be postponed, the pressing of any claim he might make on her. There were two others, who had apparently never given up an almost hopeless search, who must first be allowed to re-establish a prior claim.

Mag had said, "The kid was always dreamin' of her own folks." They, he now knew, had never stopped dreaming of her.

They would, those three, be able to make their own adjustments without any help from him or anyone else. Where they would need help would be in finding peace and privacy in which to do this.

Some publicity was unavoidable.

Knowing the newspaper business inside and out, concentrating in darkness that allowed no distractions, Steve outlined in his mind a story expressly designed to suppress rather than to invoke curiosity. It would have to be, he saw, a story that emphasized the original drama of the kidnapping while inferring that there had been no drama, as such, since. He could count on the co-operation of the miner and his wife because they loved her. He could count on Nick's co-operation because Nick loved himself. He could count on other newspapermen to let the thing drop on the basis of his own reputation for never failing to get a complete story.

Thank God, he had got in on the ground floor. With care, and there would be no lack of care on his part, it could be an overnight sensation, and that would be it.

"Psyche," he said aloud. "Psyche."

It was morning, and the sun was shining, and Psyche was again alone in the empty restaurant when he walked in. To Steve, it was as if the present time had stood still in order to allow the years to catch up with it. To be precise, seventeen years. He felt that he had known her, not briefly, but always.

He walked directly to the counter behind which she stood, and, without speaking, laid his hands palms upward on it.

For a moment Psyche did not move. Then, slowly, but without any hesitation, she placed her own hands in his.

"Would you trust me again?" he asked quietly.

"Yes, Steve."

"Then go and get your purse, or whatever you think you might need for the balance of the day. Change your dress, if you like, but you don't need to. You look perfect just as you are. I'm taking you to see some people who are rather interested in you. I'll tell you about them after we are on our way."

"But Ollie——" Psyche began uncertainly.

"I called Ollie earlier this morning."

This can only mean one thing, Psyche thought. He is taking me to see friends of his, perhaps even his family. And desperation, which had been steadily building up during two days in which she had begun to wonder if she would ever see him again, dissolved before overwhelming happiness. Happiness marred only by the desolate thought that no reciprocal gesture would ever be possible, that nowhere had she anyone of her own to whom she could introduce him.

"These—these people," she said. "Do they know we're coming?"

"Yes," he told her. "They know we're coming."

# 11 | EPILOGUE

THE chimes of the front door-bell sounded in the well of the circular staircase, musical but clear, their echoes fading softly against the thick, warm silence of the house.

A maid stepped through an archway under the stairs, to wait for a repetition of a sound she was not quite sure she had heard. And, as she stood there, a shaft of late afternoon sunlight, falling athwart the chandelier above her head, scattered a shower of prismatic colours over her black-and-white uniform, transforming it momentarily into motley out of place in time and locale.

Again the bell rang, still musical, but this time unmistakable in the prearranged pattern of a summons she had been told to expect.

Moving quietly away from beneath the soundless fall of colour, she crossed the hall diagonally and traversed a long living-room to French windows and a garden that dropped in terraced levels to a bed of delphiniums as blue in their fall flowering as the blue sky above.

Sharon, her hand in Dwight's, walking close to the delphiniums, saw the girl immediately, and walked swiftly to meet her.

"Is she here?" she asked, as soon as she was within earshot, and her husky voice broke a little on the simple words.

"Yes, ma'am, she's here. I did as you said. I didn't answer the door."

With a smile more brilliant than her wheat-gold hair, Sharon thanked the girl, dismissed her, and turned to Dwight who was now at her side.

"Dwight—darling——" she whispered, while she thought, "He was right, the waiting has been easier here than it would have been inside. And now—I must not, must not run——"

Then she was running as she had never run before.